HOMEBOUND

MEREDITH TRAPP

HOMEBOUND

A SMALL TOWN ROMANCE

MEREDITH TRAPP

This one's for the soft woman who tried so hard to please everyone else that she dug her own desires into a grave. May her people-pleasing tendencies rest in peace.

"Life is tough, my darling, but so are you."

— Stephanie Bennett Henry

HOMEBOUND

She's Texas's toughest bull rider, and he's determined to win her heart.

Dakota and Wyatt. Storm and sunshine. Growing up, they were as inseparable as a pair of cowboy boots. The best of friends—or so Dakota thought. Every summer, Wyatt would come home to his family's flower farm in Granite Falls, Texas and they'd stargaze in the fields, pinkies brushing, laughter rumbling with the cicadas until one summer... he never came back.

Dakota Cutler hasn't heard a peep from Wyatt Patterson in over three years, and a lot has changed. He's the hockey world's golden-boy, and she's developed a reputation for riding bulls and leaving men with broken hearts. After a string of one-night stands, the last thing Dakota needs is a distraction, but when her oldest childhood friend waltzes back into town, begging to move into her barn with the most adorable baby girl on his hip, everything changes.

Wyatt Patterson's back to get the girl he's been obsessing over for years, and he's doing *everything* to get her to see him as more than a friend—two-stepping at the rodeo, jumping into Cibolo Creek, even rendezvousing in outdoor showers. All Dakota wants is to keep her distance from her ex-friend, but when she learns the truth behind why Wyatt left, it turns out the scorching Texas sun might not be the only thing that burns them this summer.

AUTHOR'S NOTE

Thank you so much for diving into this story! Just a heads-up, this is the second book in a series of interconnected standalones, but don't worry—you don't need to have read the first book to enjoy this one. If you did read my previous book, you might notice that Wyatt's daughter has a new name to fit this story better. You'll see some familiar faces popping up, but you'll also get to meet a whole new cast of characters. Thanks a million for picking up my book and happy reading!

CONTENT GUIDANCE

Homebound is a small-town, slow-burn cowgirl romance full of spice, smooches, and swoons. This should ultimately be a light-hearted read, but I want to make you aware of a few things before you dive into the pages:

- Explicit language
- On-page alcohol consumption in a social setting
- Graphic description of side character's bull-riding injury on-page
- Sexist comments made by side characters
- On-page recreational marijuana consumption by main character
- Multiple explicit sex scenes on page
- On-page panic attack involving main characters
- Mention of off-page recreational drug use
- Anxious tendencies in main character; however, she does not necessarily live with anxiety
- Emotional manipulation from an ex
- Use of sex as a way to deal with and process traumatic emotions

- The main female character deals with yearning feelings of wanting to be a mother

Take care of yourselves, first and always. With love, Meredith.

HOMEBOUND PLAYLIST

Scan the QR Code for Homebound's playlist or check my instagram page for the link!

THE COWBOY KILLER

WYATT

"She's gonna have to ride 'em hard," a cowboy drawls in the rodeo stands.

My eyes slide to the two guys next to me. One has a giant mustache, and the other has one of those old Western bolo ties around his neck. They blend into the crowd with their Wrangler jeans, cowboy boots, and felt Stetson hats.

Actually, who in their right mind wears a felt cowboy hat in the middle of a Texas summer?

That's like putting a coat on your head in a dry sauna. They're sweating more than me, and I have to tie back my hair at the nape of my neck because I'm sweating my ass off.

But I'm sweating for an entirely different reason—nerves, not heat.

I shift my gaze to the arena, where cowboys kick up dust, getting ready for the bull riding. It's the main event everyone gears up for at the small-town rodeo, and it's the reason I'm scooting forward on the edge of these bleachers with my eyes glued to the chute, watching, searching for her.

The same *her* I haven't stopped thinking about since I left this town three years ago, with my heart all kinds of black and blue. I didn't expect my chest to hurt this much coming back to Granite Falls, but I can't stop googling heart attack symptoms, which isn't all that surprising.

I google *everything* now that I'm a dad.

"There's no way she can stay on that bull for all eight seconds," the mustached cowboy next to me grunts. "She's been practicing on easier ones, and this one's aggressive as all get out."

His friend shrugs. "She's only got to make it six seconds since she's in the Women's Bull Riding League."

"Yeah, but I hear our little cowboy killer's been trying to stay on for all eight since she's gunning for the PBR draft," he says.

The Cowboy Killer.

I go rigid at the nickname, scooting closer on the bleachers to hear more of their conversation. The guy sips his beer, curling a lip. "Bet she doesn't last four seconds on the back of that bull."

Asshole.

"Bet she only makes it two," the other one quips.

Make that two assholes.

I pull out a crinkled twenty, giving them my fiercest glare for betting against her. I'd bet my entire wallet on that woman. She saved my life all those years ago, so I owe her everything. "Twenty says she makes it all eight seconds on the back of that bull and then some."

The cowboys scan my white T-shirt, their gazes fixating on the smashed pea stain left by my daughter, Vienna, this morning. I won't sugarcoat it... I look like I puked on myself.

Fun times.

Thanks to my twelve-month-old baby girl, my laundry bill is through the roof, but I wouldn't have it any other way. Puke-green pea stains and all. She's my mini-me—dirty-blond waves, big green eyes, and my cleft chin (or "chin butt," as both my moms like to call it).

The cowboy with the Western bolo tie nods his hat to me. "I

take it you're a fan of our cowboy killer if you're willing to go all in on a bet?"

"You could say that," I huff out.

You could also say that I've been obsessed with that woman since I was eight, but I'm not about to get into a pissing contest with these guys. I might play for the NHL, but I'm a lover, not a fighter.

"So, how do y'all know her?" I drawl, aiming for casual and coming up short. My accent always thickens when I come back home.

They smirk at each other.

The guy strokes his mustache. "Our cowboy killer's got a bit of a… reputation 'round here in Granite Falls."

I narrow my eyes. He better not be insinuating what I think he is. "For being one of the best bull riders in the state of Texas?"

That damn well better be what he means.

"Nah, she's been having some trouble staying on lately, so it's not that…" The cowboy's smirk deepens.

I don't like that smug look. Not one bit, and I can already tell I'm going to hate whatever comes out of his mouth.

"It's for riding cowboys as hard as she rides bulls." He chortles, his mustache twitching.

It's the gut punch I was waiting for, but at least that's something that hasn't changed. She always had a boy following her around every summer I came back to Texas. I'd give almost anything to be one of those men lucky enough to be with her now.

If she's still breaking hearts, I'll gladly hand her mine.

The other cowboy slaps his knee. "She'll kill you, wreck you up nice and good if you're not careful, but it'll be a hell of a way to go. Didn't you hear what she did to Boone? Poor guy."

I tense up. Boone Bowman. There's a name I haven't heard in a while, and one I'd be happy to never hear again.

"I'd be careful how you speak about her if I were you," I grit out.

As much as I want to tell these guys off, I grind my teeth so I don't let any choice words slip out. My baby girl is a little sponge, soaking up every word I say.

I try to limit the cursing, even when she's not around. Not that I mind a woman who curses. In fact, I like a woman with a dirty mouth. But I don't want all the parents in daycare side-eyeing me if my daughter goes around squealing *fuck*.

So unfortunately, that means I can't say what I'm thinking—and what I'm thinking is that these guys playing cowboy dress-up need a weeklong seminar on how to respect a woman.

The mustache guy slides his gaze to me. "Let me guess... You've been wrecked by her too?"

My fists clench, but I stay silent out of respect for her. These small towns and their gossip. It's not the gray-haired ladies that keep the rumor mills churning; it's the rowdy cowboys who can't keep their mouths shut.

The only way to keep a secret in a small town is to tell it to your dog.

They continue talking while my grip tightens and tightens on my knees. Jealousy rips through me the more I hear about all the cowboys she's apparently *wrecked*, but I've been stuck in the friend zone for over a decade, so I'm used to the feeling. I spent all my summers watching every boy in this town fall at her boots.

Everyone wanted her. But me, I was desperate for her—still am.

Every summer I came back to Texas, she always had some new guy wrapped around her finger, and I was always, without fail, the giant third wheel.

I *thought* getting my braces off would change things.

I *thought* having my acne clear up would make her see me differently.

I *thought* she'd finally notice me after I packed on twenty pounds of pure, solid muscle.

But I'd thought wrong.

So damn wrong.

I blame it on the fact that she's two years older than me, which in the big scheme of life is nothing, but when you're fifteen and she's seventeen? It feels massive.

Not so massive now that I'm twenty-six and she's twenty-eight, though.

Growing up, she never saw me as anything more than the little boy next door, and for a while that was enough. My parents' flower farm bordered her family's property. So every summer, I'd sprint off the airplane and run straight into her waiting arms.

That was our routine.

I'd run, and she'd catch me, but as we got older, things changed. Reversed.

My voice dropped.

She got... curvier.

Soon enough, she was the one jumping into my arms, and I was always there to swing her around, feet dangling, foreheads bumping.

Until I wasn't.

"Ladies and gentlemen!" the announcer shouts.

Cowboy hats rustle in the dusty arena, and I wipe the sweat dripping down my neck. I really should cut my hair, but she always seemed to like it longer.

"Turn your heads to the chute 'cause you're gonna want to watch this next ride," he booms. "She's known for that famous scowl, and tonight, she's taking on Hammer, a beast that's thrown off every rider daring enough to face him. You don't want to mess with her, folks!"

I scan the arena, searching, searching, searching for her.

My eyes dart frantically through the dusty haze carrying the tang of manure on the hot breeze. It's been over three years

5

since I last looked into her beautiful honey eyes, but I can't find her. Where is she? Suddenly, I spot her standing by the metal chutes.

My stomach nosedives.

She's not looking at me, but I'm looking at her, and she's... Well, she's magnificent. There's really no other word for it.

She's standing there in all her rugged glory with that same fierce determination straightening her shoulders. Bull riders tend to be anywhere from five-foot-five to five-foot-ten, so at five-foot-seven, she's a good eight inches shorter than me, but she carries herself like she's the tallest person on the planet.

Those full, perfect lips I've only imagined kissing a million times are set in her permanent scowl, but I know exactly where to tickle her to make those dimples appear—the back of her knees and, weirdly enough, her elbows.

Her wavy brown hair is tied back in a braid beneath her straw cowgirl hat, and she's clad in her patched riding jacket and fringe chaps that hug every curve—and damn, there are a lot of them now.

Way more than she had three years ago.

My mouth goes dry at the thought of dragging my hands along the slopes of her thick, muscular body. I've spent too much of my life imagining doing just that.

And those freckles I know are on the bridge of her nose? A man can only handle so much.

She radiates this aura that commands attention, and not because she's breathtaking, even though she's always been that—beautiful, stunning, gorgeous—pick your adjective.

They all fit her.

It's her scowl that always teeters on the edge of a smirk as if she couldn't care less about anyone's opinion of her, which she doesn't.

My chest throbs with a painful intensity as she prepares to climb onto the back of a raging two-thousand-pound bull. She's fearless, and if my baby girl grows up to be just as bold, I'll have done something right.

The bull thrashes in the chute, and I hold my breath as I watch her strut up to the metal corral. After all these years, it never gets easier watching her face off against a bull, and as much as it scares the hell out of me, I can never look away. She's risking her life, so she deserves every ounce of my attention.

"Get ready," the guy says next to me, nudging his friend. "This one's gonna be a wild ride."

"Yeah," the other cowboy comments. "All two seconds of it, since she can't manage to hang on."

"Eight seconds," I grunt, tossing them another glower for good measure. "All she has to do is stay on the bull for eight seconds. She's got this."

I repeat the phrase like a prayer and lift the mood ring dangling from the chain around my neck. Kissing the metal, I remember the day I got down on one knee and asked her to marry me. I was eight, and she said no because she wasn't ready to get married, but I promised to keep the ring until she was, and keep it I did—for sixteen years.

Looking at her now, I realize those feelings have never gone away. I tried all kinds of vices to get her off my mind after I left.

Whiskey. Weed. Women.

They all got me in trouble, but that last one got me my daughter, so I'll never regret that choice.

But none of them worked.

Because I've always been hers... but she's never been mine.

"Alright, y'all!" the announcer's voice slashes through my memories. "Let's bring out our next rider! She's bold. She's mean, and she's got one hell of a scowl. Give it up for Kodie Cutler, the Cowboy Killer!"

The crowd erupts in cheers.

She might be Kodie Cutler to everyone else, but to me, she'll always be my Dakota.

HAMMER

DAKOTA

S *he's bold, she's mean, and she's got one hell of a scowl.*

Did the announcer *have* to say that? It's not as if I scowl at everyone. It's just my face. But heaven forbid women don't have a smile plastered to their mouths twenty-four seven.

"Remember, darlin'," my dad mutters, nodding to Hammer, the snarling bull whose name fits him since he's hammering away in the chute. "You stay loose and—"

"Flow like good tequila. Smooth and steady," I finish, backing away from the metal rails.

My dad's been repeating that phrase since I was old enough to string a sentence together, which looking back, isn't the best thing to say to a two-year-old, but that's my daddy. Bold as all get out and doesn't give a flying fuck what anyone thinks.

I'm proud that I'm just like Colter Cutler.

He's not just my father. He's my best friend.

My dad is one of the most respected bull rider coaches in the state, and no one fucks with my father—just like no one fucks with me.

I eye the brown bull with a determined frown. He's the meanest bull in this rodeo, and I'd pick him every time. I like the mean ones. They give me a good challenge. And the meaner the bull, the better my score since they're harder to stay on.

"I know, Pops. I'll try to stay loose." I slap his sweaty shoulder. The heat's oppressive today, and these chaps soak in all the heat. I might as well be swimming in lava.

This one looks like a spinner, so my dad's right. I need to loosen up, and staying loose is my biggest problem right now. I've been wound tighter than a lasso ever since Boone did that interview and shattered my confidence with one sentence. It's been tough for me to get back out here in the arena, but I'm trying.

"Right you are, darlin'." My dad grunts under his cowboy hat. "Now, look at me and listen up."

I focus on my dad's intense stare while he gives me pointers for the ride. We've got the same amber eyes, dark waves, and dimples, so he's always turning the ladies' heads, even though his brow never *un*furrows.

Ever since my parents divorced, he's been strutting about with that *same* grumpy frown with the *same* cigar in his mouth, drinking from the *same* bottle of tequila.

He plucks a cigar from his back pocket. "You got that? Hammer's a tough one. You watch out now, you hear? Stay relaxed out there. No more locking up."

I begged him to give up smoking years ago, but he still likes chewing on the tip when he's worried. His words might be steady, but I can hear the faint undercurrent of stress that always comes out before I ride, and I love that he still cares so much.

"It's kind of hard to relax on the back of a two-thousand-pound bucking animal, Pops," I try to tease, but my mom's sense of humor skipped a generation, so all my jokes fall flat. "I'll be fine. I got this."

Fine is a gamble, a flip of a coin. Heads you live. Tails you die. Bull riding... it's not for the weak.

As I watch the raging bull snorting in the chute, I'm not so sure I *got this*, but that's what he needs to hear, and what I need to tell myself. When it comes to bull riding, doubt will get you killed, but for a chronic and cursed overthinker like me, it's hard not to stress about the risks.

Most bull riders need to have a whatever-happens-happens mentality, but I'm constantly worrying that I could die in a blip without any children, a legacy—a family.

I really want to be a mom one day.

"I've got faith in you, darlin'. Always have, always will. That bull's got the makings of a champion. If you can stay on him, you'll be up there in the bigger circuits, just you watch."

I straighten with hope. "You really think so?"

"There's not a doubt in my mind."

The big circuits.

The PBR.

The Professional Bull Riders League.

It's been my dream since I first watched my dad climb on the back of a bull. All because I wanted to be just like him. I come from a long line of bull riders, so riding isn't just in my blood, it *is* my blood, and I've poured every ounce of my blood, sweat, and tears into this sport.

My dad grips the chute rails, his eyes darkening with the intense fear for me he tries so hard to hide. "You hang on for them eight seconds, ya hear?"

I gulp down my nerves. "I'll try, but no one thinks I've got what it takes, Pops. They all agree with Boone. Have you seen what they're saying about me? Some journalist called me bull riding's bitch."

I'm still bitter about that. *Bitch.* My teeth grind together.

"I don't give a flying fuck what anyone thinks. I know you've got what it takes." He waves to the rustling crowd of cowboy hats. "All that noise. All those people. Tune 'em out. You're not a flower that needs to be watered with validation, you're a cactus, darlin', prickly enough to thrive in a desert of doubt."

I used to be a people-pleaser with a soft heart, but ever since Boone claimed I'd never make it in this sport, I've hardened. I had to, so no other insults would dent my determination. Now, shit just rolls off me.

I'm damned if I care what anyone thinks, so I nod, trying to muster every ounce of confidence I've got, but inside, my stomach's twisted up. Being the only female bull rider in the Lonestar state, I've been faking confidence for so long that my whole life feels counterfeit.

Eight seconds.

It sounds like nothing, but on top of a raging beast, it's an eternity.

I try to smile for him, but I can't manage one through my nerves. "Thanks for that. I needed to hear it. Love you, Pops."

"I love you always, but you know that. Now, you ride hard, ride loose, and ride smart. Raise hell, darlin'," he repeats for good luck, and then kisses my cheek and struts away toward the animal stalls.

We keep it simple before I ride—no need for drawn-out goodbyes.

I climb up onto the chute rails as the flank man adjusts the leather strap around the bull's middle. "All right, you're up, Cutler."

"Remember, not too tight, sugar," I call out to him, heaving myself over the rails. "We don't want to hurt the poor beast."

I don't want the strap to hurt the bull. It just needs to be tight enough that he wants to buck me off. I respect these animals, and we treat them like kings.

They're athletes, just like me.

The arena's alive with cheers, but I push them aside, same as always. Securing my helmet, I lower myself onto the raging bull that could easily end me. One false move, and I'm done for.

Six feet under.

No matter how many times I ride, it never gets easier. The

pressure only gets worse because now I know what to expect. I've seen videos of broken arms, legs, hell, even deaths in these competitions, but I can't think about that, or I'll never compete again.

"Let's dance, you big ol' brute," I mutter to the snarling bull beneath me. "I'm not letting you take this round, hear me? Hammer away."

He grunts through his nostrils like he understands me, and maybe he does. I'd like to think these animals respect me as much as I respect them. It's one of the reasons I don't eat meat. I love all animals.

The gate man unlatches the metal chute, and I tighten my grip, feeling the rope bite into my palm.

"All right," he says, and I clench my chaps around the bull's sweaty hide. "Three... Two... One!"

The metal gate shoots open, and we're off.

Hammer bucks like the devil himself has a hold of his balls, and I'm jerked left, then right, then left again. The behemoth is a whirlwind of muscle, snot, and fury. I'm clinging on, every fiber of my being fighting to stay perched atop this raging beast. I'm in tune with his every move, just me and the animal moving, trying to be one.

It's horrible.

It's thrilling.

It's addictive.

Always addictive. If it weren't, I'd never ride.

The bull kicks me and kicks me and kicks me around the arena, and in this moment, I'm glad I'm able to tune out the roaring noise of the crowd. Bull riding is one of the only sports where people get a thrill out of watching you fall down, and it fucks with my head—the crowd getting more excited to see me fail than succeed.

I might not be the strongest rider in a sport dominated by

men, but I've got delusional confidence, and that's the secret to achieving anything.

Every time I fall down, I get back up.

Every time someone tells me I can't do this, I give them my most arrogant grin, even if I feel like crying, and I feel like crying a lot—not that I ever cry in front of anyone. People don't realize how much confidence it takes to be extremely vulnerable in public. It requires a give-no-shits mentality, and I'm still picking up the pieces of my broken confidence.

Hammer gives one particularly nasty jerk, and my grip loosens.

It happens that fast.

"Fuck!" I scream, scrambling to hold the rope. It's no use—I've lost control.

He kicks me off, and I fly through the air, bracing for a rough impact. The ground slams into me, dirt filling my nostrils. Pain shoots up my side, but I barely notice the fire through the adrenaline. I spit and cough to try and clear the dirt.

Fuckfuckfuck.

I roll, narrowly avoiding the bull's pounding hooves, and scan the chaotic arena for an escape. I need to get away from the charging beast fast before he comes at me.

"Shit!" I scream over the crowd's excited cheers. They love when the bulls charge, and damn them for finding my failure exciting.

I could die out here.

"Dakota! Watch out!"

That deep voice.

His voice.

For a second, I think I'm imagining it, but when I whip my head around, that's when I see him, right there in the front stands, looking like he's about to jump into the arena and save me himself.

My summer boy.

My best friend.

Well, former best friend.

Wyatt fucking Patterson.

His actual middle name is Dale, but I think fucking suits him better now. The last time I saw him, he'd kissed my cheek, told me he'd see me next summer, and then hopped on a plane back to Nashville.

That was the last I heard from him.

I called and texted and FaceTimed and hell, I even sent a handwritten card when I found out he had a kid, but I never once got a response back.

Not one.

I hate how my summer boy left me, but more than that, I hate how much I've missed those pasture-green eyes.

His knuckles are clenched tight on the railing, those eyes locked on me. He looks older. Different. He's still arguably just as cute as the little boy I stargazed with, but his dirty-blond hair is a wild mess around his broad shoulders, and it matches the frantic look in his gaze, like he's been running his hands through it nonstop while watching me compete.

Staring at him feels like getting rammed by a two-thousand-pound bull, and my focus slips. Hammer lunges and the last thing I see is his snarling face barreling toward me. I jump out of the way as fast as I can, but not before his hard body hits my side.

"Goddammit!"

Shit, that really hurts.

That'll leave a bruise.

A traitorous tear slips out of the corner of the eye. Then another, and another…

The crowd goes wild.

But I do what I always do.

I shut down those feelings, swipe away the tears, and sprint to the exit with Hammer raging behind me. But all the while, I can feel Wyatt's gaze branding me.

I'll never speak a bad word about anyone, but you can bet your ass I'll never forget the people who did me dirty, and Wyatt Patterson…

He did me so goddamn dirty.

ANCIENT HISTORY

WYATT

"*I* want to see her. Where is she?" I demand, frantically searching the makeshift medical area at the small-town rodeo.

The so-called *area* is really just a small corner off to the side of the cattle stalls, cluttered with a few chairs and a table with basic first-aid supplies. We're at a small-circuit rodeo, so they do what they can, but it's nothing fancy.

This isn't the big leagues.

"Who ya lookin' for, bud?" some bronco rider asks, wincing as he gets patched up.

I don't bother looking at him. I just continue searching for her. "Dakota Cutler."

"You mean Kodie? No one calls her Dakota."

"I do."

It's been years since I said it, so her rusty name scrapes through my throat. Watching her face off with a bull in the arena, I was seconds away from jumping in there myself, ready to distract the animal.

That would've been a dumbass move, considering I don't know the first thing about riding a bull, unless it's a mechanical one, and I've had a few buttery nipple shots to dull thoughts of a certain woman.

I try not to be a worrier because worrying makes me miss out on the present, but the panic was unbearable, and I'd been *this* close.

Then I thought of my little girl, my Vi, and my daughter always comes first now, so I stayed put in the stands because she needs me. Dakota can handle herself.

She always has.

But that'd been close.

Too damn close, so I sprinted straight back to the medical area after she finished her ride.

"Thanks for patchin' me up, sugar," someone says behind me.

I stiffen, squeezing my eyes shut for a moment at the sound of her raspy voice. The number of times she told me to *Climb higher!* or *Don't drop me, Wyatt!* bullet through me.

A paramedic who looks more like a male model is leading a scratched-up Dakota to one of the rickety chairs. She's got dust on her nose and sweaty brown hair plastered to her forehead, and she's never looked fiercer. I scan her for injuries. No blood. My shoulders sink with relief.

But I can't stop staring.

Here I am with a pea stain on my T-shirt, and this woman's only gotten more beautiful over the past three years.

The paramedic guides her to a plastic chair with her back to me, so she doesn't notice me. Not yet. He quickly gets to work, carefully pouring antiseptic on her wounds.

"Kodie Cutler," the paramedic says, eyeing a scrape on her arm. "Damn, girl, close call. You sure look real good out there, though."

I don't want to hear that from his mouth.

"Oh yeah?" she says. "You were watching me ride?"

"Yeah," he says, putting the largest Band-Aid I've seen over a

17

scratch. "I couldn't take my eyes off you, but it seems like you were having a little trouble out there, girl."

Dammit. That's my line—the eyes part, not the trouble part. He's wrong. She can do anything.

"Aw, thanks," she murmurs in her flirtiest voice, batting those long lashes. "But it's nothing I can't handle."

I'd recognize her sultry voice anywhere since I had to listen to her flirt with every goddamn boy growing up while I followed around like a lovesick puppy.

"Maybe I can take you out later," she adds.

I grimace.

He runs his tongue along his cheek. "Now, how can I say no to that? You might not be able to hang onto that bull for eight seconds, but I'm a hell of a lot easier to ride."

I swear if she goes home with him after that pick-up line, we're going to need to have a serious talk about standards.

She hunches forward like those words hurt more than her scratches, but she musters up a fake smirk. I know it's fake because I know *her*.

"I'm sure you are," she drawls.

That's it—I can't watch this anymore.

"Dakota's got everything it takes to make it on those bulls."

Her back goes rigid, and I think she winces a little. Her name falls from my lips like I've been murmuring it every day, and I need to say it again, so I do. Softer this time.

"Dakota, are you okay? I was watching out in the stands. Please look at me."

I use the same pleading tone I always used anytime I'd beg her not to jump off the highest boulder into Inks Lake. She was always trying to one-up everyone—jump from the highest point, climb the highest tree. She never listened then, so I'm shocked when she listens now.

She slowly turns to face me, and her eyes narrow, soaking me in. I'm hoping she thinks I look different. Older. Let's hope sexier. My shirt might have a pea stain, but it's a little too tight, so you can see the outline of my abs. Yeah, that was intentional. She doesn't seem to notice, no matter how much I want her to.

Her expression plummets straight into her infamous Cutler scowl. She was never one to grin all that often, which is why I used to do anything just to see her smile.

Those dimples did me in every time.

I'd let her win all our arm-wrestling matches, tickle her elbows, take her stargazing, make her flower bouquets... anything to see a flash of those dimples.

But they're nowhere to be seen now.

I hold my breath, waiting to see what she'll do. A slap across the cheek, maybe? I'd deserve that for leaving the way I did.

"Who's this?" the male-model paramedic asks, sizing me up.

She flicks her eyes over me like I'm nothing but a pile of horse shit, and that more than anything hurts the most. "Not sure. I think I might be looking at a ghost, considering I haven't heard a peep from Wyatt Patterson in over three goddamn years. How's it feel to be back from the dead, sugar? I hear it's a bitch to be resurrected."

I bite my cheek to stop my grin from spreading. She's never been all that quick with a comeback, so she must've been thinking about what to say for a while. "How long have you been thinking about that one?"

She points a finger at me. "No. You don't get to do that. You don't get to pretend like you know me 'cause you don't. Not anymore. You up and left me."

My smile falls a second later. "I know. You're right."

"That's it? That's all you're going to say?" she blurts. "No explanation? I left you voicemails every day for months. Voice-mails, Patterson. *Voicemails!*"

"I know," I admit. "And I saved every single one of them."

That stumps her for a second. Good. But she shakes her head

and sucks in a trembling breath. "And you never thought to respond? What did I ever do to you to deserve that?"

I slump forward. Even though I left, I never stopped feeling guilty about that choice. I've always had the guiltiest conscience.

Dakota once made a homemade Twinkie cake for the Fourth of July that was so sickeningly sweet, I threw up the entire thing that night. But she spent four hours in the kitchen, so I couldn't tell her it was awful. Every summer until I left, she continued to make that Twinkie cake for the Fourth of July, and I continued to eat a slice and vomit it up.

Christ, I had it so bad for her.

Still do.

"I'm sorry," I rush out my apology, not caring that we've got an audience. "For leaving. For going quiet on you. My life got crazy busy after I had Vi, and I'm sorry."

Parenthood sucked out all the old parts of my life and replaced them with something better, harder, but still better.

"Ah, yes. That's right," she drawls, rubbing her hands on her chaps. "My dad told me you had a daughter. An adorable baby girl, in fact. I thought you would have mentioned that considering you used to call and tell me what you had for breakfast, but I guess your Healthy Harvest Egg Casserole is more important news than your beautiful little girl, but hey," she says, holding up her hands. "I'm not one to judge what's important to someone."

Despite her sarcasm, I get stuck on the fact that she called my baby girl beautiful. I wonder if Dakota's been keeping tabs on me.

"Dakota," I plead, latching onto her hard gaze. "I know you're mad, and you have every right to be. I should've called, or texted, or something. I shouldn't have cut you out of my life like that, but I'm back now, and I'm determined to make things right this summer."

She blinks like she didn't hear the words and then casually flicks her scratched-up wrist.

"Hey, don't you worry about it. Becoming a parent is a huge

20

life change, and that was a long time ago. It's ancient history." She turns to the paramedic. "Why don't we head on out? It's getting a little bit crowded here, don't you think?"

That's it?

Her nonchalance is almost worse than her anger, but she's always been one to bury her heaviest emotions. She'd rather feel nothing, and I want her to feel everything when it comes to me.

"That's all you're going to say?" I ask, narrowing my gaze on those mesmerizing honey eyes.

I want her to yell, cry, fight me, spit on my boot, something, *anything*, but she doesn't do any of that. Instead, she jumps off the chair and rushes up to my face, her lips less than an inch from me.

The heat of her breath mingles with mine, and I drop my eyes to her mouth, thinking how easy it'd be to kiss her, to finally taste her. But we've never kissed, and she's not looking at my lips like I'm looking at hers.

I'm tempted to lick those lips, but she looks like she's about to bite mine off.

Her eyes lock onto me with an intensity that sends a hot shiver down my spine, but then she gives my shoulder a hard pat.

"Ah, it's all good, sugar. All's forgiven," she says in a husky murmur that sounds a lot like *fuck off.*

With a toss of her brown braid that hits me in the face, she loops her hand through the model paramedic's and pulls him away, leaving me in the dust. I can't stand watching her with him, but I deserve it for cutting her out of my life like that.

Damn, she's going to *hate* when I show up to the barn later with all my luggage and beg her to let me stay with her.

"Like I said!" she calls out without a backward glance. "It's ancient history!"

Ancient history, my ass. We're getting our happy ending this summer.

4

JAKE OR JAMES OR CARL

DAKOTA

"Who was that guy at the rodeo earlier today?" the sexy paramedic asks as I straddle him, topless, on my leather couch.

"I don't want to talk about the rodeo," I nearly growl, mostly because I want to get my orgasm over with so I can get a good night's sleep before my dad lectures me tomorrow on everything I could've done better for those eight seconds.

Well, four seconds since I couldn't manage to stay on the fucking bull.

Right now, I want a distraction so I don't have to think about my failure. Ever since I called it off with Boone, I prefer to keep things casual because the fewer people who love me, the better. That way, if I get snuffed out by a bull, the less people get hurt.

Though, I'll admit, it's getting harder and harder to find random one-night stands, since most of the guys in town have seen me from diapers to braces to prom dresses. I have to stick to tourists or cowboys passing through for a rodeo.

I swipe my tongue along Jake's bottom lip—or maybe his name was James? I can't remember, but it was something with a J... I think.

It also could've been Carl, but he's already put his tongue in my mouth, so now it would just be rude if I asked for his name. It's probably best to stick to calling him "sugar" so I don't get mixed up.

He pulls me closer on his lap. "I take it the rodeo's a sore subject?"

"How about we don't talk when I'm topless and straddling you on my couch, sugar?"

"Good point," Jake or James or Carl murmurs against my lips. "I've got a beautiful woman on top of me, and I don't really want to use my mouth for talking."

I tangle my fingers in his brown strands, leaning in for a kiss. I've always preferred men with dark hair. They just do something for me. Blond guys are too… blond. Don't ask me to explain it.

I can't.

I've always been drawn to the broody cowboys.

Call me a walking cliché, but I'm *that* girl—the one who goes after the tall, dark, and handsome types. The one who thinks she can change their scoundrel ways with a flirty wink. I view them as a challenge, and I love a solid challenge.

Give me a dark-haired man with a mean smirk who tastes like bourbon whiskey over a blond sweetheart every day ending in Y.

"That's my kind of man," I say against his lips. "Let's put that mouth of yours to good use."

He grabs my hips. "And what kind of man would that be?"

"The kind who prefers kissing over talking," I say, stealing another kiss, this one deeper, more insistent.

The guy kisses my neck, and this, this is exactly what I need, not to think about anything other than the man beneath me. To turn off my brain for one damn second and stop worrying about making it to the PBR.

It's always been difficult for me to focus during sex. My thoughts tend to wander, and right now, I'm thinking of Wyatt Patterson and wondering about his cute little girl.

I've stalked all his socials, and he doesn't post about his daughter often, but when he does, my breath always hitches. She looks just like him with those sunny ringlets and green eyes big enough to see everything.

Wyatt Patterson couldn't scare a fly, so he's going to have trouble keeping all the boys away from her one day.

I'll be honest—it hurt when I found out he had a child. He might've had a crush on me growing up, but I only ever saw him as a kid. He grew out of it, thankfully, and we became friends. Best friends. And best friends tell each other shit like that.

More than anything, he hurt me by leaving, and when I'm hurting, I get angry, but I don't want to trauma dump my feelings on him, which is why I shut down and left him at the rodeo.

"Come here," I growl, pulling the guy closer so I don't have to think about my summer boy.

Jake or James or Carl's fingers dig into my ass as I straddle him. It feels good to stretch my legs like this since my thighs are sore as all get out from the grueling bull ride.

"I want to be inside you so bad," he mumbles.

"I bet you do," I say, even though I'm not feeling the same way.

It's been a long time since I've felt desperate to sleep with someone. The last man was probably Boone, but we had a whirl-wind romance—too fast, too hot, too intense to survive.

Sex to me is mostly a routine now: kiss a little, proceed to doggie style (or reverse cowgirl if I'm feeling frisky), and then kick them out of my bed so I can sprawl starfish-style with my pooch, Luna—my ten-year-old, three-legged, rescue black lab.

Speak of the furry devil; Luna lets out a particularly loud snort-snore from her dog bed.

He jolts beneath me. "What the hell was that noise?"

"That's my dog. She's a sleep-barker, so she's probably just having a heck of a dream about running through the flower fields. Just ignore her."

"You sure you don't want to put her up?"

"What?" I gasp, lurching back. "No. She's not going anywhere. She's my fur baby."

Her black body's curled up on her dog bed. If I'm home, she's never more than a room away. She's the sunshine to my grumpy, and she always lets out the cutest snorts when I get home. I rescued her from the shelter because no one wanted a three-legged dog, and she's been my best friend for ten years.

I sniff. Great. Now, I'm tearing up just thinking about losing her one day. Sometimes, I think about how dogs can't live forever, and it's one of the few things that makes me cry.

Pets should be immortal.

There's a knock on the door.

Luna jumps off her bed and hobbles over to the red front door, tags jingling, tail wagging, leg still missing.

He jerks his head up, eyes narrowing. "You expecting someone?"

"No?" I go back to kissing him.

There's another knock.

Louder this time.

Luna barks and starts wagging her tail, peeping through the window. She barks again, and it sounds like her excited bark. It's probably my best friend, Alanna, asking me to come out with her again, so with a grunt, I get off him.

"Let me see who it is real quick," I say. "Why don't you wait for me in my bedroom?"

"Oh yeah?" He winks. "Should I keep my boxers on?"

"Nah, take 'em off, sugar."

As I walk away, my lips fall into a frown. I don't bother putting on a shirt over my bra since it's just Lana, and we have no problem changing naked in front of each other. I swing open the wooden door, but I'm not looking into Lana's familiar hazel eyes. Instead, I find a pair of emerald ones.

My teeth grind together. "What the hell are you doing here, Patterson?"

5

OLD BAGGAGE

DAKOTA

There *he* is, standing in all his sunshine-boy glory. The NHL's heartthrob—as Sports Illustrated dubbed Wyatt Patterson.

His eyes travel over my purple lace bra, and his face lights up like a stoplight, which is typical. He used to blush anytime a girl so much as smiled at him. That's why we were always just friends. Wyatt's too easy to walk all over, and I need a man who can handle me. Wyatt could never—this boy's too damn nice.

He pushes back the loose strands of hair from his forehead. "Uh, hey."

"Solid opener," I deadpan, keeping my voice level to hold back my irritation.

All those old feelings come rushing back—the voicemails that never got returned, all the texts I sent that he left on read. My eyes burn, but I'm not going to lash out at him just because I'm pissed. Instead, I push down all those emotions and keep my thoughts to myself, taking in all his changes.

With his chiseled jawline, everlasting tan, and soulful green eyes, there's no doubt he's grown into an attractive man, but I've never been attracted *to* him.

I like my men a little more rugged, a little more *scowly*, and a little looser when it comes to their morals.

Luna bounds forward, attacking him with a slobbery kiss. Wyatt grunts and nearly falls back into one of the potted cacti. "Ms. Tuna, look at you! You're still just as happy as ever. I've missed you, Toons."

I wince at the memory.

He always called her that—Tuna. It all started because Luna loves swimming, so he started calling her Luna-Tuna because she swam more than a fish. That morphed into Tuna, then Toons, Luna-Tuna, Tuna Roll, and so on…

Are you even a dog lover if you don't have a million nicknames for your pet?

Now, Luna actually answers to Tuna more than Luna. It's kind of embarrassing when I have to shout, "Tuna, come here!" at the farmer's market.

Luna-Tuna-Toons wags her tail, her whole booty shaking with the motion, and my dog's a hell of a lot more excited to see Patterson than I am, but I am curious why he's here.

He's got a suitcase in one hand and his squirming baby girl in the other. I have to hold back a smile at the drool dribbling onto her pink cowgirl shirt.

Goodness, I want to squish her against my chest. She's a right cutie, that one, but I always knew Wyatt would make cute babies. I want one of those one day, but it feels like I can't be a mother and a bull rider. If I rode on the back of a bull pregnant, everyone would have a goddamn opinion about *that*.

Hurt mingled with annoyance prickles up my spine, but I do my best to hide every emotion from my voice. I don't have time to deal with feelings.

"What the hell are you doing at my place, Patterson? Shouldn't you be back with your moms at the main house?"

"Technically," he says, bouncing his girl, "your place is my parents' barn, so that's why I'm here."

27

Ever since Wyatt's grandparents passed, we've got a deal—I help manage their flower farm during the winter months along with a team of farmers, and his moms let me live in their renovated barndominium (barn + condominium; Patterson and I used to call it "The Barndo") for free year-round.

I lean against the doorframe and cross my arms, which pushes up my breasts. "What do you want to talk about?"

He seems to notice, and his tan cheeks ignite as he looks at my topless state. "Are you busy? I can, uh, come back later if you're busy."

He's so flustered.

Bless his heart.

I curl my lips into the standard smirk I give all men. "Oh, come on now. I know your parents raised you to be a Southern gentleman, but you don't have to look away. You must've seen a woman topless by now since you've got that precious little girl on your hip."

She really is a cutie-pie.

After a lengthy swallow, he gives a gentle smile down to his daughter that would melt my walls if they weren't so thick. "She's something else, isn't she?"

The love overflowing from his words has my throat tightening. He's going to be such an amazing dad.

It's strange to see him in *Daddy Mode*, but he's truly one of the good ones. One summer, he even worked for a kids' traveling petting zoo, lugging around tiny iguanas, ducklings, and baby goats that he'd dress up in tiny cowboy hats and tinier bandanas.

A baby goat in a cowboy hat is something I didn't know I needed in life.

Not to mention, he's a two-stepping master, always makes sure a woman walks on the inside of a sidewalk, and he's got this calming demeanor that's like aloe vera for any argument. But every so often, he'll whip out a hell of a joke that will leave you laughing so hard you pee a little.

Wyatt speaks about his daughter with so much reverence that it's difficult to keep my scowl in place, but I manage. "What're you two doing back here? I thought you were too busy being the hockey world's golden boy for us small-towners."

He lifts a brow as he bounces his daughter. "You kept tabs on me?"

I go rigid.

I've read every article written about him and watched every interview, but like hell am I admitting that. I stiffen at my slip-up, glancing at my chipped pink nails. The pink makes me feel girly in a man's world.

"It's hard not to. Everyone talks about the hockey world's heartthrob in this town," I say, adding finger quotes.

He clears his throat. "Yeah, I didn't come up with that one, but I'm not here to talk about that. You left so fast after the rodeo that I didn't get a chance to tell you…"

"Tell me what?"

He hitches his daughter up on his hip, looking a little sheepish as he glances down at the wooden porch. A knot of unease coils in my stomach. It's then that I notice what's behind him—the multiple suitcases, diaper bags, extra clothes.

The man's brought enough suitcases to last all summer.

"That's a hell of a lot of baggage you've got there," I say warily.

Luna barks her happy bark.

"Yeah, I know." He rocks back on his boots. "I wanted to talk to you about staying here at the barn this summer. Like old times."

6

NOT "YES"

WYATT

Goddamn, I need to chug a gallon of water looking at her like this. It's taking a massive effort not to let my gaze drop to her cleavage, but I can do it. I'm strong.

"How long?" Dakota demands, shooting me the mother of all glares. I try not to shrivel up.

She's standing in her purple lace bra, clearly not caring that she's topless. Purple. At least her favorite color is still the same.

She always used to say it was the color of Texas bluebonnets —not quite blue and not quite purple. Somewhere smack dab in the middle.

I've seen Dakota in a bikini, underwear, even naked once, on accident, and it never fails to make my mouth go dry. For a split second, I can't think of a thing to say. But I can't look at her now. The only time I let myself think about her body is when I'm lonely at night.

I hitch Vi's giraffe diaper bag up on my shoulder, mostly to give myself something to do. "How long what?" I ask, trying to clear the gravel in my throat.

"How long are you planning on staying here?" she states flatly.

There's no emotion, no fire in her voice, and I know for a fact this woman can light someone up with her words. It's one of my favorite things about her—that fire. It pushed me to be better, do more, impress her.

She leans against the door frame, pressing her shoulder over our height marks etched into the wood. *Wyatt & Dakota 2006.* I hope she's not trying to cover up our memories.

"I'll head back at the end of August for preseason training," I say. "So just for the off-season. Maybe a couple of months? I want to help out with the farm. Make sure things are still running smoothly."

"That long, huh?" She huffs. A piece of brown hair goes flying up into the summer heat.

Okay, two months is not *that* long.

"Please? We'll stay out of your way," I beg, scratching Luna-Tuna behind her ear as she shoves her face right in my crotch.

This dog.

She's the best.

Not because her face is in my crotch, to be clear.

"Why can't you stay with your moms at the main house?" she asks.

"They're renovating the upstairs this summer, so there's sawdust and nails everywhere. I don't want Vi around that, and plus, they don't have any extra bedrooms downstairs. You've got an extra room here, so it'd be perfect for the two of us."

Her gaze lingers on my daughter before settling back on me. I want to believe her lips twitch in a smile as she looks at my girl, but I can't tell. She shifts her focus, and it feels like she's scrutinizing the dark circles under my eyes, but if she's thinking about shooting me down, she doesn't show it on her face, thankfully.

I can't handle any more awe-filled yet pitiful looks like the ones I get from women in the grocery store fruit aisle. You'd think I was performing open-heart surgery on an airplane with the way women look at me pushing my daughter in the cart.

31

I'm just being a fuckin' dad, grocery shopping with my kid. No need for a round of applause, ladies.

All she does is brush a curl off her forehead before flicking a hand to the rustic living room. "By all means, have at it. Technically, this is your parents' barn, so if you need a place to stay, you don't need to ask for my permission. The room's all yours."

My brows soar. "Really? You're not going to fight me on this?"

She rolls her eyes. "Of course not. I'm not going to be rude and deny you and your daughter a place to stay. Plus, I don't have the energy to fight you, Patterson. I've got to focus on training this summer for the Granite Falls rodeo at the end of August. I'll be traveling most weeks to rodeos around the state, so stay wherever you want. I don't really give a shit."

Her words are sharp, but I can still hear the slight wobble of hurt in her voice, and all that does is fuel my determination to make things right.

I know I fucked up. I'm man enough to admit that, but I had a good reason. "You're sure you're okay with this?"

She shrugs, but it's stiff. "Positive. Room's yours."

She grabs one of my duffle bags from the porch, spins on her heel, and struts inside without another word. That was nice of her. She's always been an acts-of-service type of woman. She spent one winter building an entire irrigation system for the flower farm all to surprise us that summer.

"Thanks for grabbing my bag," I say.

She doesn't respond, so with a heavy sigh and Vienna chewing on my hair, I follow her inside the rustic barn.

Not much has changed.

The walls are still cedar. The furniture is still leather. There's still that stone fireplace we never lit because it would be insane to light a fire in the middle of a Texas summer. Ugh. I'm sweating just thinking about that.

It's all the same, but the open floor plan seems... emptier.

That's when I realize all the random estate sale items Dakota and I collected over the years are gone. The old-school vinyls. That broken rooster clock. The cowboy frame that used to have a picture of us stuffing fresh strawberries into each other's mouths at Sweeter Berry Farm.

It seems like she threw out all our memories, which I guess is good. I'll look at the positives. We have extra space now, especially since the person I hired to babyproof the barn is coming tomorrow. The highchair can go on the granite island, and I can set up Vi's play mat in the living room. She's not walking yet, which is a sore spot for me, but we'll make this work.

We always do.

I glance around the open floor plan living room, searching for any remnants of our memories. "You got rid of that old dart board we found at that estate sale in Sisterdale?"

Dakota doesn't bother turning around to look at me, but now that we're in the light, I'm cataloging every scar, bruise, and wound on her bare skin.

She's so damn strong.

"I didn't have anyone to shoot darts with," she says with a shrug. "So I gave it to my friend, Lana. She likes getting high and throwing darts. Not the best combination, but who am I to judge?"

I chuckle. "Remember when we found that old bong at an estate sale and—"

"No," she interjects in a hard voice. "We're not doing this."

"Doing what?"

She casts a glance over her bare shoulder, and there's nothing but indifference in her gaze. "We're not reminiscing."

Her bedroom door opens, and I grimace when the paramedic from the rodeo walks out in nothing but a pair of American flag boxers. I'm all for a little Fourth of July pride if we're at a parade, but I already don't like him. "Hey, Kodie. You still coming in here, Killer?"

She bites her bottom lip, smirking at him in a way she never did at me. "Yeah, sugar. I'll be right in."

Jealousy rips through me again, but I'm so used to feeling that with Dakota that it barely bothers me anymore. I think I'm desensitized to the emotion.

"Who are you?" the guy asks me, dark brows coming together. "Wait, I know you. Weren't you at the rodeo earlier?"

"Yeah, I'm—"

"He's no one," Dakota interrupts, and I wince.

That stings most of all because I used to be the guy she'd stay up all night on the phone with.

The paramedic looks between us, waiting for more. "Oh. Well, uh, good to meet you, man."

He holds out a hand, but I'd rather change Vi's diapers for eternity than make polite conversation with Dakota's one-night stand, so I give him a stiff smile, gently rocking my girl.

I really need to wrap this up and get her tucked into bed soon. She's a champ for hanging in there all day without a nap. Did I pack her favorite blanket? I think it's in the backseat. Yeah, I shoved it in there right before we left.

Dakota struts over to the fridge, jerks open the stainless steel door, and stares at the contents for a while before releasing a heavy sigh.

"Actually, he's not no one," she corrects, closing the fridge. "This is Wyatt Patterson. He's a right winger for the Nashville Guardians, and that's his daughter, Vienna. His parents own the barn, and he's got to move his stuff in tonight, so you best be leaving."

"What? You're seriously kicking me out?" His mouth drops, and so does mine. I can't believe she's sending him away.

Hell yeah.

"I seriously am," she states.

"You've got to be shitting me," he complains. "I've been waiting for this all night."

What a prick. I've been waiting for her for over a decade, so get in line.

She picks up her T-shirt from the leather armchair and pulls it over her head. Thank hell.

"Nope. I'm not," she says. "Door's that way."

The guy huffs and puffs as he puts on his clothes but doesn't say anything. All he does is shoot her a glare before he slams the front door on his way out.

Vienna lets out a screeching wail at the noise. "Dada!"

Shoot. It's her I'm-tired-gurgle-cry.

I bounce her gently, trying to soothe her sobs until she quiets. We road-tripped straight from Nashville with my parents, and she's taking this transition like a tiny boss. Frankly, I'm shocked my girl hasn't thrown a tantrum sooner.

I coo in her ear. "Hey, it's okay, baby. Daddy's got you. I've always got you."

Dakota watches us with a concerned pinch in her brows. "How've you been holding up? Being a single parent looks like hell on earth."

I smile down at my snotty little girl. "It's not easy, that's for sure, but she's the best thing that's ever happened to me. The good days make all the bad ones worth it, and I'm lucky I've got my parents to help out."

Balancing the life of a hockey player with being a single dad has been a grind, but I have two strong women in my life to help raise my daughter. Though, I wish I had a teammate to hang in there with me through all the gritty parts of parenthood. It's been hard to find a woman who wants to stick it out with me through the shit-soaked onesie explosions.

Fuck, those were gross.

Her eyes narrow on my tipped-up lips. "You're still so positive, aren't you? Always looking at the bright side."

"I mean, yeah? I'd rather focus on the good parts of life than the bad parts."

I'm a pretty simple man because I've got a lot to be grateful for—amazing parents, a job that's my passion, a beautiful little girl, great friends. Not much gets to me anymore. If the people in my life are happy, then I'm happy.

She snorts a scoff. "Yeah, but the bad parts hit so much harder. It's the shitty things that always stay with you."

"Only if you let them," I say.

"Of course I let them. That's what keeps me going. I need to prove everyone wrong."

She's a cynic through and through, always chasing her dreams, but I've never minded her cloudy demeanor. It stems from an innate sense of ambition, which always made me better.

Growing up, watching her chase a dream made me want to go after mine, just to get on her level. My parents never pushed me in one direction or another. They wanted me to figure things out on my own, but seeing Dakota's drive sharpened me. Every summer, I'd come back a little stronger, wanting to impress her.

In all honesty, part of me always wanted to be a little more like her. Ambitious. Determined. Focused. She's what got me strong enough to play in the NHL.

Dakota's eyes shift to Vienna snoozing on my shoulder, but all she does is stare at my girl while I search her face for a hint of her underlying emotions.

I find nothing.

Eventually, she whispers, "She looks just like you."

Pride swells deep in my heart. That shouldn't matter, but it does. With her wild golden curls that I'm constantly untangling and those bright green eyes, there's no doubt she's mine. "Yeah, you think so? She's pretty darn cute, isn't she?"

"Yeah, I do." She swallows, slow and thick, before she clears her throat. "Your room's down the hall on the right, but I'm sure you remember."

I glance down the hallway and stiffen when I spot what's

sitting on the wooden cupboard. Right there, I see it—that cowboy frame with us shoving strawberries into each other's mouths.

"You kept the strawberry photo?" I ask.

She pauses. "Yeah, Patterson. I kept it."

I wait for her to add something, but she doesn't. Spinning around, she heads to her bedroom with Tuna hobbling behind her, but before she can shut the door, I stop her.

"Dakota?"

She stiffens, and I've already noticed she does that every time I say her name.

"What?"

I swallow a lump. "I heard you called off your engagement, and I'm sorry about you and Boone. Must've been a tough decision."

She gives a blasé shrug, but she's picking at her cuticles like she always does when she's nervous. "Not really. We were never a good fit, and I see that now... Night, sugar."

She closes her bedroom door, treating me like all the other men in her life.

Sugar.

I hate that nickname, but I don't hate it nearly as much as having to watch Boone Bowman get down on one knee in front of her family and her looking so damn ecstatic that I had to chug three bottles of cheap champagne to put a smile on my face. I had the world's deadliest headache the next day and vowed never to drink champagne again.

The sugary death trap.

After one last two-step dance where I lied and said I was happy for her, not dying inside, she dropped my hand, and I booked a ticket back to Nashville. After that, I cut off all communication because I needed to get over her.

What was I going to do? Fight for her? No. She thought she

loved him, and I wanted her to be happy, even if it meant I'd never be.

That day three years ago changed the course of my life. All because she uttered that one crushing word to Boone Bowman— *yes*.

SAYS EVERY FATHER

WYATT

The next morning, Dakota sprints out the door for an early workout, so I decide to help my moms plow the flower fields. All the rows are blooming in spite of the triple-digit heat, so Dakota's been doing a great job helping manage the farm. I thanked her last night, but she just she shrugged, like managing a ten-acre farm is no big deal.

It's a huge deal.

My parents' family owns Windmill Meadow Ranch—a boutique flower provider for small-town businesses in the Texas Hill Country. It's a family business, and all my aunts and uncles help manage the ranch during the winter months since we only come back from Nashville during the summers. I'm pretty sure everyone on my Southern mom's side of the family has owned a flower farm at some point, which is how I learned to make a bouquet faster than a florist.

"Jesus fuckin' Christ, it's hotter than a sauna in hell out here," my mama, Stella, complains while spraying the row of orange zinnias with her garden hose. "Since when did Texas get to be so hot? I don't remember it being this bad. Do y'all?"

"Yeah. You walk outside and start sweating," my other mom, Jessie, says.

She presses a kiss to her sweaty cheek. Over twenty years together and they're still ridiculously in love. Maybe that's why I'm such a hopeless romantic, pining for a woman who wants nothing to do with me.

"Do you say your prayers in church with that dirty mouth of yours?" my mom adds.

She winks under her sun hat. "You bet I do. Every fuckin' Sunday. If our sweet baby Jesus sends me to hell for having a dirty mouth, I want no part of that heaven."

"Mama," I groan, rubbing SPF 100 on Vi's sweaty face. There will be no sunburns on my watch. "How many times do I have to tell you to watch your words around Vi? She's repeating everything right now."

"She's only said two coherent words, Wyatt," she says. "So, if she's repeating the word *fuck*, it'll probably sound like *fuh*."

Stella Anderson scrubbed my mouth out with soap when I forgot to say "yes, ma'am," but she's got no problem cursing more than a frustrated parent. Maybe that's why she fell in love with a crass hockey coach from up north.

Jessie's my Northern mom, but Stella's my Southern mama. That's what I call them—mom and mama. My mama's got the same blond hair and green eyes as me since I'm hers biologically, thanks to a generous sperm donor, but while I didn't get my mom's brown hair and brown eyes, I got all my hockey skills from Jessie Patton. They combined their two last names— Patton and Anderson—when they got married to form Patterson.

As an NHL player in Nashville, I might've only spent my summers in Texas, but my mama was raised in Granite Falls, so I consider myself a Southern gentleman since I was raised by a true Texan. Her sister's family even owns the old dive bar in town—The General.

My mom sprays some sunflowers. "So, how've things with Kodie been? Was she okay with you moving in?"

"I don't know. I can't tell what she's thinking anymore," I say, slathering more sunscreen on Vi's face. "I almost wish she'd yell at me for leaving, but it's like she doesn't even care that I'm back."

"Give her time," my mama says. "She'll come around. She's always—"

Gravel crunches and Dakota's 1971 pale-blue Ford Bronco pulls up to the barn, cutting off our conversation. I still remember the summer she spent covered in grease, fixing up Daisy Blue, as she calls it, with her dad.

She steps out of Daisy Blue wearing nothing but a sports bra and tiny shorts that hug her athletic frame. The late afternoon sun catches the sheen of sweat on her skin, highlighting every curve and muscle. She's clearly getting back from training, and goddamn, she looks good sweaty.

"Kodie Cutler! Get over here, and come say hello to your favorite neighbors!" Mama shouts, waving her arm around with a giant smile.

Dakota struts through the field of yellow flowers and wraps both my moms in a warm bear hug. "Holy shit, it's been too long! My goodness, I've missed y'all. How the hell are you?"

Her face lights up with a dimpled grin, and I can't help the pang that hits me. I want that smile directed at me.

She releases them from her vice hug and scans my face with a frown, but then her eyes slide to Vienna, and she gives her a small grin. "Hey, girl. You're looking mighty cute in that pink bucket hat."

"Mo!" Vi giggles, thrashing in her stroller like she's trying to get to Dakota, which isn't all that surprising.

She *is* my girl after all.

A dimple flickers in her cheek. "I don't have any more hats, but I'll see what I can do for you. You're pretty hard to say no to. Just like your daddy."

Fuck.

I like hearing her call me daddy.

"Dada!" Vienna suddenly squeals, repeating her.

That dampens the heat in my body. I'm constantly swinging between *man* and *dad* so much that I get dizzy. She squirms in her shaded stroller. Her high-pitched laughter fills the space between us, and it's the best sound in the world.

"Yes, ma'am?" I coo. Her cheeks are a little flushed from the heat, but I've got those attachable fans pointed at her face.

She claps her tiny hands. "Dada! Dada!"

I kiss her cheek. She wants some attention. "Yes ma'am, that's me, baby. Your daddy, and I love you very much."

I thought I knew what love was, but when I had a child, my entire definition expanded. No matter how wiped out I am, I can't help but crack a smile when I look down at my little girl.

My mom nods down to Vienna's T-shirt that reads *Long Live Cowgirls*. "I'm surprised she hasn't had a meltdown yet. She's doing pretty well for being in a whole different routine."

"She's always happy when she's with her daddy." I pick her up, nuzzling her face in a way I know makes her laugh. "Isn't that right, baby girl?"

"That she is," she agrees. "Goodness, she's getting so big."

"I hear kids grow up pretty fast," Dakota adds.

"They do," I agree, latching on to any shred of conversation she's willing to throw my way. "I still remember the day I took Vi home from the hospital. She was so tiny. Five pounds, eight ounces. I remember being terrified that I'd trip and drop her."

Mama slaps her knee. "I forgot about that! Oh my goodness, when it was time to put her in the car seat, it took you over thirty minutes to figure out the seat belt puzzle, and then you crept down the highway at twenty miles under the speed limit. Don't you remember that, Jessie?"

"Oh, I remember, alright," Mom says. "Thankfully, you had us."

Vi cried the whole way home, this piercing sound that made my chest ache, but the moment I took her out of the car and into my arms, she stopped.

Just like that.

It was like she knew she was safe with me.

The hard parts of parenting can outweigh the good, but the good parts are so much brighter. Most people can relate to the difficulties of parenthood—changing diapers, the lack of sleep—but it's hard to explain the gut-wrenching awe that comes with hearing your child's laugh for the first time, or watching them smile, or take their first steps... Not that my baby girl's walking yet.

"She sure is a cutie though," Dakota says, reaching down to pinch her cheeks.

She stares at my little girl for a moment, and it looks like there's yearning in her eyes, but I don't want to get carried away with that thought.

"Isn't she? It's a good thing too, since that girl's got a set of lungs on her," Mom says, grabbing her shoulder. "We missed you, Kodie. It's good to see you again."

"I missed y'all too. How's Windmill Meadow Ranch look?" Dakota asks, spreading her arms in a circle to showcase all her hard work. "Up to your high standards? Y'all know if you give me a task, I have to overachieve."

"Sweetie, we would've been in a world of hurt if it hadn't been for you," Mama says. "You're an angel."

They continue to talk about the farm, exchanging *thank-yous* and *I've missed yous* while she seems like she works hard to not look at me. She continues standing there in those tiny shorts, and I don't say a word because my throat's parched from looking at her. I can never pull my shit together around this woman. It's like I revert back to that same boy-obsessed teenager. Dakota doesn't say anything to me either, and then she heads back to the barn without a goodbye.

Mama sighs, watching the screen door swing shut. "I always wanted you to marry that girl. You two were so cute together."

"I need to get her talking to me again first," I say as Vi grabs at the mood ring around my neck. I tug it out of her grabby hands because, *choking hazard.*

Mom lets out her booming bark of a laugh that always makes everyone in the near vicinity jump. "You will. You've had a crush on her since you were eight. It's a damn shame you stopped talking to her."

"I still remember all those nights you'd sprint home from hockey practice to wait by the phone for her call, remember that, Jessie?" Mama says. "It was when we still had that landline, and we wouldn't let him get a cell, so he'd lock himself in the pantry to try and get some privacy."

"Oh, but we could still hear." Mom chuckles as she waters the sunflowers and starts mimicking my voice before it dropped. "'I miss you, Dakota. No, like, I really miss you. I wish I could be with you all year, and not just the summers.'" She kisses my burning cheek. "You were always such a lover, sweetheart. Don't ever change."

I shoot my moms a hollow glare. I can admit it; I'm a mama's boy, and because of how close I am with my parents, you can bet I'll raise a daddy's girl. "How about we stop talking about my most embarrassing teenage moments, yeah?"

Mom adjusts her navy Guardians cap. "But that's the best part of being a parent. Embarrassing your children. You'll get your payback when Vi starts dating."

I grimace, glancing at my baby girl chewing on her tiny fists. I want her to stay this little forever. "The thought of her dating makes me want to puke."

Mama kisses my cheek, a gold strand of her hair getting caught in my scruff. "Says every father."

8

RIP SEXY PATTERSON

DAKOTA

I'd made peace that my friendship with Wyatt Patterson was dead and buried, but now he's turned the barn into something out of a children's fantasy playroom.

I've never seen so many toys. Just this evening, on my way to Alanna's picturesque cottage beneath the old oak trees, I almost tripped on a wooden shopping cart full of plastic vegetables that apparently... sing?

"He's staying with me all summer, Lana." I groan, sucking on the tip of the pre-rolled joint. The skunky smoke fills my head, quieting my buzzing worries.

My best friend tosses her red hair over one shoulder. "Why don't you just kick him out?"

I blow out the smoke. "Because that's mean, and I'm not a complete asshole. His daughter is stinkin' cute, so that's a plus, and he makes banana pancakes every morning, so there's that."

We used to do brunch with our parents every Sunday, and banana pancakes used to be our *thing*, so he's been constantly knocking on my bedroom door with a plate of steaming pancakes like he wants me to remember we have *things*.

It's actually pretty adorable.

"You've got to love a sexy single dad who cooks," she says, sucking until the joint's tip glows more red than her hair. "Does he have any brothers?"

"No, he's an only child."

"What a shame." She blows a smoke ring. "Hey, will you come to the farmer's market with me this weekend? I feel like I've barely seen you."

"I can't. I have to train."

"You're *always* training," she whines. "Why do you say no to everything? Just come out with me."

Guilt prickles in my skin. I want to hang out with her, but I can't sacrifice any time training, especially not with the Granite Falls rodeo coming up at the end of the summer.

"I'm hanging out with you now," I counter.

"Only because I basically dragged your ass here, which is fine. I'll reel you back in anytime you pull away."

"The world needs more Lanas," I say. "You're my favorite."

"Aw," she sing-songs. "You're *my* favorite."

I've sacrificed one too many relationships for my career, but I don't want to think about all the sacrifices I've made. All it does is fill me with this weird mix of regret and determination. I've missed out on so much that I have to make it now.

Looking out at the rolling grassy fields, I rock back in a white porch chair. Alanna's teeny cottage is nestled on an acre of old oaks, but it's decorated like an upscale designer renovated the chic interior, whereas my place is a hodgepodge of hand-me-down antiques.

I wind up my arm and toss the tennis ball high into the pink sky, watching it arc before it lands with a soft thud in the tall grasses.

Luna hobbles off. It always takes her forever to get it, but she loves fetching.

"If you're still hunting for someone at farmers markets, I'm sure Patterson would date you," I say. "He's the commitment type, so I could put in a good word."

Alanna shakes her fiery hair. "Nope. No thanks. Kids are cute, but I'm not like you. I want to keep my life as it is, and I don't want to give up my preventative Botox appointments during pregnancy."

"Why do you do preventative Botox? You're naturally stunning."

Alanna is one of those women who turns every head in the room, and she's got a killer personality, so she's basically got it all.

She gestures to herself with a snort. "You think this is *au naturel*? Babe, I drive into Austin three times a month to get work done. Once to color my hair so it's this 'natural' shade of auburn, once to get chemicals injected into my forehead so it stays wrinkle-free, and once to get my eyelash extensions. I'm a carefully crafted stunner."

"But a stunner nonetheless."

"That's because I don't scowl all the time like you," she throws back, gesturing to her forehead. "I can't afford frown lines."

"I don't scowl *all* the time," I grumble, but Alanna has a point.

My sense of humor is painfully sarcastic, my raspy voice sounds like a chain-smoker, and I don't like my face when I smile, so I rarely smile. All of that is the perfect combination for a chronic case of resting bitch face. I've had guys tell me I look constipated when I grin, so I stopped. But I care deeply about the people in my life, and all I want is for someone to love my rough edges.

People call me mean, but I'm just a little spicy.

"You do, babe," she says. "But that's why you're the Bonnie to my Clyde. The yin to my yang. The coffee to my cinnamon roll dairy-free creamer."

I laugh into the sunset. Alanna and I shouldn't work as friends, but I've been trapped in a man's world for so long that I crave female friendships. I'm an only-child boys' girl, and she's a textbook big-family girls' girl, but for some reason, we're like long-lost sisters.

Alanna's a Houston princess who comes from old money, and she's high maintenance but handles her own maintenance. She's got a closet of snakeskin boots and fringe jackets she only pulls out in winter and always manages to keep her linen jumpsuits wrinkle-free. She's what we call "cowgirl chic" because you'd never *actually* wear those clothes on a ranch.

They'd get too dirty.

She's one of the best people I know. I managed to wiggle my way into her life when she moved here from the city.

There are just some strangers that pop into your life, and when you meet them, you think, *Now, that's someone I've got to keep*, and that was Lana for me. We just work—even though she won't stop trying to get me on her thirty-two-step skincare routine.

She creaks back in her rocking chair. "Why're you so pissed at Wyatt, anyway? Don't you want to at least hear him out?"

"Not really," I say. "He's going to leave again anyway, so what's the point? I'd rather just be civil to him this summer. Like roommates."

I suck in a long drag, needing an extra moment to gather my thoughts. "But I'm pissed 'cause we used to spend every summer together and then talk almost every week on the phone when he went back to Nashville, but then he stopped returning my calls. He wouldn't even respond to my texts. Then, I read somewhere online that he had a little girl, and that was the last straw. That's the kind of shit you tell your friends, you know?"

At least, that's what I thought I'd been to him, but I'm not about to force anyone to be my friend. If someone doesn't like me, that's okay. I like who I am.

Luna comes back, dropping the tennis ball at my feet. This time, Alanna throws it for her. "You're only pissed because you miss him," she says, calling me on my bluff. "And I mean, he *did* have a kid. I'm sure that's kept him pretty busy."

"Yeah, but he still could've called," I grumble. "I know he's this hotshot NHL player, but it's not like I was asking for much. I would've been satisfied with a few Happy Birthday texts, but instead, I got ghosted by my so-called friend. Men should know how to communicate by now."

"Ugh, I know," she agrees. "And when is manspreading gonna go out of style? There's no way your balls need *that* much room."

She blows out a perfect smoke ring, kicking up her cowgirl boots on her back porch. The cicadas hum to life now that the setting sun is about to dip behind the oak trees.

There's nothing more beautiful than a Texas sunset sprawling across the Hill Country. I'm a morning person, but this is my favorite time of day—when the heat is about to burst, and the clouds look like they're on fire.

"That Wyatt Patterson's a looker though." She whistles. "The whole town's talking about him being back. I heard Ms. Thompson talking about setting him up with her granddaughter in the grocery store."

Ms. Thompson's granddaughter is in no way good enough for Wyatt Patterson, but like hell am I saying that out loud.

"Damn, it's weird hearing people call him attractive," I say, trying to picture it, but I can't. "He'll always be the little flower boy that followed me around every summer."

I toss the tennis ball again for Luna, but she must've had enough because she plops down next to me on the porch, rolling over for a belly rub.

Damn, do I love this dog.

Alanna passes me the joint, and I'm definitely high now because I'm squinting at the longhorns in the field splattered with yellow wildflowers, thinking about how one of them has a spot that looks like the birthmark on Wyatt's right ass cheek.

I saw that once when I dared him to go skinny-dipping in the stock tank the cattle drink from. He spent the whole time trying to shield his dick from me, but he did it. That boy used to do anything I asked. He spoiled me, and he was always too good for me.

"So you and Wyatt never...?" she prods, blowing another smoke ring.

"Never." I grimace. "I'm two years older than him, so I've never thought of Patterson like that. I know two years isn't a huge gap now, but when you're teenagers? It's massive. When I was sixteen, he was this gangly fourteen-year-old. He's like family. Not like a brother, but like... a cousin."

She swats her curtain of wine-stained hair over one shoulder. "Wyatt Patterson is really sexy, though. He looks like an archangel you want to rough up a bit, you know? I'm not into single dads, but you should fuck him for the plot."

"No. Even if I were attracted to him, I couldn't. Especially not after he drunkenly peed the bed *with me in it* at my eighteenth birthday party because he drank fuck knows how many beers. I ruined that kid's innocence. I had to wash all my sheets three times, Lana. It kind of killed any romantic notions I could've had."

Admittedly, at the time, I thought it was hilarious. I'm used to shoveling horse shit, so a little drunk pee doesn't scare me away. I used to tease him about it, but anytime I brought it up, the tips of his ears would turn bright red, so I stopped because I didn't want to embarrass him.

Little giggles splutter out of us.

"Yeah, there's no coming back from the friend zone after that," she says, clutching her stomach. "RIP Sexy Patterson."

I salute her with my joint. "My thoughts exactly."

9

BANANA PANCAKES

DAKOTA

"*Y*ou're the... ah, shi—darn!"

There's a loud clang and something tumbles to the floor. I rush around the corner of the kitchen to find Wyatt with his hair tied back at the nape of his neck, holding a screaming baby in one arm while running his other thumb under the kitchen sink. His white T-shirt and sweats are covered in what looks like pancake batter.

He's a right mess.

Luna is licking up something on the floor like my personal three-legged cleaning lady. I give her a good scratch as I walk by, unnoticed by Patterson.

We've developed a nice routine over the past week. I wake up before the rooster crows, sneak out of the barn to plow, mow, and water the flower fields, and then I head to the arena to practice anytime we've got animal stock in town.

I'm keeping busy, and I'm not about to let Patterson throw my dreams off track. I've got to put on at least another ten pounds of muscle if I want a shot at making it in the big leagues. My thighs better be *thique* by the end of the summer.

"Come on, baby," Wyatt murmurs, sucking his thumb. "Daddy

just burned himself, but he's okay. See? Don't cry. Please? I'm trying to make you breakfast. Your favorite. Banana pancakes. You like pancakes, right? Can you say pancakes?"

Vienna screams. Damn, that girl really does have a set of lungs on her.

The acrid smell of burning fills the kitchen as Wyatt frantically tries to turn off the stove, juggle a sizzling pan, and make coffee all while balancing a tiny human. It's actually kind of impressive watching this one-man-daddy show. But it must be tough doing all this alone.

"Need some help?" I offer.

Wyatt jumps, hitting his head on the vintage light dangling over the stove. His eyes drop to my bare legs, lingering for a moment, but it's not a sexy look. At least, I don't think it is… It's more like his gaze fell to my legs and now he's too tired to look away.

"Hey, morning. It's fine," he mumbles, shaking his head like he's jerking himself out of a trance. "I just burned myself on the pan, but I'll be good."

I don't understand how he manages to say everything so casually. This man could be in the middle of a hurricane, and as long as he had an umbrella, he'd be grinning.

He bounces his daughter in his arms, clearly trying to soothe her wails, and that's when I notice the dark circles under his eyes. Those weren't there three years ago, but he wasn't a father when he left.

I have no idea what happened to Vienna's mom, and I don't really want to think about Wyatt's romantic partners because that makes me feel all kinds of uncomfortable, but no one should have to do all this alone. It seems exhausting. There's already a mountain of clothes in the laundry room, and it's only been one week.

I point a thumb over my shoulder. "There's some antibiotic

ointment in the bathroom. Give me Vienna and go take care of that burn. I've got her."

He blinks. Stares. Blinks again, almost like he's shocked I'd even offer, which stings. I might be pissed at him for his lackluster communication skills, but I'm not going to be blatantly rude to him.

"It's fine," he says. "You don't have to do that."

"That wasn't a question, Patterson," I say. "Go take care of that hand."

Wyatt's always been a giver, giving everything to everyone, so much so that he forgets about his own needs. He needs a push when it comes to taking care of himself, and I can give him that kick in the ass.

He hesitates. "You'd really do that for me?"

"Yeah, but I'd do that for anyone. Don't go feeling special or anything." I shrug like it's no big deal, but I actually wouldn't offer to do this for just anyone. I'm doing this for *him*. "You know I've always loved kids."

"Yeah, you always did love giving all my younger cousins piggyback rides growing up," he says.

I shrug. "Kids are a good time. They're direct, tell it like it is, and they don't bullshit you."

Of course, they can be a handful, but I always wondered what it would be like to have a big, boisterous family since it was only me and my dad growing up.

When I was young, my mother divorced him for a travel vlogger, @TreytheTrekker, but I don't blame her. She was never one for the small-town life, and I'm glad she's living it up in her forties.

She's always been a free spirit, which is why she travels the world with @TreytheTrekker's backpack. But my mom never misses our Sunday phone calls no matter where she is in the world, and I love her for that.

Wyatt's throat bobs. "Thanks for offering, but Vi's in a mood this morning. I think she's got a molar coming in or something. You don't have to hold her. She'll just scream louder, and your ears will be ringing all day."

I roll my eyes, holding out my arms. "If I can wrangle a bull, I can wrangle a toddler. Give her to me and go take care of your hand. I want to help. We should probably get better acquainted anyway if you're going to be here for the next two months."

Wyatt seems to have a moment of indecision. He looks down at the burning pancakes, then back up at me, and then does that three more times until he turns off the stove.

"You sure?" he raises his voice over Vienna's snotty screams.

I wiggle my fingers in a give-her-to-me motion. "Yeah, I'm sure. I'll take care of your girl while you take care of that burn."

"Okay…" He nods to himself. "Okay, thanks. She likes looking at ceiling fans too, so if she doesn't calm down, just stick her under a fan. She'll go right into this hypnotic baby trance."

"We'll be fine, Patterson. Go. We've got plenty of fans here."

He hands her over, and when our arms brush, I jerk my fists away as fast as possible. His face falls, but he walks down the hall to the bathroom, right after giving Luna a little nuzzle.

Vienna instantly starts thrashing in my arms, but it's nothing compared to a bull. I start rubbing circles on her back, but that does absolutely shit-all for the wailing.

"Well, aren't you a little devil? You're cute but definitely a menace." I wipe the snot from her button nose with her cowgirl T-shirt. "I think we'll get along just fine, screaming and all. Seems like you're a little spicy like me. Now, what is it? Do your teeth hurt?"

She screams louder, and now I feel bad for the little girl. Her teeth must really hurt, so I scan the kitchen for her teething ring. "It's okay. Sometimes, I just want to scream at the world too. Let it out while you can, girl, 'cause when you're all grown up, you're gonna have to muster up a fake smile, and you'll feel like you're tacking on a cowboy emoji to hide all your hardest feelings."

She keeps wailing, so I start singing the first song that comes to mind. She peers up at me with her wide green eyes, and it feels like I'm looking at Wyatt. After a moment of staring, her crying turns to little sniffs.

I perk up. Holy shit. I *did* it. I'm rarely, if ever, the person to calm people down, so this feels like a tiny accomplishment.

"There we go, and look, we didn't even need a ceiling fan," I coo as she settles. She might just be the most adorable kid I've seen. "You like eating banana pancakes while singing 'Banana Pancakes' too?"

All she does is blink up at me, and I find myself smiling for the first time in a long while.

Bull riding is a self-serving sport. I do it because I thrive off the adrenaline rush, and I never have to think about anyone but myself. I don't need anyone, and no one needs me, but as I'm sucked in by her baby greens, I can't help but be a little jealous that Wyatt's got someone who relies on him.

No one relies on me.

She latches onto one of my brown curls, calming. "What?" I ask. "You like me talking to you? I'm Kodie. Can you say Kodie? Ko-die."

"No," she says in her high-pitched voice through another sniffle. "No. No. No."

"Yeah, that's my favorite word too, and a good one to know for when you're older and have to tell off all those boys or girls." I chuckle, swaying her in my arms.

She settles down as I continue to sway her, and then I turn around to find Wyatt leaning against the doorframe with a pink Barbie Band-Aid on his thumb, watching us with a small grin tugging at his lips.

I stiffen. "I didn't realize you were done."

He swallows visibly. "Yeah, I was just, uh, watching you two —" He cuts himself off, almost like he was caught doing something illegal. "You were singing our song."

"Oh. I guess I was."

He runs a hand through his messy hair, blowing out a breath. A deep V forms between his brows. "How'd you get her to stop crying?"

"I just sang to her a little and talked like a normal human."

His lips twitch. "She must like you. Most of the time it feels like she's trying to burst my eardrum."

"A girl can still love you and want to strangle you at the same time," I mutter, bopping his daughter on the nose to avoid looking at him. There was a little too much truth in that comment, so I tack on, "I better head out. I have to head to the arena for my skills session with my dad since I'm gunning for the PBR draft."

He takes Vienna from me, and his biceps clench with the movement. He's really filled out with all that hockey training. It's like his forearm veins have veins.

I never really noticed his body before because it feels strange to look at him that way, so I glance at the clock on the wall. I've got twenty minutes before I have to be at the arena for my training session.

He cocks his head so his stubbled cheek is resting on Vienna's. "You're really gunning for the draft? What team?"

"The Austin Rattlers."

Every small-circuit rodeo is a stepping stone to the big leagues. If I do well in one, it builds up my reputation. Then it grows the more I compete, and the more rodeo belt buckles I'll get.

He blows a low whistle. "Damn."

I can't tell whether that's surprise or doubt in his tone, but either way, it raises my hackles. "What?" I retort. "You don't think I can do it?"

"No, that's not it at all," he murmurs. "I think you can do anything."

My throat constricts at the sincerity in his voice. Ever since

Boone claimed I'd never make it, I've been doubting everything about myself, wondering if I'm really tough enough for this sport.

Wyatt has no idea how much those words mean to me, and suddenly, this barn feels like it's shrinking in on us. I can't stand the feeling. I prefer wide open spaces bigger than the Texas sky, so I dig through my backpack for something to do.

I pick out the stuffed longhorn I got last week when I went grocery shopping. I was originally going to use it as a chew toy for Tuna-Toons, but maybe his daughter will like it more.

"Here," I say, tossing out the stuffed animal. "I got this for Luna, but I think Vi might like it better, and it might help with the crying."

I hand it over, and she smiles and grabs it with her baby hands, squealing, "Wah!"

"That means she likes it," he says, watching the interaction with tipped-up lips. He picks up her tiny hand in a wave. "Can you say thank you, Vi?"

"No!" she shrieks. "Wah!"

I chuckle at her garbled thank you, but then my throat goes tight, thinking about when, if ever, I'll get to have a family of my own.

Wyatt and his adorable baby girl just remind me of the family I so desperately want, but I can't have yet because the sad, sad truth is that I'll always be cleaved down the middle, forced to straddle my dreams and my family.

I hate that I can't have it all.

10

SET IT ON FUCKING FIRE

WYATT

*H*ere's the thing about Dakota Cutler: she *acts* like she doesn't hold grudges, but really, she likes her grudges like her cowboy boots—old, broken in, and worn. She holds onto them so tightly because when someone hurts her, it cuts her deep.

She'll say she forgives you. She'll claim it's all water under the bridge. But she'll never forget, and you'll never be able to tell what she actually thinks since that woman doesn't speak a bad word about anyone.

It's one of my favorite things about her because that relentless tenacity saved my life, and I don't mean that like some over-the-top love confession—*you saved me from the worst parts of myself, no*—that girl actually saved my life during a flash flood at Cibolo Creek.

I'd been eight years old at the time, splashing around in the turquoise water with an imaginary sword when everyone started screaming, "Move to higher ground!"

I thought they were joking because Texas is supposed to be this dehydrated desert state, so how can there be flash floods in the Hill Country? But hills have valleys, and when those valleys fill, people drown.

If it hadn't been for Dakota's death grip, that would've been me—deader than a gaping fish.

The rain came pouring, and the water started rising. I was frantic, sweating despite the chilly summer storm. All I could think to do was to scramble onto one of the ancient cypress tree roots, but my fingers kept slipping on the wet bark as I tried to hoist myself up.

The water surged around me, filling my nostrils, and when I thought I couldn't hold on any longer, Dakota appeared, hovering over me like a dark angel. Her eyes blazed as she glared at me something fierce—even as a preteen, she could cut a man down with just a look.

"Grab my hand," she said. No, commanded.

I grabbed.

And she held.

Using all her strength, she pulled me up over the ledge until I crashed onto her chest, and then we ran to my sobbing mothers on higher ground. From that moment on, I knew I had to hold onto her like she held onto me.

"She hates me, Cruz," I groan, talking to him through my AirPods.

"Well, can you blame her?" my teammate, Micah Cruz, says on the phone.

He's our center for the Nashville Guardians and one of my best friends. He and Rhode Tremblay, our retired goalie, are my boys.

They stayed up with me through sleepless nights with my girl and sat by my side as I watched all the swaddling tutorials after she was born. If it weren't for them and my parents, I would've gone insane from lack of sleep those first few months.

"From what you've told me," he continues, chewing obnoxiously on something. Sounds like tortilla chips. "You basically came back and moved into some barn with your screaming baby. Don't get me wrong, Vi's cute but loud. I'd be pissed, too, if I were her."

Cruz gives everyone hell, but he's one of the best guys I know. Since Tremblay's off gallivanting in Argentina with his girl, Nina, Cruz answers my calls more often, and he always answers on the first ring no matter when I call.

"Yeah, you've got a point," I admit, racking the barbell in the open-air gym—Colt's Place.

Colter Cutler, Dakota's father, built a gym in Granite Falls for all the rodeo competitors to train at as part of his Give Back to the Community effort. It's not fancy, but they've got squat racks galore.

Cruz crunches a chip on the line. "What's her name again? Kodie, right?"

"You can call her Kodie, but I call her Dakota."

"Why do you call her that?"

"'Cause her dad named her after the song 'North Dakota' by Lyle Lovett, since, in his words, she came out screaming the day she was born, and it was the only song that calmed her down. He always hated that everyone shortened her name to Kodie."

Except, even Mr. Cutler can't help but call her Kodie now, so I'm the only one. It makes me feel like we've got something special.

He crunches again. "Damn, you two really do go back."

"Yeah, we do." With a grunt, I towel off the sweat on my forehead. "And what're you eating? Close your mouth."

"*Close your mouth*," he repeats with a snort. "You and those manners. What's with all your grunting? You sound like you're jacking off."

"How would you know what I sound like when I'm doing that?"

"'Cause we lived together for two years and shared a bathroom. I *know*."

"It's kind of weird that you were listening, man," I say.

"I have no boundaries. So, what're you doing? Need me to call you back so you can finish?"

With an eye roll, I tie my hair back. It's fucking steaming in here. "I'm doing what you should be doing instead of eating chips. Working out. Preseason practices are gonna be brutal if you don't hit the gym this summer."

A sharp twinge pierces through me at the thought of leaving Texas, but I push it aside and pick up my weights. This gym looks more like a renovated CrossFit studio with rubber mats and leg presses.

I can see Dakota kicking up dust in the distant training arena with the other bull riders, next to the giant white barn where they keep the animal stock. Her brown hair is plastered to her sweaty forehead, but I can't stop staring.

"So, back to Kodie," he says. "I've never heard you bring up this girl's name until you told us you were headed home to some small-ass town in the middle of fuck-knows-where, and you get quiet when you're hiding something. You in love with this woman or something?"

I stay silent.

Too silent.

"Holy shit!" Cruz yells on the phone. "Tell me everything. Right now."

He is never going to let me live this one down, and I need to talk this out. I've kept these feelings bottled up for too long, and I'm tired of acting like I'm not completely gone for Dakota Cutler.

I slump against the bench press, running a hand through my sweaty hair. "Yeah, alright, fine. I've liked her for a while now, but she has no idea."

"Damn." Cruz whistles out a long breath. "How long have you known her?"

"Since I was eight." I lower my voice to keep this private,

glancing at some guy doing pull-ups. He's sweating a shit-ton, so I should grab a towel for him.

"You've been obsessing over this woman for that long?" he shouts so loud I have to jerk the phone away. "Why the hell haven't you made a move?"

I scowl even though he can't see me. "Because every summer I came back, she always had a boyfriend, and then she got engaged to some bull rider named Boone Bowman, and I missed my chance, and that led to Vi, but I found out she called off her engagement, so I'm back now."

I stand from the bench and walk through the open garage gym door. Squinting against the bright sunlight, I spot Dakota sitting casually on the metal railing, watching one of the bull riders bucking around the arena. There's something about her intense focus that always makes me wonder what thoughts are racing through her mind.

"Are you gonna make your move this summer, then?" Cruz asks.

"I want to, but..." I shake my head even though he can't see. "It's complicated now. I've got Vi, and she's only ever seen me as a friend."

"How the hell is that even possible?" Cruz says. "You're sexy as shit."

A laugh jumps out of me. "I don't know, man. She likes guys with dark hair. Maybe I should dye my hair."

"Don't you fucking dare. You better not change a single hair on your head for any woman."

"I don't know how to change her mind." I groan, already googling hair salons on my phone, but then I close it out.

Dumbass idea. I'm not dying my hair. Then, I wouldn't look like Vi, and I love looking like my baby girl.

"You ever tried taking your shirt off in front of her?" he asks.

I chuckle.

"I'm serious, man," Cruz says. "You're fucking ripped. Whip

that shirt off every time you're around her. Guaranteed she'll notice."

My ears go hot, remembering the time I came back after gaining twenty pounds of muscle. She'd been on a big weightlifting kick the summer before, so I obviously had to bulk up to reach her level. I spent that whole summer shirtless, puffing out my chest, hoping she'd notice.

She didn't.

I towel off my sweat. "I don't know. We used to swim in this creek growing up, but she never cared. I tried everything."

"What is it about this woman?" he asks. "Why's she got you all twisted up?"

I stare at Dakota as she glares down a bull, and that same glowing sensation I've had for years flares in my chest. "She's always been the one for me. You know my parents, they're flower farmers and one's a middle school hockey coach—they never really pushed me toward anything. But Dakota? She always pushed me toward hockey."

"What do you mean?"

"She'd tell me to raise hell, to do whatever I wanted. She's the one who told me to dream big and go for the NHL. I probably wouldn't have even gone for the League if it weren't for her. She's ambitious, and I needed that 'cause I didn't have much direction growing up. She's good for me, and I know I could be so good for her."

"Fuck." Cruz snorts. "I didn't ask for a novel, man, but alright, I got it."

"What am I supposed to do?" I take a hefty swig of lukewarm water and toss an extra bottle to the guy next to me since his is empty.

"Alright..." He sighs overdramtically. "This is a tough one, but here's what you're gonna do. You're gonna grow a fucking pair, and tell her you're in love with her, and then you're gonna kiss the hell out of her so she gets the damn point. Problem solved."

Part of me is tempted to go for it, but that's a risky move. She could reject me, and then I would mess this up. Not to mention I'm not feeling as confident as I used to feel when I constantly smell like wet wipes.

It might make me old-fashioned, but I want her to fall for me naturally because falling for her was the most natural thing in the world for me.

"It's not that easy." I stand here, my eyes glued to Dakota's muscular silhouette in the distance. "I can't blurt that I'm in love with her. She hates me right now, so I've got to make things right first. What if I ruin everything?"

"That's exactly what you need to do. Ruin everything. Ruin that friendship. Set it on fucking fire. She's only ever seen you as a friend? Fine. You need to show her you're the man that got a woman pregnant *with* a condom. Those are some strong swimmers, Patty."

I huff a laugh. It's funny, but it's not.

Even though my life didn't turn out as I planned, I don't have any regrets about Vienna. She's not just part of my world, she is my world, but it's hard to ask someone to make my daughter their whole world too. "Yeah, but I've got my girl to think about, too. I come with a lot of baggage."

"Any woman who thinks your daughter is baggage shouldn't be *your* woman," Cruz declares, and dammit, he's not wrong.

"Okay, maybe you're right."

"I'm always right. You and Tremblay don't give me enough credit. The next time we talk, you better have made your move, or I'm flying down to Texas to force you, and then…"

He keeps talking, but a whistle in the distance draws my attention. The flank men open the gates, setting the bull loose with Dakota on its back.

This is only a practice round, but she's wearing that same determined expression that always makes my heart hammer.

They let her go in the arena, and then the bull is bucking wildly with her holding on for dear life.

Come on, honey. Stay on for me this round.

The bull bucks and bucks, and Dakota looks really stiff on the back of the animal. She needs to loosen up, or she's going to fall. After a few seconds, she goes flying through the air, right into the dirt.

I flinch like my pain is tied to hers. "I've got to go, Cruz."

I'm on my feet a second later, jogging through the field to get to her.

Always to get to her.

I WORK OUT

DAKOTA

"**G**oddammit!" I spit out the dirt in my mouth, looking up to see the guys wrangling Maverick, the bull, back into the training chute. It's hotter than hell out and these leather chaps are soaking up all the sweat.

That beast knocked me off good—the bastard.

Three seconds.

I smack my palms into the dirt. I can't believe I barely lasted three seconds, and that was on an easier animal. It doesn't matter who you are, it's tough to stay on for all eight seconds, but if I can't stay on, I won't even score.

A bull rider's score depends on the skill of the rider and aggressiveness of the bull, so if I want any shot of making it on the Austin Rattlers PBR team, I need to start scoring higher on some meaner animals.

"Dakota!"

I'd recognize Patterson's voice anywhere, but I don't dare turn to look, not with all the other bull riders' prying eyes on me. They're good guys, but they like to give me shit for anything and everything.

But I toss that shit right back. Well, to the best of my abilities. I've never been all that quick with a comeback.

Beneath the thick, vibrant sunlight, Wyatt rushes toward me with a few loose strands of dirty-blond hair curling in his eyes. He skids to a stop in the training arena, kicking up dirt around us, and seems to scan my entire body for injuries.

"Hey. Are you okay? You good?" he says.

The words tumble from his lips in a rush, making my jaw tense. I can't have him hovering over me in front of all the other bull riders, making me look like some damsel, even if my hands are shaking violently from that fall.

"I'm fine," I grit out, keeping my words blunt so he can't hear the tremble in my voice, but I think he might anyway. "What're you doing in our training pen?"

"You sure? That looked like a bad fall." He offers a helping hand to lift me up, but I shove off the dirt myself, dusting off my leather chaps.

I cross my arms to hide my trembling hands. "I'm fine. I'm used to falling on my ass. What're you doing here?"

He rubs the back of his neck, and the move is so familiar, so tender, it has me wanting to tone down the sharpness in my words. Wyatt Patterson isn't the type of man you can lash out at because he never bites back.

"I was working out at Colt's Place, saw you fall, and just wanted to come check you out." His green eyes pop. "I mean check on you. Not check you out." He coughs, going red, and that makes me grin a bit.

Awkward Wyatt is too cute.

It reminds me of how he was as a kid.

"You sure you're okay?" he tacks on.

The other riders holler from the fence, twirling their hats. I can't have them thinking less of me. These boys will have the rumor mill churning in no time, so I step out of his grasp. "I'm all good. You can get back to your workout."

He must hear something in my voice because he squeezes my shoulder with his calloused hand, and I'm vaguely aware of how much rougher it feels after all the years of hockey. "Hey, you did good out there. That bull was tough, but you'll get the next one."

He probably means for those words to be encouraging, but it comes off slightly patronizing. At least, that's how I take it because I know that ride was a shit show.

"Hey, Kodie!" one of the bull riders, Tyler, shouts, wiggling his dark brows. "You want to introduce us to your newest friend over there?"

"You gonna wreck him like Bowman?" Someone else whoops.

"Y'all mind your own business, or I'll wreck you!" I call over my shoulder, ripping myself away from Wyatt's firm grasp.

I wish I had a better comeback other than *I'll wreck you*, but I always think of the best ones a week later in the shower.

A few of the riders whistle at us, but I know they're only messing around. Bull riders are a tight-knit group. We've got to have each other's backs in this dangerous world, and we're all friends—*only* friends. I made that mistake once with Boone, and learned my lesson the hard way not to fuck where I shit.

Nasty visual, but it gets the point across.

Wyatt's eyes narrow on the guys. He opens his mouth like he's about to tell them off in my defense, but I instinctively press the tip of my index finger to his lips. "Don't do that."

The move startles him. "Do what?" His warm lips brush my fingers when he speaks, and I jolt back, startled by the zap of heat on my skin.

That's never happened before.

"Don't defend me or whatever you were about to do. I don't need it. I can handle myself." I lower my voice right along with my hand, flexing out the fiery imprint his lips left behind. "Not to mention, it makes me look bad in front of all the guys, so I need you to stop."

"Talking to you makes you look bad?" His brows pinch. "How?"

"No. Not that. You coming to my rescue makes me look bad." I flick a hand to the cowboys dangling their boots off the fence. "Would you have rushed over to any of *them* if they fell off the bull?"

His mouth tightens. "No. Of course not, but they're not you."

"Right. That's my point." I poke his chest. Damn, that's solid. "I need you to treat me like everyone else."

His eyes bore into mine, unyielding. "I could never treat you like everyone else."

"Well, you better start tryin', sugar."

A muscle twitches in his cheek, betraying his calm exterior, but before he can add anything, someone booms my name.

"Get your ass over here, darlin'!"

I jerk my head to my father's raspy drawl. He's got a scowl under the brim of his black hat, which means I'm about to get a lecture, but I always appreciate his advice. With one last stern look at Wyatt, I spin on my boots and stalk off past the bull riders perched on the ledge of the fence. They all start whooping as I strut past.

"Maverick almost got ya, Kodie!"

"I was on the edge of my seat watching that one!"

"You a little sore there, girl? You sure you can handle another ride?"

They're fooling around, so I breeze right by them. "I can always handle another ride, boys!"

Anytime someone tells me I can't do something, all it does is make me want to prove them wrong, and prove them wrong I will. Though, I bet I'll think of a *much* better comeback while I'm loofah-ing myself tonight.

The bull riders continue hollering playful jabs, but at least they don't placate me with meaningless encouragement. I'd rather have someone be blunt but honest than lie to me just to be nice. I can't stand when people give me empty praise like *You can do this!* when really, it's *me* who's going to have to get on the back of the bull.

Not them.

I stop in front of my father, bracing myself for his blunt critique. He looks me over with those deep-brown eyes that shine as intense as mine. "You know I'll always give it to you straight, darlin', that wasn't good. You know it. I know it. And now, let's talk about how we can fix it."

My dad's got this way of calling me out without beating me down, and it's one of the reasons I strive to be just like him, and I want to make him proud. "I know. What do I need to do?"

He uses both hands to squeeze my shoulders and then shakes me lightly. "For starters, you still need to loosen up. You're too tight. You should go out dancing. What happened to that? You used to love two-stepping at The General."

Patterson was always my two-step partner, but I stopped dancing when he left because all it did was make me miss my summer boy, which made me depressed, which had me spiraling. "No. I don't dance anymore."

"That's a shame. You always knew your way around a dance floor." He nudges my shoulder with a wink. "You got that from me."

"Why couldn't I have gotten my grip strength from you too?" I mutter, wanting to steer this conversation away from memories of Wyatt. Memories of us laughing, stumbling around a creaky wooden dance floor in high school, with him drunk off one wine cooler because I corrupted him early. "I can't even manage to hold onto the fucking rope on some of these meaner bulls, Pops."

"Hey, now." He thumps my back. "All you need to do is get back in the gym. You've been muckin' around for the past couple of months since you ended things with Boone, and I let it slide because calling that off was a big decision, but enough is enough."

"I haven't—"

My dad silences me with a sharp look. "You know you've been slacking, so don't you dare fight me on that. You've lost some of your muscle definition. Yeah, you need to be lean, but you need muscle to stay on the bull. You've got to put on some weight."

"I do have muscle." I clench my fists.

"Now, darlin'," my dad drawls, eyeing me under the brim of his hat. "I'm not saying that to piss you off, but it doesn't change the fact that you're gonna have to work your ass off to compete in the big leagues. The cards aren't stacked in your favor, but hell, that's life. Fuck the damn cards. Every hand can be a winner if you play your cards right."

My dad's a Texas Hold'em king and could bluff his way out of jail. Don't even think of leaving him at a blackjack table.

"Alright, what do I need to do, Pops?"

"You need someone to train you. Hold you accountable." He nods to the bull riders perched on the fence, their boots swinging and hats tipped low. "Hit the gym with one of them fellows over there. You've got to work out with someone stronger to get stronger."

The other bull riders are good, solid gentlemen, but as much as I hate to admit it, they're also my competition. I live in a world where I can see all their stats on the scoreboard. I don't want to spend more time with them because then I'll end up comparing myself, and I hate comparing myself. It's a vicious never-ending cycle that always ends with me feeling shitty.

Sometimes, I wish I were softer, content with what I have in life like Wyatt, but I'm not, and I blame society for drilling this ambition, the need for positive affirmation, into me as a kid.

Teachers in school always tell you to *go go go* and do *more more more* to be successful in life, and then they praise you when you do something right, but I don't want to be the type of person who relies on someone else's praise to succeed. Perpetual ambition is overrated. All it does is make me run like a hamster on a wheel. The happiest moments in my life are the slowest, the simplest.

Sipping coffee in the morning with my dad.

Calling my mom on Sunday night walks.

Strolling farmers markets with Lana.

But I can't turn off this inherent drive to succeed that pushes me to want to be the best, and if I train with those cowboys, I'll get jealous of the fact that they can lift more, do more, *be* more, without putting in the same effort as me. All because they have a Y chromosome that allows them to build muscles easier.

I dig my boot into the dirt, glancing out over the rolling hills. "Can't you train me, Pops?"

He taps the brim of my hat. "Oh, darlin', I love you more than life itself, but we spend enough time together during our skills sessions. You're better off finding someone your own age. At least in the gym, but I'll give you all the pointers you need out here in the arena."

"Who else is there?" I grumble.

A throat clears, and without turning around, I know exactly who's standing behind me. "I work out, so I can train with you."

AGAIN

WYATT

I work out? Someone glue my mouth shut, please and thank you, ma'am.

"What do you mean you'll train me?" Dakota demands.

She stares me down, brown curls whipping wildly around her sweaty face, but I'll take the flames in her eyes over her indifference any day.

"I'll train with you in the gym," I say. "I've got to stay in shape this summer, so it'll help me out too."

It'll also give me a reason to spend more time with her, since I can't get enough of her scowls. Plus, I can't *not* help her. It goes against my helper personality not to offer.

"You'll train me?" she repeats like I've got no business training her—like I'm not one of the fastest right wingers in the NHL. I'm kind of offended by her shock. Maybe she needs to watch one of my games again because I'm a speed demon in the arena.

Gritting my jaw, I dip my chin. "Yes, ma'am. I'm pretty fast on the ice, so I'm sure I can have you panting in no time."

Her brows shoot skyward.

"What the hell is *that* supposed to mean, boy?" Colt Cutler demands.

I jolt.

Shit, I forgot he was here, and now my ass is sweating from that glower on his face. It's scarier than his daughter's.

Mr. Cutler's blunter than that old pocketknife he carries around, but I look him dead in the eye. "Nothing, sir. All I meant was I could give her a good workout. We do high-intensity training in the gym, so I could apply those same tactics here."

Dakota scoffs at my manners, but it's a habit I refuse to break. I call all men *sir* and all women *ma'am*. It doesn't matter whether they're eight days or eighty years old. It was drilled into me as a kid. I got my manners from my Southern mama, and she'd kick my ass if I ever stopped being polite.

Mr. Cutler gives me a once-over with that legendary glare. His brown eyes, so much like Dakota's, strip me down.

He's only in his forties, so growing up I thought he looked more like her brother. He's always been a tough old boot, twirling around his pocketknife to intimidate the guys she brought home, but he never used to twirl it in front of me.

He pulls out the pocketknife from his jeans and starts using it to peel an orange, so that's changed. His withering stare scalds my cheek as he seems to consider something. "You know, darlin', that's not a bad idea."

Have I mentioned I love Mr. Cutler? Best man I know. Cream of the crop. Salt of the earth. He can slice my skin right off with that pocketknife if it means he pushes me toward Dakota.

"Please," she scoffs. "Patterson couldn't handle me in the gym."

Like hell I couldn't.

A muscle ticks in my jaw.

It usually takes a lot to light my fuse, but her comment strikes a nerve. Lately, fatherhood has left me feeling less like myself. The random food stains, the lack of sleep, the bags under my eyes —being a dad has become my entire personality.

"Trust me, I could handle you just fine," I grit out.

Her lips part like she's shocked by the comment, and maybe

she is because I never used to say things like that when we were younger.

She seems to collect herself. "What about Vi?" she asks, switching gears. "Who's going to watch her while we're training?"

I zone in on her, shocked the first thing she asked was about was my daughter because, usually, I'm the only one who thinks of her first.

"What?" she demands when I stay silent.

"Nothing..." I shake my head. "I'm just surprised you thought to ask about her, but my parents can help whenever I need them to. They're amazing. So, what do you say?"

"I say..." Her honey eyes bounce between mine, and I think she's going to agree, but then they narrow to slits. "No. You have your little girl, and I don't want to take your time away from her this summer. Go be with your girl. You don't owe me anything."

I've known her for so long that I can hear the double meaning in her words—*I don't want anything from you.* I'm not all that surprised. She hates relying on people and prefers doing things on her own, but I want to help get her stronger.

"Dakota, please let me help. I want to. My parents have Vi most mornings anyway, and I need to stay in shape for next season. Not to mention I owe you one for letting us stay at the barn."

"It's your place. You can stay there whenever you want, so I don't need you to train me." She tries, and fails, to keep the sharpness out of her words.

This woman. She's so damn stubborn. "Give me one good reason why not."

She struts up to me, fringe chaps swaying in the wind, and lowers her voice so her dad can't hear. "'Cause I'm still pissed at you for cutting me out of your life like that, Wyatt Patterson. What did I do to you? I get that you had a little girl, but you could've texted every once in a while. I wasn't asking for much."

Her eyes turn glassy, so despite her tough exterior, I can see the thread of hurt shining in her gaze. I stuff my hands in my jeans so I don't crush her against me. "What do you want me to say? That I'm sorry? 'Cause I am, and I've said it a million times, but I'll say it a million more if that's what you need to hear."

"No," she says, her voice rising so that a few cowboys look our way. We're causing a scene, but that doesn't matter to me. "I want you to say that you missed me as much as I missed you because I fucking *missed* you, Patterson."

Her voice cracks.

Shit.

She goes right for the heart, and I actually rub my chest.

Without giving me a chance to respond, or beg, she struts away in her boots, but at the last second, I catch her wrist and pull her into me, wrapping her up tight in my arms. My chin rests perfectly on her head.

She doesn't pull away.

"I fucking missed you," I whisper in her ear for her, and only her, to hear. "I missed our late-night phone calls. I missed debriefing all your rodeo rides with you. I missed your laugh. I missed everything about you, but you had Boone. I thought you didn't need me anymore."

"I always needed you," she mumbles against my T-shirt. "It hurt me when you left like that. You weren't like the other boys. You were my best friend."

Yeah, that was the whole problem.

And there it is—that hint of vulnerability she only shows to a few people.

I brush my lips against the top of her hair. "I'm here now, and I promise, I'm not going anywhere."

"You better not," she muffles into my shirt again.

Dakota might be a rough and tough bull rider with a mean attitude to boot, but she's got a softer side that only comes out of hiding for the people who matter most. She rarely whips it out, so when she shows you that tender piece of her, it makes you feel like someone important.

She's stiff in my arms, but the longer I hold on, the more she relaxes until her fingers dig into my back, unwilling to let me go.

I get a whiff of sweat and dirt, but she's still got that sugary campfire scent that always clings to her. She used to douse her body in that Warm Vanilla Sugar Bath & Body Works spray growing up. I only know the name because I followed her around the store one time as she tried on scents. She didn't pick the one I liked, so I trained my nose to like the too-sweet smell of burning vanilla.

Mr. Cutler clears his throat. "Doesn't this look mighty cozy. Should I grab a bottle of wine? We could all split it."

Well, that kills our moment.

Dakota rolls her eyes, stepping back, but her face is flushed. Probably from the heat. "Don't be ridiculous, Pops. You know I prefer my famous prickly pear margaritas. I've got to go, so you and Patterson can split the wine."

She starts to strut away, but I cup my hands over my mouth, calling out to stop her. "Saturday, Dakota! Bright and early. Be ready for training."

She waves a hand but keeps on sauntering away with those mouthwatering hips swaying. "Can't Saturday. Lana's making me go to the farmer's market because I've turned her down one too many times for training."

"You're not getting out of this one!" I call out, trying to follow her, but a heavy hand drops to my shoulder, squeezing hard so I can't move.

"Let her go, boy," Mr. Cutler rumbles. "You've got no business going after my daughter, so let's you and I have a lil' talk."

He makes the word *talk* sound like a prison sentence. Up until now, the man always liked me. He even ripped the Smirnoff Ice out of my hand and gave me my first bourbon whiskey when I was fifteen (the man's a rule breaker), but if there's one thing I know about Mr. Cutler, it's that he respects anyone who dares to stand up to him.

Straightening to all of my six-foot-three inches, I stare directly into the pits of his deep, dark eyes.

He's tall, but I've got a few inches on him. "With all due respect, sir. I can't stay away from your daughter. She's my..." I don't want to say this word, but it's the only one I've got for now, so I force it out. "Friend."

He releases a booming laugh but sobers quickly, spinning that knife. "Don't insult my intelligence, boy. Kodie might be blind, but I'm sure as hell not."

My heart jerks at what he's insinuating, but I play it off. "What's that mean?"

"You know exactly what that means, and here's the thing..." He grips my shoulder while tossing the orange in his other hand. "You're a daddy now, so you know us fathers will do anything for our little girls. She cried for weeks when she finally realized you weren't coming back, so I'm warning you now, if you hurt her again, well..." He takes out his pocketknife, flicks it open with a click, and uses it to slice off a piece of orange skin.

But all I'm thinking about is that one word...

If you hurt her *again.*

KNOCKIN' BOOTS

DAKOTA

*T*he next morning, Alanna drags me to the Granite Falls farmers market because she heard there was a new booth tabling organic sheep's milk beauty products called Fleece and Glow, and I agreed because if there's one thing I love, it's farmers markets.

"Here you go, Charlie," I say to the Fredericksburg Peach table owner, handing him a ten-dollar bill. Charlie Rivera's known me since I was in diapers, and he's also been giving us free peaches for that long. "You dropped a peach."

He gives me a wrinkly grin. "You keep it, lil' miss. I know you've always had a sweet spot for my peaches."

It sounds dirty, but it's not. Charlie's one of those oblivious eighty-year-olds with the best of intentions.

"Thanks, Charlie. I owe you one." I bite into the juicy skin, the nectar tartness explodes on my taste buds while we peruse the farmer's market tables.

There's no other place on Earth where you can buy homemade almond butter dog treats and turmeric and black pepper bone broth. All while chatting with a war veteran named Harold, who tells you his life story about the lavender farm he named after the love of his life who died before he made it home—Lavender.

They don't make cliches like that anywhere else.

Alanna adjusts her cleavage in her paisley sports bra. She's been trying to convince me to order new workout clothes from her favorite online boutique, but I'll never give up my cutoff denim shorts or my dad's old rodeo T-shirts. They have about a million tiny holes, but you couldn't even buy a softer shirt at a farmers market, and they're one of my favorite places to shop.

"Did I tell you Wyatt offered to train me this summer?" I tell her as we stroll around the humming market, our arms looped.

I was tempted to take Patterson up on the offer, but he looks so exhausted all the time that I didn't want to take any more time away from his little girl. He's always doing everything for everyone else, and I don't want to be like everyone else to him.

She arches her microbladed brows. "Oh, that sounds like a recipe for some delicious sexual tension. All that stretching and grunting? I'm getting hot and bothered just thinking about it."

"Yeah, but you get turned on by the pressure of your shower head."

She peals her musical laugh. Alanna even snorts beautifully. "If my water pressure isn't hard enough to have an orgasm without touching myself, it's not up to my standards."

"Why do you think I love showering in your shower?" I say, only half joking.

I lead Luna-Tuna over to the Bark Bakery booth and let her sniff all the homemade dog treats. Her whole booty wags as she peruses the table. Everything's organic and *Sourced from Granite Falls Local Farm!*

Small towns like ours don't get fancy with establishment names. We just pop *Granite Falls* in front of the business: Granite Falls Auto Shop, Granite Falls Donuts, etc.

In a small town, you'll never find yourself standing in front of a place called The Alchemist's Brew, wondering if you're about to step foot into a beer garden, coffee roaster, or an underground speakeasy with leather-apron bartenders serving dry-ice martinis.

We keep it simple.

I hold out a bag of maple butter dog treats for Luna to sniff. "You want this girl?"

Her dark tail wags.

"Okay, then you got it." I pay for the outlandishly expensive organic treats because Luna-Tuna deserves them, and I love her.

We move on to the homemade bone broth booth, and Alanna picks up a jar of jiggly brown liquid, giving me the side-eye. "So, are you over this whole thing with Wyatt then? You gonna let him train you?"

Harboring this resentment is taking more emotional effort than I'd like. I never forget the people who do me dirty, but I also have no problem forgiving them if they genuinely apologize.

Ever since he said I'm sorry and told me he'd missed me, I've been feeling a lot less angry. A true heartfelt apology normally fixes most things with me, but I still don't know how to act around him.

He's just so much *bigger* now. I never noticed it before. Not until I was standing up against his chest with the warmth of his breath coasting across my cheek. I shiver at the memory.

Shrugging, I pick up a Sage & Beet bone broth jar, examine the bloody-looking lumps, and ultimately set it back down. "Maybe? Probably. It'll make this summer a hell of a lot less awkward if I let this go. I feel like it's not even worth my energy stayin' mad when I've got better things to do with my time."

"Hah! Called it." She slaps my ass. "I knew you couldn't hold onto that grudge. You might be a badass bull rider, but inside, you're also a big softie. You just don't show that side to everyone, which is fine. It's not like you have to show your true colors to every person on the planet."

"Cheers to that."

"So, how's living with Wyatt been?" she asks. "Have you accidentally walked in on him naked yet? I, personally, am crossing my fingers for that since the barn only has one bathroom besides the outdoor shower. I would love that for you."

That thought makes this July heat feel all the more scalding. "No, I can't even imagine him naked."

And yet, the visual pops into my head for the first time ever. All those soaking wet muscles, but then I remember the drunk teenage bed-peeing incident, and it ruins the visual.

"Dakota!"

I jump at the sound of my full name, so I already know who it is, and I secretly love that he still calls me by my full name. No one else does.

I glance across the market booths to see Wyatt beelining through the crowd with Vienna on his hip, juggling a grocery bag bursting with vegetables. It's easy to spot him since he towers over almost everyone in his cowboy hat. Not to mention every woman nearby is smiling at the daddy-daughter duo. Including me.

He's wearing a T-shirt that says *Rodeo Daddy* and Vienna's in a miniature version that says *Rodeo Princess.* She's also clutching the stuffed longhorn I bought her, and my smile twitches at the sight.

She really likes it.

"Oh my goodness, they're *matching.*" Alanna smacks a hand to her chest. "That's the cutest thing. Kodie, isn't that the cutest thing you've ever seen?"

"I've seen cuter," I lie, biting my bottom lip to contain my smile. Their matching set *is* pretty adorable. I should buy a top for myself.

Wyatt stops in front of us, brushing the loose strands of hair back from his face. The buttery sunlight makes the strands look extra radiant, but his five-o'clock shadow is growing into more of a beard, like he hasn't had enough time to himself to shave.

I hope he's getting enough sleep. He needs to be taking care of himself.

Alanna shoves out a perfectly manicured hand, going right to introductions. "I'm Alanna, but my friends call me Lana. I've heard so many things about you, and fair warning, I've got high expectations for the hockey world's golden boy."

Wyatt chuckles, low and rough, and dips his hat. A few moms pushing strollers eye him with blatant interest, and I don't blame them. He looks good, but their staring is starting to border on ogling. Come on, ladies. We're at a farmers market, not a strip club.

"Well, howdy there," he twangs out, ramping up his accent. "I better live up to all these expectations you've got for us Southern gentlemen."

He lifts Lana's hand to his lips to kiss the back of her palm like he's greeting royalty. He's never been a smirker, only a smiler, but I like a man who smirks. Arrogance can be kind of hot when it's not overdone. There's something about a slightly overconfident man that gets me every time.

"Oh, no need to impress me with your gentleman tendencies," she says. "I prefer my men rugged and rowdy like Kodie."

His teasing grin falters, but he manages to keep a polite smile in place. "Rugged and rowdy, huh? Well then, yes, ma'am."

Alanna gasps, ripping her hand away. "Nope. No, no no. You are not calling me *ma'am*. That's where I draw the line."

"No can do. It's ingrained in me." Wyatt leans down to scratch the spot behind Luna's ear she loves, and Vienna reaches down too. "You want to say 'hi,' baby? Hey, there, Tuna. Can you say Tuna? Tu-na?"

"No!" she squeals.

"Jesus, she's adorable," Lana says.

"She's the cutest kid I've ever seen," I blurt in agreement.

Wyatt snaps his head up at that, and a wide smile jumps to his lips. "You think my baby girl's cute?"

I could lie, but what's the point? We've both got eyes. "Yeah, she's your kid, so of course she's cute."

He winks. "Are you saying I'm cute, Dakota Cutler?"

Something about that wink makes my stomach tighten, so I lift my shoulder. "You've got a mirror."

"Yes, ma'am, I do, but I'd rather hear it from your lips," he says.

He makes the word *lips* sound dirty, and I swallow, suddenly parched. Has his voice always been that deep?

Lana rolls her eyes. "Enough with the ma'am."

Wyatt scratches Luna again, and her back leg starts jerking in that dog-orgasmic way that, frankly, feels somewhat inappropriate to watch.

"Patterson can't help his manners," I say, tugging Luna away from him. She's obsessed with him, and waits, curled up in a black ball by his bedroom door until he comes out every morning, and I let her because he makes her happy.

"He calls everyone ma'am," I continue. "Doesn't matter if they're one or a hundred. I've never met a door Patterson hasn't held open either, and don't get me started on sidewalks. He never lets a woman walk on the side closest to the street."

Lana laughs. "I don't think I've ever heard you say more than one sentence about a man."

I'm stumped for a second, and no comebacks come to mind. Like always.

Wyatt seems a little smug at that, and it's throwing me off, so I clear my throat. All our history spills out with him since I've known him for so long. "I'm just speaking the truth. Isn't that right, sugar?"

He frowns when I say *sugar* but seems to force a grin after.

"Sure is," he says, pressing a series of three little smooch-kisses to Vienna's cheek until she giggles. "Right, ma'am? We like our Southern manners. Yes, we do."

Vienna laughs her high-pitched giggle-squeal, and I can't help the smile that peeks through my lips. Wyatt's an amazing father, and watching them, I'm reminded of me and my dad.

Colt Cutler doesn't hug a lot of people, but I've seen old pictures of us curled up together on my canopy cowgirl bed with him reading me to sleep. I've caught Wyatt doing the same thing on our couch a couple of times, and I always drape a quilt over them.

There are some guys built to be girl dads, and Wyatt's one of those sweethearts—like my grumpy father.

He gestures down to the brown bag with leafy vegetables poking out the top. "Will you be back for dinner tonight? I'm making tilapia tinga tacos. You're still a pescatarian, right?"

I freeze. "You remembered?"

His lips turn down, and he looks a little hurt by my question. "Of course I remembered."

"*And* he cooks?" Alanna interjects. "And not just tacos. *Tilapia tinga* tacos. The men I've dated think ordering takeout is the equivalent of cooking."

I roll my eyes before focusing on Wyatt's eager expression. "No, I can't. I've got a date tonight, so I'll be back late."

The conversation dries up.

Alanna suddenly finds her ombre French manicure enthralling.

"Oh." He opens his mouth like he's about to ask a question but shuts it just as fast. "Another time then. Guess I'll... see you at the barn when you get back from your, uh, date."

"Guess so," I say, digging around my bag to give myself something to do. I can feel Wyatt's stare on my cheek, and now I'm questioning this date.

I'm not all that excited, but the guy was pretty insistent at the bar last week, so I figured why not? I'm single. He's single. I'm hot. He's hot. I've got a 1971 Ford Bronco, and he's got... a lifted F150 with custom airbrushed flames on the side.

Maybe we'll take my Bronco, Daisy Blue.

And it's been a while since I've had sex, so I deserve a good orgasm. I think the last time was before Wyatt came back into town, and the guy at the bar was nice enough. We had a luke-warm conversation, but I'm not looking to marry the man.

Plus, I'm a pro at shutting off my emotions during sex and remaining detached. I might not be particular about who I let into my bed, but I'm pretty damn particular about who I let into my heart.

I pull out a package of blueberries from my bag and hand them to Wyatt. "I got these for Vi, by the way. She always eats the blueberries I put on her highchair, so I figured she likes them. She's a blueberry-eating fiend."

He stares at the package before taking it, and when our hands brush, he rubs his calloused thumb on the back of my palm, sending sparks shooting up my arm. "Thanks. She loves blueberries, almost as much as she loves the longhorn you got her."

"I'm glad she likes it," I say, meaning every word. I'm deter-mined to win over the little devil by the end of the summer.

There's a pause, and they both look at me. Alanna jams her lips together. When I don't add anything else, Wyatt picks up Vienna's tiny hand and waves at us. "Say thank you to Dakota, baby."

She shouts a garbled noise instead, nuzzling into his scruff, and butchers my name so it sounds more like Dee-Dee. I'm not even sure she's saying my name, but I like her version better. Goodness, that's cute, and a pang of yearning for motherhood hits me.

"Of course." I wiggle my fingers at her, tugging on her baby boots. "Bye, little devil. I'll see you later."

Wyatt watches us with quirked lips. "You do realize that you smile at her more than you smile at me, right?"

"That's because I like her more than I like you," I tease.

He knows I'm joking so that only makes him grin wider. "I

can tell. Well, I guess we'll see you later. Have fun on your... date."

With one last unreadable look at me, Wyatt picks up his bundle of groceries and strides through the crowded market. I watch him go until he rounds a corner into the parking lot.

There's a weight off my chest now that he's gone. I always feel like I'm being submerged in something all-consuming when he's around, and it makes it hard to get in a good breath.

Alanna bumps my shoulder. "Do you really have a date tonight, or did you make that up?"

I quirk my brows, confused as to why she's asking. "Yeah, of course I do. Why would I lie about that?"

"Because you're breaking his heart without even trying. He's like a sad little puppy dog around you, waiting for you to throw him a Milk-Bone."

At the reminder, I give Luna an almond butter treat, making her shake for it. "Patterson's always been that way. He's a big sweetie. That's why we're just friends."

"Babe." She gives me a *really?* look. "Don't play dumb. It's not a cute look."

"I'm not playing dumb. I know what it looks like when a man wants me, and Patterson's always looked at me like..." I think for a second, scratching Tuna. "Like he wants to squeeze me. Like how I'd love-squeeze my Toons."

She scoffs. "Friends don't look at each other like that. There's no way that man is 'just friends' with you, unless 'just friends' means he looks at you like he's imagining you naked then sure, you're 'just friends.'"

I toss my head to the cloudless sky and groan. Everyone has always made that assumption, and everyone is wrong. "Not you too. I mean, I thought *maybe* he had a crush on me when we were kids, but he had fifteen years to make a move, and honestly, it doesn't even matter. Patterson's the complete opposite of my type. We're better off as friends."

It's like men and women can't *just* be friends anymore, but I've always been a boys' girl, so most of my friends are men. Until Alanna, I always got along better with boys.

I've never been considered the girly type, no matter how many dresses I wear, and I love dresses. Especially lacy ones. But for some reason, men see that I'm a bull rider, and assume I only communicate with grunts and drink beer.

Sure, I love a good beer on a hot day, but I also love sipping a crisp white wine while overlooking the bluebonnet fields and painting my nails in *Flamingo Fizz*. I'm slapped around so much on bulls that all I want is to be treated like a lady for once.

Alanna puts a hand over her forehead, shading her hazel eyes as she squints at me.

"Why're you squinting at me like that?" I ask.

"I'm trying to see if you've got cataracts, because I think you might be going blind if you can't see how he looks at you, and I'm concerned for your well-being."

"Oh, please. I'm not going blind. I know I make him flustered, but all women do, and I've never been attracted to him, so that's that."

"You need to go to the eye doctor."

"No, I don't. Trust me, I know how Patterson looks at me."

"And trust *me*," Alanna says, looping her arm through mine. "You're going to be knockin' boots by the time this summer's over."

14

THE BET

WYATT

"*P*lease, baby?" I moan, rocking Vienna in the rustic living room. "I know you're tired. Daddy's tired too. I need to put this bed together for you, and then we can sleep."

Her wail drills into my already thumping headache. She's been crying all evening since I got back from the farmers market, and nothing I do can get her to stop. This is one of those moments where I wish I had someone to complain about how tired I am, and then we would cackle-laugh together because we're delirious from exhaustion.

But no. It's just me.

I sniff her diaper.

Clean.

When she's this fussy, the only thing that usually calms her down is being in my arms, which is exhausting—having her attached to me all the time. I can't even go to the bathroom alone. I miss the days where I could sit on the toilet for an hour, scrolling through random shit on my phone.

I pull her close, dropping my voice to a soothing hum. "I know you're tired, baby, and I know your teeth hurt, but I'm trying my best here."

But my best never feels like enough. Sometimes, I don't even know if *I'm* enough.

She screams.

I wince.

Her cries are the tired kind, the ones that come when there's nothing left but exhaustion. I've been running on fumes since I left the market this afternoon, going through store after store with my parents, hunting for the perfect convertible crib.

Vi's turning into a little climber, trying to pull herself up, so I need a sturdier one. The pieces of her new crib lay scattered around the barn's living room because I don't have enough arms to hold her and assemble it. I glance at the closed bedroom door and release a long breath. Maybe we can do one more night in the old crib.

"Shh, it's okay, sweetheart." I pace the living room, swaying her, when the front door suddenly bursts open.

Dakota stumbles inside, and she's not alone.

Right.

I forgot.

Her *date*.

There's a man clinging to her waist, so with a tight jaw, I yank my gaze away. We're going to have to lay down some ground rules for the summer because there's no goddamn way I can stomach watching this over and over again when I can't even remember what it feels like to have sex.

The last time I was inside a woman was Vienna's mom, and as grateful as I am to have my daughter, I try not to think about that night too often. Mostly because it makes me feel like a jackass since I was imagining it was Dakota the entire time.

The new guy groans. "Kodie Cutler, you're driving me wild. Where's your room?"

Vienna's high-pitched cry slices through the barn, drawing their attention, and for once, I'm grateful for her shrill scream. "That's my girl. Nice timing, baby," I coo in her ear.

"Shit. Thought we were alone. Who's this?" the guy asks, scanning my sweats. "You got a kid, Kodie?"

Dakota's panting, chest heaving, and every curve of hers is on display—for him. She's wearing one of her lacy blue dresses that she only wears when she goes out. Fuck. I love it when she wears dresses because it always makes me imagine sliding my hand up her thigh.

She's got on makeup too, which means she *tried* for this guy in a way she never did for me. She looks beautiful, but she always looks beautiful.

"No, she's not my kid, but she's mine for the summer," she says.

Dakota's reply is quick, her gaze meeting mine, and there's a flicker of... what? Possessiveness, maybe? It's right there in her eyes, and it warms me more than I expect—her claiming my little girl.

"This is my roommate and his daughter, Vienna," she explains. "Isn't she a cutie-pie?"

The man huffs. "Yeah, a loud one. Nothing like a crying kid to kill the mood."

Dakota shoots him her infamous Cutler glare, and suddenly, the air shifts. She points to the red front door.

"Leave," she demands.

His mouth gapes.

So does mine.

"What?" he blurts.

"You need your ears checked? Maybe a cotton swab?" She nods to the door, sounding anything but sweet even though she looks like her dress is made of blue cotton candy. "Leave. Now. You can go."

The guy's frown deepens. "Seriously? I came all the way over here."

Dakota props a hand on her hip. "Oh, you mean you drove me

five miles down the road from The General? Thanks. You're defi- nitely owed sex for that act of chivalry."

I turn my laugh into a cough. They both glance in my direc- tion, so I cough again to sell the whole act. I'm not sure what Dakota's motive is for kicking him out, but she's been doing what she wants when she wants since the day she was born.

"Fine," the guy scoffs, tossing up his keys. "I'll go. You're really living up to that Cowboy Killer reputation, girl."

"Good," she retorts.

He stalks out of the barn, slamming the door on his way out, hard enough to rattle the cedar walls. That sets my baby girl off.

"You didn't have to send him home because of me!" I yell, raising my voice over Vi's screams.

"Yeah, I did!" she shouts back. "He was being a dick to you, and frankly, the date was terrible. He smelled like dildo!"

Dildo?

"What?!" It's impossible to have a conversation with my girl screaming.

"Dil-do!" she repeats.

"Why would he smell like a dildo?" I yell, bouncing Vi in my arms. Her face is a scrunched-up tomato for all the crying.

"MILDEW!" she clarifies. "He smelled like *mildew*!"

"Ah, got it. Sorry, she's loud, but it's nice to know you aren't sniffing dildos in your spare time."

She side-eyes me. "That you know of."

Vi lets out another wail, and Dakota gestures to her with wiggly fingers. "Here. You look like you could use some help. Give me the little devil. I'll hold her while you build the crib." She opens her arms, ready to take my tiny bundle of chaos.

I clutch my girl tighter to my chest. "Thanks for the offer, but she's in a mood tonight. Doesn't want anyone but her daddy holding her."

Dakota rolls her lips between her teeth, contemplating some- thing. After a moment, she picks up one of the pieces of the crib, tossing it in her hand. "Then how about you hold her while I build the crib?"

I stiffen, surprised that she's even offering, but then a pang of guilt shoots through me for having the thought. She's a pescatarian bull rider who avoids stepping on bugs, so her generosity always runs deep.

Hell, she's the one who convinced my parents to make the farm a bird sanctuary for their agriculture exemption, and now they've saved a few endangered species, thanks to her. Not that she ever sees the good parts of herself. She only focuses on the bad things.

"You'll really help me build the crib?" I ask.

The honey in her eyes seems to warm as her gaze lingers on Vi, a thoughtful tilt to her head. Her focus drifts from my hands wrapped around my girl's tiny body to the shadows I know are under my eyes, and the lines of her face seem to soften.

"Yeah. You look like you could use a break, and I want to help."

She's right. I'm exhausted, but I don't want her pity. What I want is for her to *want* me, like a woman wants a man, but I doubt she will when I smell like a mix of baby powder and wet wipes.

"I'm a single parent. I'm always tired," I attempt to joke.

Her lips curve into a half-grin, amusement playing across her face. It's not nearly close enough to the smile I want to see. "Then let me help you build a crib. Now, where are those instructions?"

I nod to a pamphlet on the living room floor, and she gets to work. While she pieces together the crib, she doesn't talk to me, but we've always been comfortable in each other's silence, and I don't have the energy to force a conversation with Vienna wailing, so I watch her work, gratitude thrumming through me like a heartbeat until my girl starts to calm.

My eyelids droop, but I fight to stay awake so I can watch Dakota. The way her dark-brown hair brushes her forearms as she moves. How her tongue pokes out when she tries to drill a piece into the crib. Vi's eyes close, and mine start to flutter.

Drifting. Dreaming, imagining my girl giggling in my woman's arms.

Someone shakes me. "Patterson."

"Hm."

"Patterson."

My eyes fly open. "What?" I ask in a voice garbled with sleep. "What happened?"

Dakota's hunched over in front of me, shaking my shoulder, but she drops her hand when she sees I'm awake.

She's so close I can see the faint scar on her forehead from when she banged her head from one brutal bull ride, and I sat with her for hours in the hospital waiting room. That'd been torture for me. On instinct, I reach out to stroke it, needing to feel her warmth beneath my touch. Her lips part for a moment.

"You fell asleep," she says, backing away from my touch.

I rub my eyes with both hands. Wait. Two hands? I stare down at my hands, and that's when I realize Vienna's not in my arms.

I whip my head around the barn, searching for her. "Where's Vi?"

"Don't worry. She's snoozin' in her new bed. I set it up in your bedroom with the baby monitor and even hooked it up to your phone. Your password is *still* my birthday? Why? You really need to change that. I didn't go through any of your sexy messages though, don't worry."

"That'd be hard to do, considering I don't have any sexy messages," I blurt out, embarrassed she caught the birthday thing. I always say the stupidest shit around this woman.

She arcs a brow. "You sound like you want to have sexy messages."

"Oh, uh, no," I stammer. "It's fine. That's what porn's for."

Fuck me.

I wish I could take those words back, but they're out there now.

"That's what porn's for?" she repeats like I admitted to being a world-renowned serial killer.

I clear my throat. Then, I clear it again for no good reason. "No, obviously, I don't watch porn. I mean, I *have* watched porn, but a below-average amount for a man… It's like a treat."

Christ, Patterson. It's like a treat?

I blame the lack of sleep for that one.

"So, you're a porn-for-dessert kind of man then, huh?" She stifles a laugh.

I stifle a groan. "Occasionally."

She lifts her fist to her mouth, biting her knuckles as she tries to contain her throaty chuckles. "Patterson?"

I pinch the bridge of my nose, trying to erase this moment from my memory. "What?"

She cocks her head, lips lifting so one dimple flickers in a tease, and that right there makes the embarrassment worth it. "Want me to leave you some sexy messages so you can cut back on the porn treats?" Another flush of heat rushes to my face at the idea, and Dakota chuckles, raspy, rich… sexy. "Goodness, look at your face. I'm only teasing you. No need to get all flustered, summer boy."

That only makes the fire prickle higher, and now I'm grateful I haven't shaved because at least my scruff provides some needed coverage.

"It's just hot in here," I mutter lamely. "Can we stop talking about porn? All it does is remind me that I haven't had sex since Vi's mom, so I'd probably screw a horse at this point."

As soon as those words are out, we both cringe. Great. It just keeps getting worse.

"You'd…" Her lips are caught somewhere between a grimace and a full-blown chortle. *"What?"*

Blood boils in my face. "No, that's not…" I mutter a curse,

giving my head another hard jerk. I need to pull my shit together. "That's not what I meant. Obviously, I'm not into animals."

"Obviously," she laughs.

"*Obviously,*" I nearly growl.

She jerks back, seeming a little caught off guard by my low tone. "Sorry, that wasn't funny," she coughs out.

I pinch the bridge of my nose, nostrils flaring on a big breath. "What I meant was that I'm a single dad now, so I haven't had much time to date. It's just been a while for me. That's all."

"Hey, no judgment here." She shrugs a shoulder. "I don't know the first thing about being a parent, but I can only imagine that over time you lose little bits of yourself since you're giving so much to your children."

I don't know how she managed to get that so right without having kids herself. She heads to the kitchen to get a beer from the fridge and holds the bottle out by the neck. "You want one?"

"Yeah, after that conversation, I'll take all six."

I wait, hoping for her chain-smoker laughter, but she gives me a pitiful half smile instead. "I wouldn't blame you. Being a parent seems rough. I don't know how you do it all alone."

"Yeah, sometimes I wonder the same thing," I say wryly, taking the beer she hands me, ready to move past that awkward conversation. "But I've got my parents to help out, and they do a lot of the heavy lifting during the season. I'm pretty lucky I've got them."

She sips her beer, hesitating a little too long. "What about Vi's mom?"

Of all the questions I want her to ask, that's the last one I want to answer, so I take a swig of my beer to buy myself some time. "She's not really in the picture."

"Why's that?" she presses, not letting me off the hook.

She settles onto the leather couch next to me, but she's careful to put as much distance as possible between us. This is the first time she's actually started a conversation, so I'll take it, even if it means talking about my nonexistent sex life with the woman I haven't stopped thinking about for over a decade.

"It was a one-night stand," I mumble, to get it over with. "She came to me six months later and told me she was pregnant, but she never wanted to be a mom. She'd been struggling with some choices. She debated giving Vi up for adoption, but I told her that I wanted her. That was that. I got full custody of my girl."

In reality, it was the most difficult decision of my life. I went back and forth for months, talking to my parents, my boys, and a therapist. But every time I thought about my kid out in the world and never getting a chance to know her, a pit formed in my gut. And then when I looked into Vi's eyes the day she was born, I was a goner.

I haven't looked back since.

Tuna hops up next to her, and Dakota wiggles her feet beneath her black fur, cocking her head to think about something. "How can you say all of that so casually? If it were me, I'd be worrying about that decision nonstop."

I take another swig of my beer, already feeling the effects since I don't drink as often now. "Not much gets to me anymore. I thought having a kid would stress me out more, and it's still hard, don't get me wrong, but being a dad also has this way of distilling life down to the most important parts. At least for me. If my baby girl is healthy and happy, then I'm happy."

She drains her beer as she seems to consider her next words. "I wish I had that attitude. I'm always worrying about things that haven't even happened. I've got like, twenty hypothetical scenarios I'm worrying about at any given moment, and the majority end with me dying."

She laughs.

I don't. Not even a little.

"Dakota," I cut out, my voice deep and rough.

She sucks in a gasp at my tone. "What?"

I glare at her. "Don't joke about shit like that. It's not funny."

Her eyes flick over me, dropping to my chest for a second, and then she takes a long, *long* swig of beer, almost like she's overheated. I can't even think about something happening to her. Even when I was gone, even when I was trying to get over her, I still couldn't imagine a world without her in it. I always need her to be happy, even if I'm not.

"But I have to joke about it," she mumbles, scraping off the beer label. "It's the only way I know how to cope with the idea that I'm constantly risking my life. Don't get me wrong, I love bull riding, but it's still scary as hell. That's the part that makes it so thrilling, though. All that adrenaline. I'm addicted, even if I am shit at it," she says, draining the remnants of her beer.

"You're not shit at it, but let me help you train this summer," I insist, leaning forward. "Please? I need to stay in shape anyway."

"It's really fine."

I can tell she means the words, but she's not getting off that easy.

"How about this?" I gently place my beer on the wooden coffee table so I don't wake up my daughter. "What about a little bet to sweeten the deal?"

Her honey eyes spark with intrigue. As the daughter of a gambler, I know she can't say no to a challenge. "What kind of bet did you have in mind?"

A corner of my mouth lifts. "The kind I know you like."

15

TO SEE YOU SMILE

DAKOTA

"A bet?" I narrow my eyes at the smirk hinting across his lips.

Wyatt never smirks. It goes against his sweet demeanor, so I'm shocked to see one forming.

"Yes. A bet." His lip curls higher, making him look nothing like the flower boy I knew. He looks like… a man now.

There's really no other way to describe it.

I've always liked my men a little more rugged, but there might be something to be said for a gentleman like Wyatt Patterson.

He's low-maintenance and wears the same flannel he's had since he was a teenager. He says *pardon me* instead of *excuse me*. He'll never grow a full-on beard because it's "uncouth," as he says, but he doesn't want to shave every day, so he's always got a bit of sexy stubble. I look down at the dirt under his nails from where he was plowing the flower rows.

He's not afraid to get his hands a little dirty.

It's different, thinking of him like this, but the only thing I want is a one-night stand. I need a few more palette cleansers after Boone, and Wyatt may as well have *Looking for Commitment* tattooed over his heart.

"Why do you want to help me train me so badly?" I drop my voice to a whisper, careful not to wake up little Vienna. The cutie needs her beauty sleep after wailing for who knows how long.

He shifts to me and rests his elbows on his knees, giving me his undivided attention. It's unnerving. Men typically give me a two-second flirtatious head nod, not a full-blown penetrating stare. "I need to stay in shape this summer for next season, and I owe you one."

I cast a quick, assessing glance his way, trying to determine if he has some ulterior motive.

Probably not.

Wyatt opens doors for gray-haired ladies and stops to fix a stranger's tire on the side of the road. My guess is that he's simply doing this because he's got a good heart—one of the best.

"Consider this a thank you," he adds. "I know it's not *ideal* having a twelve-month-old move in with you. She's already got her toys everywhere."

I typically come home to an empty barn after a ride, and coming off the high of the crowd makes the silence scream. I can hear everything in that quiet—my worries, fears. But not with them here.

"It's actually nice having the barn a little messier," I admit. "The place was starting to feel like a hotel, so I'll take little Vi, crying and all. Sure, she's a bit of a handful, but what girl isn't?"

"True." He studies me, and his voice lowers to a rasp. "Any woman worth having takes a little bit of handling."

A zing of... something shoots right through me at the rumble in his voice. I can't stop imagining my sunshine-boy Wyatt *handling* a woman, so I take a hefty swig of my beer to squash the searing visual.

But it doesn't work.

Now, I'm looking at his hands, and wondering if they've always been that big.

"Anyway..." He clears his throat, biceps popping as he lifts his bottle to his lips. "I still owe you, so let me do this for you. It'll make me feel better 'cause I'm still sorry about leaving."

I cross my arms over my chest, forming a barrier between us, and my next words are nothing more than a broken whisper, to my embarrassment. "Then why'd you leave like that? You used to be the one person I could always depend on besides my dad."

He seems to struggle to find the right words.

"After you got engaged to Boone," he grits out, unwilling to meet my penetrating stare. "He told me to keep my distance from you. Threatened, really. He said it was 'fuckin' weird' that you had a guy best friend and that I followed you around like a 'pathetic lap dog.' Those were his exact words. I wanted to give y'all some space. Then Vi happened, and my whole life changed. After that, I felt like too much time had passed to just pick up the phone."

He looks so guilty that my shoulders drop. It's hard to stay mad at a man like him, but I can stay angry at Boone for saying that to him.

"Boone *never* should've said that," I tell him fiercely. "You were the best part of my summers, and don't believe a word of what he said to you. He was always a controlling prick. I'm not sure what I ever saw in him... I think I was blinded by the hot sex."

He grimaces and drinks a big gulp of beer, saying nothing.

I thought passion meant you'd have a good relationship, but I think relationships are all about finding someone who balances you out. Passion burns everything and dies out quickly. Only in those ashes do you realize the relationship wasn't made of anything substantial.

Eventually, Wyatt sets down his beer on the wooden coffee table. "Yeah, I always thought he was all wrong for you."

"You should've told me."

He gives me a grin that seems a bit sad. "You wouldn't have listened."

I salute him with my bottle. "That's the truth. Once I get something in my head, there's no reverse, only mistakes."

Our lips hitch up at the corners, and we're quiet, just staring for a moment. I always liked the girl I was around Wyatt. She was more carefree. Really, all she did was smile more, but it made a world of difference. Bull riding is such an intense career that I could use more wispy smiles.

"So, how about that bet?" he asks.

I face all challenges head-on, no matter how small, but I pretend to take a slow swig of my empty beer like I'm debating, just to keep Patterson on his toes. "Okay, let's hear it. What's the bet?"

He grins as if he knew I'd say that. "We arm wrestle. Like old times when we used to have to decide who had to shovel horse shi—" He glances at the bedroom where his daughter's sleeping, quickly correcting his choice of words. "Shovel the stalls. If I win, I get to train you. If you win, you don't have to spend any more time with me."

The thought of spending *less* time with Wyatt isn't all that appealing, and now I'm contemplating throwing the match, but I know myself. I'm too competitive, so I can't do that.

"You sure you want to do that?" I drawl. "Don't you remember who always won growing up? *Me.*"

His eyes flick over my body, and the corners of his lips lift even more. "Yeah. You're a lot stronger than you look but give me some credit. I bet I could take you now."

"Not a chance," I say on reflex.

He arcs a brow. "You sure about that?"

I scan his broad chest, covered only in a white T-shirt that's straining against his defined muscles, and continue my perusal up to the strong column of his neck, all the way to his wide shoulders. He's got veins in his biceps now, and he's not even flexing.

Maybe there's a *slight* chance he'll win.

"Damn, Patterson. All those hockey workouts have really worked to your benefit. It's no wonder you got someone pregnant."

Blood rushes to his face at the compliment, but I rest my elbow on the coffee table, wiggling my fingers. "Alright, sugar. You're on. Let's arm wrestle."

His face scrunches in a frown. "One more thing... If I win, you have to stop calling me 'sugar.'"

"Why?" I ask, confused. "I call everyone that."

"Exactly. I'm not everyone." There's a note to his voice I can't quite unravel. "So, do we have a deal?"

It's getting harder and harder to keep my distance from Wyatt, and I'm also practical. He's one of the best players in the NHL, so if anyone can motivate me, push me to be better, it's him. I should just throw the match and accept his offer, but I like winning.

I set my beer on the coffee table with a clink. "Fine. You've got yourself a deal. Should we do this here in the living room?"

He nods to the front porch. "Let's go outside so we don't wake up Vi."

"Good call. She needs her sleep."

He checks the baby monitor app on his phone, and we step into the heat of the night. Sweat instantly prickles on my skin as the door closes behind us with a creak. The summer air hums with the serenade of cicadas, vibrating loud enough to ripple the twinkling blanket of stars.

Wyatt steps onto the front porch, eyeing the rickety patio table. He gives it a wary shake. "Think it's sturdy enough?"

I drop my elbow on the wood. "Guess we'll find out."

He wraps his hand around mine, and the familiar brush of his calluses sparks years of rivalry in me. Bets, gambles, games—that used to be how we'd settle any argument, and right now, all I'm thinking about is winning this one.

I grip his hand, determined to beat him, but he only brushes his thumb on the back of my skin. I freeze at the unfamiliar contact. That's something he never used to do growing up. We would hold hands, but we never interlaced fingers, never let our touches linger. It feels new, exciting, and my heart starts beating a bit harder.

"On three," Wyatt says, arm flexing. Thumb brushing. Touch lingering. "One."

I squeeze him tighter. "Two."

Another hot brush. "Three."

I clench his hand with all my strength, and he does the same. The veins in his biceps pop, straining with tension as he seems to put all his force into our wrestling match. I'm strong, but shit, he's a lot stronger than he used to be. Sweat beads on my forehead as I muster all my energy to win.

"That all you got, Cutler?" Wyatt grunts.

"Not even close, Patterson," I grit out, trying my hardest to put all my force into the match, but it's not enough.

I lose an inch.

Then another.

And another.

Until finally, the back of my hand smacks against the table. "Dammit!"

Wyatt leaps from the chair, whooping in victory, while I slump forward in defeat. "Better be ready at eight AM sharp tomorrow." He claps his hands together. "We'll start with farmer's walks since your grip strength clearly needs some work."

A smile breaks across his face, quick and bright, and I stare at it like I do every sunrise. Seeing that genuine grin stirs something in me that I thought I forgot, and suddenly, I don't feel all too bad about losing.

Wyatt always made me notice I was breathing. Everyone breathes, but it's this innate, mechanical thing. Not with him. He makes breathing feel like a luxury, slow, pleasurable, relaxing.

With Boone, everything between us was go-go-go, hopping

from rodeo to rodeo to compete. He always wanted to go for the bigger competitions, so his competitive spirit amplified mine. My life was all about bull riding, and there was no room left for anything, or any*one*, else.

It became exhausting. I barely noticed I was breathing with Boone, took it for granted, but with Wyatt, life seemed to move slow enough for me to sit and enjoy inhaling the country air.

"Damn, sug—" I stop, remembering my promise. "Patterson. When did you get to be so strong?" My knuckles pop as I flex out my hand.

He throws me a sidelong glance. "Dakota."

"What?"

He keeps on staring at me with that same playful sparkle in his eyes. "Dakota," he repeats as if he's trying to explain something glaringly obvious.

"What?" I grumble, though the fight's gone out of my words. "I should've won. I always used to win."

He leans against the porch railing, chewing on his bottom lip like he used to do when he was thinking hard about something. After a few breaths, he comes to a decision about whatever is on his mind. "So, here's the thing… I might've let you win a time or two back in the day," he admits sheepishly.

My mouth drops, and, for a moment, I'm speechless.

That ends quickly.

"What?" I nearly shout, but then remember Vienna sleeping, so I lower my voice. "How many times?"

All he gives me is a casual shrug.

I tilt my head and lean in close, so close that the tip of my nose nudges him. He's still got that wild and sweet mountain laurel scent clinging to his massive body. I always loved the way he smelled, so he still must wear the same cologne. There seems to be more of the smell because there's more of him.

I give his chest a poke, right above his heart, and I'll be damned if his pecs aren't hard enough to break a nail.

"Patterson," I demand, leaning toward him. He backs into the barn door. "How. Many. Times?"

He runs a hand through his blond hair, a rueful grin playing across his lips. "Just a few times. Not that many."

"What!" I gasp, lightly slapping his chest. "Why would you do that? Did you *like* shoveling horse shit?"

He meets my gaze and holds it, never once looking away. "No. I hated that, but…"

Slowly, so very slowly, he lifts his thumb and strokes the corner of my dimple. The movement is so unexpected that I lurch back, and when I hear the next words out of his mouth, I regret jerking away so fast.

His teasing grin fades faster than a Texas sunset, all too quickly, and then—it's gone. "I let you win because it always made you smile, and I would've done just about anything to see those dimples."

SO CLOSE

WYATT

"It's official," Dakota says, dropping a fifty-pound dumbbell in the open-air gym. "I hate farmer's walks, but we're not stopping."

"No, ma'am. We're not."

It's hot as hell out, but I don't mind. I'd rather sweat my ass off than freeze in the winter. We've been working out for over two hours, doing planks, burpees, and lunges. I'm exhausted, but if Dakota's not quitting, then neither am I. When she sets her mind to something, she's an unstoppable force that I wouldn't dare try to tame.

The sweat's dripping into her eyes, so I toss her a towel that she catches with ease. "You've got to work on your grip strength, and carrying around fifty-pound dumbbells is one of the best ways to do that."

"I know, but it doesn't mean I have to *like* them." She wipes the sweat off her forehead, a corner of her mouth hooking up, but her lips ultimately stay in a frown.

I'm so close to getting one of her beautiful smiles, *so* close, and I want it bad.

"Okay, that's it," Dakota says. "What's next in Patterson's workout from hell? Plank holding for eternity?"

My teeth clash together. Her calling me by my last name isn't all that much better than "sugar," but I shrug it off. "Next, we stretch. Your body needs a break."

She salutes me with two fingers. "Yes, sir."

Goddamn.

The way she says *yes, sir* makes me a little hard, and that combined with how her thick thighs are splayed wide open on the mats has me imagining some very *un*gentlemanly things, which isn't helping the situation.

She squirts water all over her face, making her tan skin glisten. I zone in on the droplet sliding down her neck, dipping to her collarbone, and heading straight between her... I rip my eyes away to the guy grunting on the leg press.

Her strong body is slick with sweat from the intensity of our workout, but I refuse to let my eyes veer from her face. My parents always said if a woman's looking you in the eye, you better be looking back. It requires a massive amount of restraint not to let my gaze drop down her body, but I'm nothing if not restrained when it comes to her.

I clear the gravel in my throat. "So, how about we—"

A man whoops in the distance, drawing our attention. We turn our gazes to the training arena where some of the newer bull riders are practicing. She watches one of the guys bucking on the back of a bull with pinched brows. Her eyes are locked on them, and mine are on her.

She's mouthing, counting to herself, and when she reaches eight, she curses when the guy jumps off the bull, and everyone ropes the animal.

"Goddammit," she mutters, standing from the mats. "I rode that same bull last week and couldn't stay on, but that boy had no problem lasting eight seconds."

She grits her jaw, and the way she beats herself up tugs at this need I've always had to make her feel better, so I gently grip her sweaty shoulder.

I'm shocked when she doesn't pull away. "Hey, you're strong, and you're only going to get stronger this summer with all our training. I'll make sure of it. You've got everything it takes to make it on those aggressive bulls."

"Not enough, apparently," she mutters. "I've only got six weeks until the rodeo, and if I don't make it then, everyone's going to be patting me on the back and saying, 'I'm proud of you for trying.' Fuck that. I want to be the best."

Dakota tries to pull out of my grasp, but I refuse to let her go this time, so I grip her tighter. Her brows shoot up, and she seems surprised by the motion, but I force her to look at me by tilting her chin.

"Listen up," I command. She goes rigid. "Yeah, you've got to work harder to get on their level, but you've got something they don't. Grit, and that'll take you far. Success is made of a hell of a lot more grit than luck. People respect that. We'll get you on the right macros, keep training in the gym, and you'll be ready for the bigger bulls."

She nibbles her bottom lip, suddenly looking like the little girl who stole my heart with one crooked smile. "You really think so?"

"I know it." I squeeze her again. "I'll always bet on you, Dakota Cutler."

I keep my hand on her shoulder, and she doesn't pull away. She gazes up at me with something like gratitude shining deep in her brown eyes.

Dakota's not a sunshine girl; never has been and never will be. She's an ambitious cynic with a crazy drive to succeed, and I couldn't think of a better role model for my daughter. I want her to see that she can be anything, whether that's a teacher, a mom, or the president, so she never feels limited by the world around her.

"Thanks, summer boy."

And then she does it—she smiles for me, and those dimples pop, right along with my control.

There's something in her honey eyes. I think she's looking at me like how I'm devouring her, and all the clattering sounds of weights fade away. I let my gaze skate over her flushed face, but that sweat only has me picturing her sweaty for a whole different reason.

I lift my arm, giving her a chance to pull back, but she doesn't move away, so without thinking too hard about my next move, I step forward until my chest brushes hers. She freezes in shock or anticipation, I can't tell, but I need to taste her.

I'm done waiting.

I tilt her head back, and zone in on her full lips. My heart's racing, pounding, *throbbing*, but I'm not stopping. Shit, I'm nervous. My body shudders because she's always had that effect on me, but just when I'm about to kiss the hell out of her, my fucking phone vibrates in my pocket.

She jumps a bit in surprise, feeling it against my thigh. "You need to get that?"

So close.

I pinch my eyes closed, muttering a colorful curse as I look at the screen. I never used to answer the phone when I was on a date with a woman, but now that I have a daughter, I have to check.

Grumbling under my breath, I pick up my phone to see that my mom sent a picture of Vi covered in pancake batter squished between her and Mama's smiling faces, and I'm thrown back into *Daddy Mode*.

My baby girl looks so happy, which has me grinning, but then this shot of regret hits me because I'm missing out on this moment with them. My grin dips lower as I continue to stare at the picture.

"Checking in on your girl?" Dakota asks.

Jerking in surprise, I twist around to find her sitting back down and resting her hands on the mats, her head cocked in a curious tilt. She seems completely at ease, and maybe I misread that entire almost-kiss.

It's probably for the best I don't kiss her for the first time in the middle of a sweaty gym.

"Yeah, my moms are making banana pancakes with her again. Seems like they're having fun."

A crease forms between her dark brows. "*You* don't sound like you're having much fun. I mean, I don't blame you because this is the workout from the devil himself, but at least you don't have to worry about Vi with a nanny who might try to use your hot tub."

"It's the middle of summer in Texas. No one's sitting in hot tubs, but yeah, I guess you're right."

She squints, stares, *sees*. "What's wrong?"

"Nothing..." I blow out a breath, debating whether I should talk to her in the same way we used to—comfortable and breezy.

"Tell me, Patterson. I'm waiting."

She might sound harsh, but I can hear the joking undercurrent. It's the first time she's demanded anything from me, and it has me wanting to talk like old times, so I toss my gym towel over my shoulder.

"Well, since you asked so nicely," I tease.

She shrugs. "You know me. I'm not sweet; I'm spicy. Now, tell me what's on your mind."

I sigh, relenting. It's actually nice to have someone to talk to about all this. "Sometimes, I feel bad leaving Vi with my moms. It makes me feel like I'm missing out on parts of her life, like what if I miss her first steps?"

"She's not walking yet?" Dakota asks carefully.

I rub my chest to get rid of the ball of stress that randomly formed. "Not yet... It feels like I'm doing something wrong, even though I know I'm not."

She's quiet for a while like she's trying to pick out the right words, and then stands from the mat, wiping her hands on her thigh. "You're doing everything right. My cousin's kid didn't start walking until eighteen months. I know that's late, but some kids just take their time. You don't have to be here training me if it adds more stress. Go be with your girl, or do whatever you want. Relax or something. Bake."

"Bake?"

"Yeah, *bake*. Some people find it relaxing. Lana does."

"What do you find relaxing now?"

"I don't have time to relax. I need to train, but I can find someone else to work out with. I think one of the Bronc riders has some free time, but I kicked him out of my bed a few months ago, so it might be kind of awkward now."

The last thing I want is her spending *more* time with some other guy. "No, I want to be here with you," I say too eagerly, so I slow my next words. "As much as I want to be with Vi, it's also exhausting spending every moment with a one-year-old. This is good for me. I need some time to myself. Time to..." I trail off, not sure if I want to admit this to anyone.

"Time to what?" she prods, bumping my shoulder with hers.

A gulp travels down my throat as our stares meet. Her steady eyes could always pull the truth out of me. "Time to feel like a man and not just a dad. Sometimes, it feels like my entire identity is tied to my kid. I can't remember the last time I had a night out, but I feel bad leaving her."

As soon as the admission falls out of my mouth, I turn my head to the pull-up bars because if there's pity on her face, I don't want to see it. There's nothing better in the world than being Vi's father, but that's not all I want to be.

"There's nothing wrong with being a little selfish, Patterson," she says. "If you give everything away to everyone else, you'll have nothing left for yourself."

My parents are always telling me to take time for myself, and I still want to have things that belong to me and only me.

"Yeah, maybe you're right," I admit, and this is why I fell for her in the first place. She's always pushing me to prioritize myself.

When she stays silent, I turn back to find her staring at me with a tilted head like she's contemplating something.

"Come on," she says, grabbing my hand. "I have an idea. Let's get you showered. You deserve to have some fun this summer, so I'm taking you out as a thank-you for training me."

"Where are we going?"

She winks at me over her shoulder. "To the General. We're gonna have some fun tonight and find you a cowgirl to ride."

I'm going to die in the friend zone.

17

THAT'S MY BOY!

WYATT

"No, Cruz. She's taking me out to meet another woman tonight," I mutter into the phone, glancing at my daughter, slapping her soapy hands in the tub. "I'm giving Vi a bath before we go."

"Dada!" She squeals, splashing around in the bubbly water.

I reposition the phone in the crease of my neck. "Yeah, baby?"

"Dada! Duh!" she giggles, shrieking. The tingling sound warms me up from the inside. The "ck" sound is one of the last ones kids get, but I know what she wants. Her duckie.

She had a meltdown earlier because she was overtired and didn't get her nap, so it's nice to hear her laughing instead of screaming.

"You want your duckie? I got you, baby girl." Sitting on the edge of the bathtub, I hand her the plastic duck.

She always gets this toothy, picket-fence grin on her face during bath time. I swear she's going to be an Olympic swimmer or something because she loves the water.

"Sorry, she wanted her duckie," I explain.

"No worries," Cruz says. "Hey, is she walking yet?"

I clench my teeth, watching her splash in the tub. I've been debating calling her pediatrician to see if I should be concerned, but my parents are telling me not to worry, and I don't want to helicopter over her.

Realistically, I know every child develops at their own pace, but I keep watching, waiting every second for her to take those first steps. I mean, she's over a year old. She should be walking by now, right?

I don't fucking know.

"Not yet," I say. "But she did pull herself up on the coffee table, fell, and hit her head."

I went from ecstatic to freaking the hell out in a millisecond, and then I spent over an hour googling *what to do if your kid has a concussion* and had to call my pediatrician (again) to ask about stunted brain development. Dr. Bigham is going to block my number.

"She okay?" he asks, sounding concerned.

"She's fine. Just a little scratch," I say, gently stroking the bump on her forehead. No need to make this into a bigger deal than it needs to be. "Isn't that right, baby?"

I stick out my tongue to make her giggle. Her laughter fills the bathroom. "Dada! Mo!"

"Is Daddy funny? You want more tickles?" I coo, tickling her belly. She kicks around in the tub even harder.

I never realized how dangerous the world was until I had a kid. She could so easily knock her head on a kitchen counter or, I don't know, put her hand down the garbage disposal one day.

People weren't joking when they said having a kid is like having your heart ripped out of your chest and walking around freely on this planet, but worrying only makes me miss out on all the good moments with my girl.

"She'll get there, man. When she's ready." Cruz must be able to sense that I don't want to talk about that because he does a loud throat-clearing before changing the subject. "I still can't believe you made a porn joke with Kodie. Do you need me to come down to Texas? Sounds like you need some reinforcements after that one."

"Can we stop talking about that?" I pour some water over Vi's head, dampening her golden curls to bronze. Every time I think of that, I cringe. "And no. Your 'reinforcements' would probably involve tequila, which would be a disaster. The last time I got tequila drunk, I rode a mechanical bull 'cause it made me think of Dakota."

"I mean this in the nicest way, Patty, but you're so down bad for that woman. You've got to get her, man. We're gonna make this shit happen."

I cast a quick look at the closed bathroom door to make sure she can't overhear. There's only one bathroom in our barndominium, and the door needs fixing, so it only locks if you slam it hard.

"What am I supposed to do?" I add, scooping up more water. "She's taking me out to meet someone else tonight."

He pauses, thinking. "If she wants you to be with someone else, then you should go for it. Make her see what she's missing out on. Sometimes, people don't know what they want until they see what someone else has."

"No," I say in an instant. "I can't do that again."

The idea of touching or kissing someone who isn't her has my stomach twisting. I already tried getting over her that way, and it threw my life off track. Even then, I was the asshole who imagined it was Dakota when I was in bed with another woman.

"I'm not a one-night-stand kind of guy," I admit. "So I'm not using someone else to make her jealous. That's not fair to anyone, and I hate playing games."

"It's not playing games," Cruz says in a low voice. It's too quiet, like he's trying not to say the wrong thing. "You're a goddamn catch with an even cuter little catch. You deserve a woman who wants every part of you, Wyatt."

Wyatt. Not Patterson, not Patty—*Wyatt.*

I squeeze my eyes shut.

"Aw, come on, Cruz," I groan. "You're really first-naming me?"

"That's how you know I'm serious. I want you to be happy."

I glance at the closed door to make sure she can't hear me. "I still don't think I can do that. It's always gonna be her for me. She saved my life, and anytime I picture the woman I want my girl to grow up to be, it's always like her. Determined. Hardworking. Caring... She's it for me."

Cruz pauses again. "Okay, then you've got to go back to the basics, man. Flirt with her."

"What?"

"Dial up the charm. Stop acting like her fucking friend. Kiss her on the cheek. Put your arm around her. Let your hand drift down her lower back when you hold her. Act like it's all normal. That way, when you make your next move, she'll think it's normal since you've been planting all these seeds in her subconscious. It's psychology."

There's a gentleness in his voice I rarely hear. As much as I hate to admit it to myself, he might be right. I consider it. "That's not a bad idea, actually—"

The door bursts open, and Dakota struts inside the bathroom —in nothing but a towel.

Her brown hair is piled up in a messy bun with little curls brushing her face, and I almost drop my phone in the soapy water at the sight of her. Christ, this woman.

If that towel falls, I'm going to have a problem in my jeans.

A big problem.

That might be the tiniest towel I've ever seen, and now all I can think about is what's underneath, and that's bringing up the visual of her in all that tight workout wear, and heat shoots to my groin. I have to think about saying goodbye to Grandma Patterson on her deathbed so I don't get hard.

May she rest in peace along with my boner.

Her eyes land on me when she realizes she just walked into the bathroom in nothing but a towel. Both our lips part in sync.

She goes rigid and pulls the cloth up her body while I'm praying it falls to the floor. "Oh, shi—shoot," she corrects with a glance at my daughter. "Sorry. I thought you were done with bath time. We need to fix this because it never locks."

"Is that Kodie?" Cruz says on the line. "Tell her I say she needs to kiss the hell out of you."

I don't tell her that.

My voice is lost in the dryness of my throat because I'm too focused on her tan legs, those muscular, thick thighs that I want wrapped around my waist. I know how difficult it is to put on muscle, which makes her toned body all the more impressive.

I'm still staring.

I need to *stop* staring.

"Dee-Dee!" Vienna suddenly shouts, breaking me out of my trance. It's actually pretty cute how she's started calling Dakota *Dee-Dee* since she can't say Kodie.

Dakota visibly swallows as she looks at Vi, and it seems like her eyes shine a little. After a moment of hesitation, she walks right up to her in the bath and smacks a loud kiss to her damp cheek while I try very hard not to look at the way her towel climbs up her thigh when she bends over.

"Hi, little devil. You look like you're having a mighty fun time with all those bubbles. Can you say Kodie like we were practicing this morning with our peek-a-boo sessions? *Ko-die?*"

They played peek-a-boo this morning? My heart feels like it's growing.

Vi garbles something unintelligible and then squeals, "Dada!"

Dakota chuckles, clutching the towel tighter as she brushes the hair back from Vi's forehead. "Well, it seems like we all know who the crowd favorite is. I'll let y'all finish bath time before we go."

She winks, and having her standing there, smiling at my

daughter, winking at me in a damn towel is too much for me to handle, so all I can do is nod because, apparently, I've lost the ability to string words together.

She drops another kiss on my girl's head before striding out of the bathroom with a soft click.

She kissed my girl.

"Alright, forget about flirting with her," Cruz says into my ear. I forgot he was still on the line, so I jump against the phone. "We just need to get you *talking* to her again because listening to that was painful. Stop acting like some flower boy, and start acting like the best fucking winger in the NHL with a massive cock."

He's right.

Dammit, he's right.

Not about the cock thing, but everything else. I'm big, but I don't think I'm *that* big. Then again, I'm not really measuring myself up against other guys' dicks in the locker room.

I'm still acting like a flustered teenager around her because it's too easy to get stuck in the old versions of yourself when someone's known you as a kid.

I call it *revertigo*—reverting back to the person you've always been around people who've known you forever. I like that I'm a gentleman around Dakota, but I can be so much more than her friend.

I can be the man she needs.

The man she craves.

"Yeah, you know what?" I grit out, clenching the phone. "Enough's enough. She's gonna be mine by the end of the summer."

"There he is!" Cruz whoops. "Now, *that's* my boy."

18

THE GENERAL

WYATT

*D*akota's red sundress has the tiniest straps I've ever seen. How the hell is that thing staying up?

Some cowboy whistles across the hazy bar. "You're lookin' real good tonight, Killer! Save a dance for me, would ya?"

I clench my long-necked beer. Can't catch a break.

"Thanks, Brodie," she calls back. "But I'm gonna have to pass on that."

"Brutal!" someone shouts, and the group of cowboys laugh.

She sips her purple-pink margarita, but all I'm focused on are the amount of looks she's getting in that dress—that damn red sundress. I've had to keep my arm around her shoulders all night to ward off all these cowboys.

"Look at you in that pretty little dress," I murmur, tugging her closer to my side, ramping up the flirting. "You're driving everyone in here wild."

"Aw, you think my dress is pretty, Patterson? Thanks," she says, completely unaffected as she ducks out from under my grasp to say hello to the cowboys.

Dammit.

Margaritas tend to turn her scowl into a grin, so she's been handing out shiny smiles to everyone tonight. I release a frustrated groan, dropping my arm to my side.

After we finished getting ready, Dakota put her cowgirl-riding plan into action and dragged me to The General—a podunk dive bar/dance hall/restaurant that was named after the Granite Falls general store that was established in 1871.

The place has so many beer stains that all the pool tables look discolored, and there's a permanent haze in the air thanks to the bikers who never follow the no smoking sign.

It's nestled in the middle of the old town square, and they've got a revolving door of country cover bands that play every night with at least three encores. There's also this smoky scent that sticks on your clothes more than a campfire, but it's home. I've seen at least twenty familiar faces here.

My cousin, Willie (not Nelson, he always clarifies) works the grungy bar. He's got to clarify since the guy's got a brown mullet, caveman beard, and always wears a red bandana.

"You want another round, Patty?" Willie grits out, patting the counter. "You look like you need a drink."

Our Willie's in his late twenties, but it's impossible to tell his age with all that dark facial hair. His only distinguishing feature is his bright-blue eyes that are almost turquoise. Caribbean eyes, my mama always said.

I shift on my beat-up, torn leather-back chair that's duct taped together. "Nah, I'm still nursing my beer. Thanks, Willie."

He flicks a bar towel over his shoulder. "We missed you down here, Patty. I know you're a hotshot hockey player, but don't forget about us small-towners."

I hold out my fist, and he bumps it back. "Never, my man. My body might be on the ice, but my heart's here in Texas."

"You ever think about transferring down south?"

"Every day," I admit.

There's a reason everyone in the country is flocking to the Lone Star State (a.k.a. Texas) in droves, and it's not for the cowboys. People are down-to-earth, open-minded, and know how to have a damn good time.

I've missed it here.

I've heard Austin's getting a new NHL team, and I've thought about transferring. It's sounding like a good choice, but part of me is worried about leaving Cruz.

"*Please* come back to Texas," Dakota begs with a lopsided smile, popping up out of nowhere. "That would be so much fun for us. Our kids could be best friends too!"

I wince at the thought of putting my future son through that absolute torture, but still chuckle at her half-drunk state. "I'll think about it."

"Willie!" a bar patron shouts, grabbing his attention. He moves to the opposite side of the scarred wooden counter, leaving me standing there with Dakota as she sips a margarita.

She sniffs me. "Have I ever told you that you smell like heaven? I love the way mountain laurels smell. Like sweet, floral grape Kool-Aid. It's my favorite."

I pull her closer into my side, murmuring against her cheek. "Yeah, I know it's your favorite."

I spent one summer going through every store at the mall, trying to find a cologne that smelled like mountain laurels, all to see if it'd set something off in her pheromones to make her like me. It didn't work, but it does smell good, so I still wear it.

She scans the hazy bar, her eyes widening when they land on someone.

"Okay, you've still got it. That woman right there can't stop staring at you," she says, using her prickly pear margarita to point to someone. "See? She just did it again!"

I don't even bother looking. "Not my type."

"What's your type?"

"Women who want nothing to do with me, apparently," I mutter.

She snorts. "Seems like we have the same type. Give me a man who wants nothing to do with me, and my traitorous legs spread on their own. That's why I fell for Boone. I had to win him over. Now, stop putting your arm around me. People are gonna think we're together." Dakota shrugs off my arm for the tenth fucking time, nodding to a woman in the corner. "Okay, what about the cute brunette in the jean strapless jumpsuit?"

"Nope." I keep my eyes on her, not that she notices because I'm a doormat to this woman.

"Look," she commands, gripping my chin and forcing me to turn.

Holding back a frown, I look past the couples twirling on the dance floor, their boots scuffing against the old planks. The neon Coors sign flickers while a country band plays a cover of "I Like It, I Love It" by Tim McGraw, but I finally spot the woman.

"Yeah, I see her," I say. "What about her?"

"That's Emmylou," Dakota says, her warm breath fanning my cheek. She rests her hand on my forearm, oblivious to the fact that she's driving me absolutely insane. "She's a second-grade teacher at Granite Falls Elementary, and she's sweeter than a Fredericksburg peach, so she's perfect for you. You should go talk to her."

The only thing I'm thinking about is how Emmylou is the name of the girl in the song "Check Yes or No" by George Strait, and how Dakota's stereo broke one summer, and that song played on repeat every time she drove us around in Daisy Blue. "I don't really want to talk to any women tonight. I'm not feeling it."

"Why not?" she asks.

"Because I'm here with you," I say, lowering my voice. "You're the only woman I plan on taking home."

"That's because we live together." She sets her drink down to undo one button on my shirt, and I get all kinds of sexy ideas that involve her red dress coming off.

"No, it's just because I want to take *you* home," I counter.

"You're too sweet for me. You look great in that button-down and those Wranglers, by the way," she says, unperturbed. "You just need to roll up the sleeves."

She waves Emmylou over to us, and her eyes snag on me. Dakota starts rolling my sleeves up herself.

I pinch my brows. "I don't get it. Why do I need to roll up my sleeves?"

"Because women want to see your forearm veins. They're sexy. There." She nods, satisfied with her sleeve-rolling.

I grin at that. "You think my forearm veins are sexy?"

"Yeah, women are obsessed with forearm veins."

"I didn't ask about women; I asked about *you*."

"*I* don't matter. Now, quick. She's coming over here. Go ask her to dance, but if you kiss her, just don't do that weird lip purse thing you did when we played spin the bottle that one summer and you kissed Laura Jean."

"What the hell is a *lip purse* thing?"

"You know, like fish lips." She smooches the air, doing a loud demonstration.

Fucking fish lips? Is that really how she thinks I kiss a woman? Goddammit.

I take a giant swig of my beer, keeping my arm draped around her shoulder. "Alright, I know it's been a while for me, but I know how to kiss a woman, and I know *damn* well how to please a woman."

Her mouth parts, but I don't have it in me to be embarrassed.

It's the truth.

I was raised by two women, and let me tell you, when it came time for the birds and the bees talk, they got way too graphic, detailed, and personal.

We stare at each other for a moment, but then she glances

over my shoulder at something and shakes her head. "Okay, um, well, good to know, but I don't need the details about your love life. Emmylou's walking over here. You should tell her I'm your cousin so she doesn't think we're together."

"Yeah, there's no chance in hell I'm telling her that."

"Then tell her I'm your second cousin," she whispers as Emmylou beelines across the dance floor.

"Sorry. Not doing that either."

Emmylou walks up to us with a shy smile, and Dakota introduces me. "Emmylou! You look amazing tonight. Love the jean jumpsuit. This is my third cousin, Wyatt. He's a two-stepping king."

"No," I cut across her. "We're not blood related. At all."

Dakota glares at me.

I smirk right back.

"It's so nice to meet you, Wyatt. Would you like to dance?" Emmylou asks, batting her lashes. "Given you're a two-stepping king and all."

She looks up at me, and she really is cute with her freckles and blue eyes, but I don't get that same nervous-nauseous flutter I've had for years with Dakota.

I'm about to let her down easy when Dakota practically kicks us onto the dance floor. "Go. Dance. Get married."

I shoot her a scowl over my shoulder, which she returns with a wink. I count about ten cowboys already eyeing her up.

One of them lets his eyes roam a little too far down her body and starts making his way to her. Yeah, I'm not letting that happen, so we're leaving. I wrap my arm around Dakota's waist, trying to let Emmylou down easy.

"Actually," I say, tightening my arm around Dakota's curves. "We were just heading out. Isn't that right, honey?"

Dakota's brows jump in surprise. "*Honey?* Since when do you call me honey?"

I've always wanted to call her that, so I keep my gaze on her, leaning in so my stubble brushes her cheek. "Since right now, honey. Let's get out of here. Just you and me. The sun hasn't set yet, and my mom already tucked Vi into bed, so how about we go to our old spot? There's only one cowgirl I want to be with tonight."

19

OUR SPOT

DAKOTA

*H*oney.

It's new, but surprisingly, I don't hate when Patterson calls me that. No man's ever given me a sweet pea nickname before. People always give me ones like Cutler or Cowboy Killer, but honey is... cute.

Girly.

I've never been girly to anyone.

"Oh my god, Patterson," I say as we drive. "Do you remember that time you got arrested in South Padre for drunk peeing on the beach and made me bail you out of jail? What's with you and drunk peeing?"

He gives me a sidelong grin. "Hey, I've got better bladder control now, so how about we move past that?"

"Okay, I'll try, but it's still one of my favorite memories, bailing you out. We blasted Sturgill Simpson into the sunrise the entire drive home."

The hot wind whips through the open windows as he drives down back roads to our old spot at Cibolo Creek, the sunset spraying us with orange rays. He's got one arm draped over the steering wheel, and the other is rubbing distracting circles on my upper thigh.

It's how we always used to drive. Except, come to think of it, he always had his hand on my knee, not my thigh, growing up. And those tiny circles used to be comfortable, not blazing my skin. But it *is* a million degrees outside. Sweat won't stop dripping down the back of my neck.

"But that wasn't nearly as bad as the time you made me meet that random stranger in that fast-food parking lot to sell your lava lamp from Facebook Marketplace," he retorts with a laugh. "Who even uses Facebook Marketplace?"

I slap a hand to my chest. "Me. I'm an old soul."

"Well, I thought I was going to die when that guy pulled up in a white sprinter van."

"Oh, please," I say with a roll of my eyes. "Don't be dramatic. You were *fine*."

He throws me a playful scowl from the driver's side. "His username was a play on some famous serial killer."

I chuckle into the wind, feeling the lightest I've felt in a long while. "Oh, shit. I forgot about that. Well, at least we made eighteen dollars off the lava lamp."

"Yeah." He snorts. "Risking my life for eighteen dollars was definitely worth it."

"Goodness, the NHL has made *someone* a wee bit high-maintenance, hasn't it?" I nudge his shoulder. "It's a good thing we're going back to our spot because we need to get you back to your roots."

"My roots? I grew up in Chicago before moving to Nashville."

"Yeah, but you were born in Texas. Therefore, you're a Texan. Oh!" I blurt, remembering another thing. "Do you remember that mood ring proposal you did when you were eight? We were so fucking cute, planning our little wedding. What happened to it?"

He scratches his jaw. "I don't know. I can't remember."

"Damn. I always wanted that ring back."

That's how the rest of our drive to Cibolo Creek continues. We volley stories back and forth, reminiscing about summers spent picnicking under oak trees and stargazing in truck beds until we pull up to the creek where I saved Wyatt's life in that flash flood.

Most people would avoid the place where they nearly drowned, but it became "our spot" because he doesn't remember this place as a death trap, but as the spot we met each other. To him, life isn't just half-full; it's full to the brim, and I wish I could be more like that…

I'm a half-empty kind of gal.

It's easier to live life expecting people to let you down because they always do, which saddens me because before Boone, I believed the best in people.

We step out of Daisy Blue and walk up to the towering cypress trees at Cibolo Creek. Sunlight filters through the leafy canopy, casting dappled patterns on the little minnows darting through the crystal water. I can see all the way down to the rocky bottom. The old tire swing sways gently, still hanging from one of the massive branches, like something out of a country song.

"Come on!" I shout, stripping out of my red sundress dress. "Let's jump in. See if that old tire can still hold us."

He doesn't answer, so I look over my shoulder to find him staring at my exposed skin. That's when I remember I wore my fanciest red lingerie tonight because I thought I was going to end up in bed with a tourist. I like my muscular body enough, despite all the scars from bull riding, and he's seen me naked thanks to a few *whoopsies* over the years, so this is nothing new.

"Come on, Patterson. Stop gaping and get in here."

I expect him to blush and get all flustered like normal, but instead, his lips curve into this slightly arrogant half-grin.

"If you say so," he drawls.

He keeps his eyes fixed on me as he unbuttons his plaid shirt, revealing his stacked eight-pack. I can't seem to look away.

Reaching down, he undoes his zipper. The sound scrapes through the babbling creek, and the pièce de résistance—he undoes his belt with one hand.

My mouth gets a tad dry, watching him undress so casually. When did undoing a belt with one hand become sexy? If that's the new bar for men, women everywhere are ruined.

He strips out of his jeans until he's standing there in his black boxer briefs, and heat slides down my spine. I can feel the ghost of his fingers rubbing circles on my thigh.

He really has turned into an attractive man. If he weren't my oldest friend, if we didn't harbor all these secrets together, I'd seriously consider dragging him back to my bedroom. But Patterson deserves more than a one-night stand, and every time I even think of kissing him, all those memories of our younger selves pop into my head.

I don't even think the sex with him would be all that great because we were friends first. I'm imagining bumpy, flavorless sex, which isn't worth ruining a friendship.

It's beginning to feel borderline inappropriate, my staring, so I pull my gaze away to the worn rope and tug. "Think this tire swing can hold me?"

"Don't you dare do it, Dakota," he warns. "That branch looks like it's about to fall off."

"Oh, Patterson," I say with a flutter of my lashes. "You should know by now that if you tell me not to do something, I'm damn well gonna do it."

"Dakota Rae Cutler, don't you dare—"

I leap onto the rope and swing out over the creek.

At the peak of the arc, I let go, plunging into the cool water below with a hearty splash. The water is deep enough that my toes don't touch the rocky bottom.

I pop my head back up to see Wyatt jumping in after me, and then he breaks the water surface, shaking off the droplets that cling to his hair. The sunlight catches on the strands, turning them into a shimmering halo.

For a second, I just look at him, forgetting about the PBR and everything else. My life has always been so fast-paced that I want to appreciate this slow moment.

"I told you not to jump," he teases, shaking his hair.

"What're you going to do about it?" I challenge.

He catches my wrist, dragging me through the cool stream into his warmth. "Keep you close. I'm not letting you get away this time."

He moves through the glittering water until his bare chest brushes mine, and every breath of mine brings my chest closer to his. Wyatt grabs my waist, then trails his hands down my thighs to hook around the backs of my knees, guiding my legs to wrap around him beneath the sparkling water. I'm so surprised by the motion that I let him handle me. I can feel all the places our bodies are touching—and all the places they aren't.

"What're you doing?" I breathe out.

"Holding you."

"Why?"

"Because I want to."

He captures my gaze, and the cicadas, the rushing water, it all sounds quiet compared to my heavy gasps. He was always a physically affectionate man, but something about this feels different. I want to swim away from him almost as much as I want to stay wrapped around him.

"I missed this place," I whisper, clinging to his wide shoulders. "It's been a while since I've been back here."

"Me too. Did you ever take anyone else here?" he asks, swaying me in the stream. "To our spot?"

"Never. This is *our* spot. I didn't want to bring anyone else here after you left."

He pauses, frowns. "Not even Boone?"

"No. I'd never take Boone here."

Wyatt stares at me, a pinch in his brows as he seems to wrestle with a question, until he finally blurts, "What happened between you two? I never knew why you ended things."

I don't want to have some deep conversation about the hardest parts of my past. It's exhausting. I'd rather crack open some chardonnay with Lana and watch a random dating show than talk about my broken engagement, but Wyatt's asking, and he has a way of making the deep things feel lighter.

I focus on the minnows nibbling my toes rather than his penetrating stare. "Boone and I... We were too competitive with each other. When he got offered a spot on the Vegas Stampede PBR team, he asked me to move with him. He wanted me to give up *my* dream and gave me an ultimatum. Him or bull riding. I chose bull riding, and he didn't like that, so I called it off."

It surprisingly wasn't a difficult decision, which made me realize we were never destined. I got caught up in the passion and thought that meant the flame of love would burn forever.

Wyatt's arms wrap around me in a solid embrace, urging me forward until my head is tucked beneath his chin. "I'm sorry, Dakota. It's never easy to make a big decision like that."

I interlace my hands behind his back, locking him against me in the water, feeling at peace in his arms despite my racing heart. "It was for the best. Any man who asks me to choose between *who* I love and *what* I love isn't the man for me, but that's not even the worst thing he did..."

His back muscles are taut under my touch. "What else did he do?"

"After I called things off, he was pissed. Real pissed. He did an interview for the PBR and made this comment about how I'd never be a threat to anyone 'cause I'd never make it in this sport. He said I didn't have what it takes, and never would. Some of his biggest fans came after me, and that's why everyone started calling me Cowboy Killer, since it was clear from his attitude that I broke his heart."

Wyatt goes quiet, which he always does when he's angry, so I continue. "But it still put all these doubts in my head. After that, I questioned *everything*. Whether or not I could really do this. If I had what it takes. It's really thrown me off my game, and I hate him a little for putting all those fears in my head. I think he broke me. Bull riding requires a lot of mental resilience, and that's why I can't stay on now because there's all this doubt in my mind."

His fingers dig into my waist. "You don't need me to tell you this, but you can do *anything*, Dakota Cutler, so don't listen to a fucking word out of that prick's mouth."

Well, shit.

I like hearing him spit out dirty curses.

It takes a truckload of problems to rile up Wyatt Patterson, so rage is an emotion I rarely see from him, if ever.

But it's refreshing to see him feeling this injustice as deeply as me. I've spent so much of my life fighting my own battles and carving out a path in a male-dominated world, that it's nice to have someone by my side who wants to fight on my behalf.

But a second later, his bubble of anger pops. "You know, I never liked that guy. He was never good enough for you."

I smile up at him, the sunset making his blond hair glow like a halo. I knew my summer boy couldn't stay mad for long. Grumpy™ is my modus operandi, not his.

"Yeah, he's an asshole," I agree.

"Why do you always date assholes?" he says, pulling us deeper into the water.

I don't miss a beat. "I don't *date* assholes, not anymore. I sleep with them. There's a difference."

"Fine," he says with an eye roll, his hands skating up my waist, leaving a prickly path of goosebumps. "Why do you only *sleep* with assholes?"

I shrug against his solid chest. He's so warm. "Because they tend to be good in bed, unfortunately."

"You know…" He arches a brow. "Nice guys can be good in bed, too."

My breath hitches at his low tone.

"I wouldn't know." I gasp a little, unable to look away from his penetrating stare. "I've never dated a nice guy."

"Maybe you should change that." He leans forward to murmur in my ear. "Us gentlemen can be really generous."

My throat goes from dry to parched. "Are you offering up your services in the bedroom?" I try to joke, but my voice is too tight.

I'm imagining it now. Him. *Us*, tangling in bedsheets, scraping toes down each other's calves. I shouldn't be thinking of this, but I can't stop. He's acting so different tonight, and I'm not used to this brazen confidence from him. This is starting to feel too *friendly*.

His calloused fingertips brush my bra clasp beneath the water, tracing the valley of my spine, and my shiver has nothing to do with the cool river. "I'm just saying, if you ever get tired of sleeping with assholes… my bedroom's only a few steps away from yours."

All I do is nod because, for the first time ever, Wyatt Patterson has left *me* speechless.

20

EVERYTHING'S BIGGER IN TEXAS

DAKOTA

*P*atterson sure knows how to work out a woman.

After a week of planking and more lunges than I've done in a lifetime, my muscles need a yearlong soak in an Epsom salt bath. I'm tempted to down a bottle of pain killers if it wouldn't wreck my kidneys.

The bigger bull riders have private massage therapists, weekly acupuncture appointments, and chiropractors on speed dial, but I'm not to that level yet.

I'm still treading in the minors, which is fine. My thighs are getting thicker. I can keep treading water.

But I need a break, so after Patterson's workout from hell, I grab a blueberry scone from the Granite Falls Bakery, and now Lana and I are tending to Windmill Meadow Ranch's fields with Tuna-Toons frolicking through the rows.

Wyatt's family and their ranch managers do most of the heavy lifting, but I like to help out where I can. It's satisfying, helping things grow.

The scorching Texas sun blazes down, barely filtered by my straw hat, as I send a sharp whistle slicing through the air with my fingers.

"Luna! Hobble your ass back here, girlie! There are rattles out in those fields, and I don't want you getting a snake bite!"

Her recall is amazing, so she wobbles her way through rows upon rows of orange zinnias, Texas sage, and violet coneflowers. I release a breath when she reaches my side. The nearest emergency vet is over an hour away, so if she got bit by a snake, she'd be a goner, and I'd be destroyed by the loss of my furriest friend.

Lana sprays a patch of sunflowers with a garden hose. In her typical fashion, she got dressed up in a white sundress and floppy hat on the not-so-off-chance she meets some rancher in the fields. I'm still in my workout clothes, but now I'm tempted to change to match her vibe.

"So, how've things been since your little romp in the Hill Country creek with the hockey world's heartthrob?" she asks.

That had been… a shock.

Everywhere our bodies touched, it felt like a current of energy fizzled through my veins, charring me from the inside, and it surprised the hell out of me.

I didn't like the feeling one bit.

I've been with a lot of men, and it's never felt like I'm being electrocuted. Sex is supposed to be something a person can easily sink into—something luscious and languid.

It's not supposed to jerk a body back to life.

"It wasn't a romp," I counter, spraying the flower rows. "We were only swimming."

"That's a shame," she adds. "I was really crossing my fingers that you two would end up knocking boots. I think you should, for the record."

"I can't go there with him, Lana. I've known him for years. We'd ruin over a decade of friendship."

But even as I say it, my mind drifts back to the creek and how close our bodies had been. How close we'd been to what seemed like a kiss, and I'm shocked at how much I'm still thinking about that moment.

"Why not? What's the worst that could happen?" she asks.

"We have lackluster, terrible sex and completely fuck up our friendship, and then we'd be cursed to awkwardly run into each other at the grocery store, and I'd have to live a perpetual life of cringeworthy encounters."

"I forgot you're such a pessimist. I shouldn't have asked you to come up with a worst-case scenario." She sighs. "I still say go for it. Fuck him and see if there's chemistry. If there is, great, you'll have a fun summer fling. If there's not, then you can go back to being friends."

"*You* need to get this idea of us out of your head." I playfully splash her with hose water. "I'm too intense for him, and Vi deserves someone sweet and loving for a mom. Not a bull rider with an overthinking complex who will probably end up dead in the next ten years. I'm not cut out for motherhood, no matter how much I want kids."

"Okay, that spiraled fast. Stop talking about you dying. It's depressing." She blinks, and her lash extensions make it look like a fluffy caterpillar is landing on her sharp cheekbone. "And babe, you can be sweet *and* salty, kind *and* demanding, a bull rider *and* a mom. You can be whatever the fuck you want, so stop overthinking everything. You need to learn how to under-think."

"Thanks, let me just learn to breathe underwater first."

It's impossible for me not to overthink every possible situation. I've got my life mapped out, and backup plans for my backup plans.

"Can we talk about something else?" I ask, not wanting to dwell on my worries. Living in Wyatt's sunshine world is better. "I've got the Sisterdale rodeo coming up next week, and I need a distraction 'cause if I think too hard about all those shitty things, I'm just gonna spiral."

Alanna plucks a sunflower from the garden. "Okay, we can move on to my romantic life. Have you seen the bartender at The

General? He's the one with the beard-mullet combo who always wears those cut-off denim shorts and looks like a caveman."

"Have *you* seen him? Normally your type is suits and boots," I say. "And that's Wyatt's cousin. Willie."

"Oh, good to know. I'm trying to figure out if there's a marble jawline under all that hair. What do you think? I'm taking bets, and I'd say it's looking good if he's Wyatt's cousin, considering his jawline could chip a nail."

"Really?" I quirk my head, considering. Wyatt's jawline *is* pretty square. "You might be right."

We make our bets as the shadowy sun slants across the rainbow of flowers, and Lana talks about Willie (not Nelson) for the next thirty minutes.

She can chat it up with anyone, but I call her a firefly because she lights up in social settings but needs to hole up for at least a week of alone time to recover. I like my alone time too, but I also like the spotlight, so it's an even split.

We hug our goodbyes, and she drives off in her Porsche. I meander back through the vibrant flowers in the heat of the setting sun.

I nuzzle Luna's head, taking the walk back slower to match her three-legged pace. "You good, Tuna Roll?"

She looks up at me, tongue lolling.

Yeah, she's good.

Luna is one of the brightest parts of my life. There's no other being on this planet I can whisper all my deepest darkest secrets to, and always get a slobbery, judgment-free kiss in return. Sometimes I look at my girl, and I get this urge to squeeze her until her ribs crack because I love her so much.

When we reach the red barn, I gently creak open the door. Luna finds her indented spot on the leather couch, and I poke my head into Wyatt's bedroom. I spot Vienna, asleep with the baby monitor camera pointed down.

A grin steals across my face. There's nothing better than

coming home to her, and I'm always looking forward to coming back after training and playing peek-a-boo. We're also working on new words. We've finally got Dee-Dee down, so now I'm teaching her how to say Tuna. It's coming out like *toha,* but she'll get there.

I glance up, noticing the ceiling fan is off, so I turn it on for her in case she wakes up and wants to look at it spinning. That girl loves her ceiling fans.

Wyatt's not there, so I quietly shut the door and glance around our rustic living room. The space is a hurricane of toys, and I never thought I'd love coming home to a mess every day, but I do.

He's got the monitor app on his phone, so he must be watching Vi from somewhere. He takes that thing everywhere. He even showers with his phone since he's got access to the app.

Sticky with summer heat, I grab my towel and head to the outdoor shower—my own little sanctuary that offers a sprawling view of the endless fields. There's nothing better than a shower under the sunset or stars, and it's one of my favorite ways to unwind.

I step out onto the back porch and head toward the wooden stall, only to grind to a halt as the sound of running water reaches my ears. Through the slatted wood, I catch glimpses of Wyatt. Water cascading over his sculpted back. Droplets glistening on his tan skin.

He's naked.

So naked.

I shouldn't be looking. No, I *really* shouldn't be looking.

I especially shouldn't be looking at the curves of his muscles leading to the firm, smooth contours of his lower back. He might not have dimples on his face, but he's got dimples above his round ass, and that body is hard enough to carve a statue out of it. Michelangelo should've named that statue Wyatt, not David.

His hair is wet from the shower, curling at the nape of his

neck. He tilts his chin up to the stream of water and shakes his head so a few droplets sparkle off his skin, and I get a full-on view of what's dangling between his legs.

My chin drops.

I guess everything really *is* bigger in Texas.

Suddenly, he turns around and looks up.

Our eyes meet, and surprise brightens his features. I expect him to lurch for a towel to cover himself up, but he doesn't. He stares at me, and I stare back, and then, to my absolute shock, my oldest friend starts getting hard in my periphery the longer I focus on his naked body. If I thought he was big before, it's nothing compared to now.

I don't even know how that fits inside someone's body, and I'm never going to be able to unsee this. Now, every time I eat banana pancakes with him, my brain is going to be shouting *REMEMBER THE SHOWER INCIDENT!* at me, which is going to be exceptionally distracting as I drizzle maple syrup.

I'm not a blusher, but right now, my face might be flaming.

"Sorry, I'll, um, let you finish," I stammer out, soaking up one last glance at his hardening cock. "Showering, I mean."

21

YOU CAN LOOK LOOK

WYATT

akota hauls ass out of the outdoor shower, and all those workout sessions are really paying off because the woman can *run*.

My dick is still a little hard from feeling her eyes on me, so I lurch for a towel, tuck it away, and sprint after her into the barn.

"Dakota, wait!" I stop her right in front of the screen porch door, clutching the cloth around my waist. "Hey, hold up. I'm sorry about all that. I didn't think anyone was home."

"Why are you sorry? You don't need to be sorry," she pants, stepping out of my grasp and up against the screen. "I'm the one who accidentally walked in on you in the shower. I should be sorry. I didn't mean to, uh, intrude."

Her voice is all tight, and I don't want to make her uncomfortable, so I wave a hand, gripping my towel at my hips to make sure it doesn't slide down.

"Don't worry about it. I'm good," I say, trying to de-escalate this situation. "This isn't the first time a woman's seen me naked, and it sure as hell won't be the last."

We stare at each other, and then her honey eyes drop to the V in my waist, lingering there. That's... new. It seems like they light up with something, but she's never looked at me like this before. I can't tell what she's got hiding beneath her frown, but then her breathing starts to pick up, and I think she's looking at me like she wants me.

Holy shit.

The biggest fucking smirk jumps to my lips. "What're you lookin' at, honey?"

She jerks her head up at that and clears her throat. "Nothing, um, sorry. I wasn't looking. You're not embarrassed or anything that I invaded your privacy, right?"

Embarrassed? No. But the fact that she's asking is somewhat irritating. Maybe I'd imagined that fire in her eyes.

It sounds like she thinks I *should* be embarrassed, but I don't care that she saw me naked, and I'm tired of her acting like I'm some fragile guy she can crush with one word. I can still like buying matching daddy-daughter clothing sets and go down on a woman for hours without coming up for air.

I'd say that makes me a goddamn catch.

Using my height to my advantage, I take a step forward until she's pressed against the screen door, and I'm towering over her.

I brace my hands on either side of the screen and dip my chin. I don't give a shit if this towel falls now. "No, I'm not embarrassed. I work hard for my body, so what do I have to be embarrassed about? Or are you talking about the fact that you've seen my cock now? 'Cause that doesn't bother me either. Not one bit. Look all you want."

Her eyes bulge, and then... hell yeah, red splotches start dotting her chest. Dakota's never been a blusher, so that's her only tell. This woman's actually turning red at something I said.

I smirk. Oh, do I smirk *big*.

She coughs into her fist. "No, you're right. You have absolutely nothing to be embarrassed about. Nothing," she fumbles out, and then snaps her jaw shut.

Her eyes track over my chest, then dip lower, and something

flares to life in her gaze that lights me up. My dick twitches at the attention. I think that's heat in her eyes, and it's the ego stroke I've been needing. She's not looking at me like I've got peanut butter fingerprints all over my ratty T-shirt.

No, she's not.

She's gazing at me just as she's looked at every other man she's slept with, and I'll take what I can get from her. Confidence sparks in my chest, and the longer she stares, the more it grows into a flame. She's usually so intense, so assured, that it's fun to see her knocked off-balance for once.

I'm normally fumbling over *her.*

She coughs again for no apparent reason. "Anyway, um, I didn't mean to look. Well, I mean... *look* look," she continues while I try to stop my grin from growing.

I'm still shirtless, and she's still staring.

I can't help it—I flex a little.

I let my gaze rake over her body, looking at her in a way I always used to hide, but not anymore. I'm done hiding.

"You can *look* look, you know," I murmur with a nonchalant shrug. "I don't mind. Like I said, my bedroom's just a few steps away."

Her mouth drops in shock, and she looks like she has no idea what to say, which is perfect for me. There's a pause, but this time, I relish in the awkwardness because it's one-sided—hers.

I'm fucking peacocking.

"Very funny, Patterson," she rasps, panting.

"That wasn't a joke, honey."

"Duly noted," she says on an exhale, backing away. She knocks into a bucket on the ground before righting it with her quick reflexes.

My smirk triples in size.

PROGRESS IS PROGRESS

DAKOTA

*W*yatt Patterson has shattered the image I had of the little summer boy who likes making floral arrangements. I mean, he's still that guy, but he's also the man I can't get out of my head now.

And all my worries are spiraling.

How is he so casual about this? Is he worried about ruining our friendship? What if the sex is terrible?

Oh my god, I bet he'd spread flower petals on the sheets, and we'd make sweet, sweet love to some classic sixties love song like "Moon River" by Henry Mancini.

I can't do this.

I should think this through, but I want him, and it's becoming a problem. Even when he does something sweet and dad-like, I'm still reminded of the shower incident.

He cuts up a watermelon for me and Vi? I'm thinking about him naked.

He tugs on that *Rodeo Dad* T-shirt? I'm thinking about that shower again.

Every time he makes banana pancakes, I watch the way his back muscles flex beneath his T-shirt, wondering what it would feel like to scrape my nails against his skin. I never used to look at him like that, and it's hard to reconcile my best friend with the man I saw naked in the shower.

He's my friend, but now he's my sexy friend, and I can't sleep with him because there's no such thing as casual with a man like him, but oh, am I tempted.

So tempted.

We pass the next week knocking into each other like those bumper cars we used to ride at the rodeo fair, except he doesn't seem the least bothered by the encounters. If anything, he's all smirks and winks as he saunters around shirtless.

I need some space to breathe.

By the time the Sisterdale rodeo rolls around on Saturday, I'm wound tight, and I'm ready to let out some of this frustration on a bull. I'm riding Tacoma today, and it's exactly what I need, a solid adrenaline rush to get out this pent-up energy.

"You seem stiff. Did you do your warm-up, darlin'?" my dad drawls.

I can barely hear him over the bustling sounds of the rodeo. We're in the back pens, warming up with the other cowboys by the animal stalls.

I strap on my spurs. "Course I warmed up. I always do."

"I'm just checking on you." Using his boot, he scoots a small hay bundle to the side as cowboys scurry around the snorting horses. "You worked on those visualization techniques we talked about, right?"

"Yes, Pops," I repeat with a hefty sigh. "I *visualized* not falling off the bull. Not sure how much good that'll do, though."

It's the fifth time he's mentioned those visualization techniques since we arrived at the rodeo. Colt Cutler puts the *over* in overprotective when it comes to me, but he tries not to show it. I tighten my leather chaps with jittery hands, trying to visualize staying on the back of angry snorting bulls.

145

He dusts his hands on his jeans. "And you've been working on your grip strength with that boy, right?"

I shoot him a salty look that he shoots right back. "That boy has a name."

Wyatt and I are finally on better terms, but my dear ol' dad is *not* agreeing to those terms. It doesn't seem to matter how much he's helped me, and he's helped me a lot in the gym. He might be a sweetheart in the streets, but he's relentless when it comes to farmer's walks. And when his voice takes on that gritty, low rumble? I start sweating for a whole different reason.

"Yes, Pops. I've been training with 'that boy' every morning in the gym, so I'm good and ready for today. 'That boy' is out in the stands right now."

He chews his bottom lip. "And he's treatin' you right?"

That shower inconveniently pops into my head again.

All those muscles.

All that water.

I clear my throat. "Yes. He's being a perfect gentleman, like always," I say, scanning the crowded stands for Wyatt. He shouldn't be hard to find considering he towers over most people.

"Good," he fires off. "Now, no more talk about boys—"

"Boy," I correct. "Singular."

He guffaws, and a few cowboys jump at the noise. My dad doesn't laugh often, but when he does, it makes an impact. "Ah, please. Back in the day, I was just like you, darlin', so you can't fool me."

Now that I think about it, there have been a lot fewer boys in my bed since Wyatt came back to town.

Zero, in fact.

He grips my shoulders, nodding to the dirt arena. "Don't forget to stay loose out there on the bull. No more locking up your joints, or you'll get thrown off. You got it?"

"Yeah, I got it. You don't need to worry about me."

The words are more to convince myself because, truthfully, I'm always a nervous wreck before rodeos. My thoughts race and race ahead of me, thinking of everything that can go wrong, and there's nothing I can do to stop my worries from running wild other than get on that bull.

Sometimes, I wonder why the hell I even put myself through this. There's really no point. It's all for the sake of entertainment. I'm not saving the world, or changing lives, but I've poured so much of myself into this that if I give up now it will all be for nothing.

Not everyone finds their passion in life, and I think the ones lucky enough to find something they love owe it to themselves to go after their dreams with everything they've got.

My dad taps the brim of my hat again. "I'll never stop worrying about you, darlin'. I'm your dad. That's what we do for our little girls."

"Little?" I scoff. "I'm in my late twenties. I think you can stop worrying now."

"And I'm only in my forties." My dad's mustache twitches in a grin. "I don't care if you're hobbling around as an eighty-year-old, you'll always be my little girl. I love you, darlin'. Always have. Always will." He kisses my cheek. "Go on and finish up those warm-ups. You've got five big ones riding on tonight. Remember, stay loose and—"

"Flow like good tequila," I finish. "Smooth and steady."

"Right you are. Go raise hell."

He strides through the animal corrals, and I watch him go, breathing in and out, in and out. My dad has been my constant, standing by my side through every high and low, and if something happened to him, it would end my world.

He's not just my people—he's my person.

I don't keep secrets from my dad. After my mom left with @TreytheTrekker, I never had a choice, but he made sure to raise me right, knowing that nothing I could say would ever scare him away. That's exactly the kind of parent I want to be.

When I got my first period, I asked him to buy me tampons, and he didn't bat an eye. After I gave my virginity to the wrong boy, I cried in my dad's arms, and he vowed to hold me until I ran out of tears. (I learned later he slashed a hole in the guy's cowboy boots, but that's neither here nor there).

Colt Cutler is my teacher, my best friend, and my role model, all wrapped up into one gruff-looking cowboy. There's no doubt in my mind that Wyatt will be just as good of a father to Vienna as my dad was to me.

I head to the back pens where everyone warms up to do some stretches when voices drift from the animal gates.

"You worried about Cutler?" some cowboy drawls.

I peer around a horse stable, spotting some guy with red hair and a Texas tattoo on his bicep standing next to Brodie, one of the bull riders I've known for years. Brodie's always cheering me on during my training rides, so he's one of the good ones.

"Nah," Brodie says, waving a hand.

"You're not? Why?" the redhead cowboy asks.

Brodie straps on his spurs. "Cutler doesn't have what it takes. She's in her head too much. I doubt she'll make it to the PBR. Honestly, I don't think she'll ever be good enough, but I'd never tell her that 'cause she'd probably kick me in the balls."

Tears spring to my eyes.

Why don't you go ahead and rip my heart to shreds?

My hands tighten into fists. I can't stand people who tell you one thing to your face and then turn around and say something else to their friends.

I'm tempted to tell them off, but I'm so damn tired of dealing with this two-faced bullshit that I'd rather save my energy for the ride. They're a waste of my brain juice, and I can do this even when I feel like curling into a ball.

148

I head to the arena, feeling more determined than ever, but that comment stays with me the entire walk to the corrals.

"And next up, we've got Kodie Cutler, the Cowboy Killer!" the announcer shouts.

I suck in a shaky breath. I wish I could press a button and make all this self-doubt disappear, but the only way I've learned to combat this is to chant positive self-mantras in my head while imagining proving all the assholes wrong, which is exactly what I do as I scan the crowded rodeo stands for Wyatt.

I spot him in an instant.

He's sitting in the front row, wearing jeans, a white T-shirt, and his straw Stetson cowboy hat, but he's not alone. There's a woman next to him with golden hair that matches her tan skin.

She's beautiful, but they look like they could be siblings. Except, the way she's tightly gripping his jean-clad thigh is definitely *not* how I'd touch my brother if I had one.

She says something, and Wyatt leans in closer so she can whisper in his ear. He's close enough that her lips brush his stubbled jaw. A sharp pang pierces my gut. It rivals the swooping lurch I get when I'm thrown off a bull, and I can't stand the feeling.

It *stings*.

Her hand climbs higher and higher up his thigh, and...

Wyatt shifts out of her reach, putting distance between them and turns to me, almost like he can feel my stare on him. My whole body relaxes when our eyes meet.

A huge grin spreads across his face as he gives me two thumbs-up. *You got this*, he mouths.

I smile back for him, and only him. *Thank you*, I mouth back.

He blows me a kiss, and I swear teeny butterflies start to flutter in my stomach. I feel like a girl with a crush back in elementary school, looking at him. How the hell is that even possible? I've known him for over two decades.

After overhearing what Brodie said, those two thumbs-up

mean more to me than he'll ever know. But when my name is called, and I climb on the back of the brown-and-white-colored Tacoma, I'm still thinking about those doubt-soaked words.

As much as I try not to let people get me down, sometimes, they still sink their claws into my confidence.

I blame that for the reason I face-plant into the dirt after six and a half seconds. It's longer than I've ever stayed on, except it's still not enough.

But hey, progress is progress. Maybe Wyatt's positivity is rubbing off on me after all.

23

I KNOW WHAT YOU NEED

WYATT

"Come on, Killer, don't be like that. You'll get 'em next time," a cowboy in dark chaps says as I stride up to the rodeo stalls.

Dakota's fall hadn't been all that bad, but I still need to see her to make sure she's okay, so I headed straight for the back pens after she finished.

Now, she's the center of attention in a circle of fringe chaps and straw hats. The bull riders are the rock stars of the rodeo, so they tend to stick together, picking each other up after a bad ride, while also keeping to themselves.

There are a few little brown curls flying around her face, and I'll never know how she manages to look so fucking stunning after getting thrown off a bull, but she does, and she does it well.

Another cowboy drapes an arm around her shoulder, and the move has my jaw tightening, but I'm not going to do anything about it because, for all I know, this guy could have *also* been stuck in the friend zone for over a decade.

Turns out, I don't have to do anything since she shrugs him off herself. "Get your arm off me. I don't want to hear it, Brodie. I'm fine."

I can hear the wobble in her voice, but I don't think they can.

The other cowboy smacks her shoulder. Her glare magnifies.

"You could always try practicing on some easier bulls again," Brodie says. "It's not like you're on a time crunch. You can go for the PBR draft in a couple of years."

She's quiet.

Fuming.

The guy, Brodie, slowly lets go of her, taking a step back. Then another, and another. Until eventually, she grits out, "I'll make sure to consider that next time, but just so you know, I *will* be gunning for the draft. I've got my sights set on the Austin Rattlers, so you can expect to see me on those aggressive bulls again."

Brodie holds up his hands in an *I Swear I'm Not Guilty* gesture. "Goddamn, Killer, I was only trying to be nice."

She gets up in his face but keeps her voice steady. "I don't need you to be nice, Brody. I heard what you said earlier, so don't spew this bullshit. Just be honest."

Now I need to know what's got her so pissed off. I stride up to the group of cowboys, nudging one with my shoulder. "What the hell did he say earlier?"

Dakota must not be surprised I'm back here because she keeps that glare fixed on him. "He said I'd never make it to the PBR, isn't that right, sugar? You've been lying right to my face with all that room-temperature encouragement."

Now, I'm the one fuming.

Brodie takes off his hat, running a hand through his dark hair, looking somewhat sheepish. That's not good enough for me. Dakota steps back, and I stride right up to him, towering over Brodie with my extra few inches of height.

That's one thing we hockey players have on bull riders—we're taller.

"You've got two options. Either apologize or own up to what you said," I demand.

In my periphery, Dakota's brows shoot up in a look that seems half surprised and half impressed.

Brodie's jaw works, and he glances at her like he's debating what to do.

"Fine," he mutters. "I don't think you'll make it. You're too in your head. It's gonna be a while before you get on the level needed for the PBR. Boone called it in that interview."

I see Dakota sniff out of the corner of my eye, but she remains silent. I'm not expecting her to throw a punch because she doesn't stand up for herself unless it's something worth fighting for. She'll let all the bullshit roll right off, but when it comes to her friends? Her family?

She would do anything for them.

Which is why I'll always stand up for this woman.

I grip Brodie's fringe jacket with everything I've got, lowering my voice to a vicious growl. "I can't wait for her to prove you wrong."

He stares.

I glare back.

Releasing him, I step away as Dakota spins around, colliding right into me. I catch her shoulders to steady her, and she grabs my wrists. There's something in her eyes—gratitude, maybe? I can't be sure because she shakes me off and strides toward the horse stalls. She's not getting away that easily. I follow her instantly, but I catch the tail end of the cowboys' discussion.

"Guess the rumors are true. I'd heard Kodie Cutler could be kind of rude, but that glare is something else. Sexy as shit, but terrifying."

I slow my steps.

"Woo yeah, buddy, you do *not* want to get on her bad side," Brodie agrees, his footsteps echoing.

"Boone lucked out," he says, voices dimming. "Could you imagine spending a lifetime with *that*?"

"Fuck no," he says. "One night, sure, but not a whole life."

That makes me grind to a screeching halt.

"Careful, boys," I call out with clenched fists, trying not to let my fuse snap. "You should watch that tone, or she might come after y'all."

At least they have the audacity to look a little guilty. I'm seriously tempted to knock some sense into them, but they aren't worth my time, and I'd rather go after Dakota to make sure she's okay. Her outside might be steel, but her inside is pure gold. These guys don't know her like I do.

She's been keeping the fridge stocked with blueberries for Vienna, and she claims it's because she likes them, but I know it's really because I told her my baby girl loves them.

No one buys five boxes of blueberries at the grocery store *just because.* She softens for the people close to her, and I'm lucky that Vi and I are two of those people.

I follow her to a quiet area by the wooden horse stalls. She's hunched over on a hay bale, feeding a lump to one of the brown and white Broncos. She's always been an animal lover, so I'm not surprised to find her watching him chomp through the metal grates.

"What're you doing back here?" she mumbles, looking at the horse through the bars and not me. "I'm not going to be good company tonight. Not after that fall, so you best be on your way. Leave me with my bottle of painkillers and Epsom salt. Maybe throw in some tequila."

"Let's get one thing straight." I move closer to her back, breathing in the salty smell of her sweat mixed with leather. It's rugged and fucking sexy. "I don't care if you're good company. The reason I came tonight is because I wanted to support you after all the training we've been doing, and don't you fuckin' dare listen to a word out of that asshole's mouth. You've got everything it takes."

"Yeah, sure." She makes a noise that's louder than the horse snorting, feeding him another bundle of hay. "I lasted a whole six and a half seconds, didn't you see?"

Her voice doesn't crack, wobble, or waver. It's bursting with sarcasm so heavy it can only mean she's trying to hide her hurt, but I can see through her.

I always do.

This is her norm, tearing herself down before anyone else can. She imagines the worst-case scenario first, that way if it ever happens, she can claim she saw it coming. But if she needs someone to lift her up, I can be that man.

I can be her best-case scenario.

I straddle the hay bale behind her and start massaging the back of her neck. She goes ramrod straight against my chest, but when I knead my thumb at the base of her neck, she lets out a moan that goes right to my dick.

I put some distance between our bodies so she doesn't notice me getting slightly hard.

Now is not the time.

"What're you doing?" she asks.

"Massaging you," I say nonchalantly, though I feel anything but. My body's buzzing with need.

"Why?"

"'Cause you're tense. Stop fighting me on it, and let me take care of you," I murmur in the shell of her ear.

"You're too good for me," she mutters, more to herself.

"No," I counter. "I'm just good *for* you, and you're good for me."

Goosebumps pebble on her neck, and her brows quirk like she's not sure what's happening, but I'm done holding myself back.

"Now, listen up." I lightly slap her thigh, and she jerks, staring down at my hand.

She sucks in a deep breath, seeming to shake off some thought, but all I do is grip her tighter. "No more beating yourself up. Yeah, you fell down, but you're damn good at picking yourself back up. That's what you're gonna do because it's one of my favorite things about you. You know who I always imagine Vi growing up to be like?"

She twists her head back to meet my gaze. "Who?"

She's picking at her nails again, so I interlace my fingers through hers to stop her from hurting herself. "Someone like you. Brave. Strong. Caring for the people you love."

"I don't feel like a very good role model for anyone right now." She blinks rapidly and tries to turn away, but I grip her chin, forcing her to focus on me. Her lips part.

I know that means something to her, but she's not good at accepting compliments, so I press on. "You are. Now, you've still got a few weeks until the Granite Falls rodeo, so all you need to do is loosen up. I was watching, and you're still stiff."

"I know, okay?" she says, sounding slightly breathless, and I'm hoping it's from my touch and not the ride. "I'm trying to loosen up out there, but it's tough when I'm being thrown around by a two-thousand-pound animal. All those doubts come flying back in. My instinct is to hold on, and then I lock up."

Pulling away, she tightens her arms around her body in a barricade. When she was younger, she used to run around wild and free, but her spirit's been caged. It's still there, but she needs someone to open the door. She needs...

A slow grin unfurls on my mouth, and I reach for her hand, interlacing our fingers together. "Why don't you put on one of those pretty dresses? We're going out."

"Oh?" she says, straightening with a small grin that makes me feel like I won the lottery. "You're taking me out this time?"

I quirk a half-smile, rubbing her arms while trying very hard not to think about taking her home to bed. "You and I are going two-stepping. A little dancing's just what you need, honey."

24

THE CUTE FIDDLER

DAKOTA

*P*atterson sure is getting some flirty looks tonight at The General. I can't blame all these women for biting their lips because I can't stop staring at him either.

Wyatt's hair is pulled back into a loose, low bun at the nape of his neck, and it's making me chug my prickly pear margarita in triple time. And those top three buttons undone on his button-down? I can't stop imagining all those tanned muscles dripping wet in the shower.

I always thought I wanted a broody bad boy, but loyalty? Tenderness? Responsibility? Those are some pretty sexy qualities in a man. And apparently everyone else in this goddamn bar thinks so because these women can't keep their eyes off him.

The rusty old bar is alive with couples twirling, two-stepping the night away, but Wyatt's barely looked at anyone else tonight.

His eyes are on me, and mine are on him.

"I told you the rolled-up sleeves work," I whisper in his ear, my tongue loose from the pink prickly pear margarita I've been sipping. If there are any poor decisions tonight, I'm blaming them on the salt rim. "That redhead by the bar's been staring at you for the past thirty minutes."

I would know. I clocked that when we walked inside. Between the redhead's short jean skirt and Wyatt's button-down, they look like the perfect two-stepping duo. I try not to let that bother me. As I watch, she peeks over her shoulder at him but quickly looks away when she finds me staring (okay, glaring) back.

"Really?" He keeps his eyes anchored to mine, never once leaving my face. "I didn't notice. You're the only woman I'm looking at tonight."

The deep, guttural way Wyatt says that has my breathing turning shallow. I'm not sure if it's the margarita or that damn shower memory, but he's starting to feel nothing like my old friend and everything like a new man.

Maybe it's because he hasn't let go of me all night. Maybe it's the way he can't stop staring at the white cotton dress I borrowed from Lana. Maybe it's how his hand keeps climbing higher and higher up my thigh, making my core ache. But it's *definitely* because of the way he stood up for me to Brodie when no one else has.

I down my entire margarita in one gulp. "Who are you, and what have you done with my summer boy?"

His hand rubs burning circles on my thigh. "He's still in here, but he's grown up, which is something *you* need to realize."

He pinches my chin, and a zing of need shoots right to my core. I lurch back on reflex, surprised by how turned-on that made me. His jaw visibly tightens at the new distance between us.

He picks up his whiskey on the rocks and takes a lengthy swig. When the glass is nearly empty, he sets it on the table and releases a huff, changing the subject. "Are you feeling better now after the ride?"

Thinking about that is going to ruin my night even though the tequila's burned right through my garbage mood. Sometimes, I rely on alcohol to make me happy, which is a trash tactic, and one I don't like doing all that often, but if there's one thing that puts a smile on my face, it's tequila.

"Let's not talk about my failure today," I mutter. "Yeah, I stayed on for six and a half seconds, so it's progress, but until I make it for all eight, I won't even score. I just need to stay on."

His thumb moves to my forearm, and he begins tracing those little patterns there instead.

Burning patterns.

Branding patterns.

"You're not a failure, Dakota," he whispers the words, swollen with conviction, like it doesn't matter whether or not I believe him because he'll believe in me for the both of us.

I glance away so he can't see the vulnerability etched into my frown. It's difficult for me to talk about my deepest worries, mostly because it's emotionally draining, ruminating on the hardest things about my life, but Wyatt's a judgment-free zone, so my guard falls.

"No matter how hard I train, I can't even last eight seconds on these more aggressive bulls, but sure, I'm doing just fine."

Rough fingertips brush my chin, and he turns my head, forcing me to look at him. "Do you love bull riding?" he murmurs, staring at me like he sees something I can't.

I clench my margarita tighter, needing something to hold onto. "Yes. I love everything about it—the thrill, the adrenaline rush, everything. It's terrifying but addicting."

He smiles like he expected me to say that, and his thumb climbs up to the inner crease in my elbow. He lightly digs his thumbnail into my skin. It's a gentle, innocent touch, but it makes me all too aware of the mere inch of space thrumming between our bodies.

"Can you imagine doing anything else with your life?" His question pulls me back to the conversation.

I don't even need to think about my answer. "No. Even when it's hard, there's nothing I'd rather do."

He lightly pinches my skin, and another zap ricochets to my core. "Then you'll never be a failure. No one can call you a failure if you're doing what you love."

I hold his gaze, and he holds onto mine.

"But what if I'm really not cut out for this?" I whisper my deepest fear, all those doubts floating to the top of my worries.

"You are," he says, almost ferociously. "Don't let Brodie's opinion drag you down. Listen to the people who've got your back. It might take you longer, but you'll get there."

Wyatt's simple, heartfelt words ease my concern, and I'll never know how he manages to say exactly what I need to hear. He always used to have this way of distilling the most complicated emotions into the simplest feelings.

My lips tip up. "You sound like my dad."

"He's a smart man, even though he is somewhat terrifying." He strokes my dimple, and I find myself imagining what it'd be like to suck his thumb into my mouth.

"There's that smile," he whispers against my ear, and I shiver.

I can't stop shivering, and it's at least eighty-five degrees in this bar because Willie's family hasn't updated the AC since the mid two-thousands.

His thumb continues its distracting swirls, pulling all my focus to him and his rough hands, until the lead singer speaks into the microphone on stage. "Alright folks, we're gonna start off with a few covers here in a bit, so finish off those beers, grab another round, and find yourself a pretty dance partner."

"Hey, Killer!" Tyler, one of the Bronc riders, shouts across the bar. "Dance with me!"

I cup my hands around my mouth, earning a few looks from the crowd. "You're gonna have to ask me nicer than that, sugar!"

Tyler's a decent one, so he scoots back from his chair and starts heading toward me. Wyatt releases a noise that sounds like a snarl, and beneath the table, I notice his fists clenched.

He slams back his whiskey right as the rest of the band meanders on stage. The lead singer looks like a flannel teddy bear while the fiddle player is a particularly cute brunette with a tattoo sleeve and fluffy curtain bangs.

Wyatt eyes the curtain-banged fiddle player a little too long, and something tightens in my chest the longer he stares. His gaze narrows on her, and then all of a sudden, his mouth curls up into a leisurely curve.

A second later, he smacks the wood. "I'll be right back."

"Where are you going?"

I'm almost tempted to stop him because I want him here, next to me. But if he wants to go after another woman, I don't want to block him. This man deserves all the happiness in the world.

All he does is shoot me a saucy wink over his shoulder as he saunters away. He walks right up to the pretty fiddle player. Then, he starts flirting with her. My stomach plummets.

I know he's flirting because he does a finger-crook to get her to come closer and then dips his cowboy hat low, whispering in her ear. He says something to make her laugh, and her giggle bullets through me.

I slam back my margarita, only to remember I've already drained the whole thing.

My body heats about twenty degrees, and I wonder if people can spark spontaneous fevers. Turns out, I don't like watching him flirt with other women.

Not one bit.

TUPELO HONEY

WYATT

The fiddle player is a *talker*, and I like talking to strangers after a few drinks, which means we get lost in conversation for a solid twenty minutes, delaying the start of the band, The Outlaws.

Tyler and Dakota are chatting by the bar, heads dipped close together. This woman—she's always got a man ready and waiting at her heels. I blame the white cotton dress she's got on that's turning everyone's head.

She keeps glancing over at me, and yeah, I'm jealous, but I'm not worried. I'm kissing Dakota tonight, and no one's stopping me.

Not a goddamn thing.

I came over to the stage because I have a plan, a damn-near brilliant plan if I do say so myself, but I'm quickly sucked into the fiddle-player's captivating story about the love triangle she's stuck in between the gruff lead singer and the himbo saxophonist.

She taught me that word. Himbo. Fun word.

By the time she finishes, I feel like I've known Saoirse—*it's pronounced Sersha, Wyatt! Ser-sha*—my entire life.

After she begs for my advice on her love life, I hiss in a breath through my teeth. "I wish I could tell you what to do, Saoirse, but I've never been a fan of love triangles."

"Me either." She huffs into the whiskey-laden dive bar as people rustle about. "Anywho, enough of my boy problems. I'm assuming that's not why you strutted your fine ass over here."

"No, it's not, and thank you ma'am for calling it fine." I sling an arm around her shoulder, turning her to face a scowling Dakota across the smoky bar. Her frown intensifies as she watches us bonding, but that's her norm, so I don't take it personally. She flicks her dark hair over her shoulder and turns back to Tyler, leaning even closer to him.

My teeth grind together, but it's fine—I'm taking her home.

"Don't make it obvious," I say to Saoirse. "But you see that gorgeous woman over there sipping the pink margarita and talking to that guy in the black Stetson?"

She follows my gaze with a knowing smirk. "The one glaring at you like she hates you?"

"Ah, don't worry about it. That's just her face. She likes me. Not as much as I like her, though." I grin, slipping a crinkled twenty into their tip jar. "I've got a plan, but I need a little help setting the stage, if you know what I mean."

Her eyes twinkle with mischief. "Oh, you trying to get the girl?"

"Yeah, for years now."

I end up spilling my entire pathetic love story to Saoirse, and by the time I'm done, she claps her hands together, bouncing up and down. "Oh, hell yeah. I love playing matchmaker! What can I do?"

I thought I'd feel nervous about this plan, but her excitement is contagious. "Do y'all know the song 'Tupelo Honey' by Van Morrison?"

"Am I a fiddle player in a cover band called The Outlaws or

not?" She gives another bouncy nod. "Of course I know it. Very sweet for trying to get the girl."

"I'd like to think so." I tap my knuckle against her forehead, glancing at Dakota again.

Her scowl seems to have grown another scowl as she watches us. I've never gotten hard from a woman's scowl before, but Dakota's?

That always does it.

I crook two fingers at Saoirse, and she lifts on her toes, bringing her ear closer to me. "See, I really want to kiss that woman over there tonight, but she's got it in her head that we're just friends, so I'm gonna need a little help from you to make that happen..."

I whisper my plan, and by the time I'm done going over the details, she plants a hand on her chest. "Oh my goodness, that's the sweetest thing. Yes, we can do that."

"Thanks, ma'am. I owe you one." I give her a chaste kiss on the cheek, the same way I kiss my mama, before heading back to Dakota and Tyler, talking closely at a table by the bar.

I've seen Tyler around town before, so I know he's a good guy, but he's not as good for her as me. He's clearly trying to take her home, and that won't be happening on my watch.

They're drifting closer to each other at the table, and I'm not sure if it's a natural gravitational force, but either way, I'm inserting myself into their conversation.

I strut right up, scrape out a chair, and throw my arm around the back of Dakota's shoulder in a move that all men know as *stay back; she's mine.* "How are you holding up, honey?"

"Oh shit," Tyler drawls, giving me an apologetic shrug. "I didn't know she was yours now, man. My bad."

"We're not living in the eighteen-hundreds, so I'm not *his*," Dakota counters with a roll of her eyes. "Women can own property now. Shocking, I know."

"It's all good," I accidentally speak over her, which I'm not all that pissed about. She might not be mine, but I'm hers.

She shoots me a glare.

I shoot back a smile.

Tyler's head bounces between us, and he creaks up from the table, leaving us alone. "Well, you folks have fun now. See you at training next week, Killer."

"You don't have to leave, Tyler," Dakota says.

Uh. Yeah, he does.

He eyes me, and I tug her chair closer, fixing him with a narrow-eyed stare.

He dips his hat. "I think I do."

I lift my whiskey tumbler, giving him a wink. *Good man*, I mouth. He salutes me with two fingers before walking away. We Southern gentlemen understand the unspoken rules.

The band settles on stage, and she lifts her empty margarita, dumping a piece of ice into her mouth as she chews violently. "Sure looked like you were hitting it off with the fiddle player. She's super cute."

I narrow my eyes. I'm used to her scathing tone, but there's a murkier edge to her voice this time, and... I think she's *jealous.*

My smile explodes, and I start toying with one of her brown curls. "If I didn't know any better, I'd say you sounded jealous, Dakota Rae Cutler."

She flutters her lips, puffing. "Oh, please. I would never stoop so low as to feel jealous of someone. It's a pointless emotion and never does any good."

Her retort is too quick to be honest, and I try really fucking hard not to smile at that thought, so I lower my hand beneath the table, tracing my fingers up her bare thigh to the edge of her cotton dress. It's a risky move, but I'm done playing it safe. I'm finally starting to feel like myself again, being out here with her.

She looks down but doesn't stop me, and I don't go further. I just toy with one of the loose white threads of her dress, tugging, unraveling. I can't believe I'm finally touching her like this, and she's not pushing me away.

I slip my pinky up her inner thigh.

Her mouth parts on a breath.

"Yeah, but that's the thing," I say, leaning closer so my lips brush her cheekbone. "We can't control how we feel, but you have no reason to feel jealous. I can't stop staring at you in that pretty little dress. You look beautiful tonight, honey."

"I'm *not* jealous," she huffs, but her breathing is too heavy. Her face too flushed. I think my words hit their mark. "At least, I don't want to be, and um, thank you," she adds, toying with the hem of her dress.

I bite the inside of my cheek to keep my smile zipped up, trailing my nose down the curve of her neck. "Course you're not, and you're welcome."

I press my lips to her temple, letting them linger on her warm skin.

She sucks in a light gasp.

My jeans suddenly feel like they're constricting every muscle, and all I can think about is taking her home, ripping off that dress, and watching it fall to the floor.

Just being this close to her, I can't believe how much it turns me on, and based on the flush in her cheeks, I think she's feeling the same, but she needs a little push. She's so stuck on our history that she can't picture our future, and I need her to want this as much as me.

The lead singer speaks into the microphone, and Dakota jumps at the noise. "Alright folks, we're gonna start off with a cover of 'Tupelo Honey' by Van Morrison, so grab your partners and get on out here on the dance floor."

Saoirse winks at me from the rickety stage, and I try not to look too smug at my perfectly laid plan. The lead singer strums his guitar, and a rugged twang fills the smoky bar as he begins singing.

I set my whiskey on the table and hold out a hand. "Alright, it's time. Dance with me. It'll help you loosen up."

"No," she grumbles.

"Yes."

My parents taught me that when a woman says no, she means *hell no*, but they also taught me that sometimes a stubborn woman is like a mule—she needs a good kick in the ass to move.

And every good Southern gentleman knows when it's appropriate to give a woman a solid ass-slapping (Hint: 100 percent of the time, it's in the bedroom).

"Wyatt..." She complains with a groan, chewing her bottom lip as she nervously eyes the couples dancing. "I haven't danced in years. I'm not good anymore. I'll just step on your toes."

I wrap my arm around her tight waist and drag her onto the creaky floor. "Go on and crush all ten of my toes 'cause that wasn't a question, honey."

Crush my toes, my fingers, every bone in my body, so long as you don't crush my heart again.

"Why do you keep calling me honey? Wait," she says, holding up a finger. "Let me guess, it's because it's the color of my eyes?"

"No. That's not why." I loop my fingers through hers. "It's because "Tupelo Honey" is the first song we ever two-stepped to. Now, would you make me the luckiest man in this bar and dance with me, honey?"

And then she smiles, dimples and all. "Okay, summer boy. I'll dance with you."

MAKIN' BABIES ON DANCE FLOORS

DAKOTA

"You remember the first song we danced to?" I ask, taking his hand. The heat from his fingers flies directly into my heart, warming me up from the inside.

"Course I do, 'cause I don't have a terrible memory like *someone* I know," he teases, guiding me from the sticky table onto the stickier floor. "I remember everything about that night. We were just teenagers, but I'd been practicing dancing with my mama the night before, and I couldn't wait to impress you with my new moves."

He wiggles his brows.

My heartbeat stutters, and I can only manage to get out one word. "Really?"

"Oh, yeah. When you showed up in that pink lace dress, I couldn't take my eyes off you. I had a pretty big crush on you then, not that you noticed."

"You did?" I breathe out, my stomach tightening, core igniting.

"Still do." He shoots me a wink, dropping that truth like it weighs nothing.

I think we're both feeling the effects of the alcohol, but drunkenly sleeping with my best friend doesn't sound like a terrible idea tonight. In fact, dragging him into the outdoor shower sounds like a brilliant idea.

I can't tell if he's teasing or serious, but thanks to the margarita, I'm feeling playful. "Wyatt Dale Patterson. Are you *flirting* with me?"

His fingers inch up my waist, climbing higher and higher. "Yes, ma'am. I have been for a while now. You gonna put me out of my misery and flirt back?"

Before I know what's happening, he's swinging me around the dance floor, my hair fanning in an arc of waves. "Wyatt!" I laugh-shriek, feeling bubbly thanks to the margarita and his words.

He stops twirling me all of a sudden and gazes at me with such intensity, I forget we're in the middle of a packed dance floor. Couples circle around us, but he just stares at me with parted lips.

"What?" I pant, brushing a piece of hair stuck to my lip gloss. "Why're you looking at me like that?"

He swallows.

I wait.

"You called me Wyatt." Everyone two-steps, moving in a coordinated circle, but we still. Chest to chest. Heart to heart. He leans in so his stubble velcros to my cheek. "I forgot how much I like it when you say my name. Say it again for me, would you?"

My breath hitches at his rough tone. He notices. His Adam's apple bobs again.

When I don't say anything, he scrapes a hand down my back and fists the cotton of my dress. "Say. It. Again," he rasps.

His rumbly words send a ripple of desire down my spine. "Wyatt..."

It's a plea. It's a moan. It's a revelation.

It's all of the above.

This feels a lot like flirting, but I think it's the alcohol making his voice sound all gritty. But it's not the tequila making his thumbs brush my hips. Or making me lean into his touch.

That's all on us.

I lift my chin, aware of prying eyes in this bar. "Everyone staring at you is going to think we're together if you keep dancing with me like this, you know? You'll have the whole town talking."

"Good." With a firm tug, he jerks me forward into his warm chest. "I want this whole town talking about us."

Before I can even process the way he just handled me, he starts twirling me around the dance floor with a confidence I've never seen from him. He was always a good dancer, but now he's got this casual saunter to him that, I'll be honest, is ridiculously sexy.

I think men who know how to dance also know their way around a bedroom. Nine out of ten times, if he's got moves on the dance floor, it normally means he'll have moves in bed, so maybe I'm wrong about Wyatt. I can't stop imagining what it would be like to have his head between my thighs, looking up at me with glistening lips.

I step on his boot, and his low chuckle sinks into my body, then drags lower, and lower, until my legs clench.

Damn legs.

"Someone's a little rusty," he murmurs, close to my lips. Has his voice always been that sexy, or is that the margarita haze?

"It's really easy to overthink a two-step," I retort, staring down at my treacherous feet. "And the tequila isn't helping."

"Then stop overthinking and follow my lead." He lowers his hand so it rests just above the curve of my lower back, refusing to let me go. "You're trying to take control like you always do, but you can't control a bull, and you can't control me. Now, listen," he whispers, warm breath coasting the shell of my ear. I shiver, and I feel his smile against my cheek. "Close your eyes for me."

"What?" I rear my head back, but he reels me back in. "I can't dance with my eyes closed. I need to watch where I'm going."

"No, you don't. I've got you." He squeezes my waist harder. "Close. Your. Eyes."

That demanding voice is doing things to my body. My eyelids flutter closed like they can't help but agree to his command.

"That's it. Now, follow my lead, like this. One-two-one," he chants. "One-two-one. There. Just like that. You're doing so good, honey."

My heart races. That praise shouldn't sound so sexual.

Heat singes my core as he begins leading us in a smooth two-step around the dance floor, and I lean into him, closing my eyes. I can't stop myself from resting my cheek over his heart, but it used to be *his* heart that pounded harder than mine, and now my heart's beating at a rapid pace.

As he leads and I follow, I'm thrown back to all those times we would go two-stepping over the summer, but when we were young, we would both fumble around the dance floor. There's no fumbling from Wyatt now—only me.

He's smooth confidence for miles.

For the first time, I let go and stop overthinking. All my worries over my dreams, our friendship, the PBR, they drift away on the sound of the fiddle. I let myself feel and dance, and before I know it, he's whispering in my ear.

"Look at me, honey."

And I do.

The tip of his nose skims mine, and his hands trail higher up to brush the underside of my breast. "See, *that's* what you need to do when you get out on a bull. You can't control the ride, so just roll with it. Sometimes, the best things in life happen when you let it be."

I close my eyes, flowing with him. I've been fighting so hard for control—control over the bull, over my future, my career, my love life—that I forgot what it was like to just *be*. When there are so many doubts buzzing through my head, I think, sometimes, I latch onto the things I can control so I have power over something.

The song fades out with a soft strum, and the fiddle player steps up to the mic. "Alright folks, unless you're dancing with a family member, I want you all to lean in and kiss your partner good. No pecks allowed in this here bar."

"What?" I balk up at him. "She wants us to kiss?"

He sucks in a breath through his teeth. "Yeah, looks like it."

The fiddle player zones in on Wyatt. "I'm lookin' at you and that partner of yours, cowboy. If your lips aren't locked in the next five seconds, I'm coming down there to push you together myself."

It feels like every head in the bar turns to stare at us. I've always liked the spotlight, but still... I can't kiss Wyatt in front of all these people. Except, I kind of want to. And the fiddle player is still staring, and now there's a half amused, half resigned smile playing across Wyatt's mouth, as if to say *well, what're you gonna do?*

"What do you say?" he breathes the words against my lips. "Should we give 'em what they want? Your call."

My shrug turns to putty when his hands skate up my waist. It's only one kiss. What harm will it do? I've kissed plenty of men before, and he does look damn good in those Wranglers hugging every inch of his perfect ass.

I tangle my fingers in his hair. "I guess we have to. Let's give 'em a show."

"I don't care about what they want. I only care about what you want," he says, brushing his hand beneath my hair to cradle my neck. "Do you want me, honey?"

His green gaze is right in front of mine, and his hand travels higher and higher up my ribcage, close enough that just an inch more and he'd graze the underside of my breast. He doesn't though. He stops while his other hand cups the back of my neck. I never realized how *big* his hands are.

Big and warm.

He's leaning in—closer, closer, closer—and I'm not pulling away. The tequila, the smoke, his mountain laurel scent, it's all a heady combination, jumbling my thoughts.

When he cups my jaw in his rough hand, I stand on my toes to reach his height.

And when he dips his head, I loop my arms around his neck.

And then, when he kisses me, I kiss him back.

Oh, do I kiss him back.

I expect it to be clunky, but the moment our lips touch, they start moving together like muscle memory. His breath is tinged with the whiskey he's been sipping all night, and my lips part in an invitation. His mouth moves slow and deliberate against mine, almost like he's trying to start slow and make this last.

Most men treat kissing like a pit stop on the way to sex, but not Wyatt. He kisses like it's the main event, not the lead-up.

He moans when I trace my tongue along his bottom lip, hoping to capture more of his taste. His tongue flicks against mine in response, and it's just a little test, but it opens the gates to a more ferocious kiss.

We absolutely devour each other, and I forget all about the fact that I'm kissing Wyatt Patterson, the boy I've known for years. All I can think about is how I want more, more, *more* of this man. My hands tangle in the strands of hair peeking out beneath his cowboy hat. When I tug, a groan falls from his mouth into mine, and I suck in the noise, wanting to hear it again.

His hands travel down my spine, squeezing me against his tall frame, and I trail my fingers down his chest to dip them into his belt loops to pull him closer until there's no space left between us. He takes me with his mouth. A deep groan scrapes through his throat, and my nipples tighten to hard points at the noise.

He tugs my hair back to get better, deeper access to my mouth. I arch into his body, and a rush of heat tingles down my spine when I feel him hard against me. He's hard enough that people will notice, and I start blazing with need. I imagine having him inside me, and the heat just continues to spiral until I'm gasping.

This might be the best kiss of my life.

A throat clears into the mic, and the noise snaps me out of Wyatt's spell. He stops kissing me first and pulls back with the smirkiest smirk I've ever seen on a man, but on him, it still manages to look boyishly charming.

"I said to kiss your partner good," the fiddle player chastises in amusement, for everyone in the bar to hear. "Not make a baby on the dance floor."

Wyatt gives her a half-sheepish, half-blasé shrug, but there's something simmering beneath the surface of that expression, something intense.

He tucks me against his side, and from the tightness of his grip, I'm not sure he'll ever let go.

"Have you seen this one?" he calls back to her. "I couldn't help but get carried away, but we should probably head out, so we don't accidentally make any babies on dance floors."

The fiddle player winks at him. "Good call."

27

PRESS PLAY

WYATT

*W*e don't make it home.

It turns out that we barely make it to my truck in the parking lot because I have to stop every few seconds to kiss her.

Step. *Kiss.* Step. *Kiss.* Step.

I push her against the cool metal of my truck, cupping my hand around the back of her head so she doesn't bang her head.

I'm feeling pretty damn cocky about my master plan right now. I can't believe that actually worked. I need to buy Saoirse a new fiddle. No, a whole collection of fiddles. No—what I really need to do is to stop thinking about fiddles when I've got this woman in my arms, kissing me like I'm oxygen.

All we do is kiss, but I don't mind that it doesn't lead to anything else. I could spend days just kissing her.

"Fuck, I can't stop kissing you," I mumble against her lips, the heat of the summer night draping over us. It's hot out, and that's only making me think about getting her out of that cotton dress and feeling her warm skin pressed against my body.

I want to make her sweat.

I slowly trace my tongue on her bottom lip, and then swipe my thumb along the underside of her breast. She releases this needy moan into my mouth that I want to replay over and over again for the rest of my life.

I can't believe I'm finally kissing Dakota Cutler, and she's kissing me back.

I could breathe in her prickly pear margarita taste all night until I suffocate and die a happy man, but I need to keep my shit together. Take this slow, tease her, so she wants more. She tugs on my hair, and it's like that move is tied directly to my dick because it jerks to attention. My body is on fire, every nerve ending screams for more as I press into her. She feels incredible against me—so perfect that the thought of stopping, even to drive us home, feels like torture.

I pull out every technique in my arsenal to make it the best goddamn kiss of her life. I nip her lip. Suck her tongue. Flick the roof of her mouth. Her tight body feels so good pressed against me, and all I can think about is taking her home, but to take her home, I have to stop kissing her. I don't want to do that, so I just keep sucking and biting, and hell, even licking up her neck.

"Wyatt," she moans. Damn, I love hearing her say my name like that. "I can't believe I'm kissing you. When did you become such a good kisser?"

"I've always been a good kisser, so it's too bad you're just now finding that out," I say, nipping her lip again.

"You should've kissed me sooner," she moans against my mouth.

I smile against her, teeth bumping. "Believe me, I tried, but you weren't ready for me then."

She tugs me forward by my belt loops, pulling me as close as possible. "It's because we were always just friends. I didn't think of you that way."

I bite her bottom lip at that. "Call me your 'friend' one more time, and I'll drag you back to your bedroom, hook those pretty legs over my shoulders, and show you just how *friendly* I can be."

Her mouth drops, and for the first time, I think I've left her speechless, but then she says, "Then, it's really too bad we're not closer to a bedroom."

That does it.

I go in for another bruising kiss and quickly get lost in the sensation of her. The feeling of her on my lips. She's devouring my taste the same way I'm devouring her, and the only thing I'm thinking about is how badly I've wanted this for years, and how the real thing is so much better than I ever imagined.

"Get in the truck," I say. "I want to take you home and see what's under that dress."

Her lips part. Good. Let that sink in. I lift two fingers to pop her lips closed.

"Black lace panties," she finishes, chest heaving.

"Oh, yeah?" A corner of my mouth hooks up. "Did you wear those for me?"

"No, I wore them for *me*," she retorts with an arch of her brow.

"I guess I'm not surprised," I murmur. "You've always loved wearing the pants in your relationships."

She raises a casual shoulder. "What can I say? I look good in chaps."

"Damn right, you do." I dip my hat in agreement, and I love that her confidence is coming back out when she's been so down on herself. "You can wear the pants as long as I get to take them off."

That makes her shut right up.

She digs her fingers into the rim of my jeans, pulling me closer until my dick is throbbing right over her center. "I didn't know you could be like this, Patterson."

"Wyatt," I correct in a low voice, kissing the soft skin behind her ear. "You call me Wyatt from now on. No more of this teammate's last name bullshit, alright? I'm not your fucking friend. Not when all I'm thinking about is getting you out of that dress."

I drag my hand down the cotton over her stomach, lower and lower, and then ever so carefully, I brush my knuckle right down her center, just hard enough to leave her aching, but soft enough to leave her wanting more.

She gasps.

I suck in that noise like air.

"Let's go home." I lean in, gripping her hips. "I want to get you nice and—"

My phone vibrates in my pocket, cracking through the moment. I pinch my eyes shut at the interruption.

Pre-Vienna Wyatt never would've considered looking at his phone while kissing the woman of his dreams, but now that I have a daughter, I need to check. I wrench myself free from her addicting lips.

"Do you mind?" I tuck a strand of hair behind her ear. "It might be my parents."

"You don't even need to ask. You're a father first," she says, and that makes me want to kiss her all night.

I find that a lot of people who don't have kids understand the pop-up problems with parenthood, but they can't help but get irritated sometimes, and I don't blame them. I get irritated too. Dakota doesn't seem annoyed in the slightest, though, and there's genuine concern shining in her dark eyes.

After pulling out my phone, I look at the screen, and when I read the message, it feels like someone dunked my body in ice water. Everything in me stops. Panic clenches in my chest as my thoughts turn to my baby girl.

"It's from my mom," I say.

"What's wrong?" She cups my jaw, and I lean into her comfort.

As much as I want to kiss her up against my truck all night, I can't. My girl needs her daddy, and I'm a father always. "It's Vi.

She's got a fever, so I need to get home. Do you mind if we press pause on this?"

"Pause? No." She loops her hand through mine. The one that's always callused from all the riding. "Press play 'cause I'm coming with you."

28

OUR GIRL

DAKOTA

"Where's a thermometer when you need one?" Wyatt grunts, shoving aside one of the million keychains in the junk drawer, trying to keep the frustration from his voice. "And why are there so many damn keys in here? We don't even have that many doors in the barn."

He starts to slam a kitchen drawer shut, but he seems to remember the sleeping, flushed baby in his arms, and slowly closes the handle with a defeated sigh. Vienna's forehead is so hot, she's not even crying, and it breaks my heart when she sniffles, nuzzling into his scratchy neck.

Our eyes connect from across the kitchen, and I give him a look that hopefully he reads as *What can I do?*

And he gives me one back that could either be *nothing*, or maybe, *you're already helping.*

He's been a worried mess since we got back to the barn, and it's so at odds with his typical laid-back mood, that I've been forced to dial into my calm demeanor.

We were always like a see-saw—when one person went down, the other person went up. He needs calm, so I dial into the side of my nature, even if it doesn't come as naturally.

When his moms texted him, he flipped the switch from sexy cowboy to concerned daddy in a second, so I forced my body to cool down after that flaming kiss.

He seems like he's too concerned about his daughter to think about the kiss, but not me, I'm still overthinking it, and watching him fawn over his little girl reminds me that he isn't like the other men I kick out of my bed.

He's more, a lot more, and that terrifies me a bit.

I can't remain emotionally detached with Wyatt. If I sleep with him, it's going to mean something. I need to think this through because this could end up ruining everything, which will probably happen anyway, so maybe I should just go for it.

I'm not a lucky person, so I don't believe in happy endings. I believe in working your ass off to get what you want because no one owes me a damn thing in this life.

But as I gaze at him rubbing circles on Vi's back, I can't help but hope for that futile happy ending. I feel it then, the yearning for a family. Vi's not even mine, and I'm already starting to feel this new protective urge over her because she's Wyatt's. I go all in when it comes to my people.

I might not know the first thing about being a parent, but I don't want to add *more* stress to this situation, so on the way home, I was looking up best things to do if a child has a fever, reading them off to Wyatt, because I feel like solutions are better than questions in these scenarios.

"She's going to be fine, sweetheart. Her forehead doesn't even feel all that hot," his mom, Stella, says, wrapping an arm around his shoulder. He leans into her touch in that same seeking-comfort way I lean into my dad's. "We debated even calling you because all kids get sick, but she wanted her daddy."

"Yeah," his other mom, Jessie, adds, nodding her navy Guardians cap. "Kids get fevers. It happens all the time. There's no need to worry."

"Of course I'm going to worry," he counters, dampening a

cool washcloth to put on Vienna's forehead. "She's my daughter, and she's sick. I can't *not* worry when things like this happen."

Stella kisses his stubbled jaw. If Vi's the spitting image of Wyatt, he's the male version of his mom. "There's only so much you can do, sweetheart. Kids get sick. You had a million fevers as a kid, and you're still alive."

Jessie sprays some Lysol lemon cleaner, wiping up the already clean granite counter. She's always been a neat freak. "Give her a lukewarm bath, and you both get some rest."

They both pull him into a hug, and the four of them form a tight circle. It's so intimate, so raw, that it feels like I'm intruding on a private moment. Wyatt's always been a hugger, and so are his parents, so they stay wrapped around each other long enough that I debate leaving.

That's the kind of family I want one day—the come-to-us-for-anything type. The kind where you spend ten days straight together on vacation in a cramped rental, annoying the hell out of each other, and by the time you leave, you're ready to *never* speak to them again. But then you say your goodbyes at the airport, wake up the next morning in your own bed, and find you miss all that loud fighting because your tiny apartment feels empty without them.

"Get some sleep. You too, Kodie," Stella agrees, nodding as she finally pulls back. "We're going to head back to the main house, but holler if you need us."

They give me a firm hug before walking out the front door, and now, it's just us in the barn, and the ticking rooster clock on the wall.

Wyatt opens cabinet after cabinet, peering into the contents.

"Are you sure we don't have a thermometer?" he huffs, blowing a strand loose from the bun at his neck. "I want to check her temperature."

I yank open one of the kitchen drawers, scanning the clutter. I'm not sure how to help, but I'll do what I can. "The only thing we've got is a meat thermometer, and sticking it up her bum would be messy and sharp, so that's not gonna work."

Wyatt's lips twitch like he wants to smile, but ultimately, they stay rooted in a worried twist. He walks around the kitchen counter, bringing his daughter to me. "How hot does she feel to you? Think it's over a hundred?"

I swipe a hand over her forehead, warmth emanating from her flushed skin. I feel so bad for her, and I hate that there's nothing I can do. The sweet little devil leans into my palm, a mess of flushed gold, and my heart constricts.

"Yeah, she's warm, but she doesn't feel too hot." I realize that's an unhelpful statement after I say it, so I add, "Want me to see if we've got some aspirin?"

"No!" Wyatt shouts, making me jump a bit.

"Okay, whoa," I say, holding up my hands. "I didn't realize you felt that strongly about aspirin."

He shakes his head, bouncing Vi gently, who must not be feeling good because she didn't even get fussy at that noise. "Sorry. It's not that. It's just that you can't give kids aspirin. It's one of the things that can kill them, apparently, like everything else in this world, according to the internet."

My mouth gapes. "Aspirin kills children? They should put a warning label on the bottle."

"That's what I said," he chuckles, but his laughter dies a quick death.

"Okay, got it. No aspirin. I can search for some infant's Tylenol if you want?"

"No, it's fine. I already checked all the cabinets." He mutters a curse. "I can't believe I forgot to get infant's Tylenol. It's like I always run out of things when I need it. I'm such a shitty dad."

"Hey, listen to me." I grab his cheeks. "There's not a chance in hell I'm letting you think that for a second. You're not a shitty dad. You're a great dad who forgot to write down one item on his grocery list. Don't beat yourself up over this."

That crease between his brows smoothes, but he still watches his daughter with concerned eyes.

He carefully brushes her damp hair from her fevered brow. "I don't know. Should I take her to the doctor? Wait, never mind. They aren't open. Maybe we need to go to the emergency room?"

I find his arm with my hand, trying to offer some comfort even though comforting people isn't my strong suit. But I want to be that person for him. "Let's listen to your parents and put her to bed. She needs rest, and if she's still burning up in the morning, we'll take her to a doctor."

"Yeah, you're right," he whispers, pulling her closer, lips lingering on her sweaty forehead. "I just hate feeling helpless when it comes to her. Sometimes, I don't know if I can do this."

I brush Vi's warm back, rubbing circles to give her more comfort. "Do what?"

"Be everything she needs."

His voice sounds tattered, and I want to make it shiny again, so I place my hand on his cheek. "You don't need to be everything she needs. You just need to be there when she needs you."

He pinches his eyes closed, and then murmurs a soft, "Thank you."

"I haven't done anything," I say, stroking my thumb on his stubble.

"You're here when *I* need you. That's enough."

He leans forward, resting his forehead against mine, but he doesn't say anything. He's a Cancer, so he always goes quiet when he's exceptionally stressed, but we don't need words to communicate. We've got our own language full of deconstructed touches and looks that we've been speaking for years.

The way he's gazing at me combined with the way I'm holding him feels like *more*, and I need to think about this before I dive into anything with him. Being with him also means being with his little girl, and I need to make sure I'm ready for that.

Yeah, I've always wanted to be a mom, but it's still a massive commitment.

I pull back, letting my hand drop, but I still want to do something to help. "Want me to go over to my dad's and see if he has a thermometer?"

Wyatt perks up, but then his shoulders slump. "No. You've been drinking, so I don't want you driving."

"I can walk, and it's less than a half mile from the barn." I head to the red front door. "You cuddle up with our girl. I'll be right back."

He works his jaw, and the muscles tighten as he seems to wrestle with his decision. I tug on my boots, not giving him an option. Wyatt will put everyone else before himself, so I know he doesn't want me walking alone almost as much as he wants to know his daughter's temperature.

He needs someone to make the decision for him, so I say, "I'm going. I know this property like the back of my hand, so I'll be right back, and I don't want to hear any complaints."

"Dakota, I don't—"

"No complaints!" I shut the door on the very complaint I don't want to hear, and it's only when I'm outside that I realize what I said.

Our girl.

29

I HATE THAT WORD

WYATT

"*S*hhhh, I know your fever's gone, little devil, but you've got to be quiet 'cause your daddy's sleeping on the couch."

My eyes drift open at the sound of Dakota's low murmur, and I peek through my lashes to see her dancing around the open kitchen in nothing but a tiny cotton tank and little plaid shorts with my smiling girl in her arms.

I'm dazed with sleep, so it takes me a second to remember everything that happened last night. I must've fallen asleep before she got back from her dad's. But my baby girl is smiling big, which means I'm smiling. Her cheeks aren't flushed either, so she must be feeling better.

Relief hits me like a runaway train.

I almost jump off the couch to check on my girl, but then I remember Dakota said that her fever's gone, and I notice the morning light glinting off Vi's curls. Dakota's grinning down at her. My breath stops.

There they are—*dimples.*

Not for me, but for my little girl, and that's even better. I let myself stare, watching, soaking up this moment. I can't capture this, so I'd rather watch a little longer. I shove my feet under Tuna's warm body, snoozing peacefully at the end of the leather couch, and stay right here.

"It's like this," Dakota whispers, picking up Vi's tiny fist. "One-two-one. One-two-one."

She mimics my chant, her voice soft and playful, as she two-steps around the granite counter with my daughter in her arms. If I hadn't already loved her before, this would make me fall for her now. I keep my eyes barely open, just slivers of light peeking through my lashes, so she still thinks I'm asleep.

The sweet, familiar melody of "You're Gonna Miss This" by Trace Adkins hums under her breath as she twirls and sways in the kitchen.

Seeing her melt for my little girl makes this big world shrink to the three of us, and I can't help but stare at them. This right here is what I want. Simple, slow mornings with two girls I love. The hockey season can be brutally fast-paced, so I always appreciate the slower things in life.

She kisses her cheek, making her baby hands clap and trying to grab at her face. "Your daddy taught me how to two-step," she whispers. "He's pretty good, but don't tell him that 'cause he already knows it. He'll teach you one day too."

Vi's curls are a mess, but her chubby cheeks are flushed with happiness. She giggles as Dakota two-steps with her, and her tiny feet try to kick at the rhythm.

After seeing her sniffling last night, the joy rolling off my daughter is a massive relief. It's these moments that make all the snotty tantrums worth it. I swear parenting is a roller coaster of little moments filled with the biggest emotions.

And laundry—so much laundry.

She continues two-stepping, and as much as I like watching them, I want to be a part of this now, so I get up. Tuna doesn't even budge. She just blobs on the couch.

"Looks like you're getting better, but you're still a little stiff," I tease.

"Oh, you're awake." She whips her mess of brown curls to me. "I didn't mean to wake you up. Vi's all smiles and no fever this morning. It must've broken in the middle of the night. I changed her diaper, oh, and made her some breakfast. Banana pancakes. I figured I'd let you rest."

I glance at the rooster clock.

It's 10:00 AM.

My brows fly up in surprise.

"Thank you," I say. "I can't remember the last time I slept this late. Or the last time I woke up with my girl fed and her diaper changed by someone other than me or my parents. How's she doing?"

I drop a peck to the top of Vienna's head, and then feel her temperature. Her forehead is cool, and my shoulders loosen in relief. I feel like parenting is always like that. Kids get fevers, and they randomly go away.

She flashes those dimples again at my baby girl. "She's all smiles, just like her daddy."

I sway them both in my arms. Most bull riders are pretty small, so she fits snugly in my embrace. "Can I join in on this dance party with my girls?"

Dakota's brows shoot up. "*Your* girls?"

Using my knuckle, I lift her chin. "Yes, my girls."

I smush Vienna between us, settle my hand on Dakota's lower back, and start leading them in a two-step. Vi giggle-screams, and this right here is everything I want. Two-stepping in the kitchen with my girls.

Both our lives are so intense that I want to come home to something as easy as breathing. There's no other woman who would trek through a half-mile of cacti in the middle of the night just to get my daughter a thermometer.

Well, there probably are, but I only want this one.

The song comes to a gentle, final strum.

I twirl them both in one last spin. Vi tucked safely against Dakota's chest. "See honey, *that's* how you two-step."

She bites her bottom lip, and it seems like both our thoughts drift back to last night. At least, I'm thinking about the way our bodies felt pressed together, and how I want everything from her. But then she looks down at my daughter and gives her a big smack of a kiss on her cheek, and I think that might be even better than her thinking of me.

Vi starts squirming in her arms, which usually means she wants some space to move around, so I take her and navigate the sea of toys in the living room.

"Here you go, baby." I drop her into her enclosed playpen. She crawls forward, and I watch to see if she'll stand, holding my breath, but she doesn't.

"What's wrong?" Dakota asks. "Why are you frowning?"

I sigh, trying to push the worries away. "I'm waiting to see if Vi will walk. I'm trying not to stress about it, but it's hard."

Dakota starts washing one of her orange-juice-crusted sippy cups. "Hey, she'll get there. She's so close. I've seen her pull herself up on furniture, so maybe she's just not ready yet."

"Maybe," I mumble, wrapping my arms around her from behind. It's nice to have someone to share my worries with because normally, it's just my parents, and they always listen, but they have each other.

I have no one.

I kiss the curve of her neck. "Thank you."

"For teaching your daughter my amazing dance skills?" she teases, drying the sippy cup.

"No, for everything you did last night. It's nice having someone during the hard parts."

She turns around to face me, gripping the granite counter. "It's nice feeling needed during the hard parts."

She sucks on her bottom lip *again*, and the motion has me

remembering last night *again*, and the way she bit my lip. I want her, so I press her hips back into the sink.

I'm trying to keep this PG, since Vi is ten-feet away playing with her singing vegetable toys, but with the way my boxers are tightening, this is quickly bypassing right into PG-13 territory. And with the way her nipples are hardening in that tiny tank, it might go straight to an R-rating.

I lift her chin with two fingers and go in for a kiss right as Vi lets out a high-pitched wail that travels into the kitchen.

"Dada!" she screams, slapping her toys. "Mo!"

With a heavy sigh-groan, I drop my head to Dakota's shoulder. "That means she's hungry."

Her shoulders shake with a chuckle, and she kisses my cheek. "You're a daddy first."

"Yeah, but it's hard to remember that with you in those tiny shorts," I drawl, navigating the land mine of toys again to my daughter.

"Want me to take them off so you forget?" she challenges.

Fuck me. I do *not* need to be thinking about that right now.

I focus on my baby girl, ignoring the smart-mouthed, sexy-as-hell bull rider bending over in my kitchen like she knows exactly what those tiny shorts are doing to me.

I scoop Vi up from the playpen, dump some more blueberries onto her highchair, and start putting her hair into pigtails. I'm getting damn good at pigtails. Braids are a whole other beast, but I've been practicing on my own hair, so that's one benefit to keeping it longer.

Dakota watches with quirked lips, but a thought seems to occur to her the longer she stares, and she frowns. "How're you so calm right now? We kissed last night. That's a big thing, but you're over here acting like it's nothing."

Play it off, Patterson. Stay calm to keep her calm.

"I'm not worried because it felt normal to me, and I hope

you'll let me kiss you again 'cause I can't stop thinking about it," I admit while finishing with Vi's hair.

Her pigtails are lopsided, but oh well. At least it's not the pigtail-tantrum-fiasco that happened in the Target candle aisle.

"Normal?" Her mouth falls. "Kissing me feels normal to you? How? We basically did a one-eighty and went straight from friends to a hell of a lot more."

"Yeah, I know," I say, trying to play it off. Act casual. "But it feels very normal. Like I should've kissed you a lot sooner."

She groans, burying her face in her hands.

Okay.

Not the reaction a man wants.

I can almost hear her thoughts spiraling, so I walk over to her and cradle her cheeks. "Hey. What's wrong? Talk to me."

Her honey eyes search mine until she releases a breath, and then all her worries spill out in one massive string of oxygen. "I'm just a little overwhelmed with all this. You two mean more to me than anyone else, so I want to think this through. I know I can't do the whole summer fling with you."

Being with me comes with a lot of big decisions. Capitalized Big Decisions, if I'm honest. If a woman's going to be with me, she has to be okay with potentially being a mom to my daughter.

I'll never be a casual fling again. My life isn't easily *flung* anymore.

I press my lips to her forehead. "I know I come with a lot of strings, being a dad, and I don't want to force you into anything you're not ready for, so let's take this one day at a time."

"Hey, your daughter is not a string," she says in a passionate voice. "She's one of the best parts of being with you. It's like a two-for-one package, but I still occasionally smoke weed on the weekends with Lana." That thought seems to make some light bulb go off in her brain, and she rubs a hand through her dark hair, seeming stressed. "Oh my god, what if we really do this whole thing, Wyatt? I just realized I'd be Vi's *mom*."

Mom.

She said mom.

I should be surprised she jumped to that conclusion so fast, but I'm not. Her mind always spirals, imagining every possible outcome. The good, the bad, and the ugly.

I shrug like that one word didn't spark a swarm of hope in my chest while I pepper her inner wrist with kisses. "You're fine. Legal occasional marijuana consumption doesn't make you a terrible parent."

"Technically, it's not legal in Texas. I'm breaking the law. Do you really want her to have a criminal for a mom, Wyatt? How does this not bother you?"

"Well," I say, still stuck on the word *mom*. Still trying not to react. "For one, I like that you're thinking long-term about us, and two, she already has a criminal for a dad. Don't you remember that one summer the cops busted me for stumbling around on the beach in Corpus? I spent the night in the drunk tank, covered in someone else's piss, and she still calls me daddy, so... We do our best, but no parent should be expected to be perfect. That's like expecting your kid to be perfect all the time."

"I forgot about that. You and beaches." She huffs a laugh. "Still. I'm mostly used to keeping things casual since Boone, so this is a lot for me to process."

"We can keep things casual," I blurt without thinking.

All the happiness in me comes to a screeching halt.

Goddammit.

I hate that word. *Casual.*

I don't know why I said it, and I want to take it back, but her eyes brighten with something that looks like relief. "Are you sure?"

I don't want to be like the other guys she only calls when she's drunk, but the last thing I need is to scare her off before this starts, especially if she's not ready to be a mom. I don't want to force her into anything.

"Sure, we can," I lie, swiping my thumb along her bottom lip. "But just to be clear, if you want to sleep with someone, you better be knocking on my bedroom door. No one else's. I'll take real good care of you, honey."

She bites her bottom lip in a challenge. "Oh, I bet you will. I already know how *nice* you are."

"Damn right." I trace my tongue along the shell of her ear, and she releases this breathy little moan that nearly destroys my self-control. "Us nice guys might always finish last, but that's only 'cause we know our ladies get to finish first."

30

KEEP ME CLOSE

DAKOTA

*W*yatt Patterson is not acting *casual.*

On Tuesday, he makes me a bouquet of wild-flowers filled with fiery shades of sunlight—zinnias, marigolds, Indian paintbrushes. On Wednesday, he does the same thing except, this time, it's blue. And over the next week, I bounce out of bed, eagerly waiting to see what bouquet each new morning will bring.

Friday is different.

We load Luna-Tuna into the truck, strap a giggly Vi into her car seat, and take a drive through the back country roads with the windows rolled down. The sun-baked earth and lingering wildflowers perfume the hot breeze.

It's my favorite drive—the Willow City Loop—and even though my favorite season, bluebonnet season, is long over, the yellow perennials coloring the pastures in waves of gold are just as lovely.

Wyatt interlaces his fingers through mine, draping one arm over the steering wheel. He doesn't let go as we curve down windy roads, whizzing past brown longhorns grazing beneath gigantic oak trees. As I gaze out at the blur of blue sky and green grass, I try to think of the last time I drove without going anywhere.

Nothing comes to mind.

We spend the day doing all the things we used to do growing up, except this time, we've got a cute third wheel.

We pick the juiciest strawberries at Sweet Berry Farm while the owner writes down his secret recipe for strawberry pie (it's the rhubarb!). We let Vi pet baby goats while sipping a 2018 Mourvèdre at a winery.

I'm surprised by how natural it all feels, but more than that, I'm surprised by how badly I don't want him and Vi to leave at the end of the summer.

On Saturday, I tell Alanna all this at The General, and she goes off on a rant about how Texas wine isn't on par with California, but I dig my boots in, and tell her that it's delicious none-theless. Eventually, after a heated debate about wine country, we get to my deconstructed feelings.

"Day one!" Lana shouts after I finish telling her about every-thing that's happened with Wyatt. "Day *one*, I called this, and you called me crazy. I knew I was right. I'm always right. You fucking knocked boots."

"We haven't knocked anything yet," I counter. "It's surpris-ingly difficult to find time to have sex with a toddler in the house."

I'm also nervous to sleep with him, if I'm being totally honest with myself. Sex and emotion rarely mix for me, but I can't sepa-rate the two with Wyatt.

Lana wiggles her red brows, *cheersing* me with her glass. "Here's to hoping the boots will be knockin' soon."

There's that nervous-achy feeling again. I take a swig of my margarita.

Lana's got her hair in braids and is wearing a silk, champagne dress that ends mid-thigh. We look like complete opposites with me in a jean skirt and cotton tank, but anything goes here.

There's a motorcycle biker gang tucked into the back corner next to a table of girls in feather boas with matching shirts that say *Buy Me a Shot. I'm Tying the Knot!*

I sip my margarita, ignoring the shot-shot-shot chants. "I can't believe you were right about us."

"I'm sorry. What?" She cups her ear, leaning on the bar counter, and drawing a few gazes from the cowboys nearby. "Could you say that again? It's hard to hear over all the chanting."

I bump her shoulder. "Shut it. Your hearing is just fine."

"I know, but I like hearing I'm right." Alanna strokes one red nail over her empty vodka soda, calling out to Willie. "Hey! Bartender! Can I get a martini this time? Three blue cheese olives. Black, not green. Thanks in advance, sweetie."

I think Willie's glaring at her, but I can't be sure with all that facial hair. He gestures around the bar. "Does this look like the kind of establishment that has blue cheese olives on hand, Barbie?"

Oh, shit.

Lana's eyes bulge. "*Excuse* me? Did you just call me 'Barbie'?"

"Yeah, *Barbie*, I did." He crosses his arms over his ripped jean jacket.

She scoffs. "My name's—"

He cuts her off. "I know your name, *Alanna*. You don't need to introduce yourself."

She snaps her mouth closed for a second.

"How do you know my name?" she asks in a softer voice this time.

He flicks a dish rag over his shoulder. "'Cause you're the reason I have to drive all the way to Horseshoe Bay to get Grey Goose vodka since our house vodka isn't good enough for your prissy ass."

In a flash, she scrapes back from her stool, pointing a mani-cured fake nail at him. "Oh, you prick. I'm not fucking prissy. Who even says that anymore? Let me tell you something..." she trails off, her face scrunching like she's trying to remember his name.

He crosses his arms over his jean-clad chest, patiently waiting. I can't tell if he's smirking with the bandana and all that facial hair, but he seems smug.

Lana tosses her artificial locks over one shoulder. "Okay, Sasquatch, let me tell you something—"

"Nice try. It's Willie," he says, giving her his broad back. He's even bigger than Wyatt.

Her eyes bulge when he legitimately walks away from her mid-sentence, completely ignoring Lana's talon nails.

I have to use my hand to stifle my laughter. Willie mostly communicates with grunts and scowls, so I'm shocked he's actually talking to Lana, but I guess he got his city girl fill now that he's walking away.

She plops back down on the duct-taped leather stool, huffing. "Can you believe him? How rude. He just put himself right on the top of my shit list. He's absolutely not getting a tip."

"I mean, he's probably just pissed. Horseshoe Bay is an hour-long drive from here."

"It's not like I *asked* him to go. Never mind. We're not talking about Face Beard. So, how was the kiss?" she prods. "Explosive? Legendary? I want all the dirty details."

"It was…" I try to find the right words because yes, it was all of the above, but it was also so much deeper. I'm not sure I want to share all those details, even with Lana. That would make the moment less *ours*.

"It was great," I finish lamely.

"Great?" she states, slapping a hand on the sticky counter, then immediately wiping it on her napkin with a look of disgust. "That's it? *Great*? I need more adjectives."

"Fine," I relent, fluttering my lips. "It was amazing, but I don't want to talk about it."

"Why?" Lana whines. "You know I love gossiping when it's not about my life. I want to know everything."

I take a swig of my margarita, regular, not prickly pear this time. "Because it's complicated. He said he was okay with keeping things light, but he's still got a daughter, and I'm starting to get attached. I don't know if I can keep this casual, and I want to make sure I'm doing right by him because that's a huge commitment."

She pops a peanut between her red lips, chewing, thinking. "He said he was okay keeping things casual? That's actually shocking. That man might as well be walking around in a floral apron that reads *Looking for a wife,* then in parentheses, *I love going down on women.*"

I snort, wiping the lime juice off my lips. "What makes you think that?"

"'Cause you can just tell with some guys. They're the selfless types." She glares at Willie, who's opening a beer by slamming the top against the counter. "Like Sasquatch over there is no way burying that face-beard between a woman's legs."

"You're right," he drawls, instantly glancing up like he's been eavesdropping the whole time. "My apron says, *Don't worry. It'll fit.*"

Lana looks like she has no idea what to say to that, and Willie goes back to opening beers, but there's a bounce in his step this time.

"What will fit?" a low voice interjects.

My head snaps toward the bar where Wyatt's leaning casually with his hair pulled back beneath a rugged cowboy hat. There's a devilish smirk playing on his lips, and I want to drag him away and kiss him silly.

He saunters forward, radiating confidence, and closes the distance until he's towering over me. Without an ounce of hesitation, he plants his mouth on mine, and kisses me so thoroughly, I'm gasping by the end, and Lana's fanning herself.

"Hey there, gorgeous," he drawls, pulling back to kiss the tip of my nose.

I'm one lucky woman.

"God*damn*, I wish you had brothers," Lana says.

"I've got Willie," Wyatt says, keeping his eyes on me.

She grimaces. "I would need a three-day spa retreat with a full-body exfoliation session after sleeping with him."

"Well, we all know how much you love those spa days, Barbie, so it's too bad you'll never find out what it's like to fuck me," Willie grunts while casually drying a margarita glass.

Lana's chest flushes, but she regains her composure quickly. "I wouldn't fuck you even if you were hiding frat-boy Harry Styles under all that hair."

Wyatt only chuckles, and then slips behind me, draping his arms around my bare shoulders in a casually possessive move that's going to ward off all the cowboys in this bar, which I don't mind. He's mine for the summer.

"What are you doing here?" I ask, snuggling closer because he's oh so warm. "Where's Vi?"

"I love that you always think about her." He kisses my shoulder, the heat of his lips lingering on my bare skin. "My parents are watching her because I wanted to see you. You've been at the gym all day."

"I know," Lana huffs. "It's like she never leaves."

"I'm getting ready for the Fredericksburg rodeo next weekend," I say, defending myself despite the ball of guilt in my stomach.

Wyatt's hand ventures forward, snatching up my nearly empty margarita. He puts his lips right over my lip gloss imprint, licking it right off the glass rim. I had no idea that could be so hot.

"Running low? You want another one, honey?"

The slight drawl, the hint of a smirk, the casual confidence... Wyatt's aged into quite the man, and I can't be held accountable if

I end up straddling him in a bar bathroom tonight due to the margaritas. All the alcohol has soaked up my nerves, and maybe that's what I need. To sleep with him when I'm drunk so I stop overthinking this, but no. That's a crap tactic.

He's not the man I want to call when I'm drunk; he's the one I want to call when I'm happy.

"I'm not sure that's a good idea," I say.

His breath is a whisper against my ear. "And why's that?"

I swipe my thumb along his bottom lip, picking up a droplet and sucking it into my mouth. "Because tequila has a tendency to make my clothes fall right off my body."

His eyes flash.

"You're right," he rumbles, brushing his nose against the tip of mine. "Another margarita would be a terrible idea. Your skirt might fall right off, or worse… your panties." He nips my earlobe. "God forbid."

Heat simmers in my core at the huskiness in his playful words. Flirty Wyatt's even better than Friendly Wyatt.

"Exactly." I take a deliberate, long gulp of the alcoholic beverage in question, draining the whole thing as I play along. "It'd be catastrophic."

"Apocalyptic." His tongue traces a fiery path just behind my ear. "Those panties of yours might go up in flames."

I tilt my head, catching the glint of mischief in his green eyes, and our gazes lock. "I think my panties are a little too wet right now to catch on fire."

His eyes blaze with heat.

"Oh my *god*," Lana exclaims, slamming back a shot of vodka. "If you two don't tone down this sexual tension, I'm going to self-combust in an orgasm."

"I'd pay good money to see that," Willie deadpans across the counter.

Wyatt tugs me back to his chest, and there's a tenderness in his confident grin that has me melting against him. "Dance with me?"

"All this flirting is making me want to do more than dance, so I have a better idea," I murmur, wrapping my arms around his waist. "We could go home? Maybe take an outdoor shower together?"

"Hm," he says, intertwining his arms around my back. "That *would* be nice, but see you've had one too many margaritas, and I want you to remember everything when we're together, which is why we're only dancing tonight. You're still looking a little stiff out there."

The memory douses the heat. This past week has been hell on earth. At the rodeo, Teton, the bull, rammed into my shoulder something fierce. I had to sit in the bath for over an hour, so staying on during practice has been even tougher.

"You and two-stepping, huh?" I say. "You really think it'll help?"

Wyatt touches his thumb to the corner of my mouth, lifting it back up. "I *might* have an ulterior motive."

"Oh?" I lift a brow. "And what's that?"

The cover band starts playing the song "Damn This Heart of Mine" by William Beckmann. With an infectious smile, he guides us to the dance floor, twirling me effortlessly, and just when I'm about to spin out of control, he tugs me against his solid chest. "It's the perfect excuse to keep you close."

And keep me close he does—all night long.

COME HOME TO ME

DAKOTA

*L*ust is such a little shit.

On Sunday, I can't stop staring at the dimples on Wyatt's lower back, just above his ass cheeks, as he reaches for a coffee mug in the kitchen, wearing nothing but a pair of workout shorts slung low on his hips.

"See something you like?" he drawls.

I snap my gaze up to find him smirking that smirk that reminds me nothing of my summer boy and everything of the sizzling kiss at The General. But I don't have the headspace to be thinking about electric kisses today, no matter how much I want to. I need to focus on the rodeo that I have to leave for in... I check the time on my phone.

Dammit. Ten minutes.

I scoot back from the granite counter, half smiling up at him. "Yeah, *you*, but I have to go. I was just leaving."

"You sure about that?" He cocks a brow, sipping his coffee. "'Cause it looked like you were admiring my ass, not walking out the door."

"It *is* a nice ass," I say, aiming for casual, but the words are tight, like I've been sucking helium. "Looks like it's carved out of marble. Michelangelo would be admiring that view."

He rests his elbows on the counter, leaning forward. "I do a lot of lunges. Maybe I'll let you feel it sometime."

I mimic his posture. "How about you let me feel it now?"

"Mmmm." He leans back, sipping his coffee, teasing me. He looks too good in the morning. "See, I would let you feel me up, but you have to leave for the rodeo, and I want to take my time with you, honey."

This new blasé confidence makes my heart pound a little harder. He looks so unaffected, sipping coffee in the kitchen with his hair tied back and a few strands falling across his forehead. Meanwhile, I'm finally understanding exactly what historical romance authors mean when they claim their *loins are burning.*

I can't do anything about my burning loins now, so I grab my boots. "Fine. You'll have to let me feel up your marble ass another time. Let's hope a bull doesn't get me. I hear they've got some mean ones to pick from this round."

That comment is 60 percent joke, 20 percent gut-wrenching fear, and 20 percent unadulterated excitement.

A second later, my back is being pushed up against the wall.

Wyatt grips my chin, turning me toward him, and then his lips crash against mine. I'm so stunned that I don't respond at first, but then his tongue invades my mouth, and I'm kissing him back just as fiercely.

Our teeth bang together, and there's this urgent edge to his kiss that sends a ripple of fear through me. It feels like one of those scenes from the forties, where a newlywed husband kisses his wife goodbye before heading off to war—desperate, frantic, and tinged with worry.

He pulls back just as quickly, and whatever emotion he poured into that kiss, he hides from his face, stroking my cheeks with his thumbs. "Stop talking about a bull getting you. You'll be good. I wish I could be there, but I've got to watch Vienna today since my moms are delivering flowers."

"It's okay," I pant out, still gasping. Wyatt Patterson is one hell of a kisser. "I'll be fine. Take care of the little devil. She needs you more than me."

"*I* need you, though." He kisses me again, rough. "Don't forget that. You're important to me."

That shoots two jolts of emotion right to my heart—unease and warmth. Unease because I can't make any promises, and warmth because I've never been needed. It makes me want to hold onto the rope with everything I've got so I can come home to them.

I stand on my toes to reach his lips, giving him a sweet kiss. "You're important to me too."

My life might be unpredictable, but I channel Wyatt's energy, push those thoughts aside, and head to the front door. Except, I forget to give Vienna a kiss goodbye, so I turn back around and drop one to her blonde curls as she clashes two plastic vegetables together on her play mat. Wyatt watches the entire time with a blank face, as if he's shielding his emotions.

I almost make it to the door handle before he stops me again. "Hey, Dakota?"

"Yeah?" I glance back at him, and a stiff smile jumps to his lips.

He winks, a spark glinting in his eyes like fool's gold. I can't tell if that happiness is real. "Ride 'em hard, honey, and then make sure you come home to me."

I salute him with two fingers, even though it's a promise I can't keep. "Yes, sir."

* * *

THANKS TO WYATT'S drugging kisses, I forgot one very important thing before I left for the rodeo this morning—my protective vest.

Rookie mistake.

Ever since a famous bull rider died from being gored by a bull, the rodeos won't let anyone compete without one.

"Dammit," I mutter, frantically searching my bag in the back pens. It's where all the competitors hang out before they ride, so it's always a bustling area. "Where the hell is it?"

"You all good there, Cowboy Killer?"

I glance over my shoulder and see Nash, one of the younger bull riders, watching me with a grin. Everyone calls him Smiley because he's always wearing a goofy-ass smile. He's just turned eighteen, so he's one of the only bull riders who's still grinning because he's full of naive excitement.

"No, Smiley. I'm not fine," I say, rummaging through my bag. "I think I left my protective vest at home."

He hops off the metal fence, striding forward in his worn boots, his baby-blue eyes assessing me. "You can borrow mine for your ride. We look to be about the same size, but just make sure you give it back, or I'll be in a world of hurt."

Nash's always been a thoughtful one, but being an inner cynic, I say, "Why would you do that for me?"

He shrugs. There's that goofy grin again. "Because we're a team. We're all risking our lives together, so I've got your back. You ride after me anyway, so I'll make sure it's nice and sweaty for you." He laughs.

I can't stand toxic positivity, but Nash's got authentic positivity, which has my dimples popping in a rare smile. "Thanks, Nash. Really. I owe you one."

Technically, we all compete individually, but we're a team because we have each other's backs in this sport.

"Damn, girl! Look at those dimples! You *can* smile," he teases, waving a hand. If anyone else said something like that, I'd be scowling, but Nash pulls it off because he oozes a good-natured spirit. "And you don't owe me a thing. It's all good, Cowboy Killer. Best get ready for the draw."

The draw is where all the bull riders gather to get paired with the bulls. It's random, and we all sit on these uncomfortable wooden stools as the announcer booms out pairings, anxiously waiting to hear our fate.

Nash struts away, giving high-fives to every cowboy in sight, and I head over to the dusty warm-up area to meet my dad. The rodeo grounds are alive with energy, punctuated by the snorts of restless animals. Dust swirls around us as cowboys prepare for their rides, adjusting gear and bantering.

I find my dad by the water coolers, coiling a lasso for a calf-roper. He hands the cowboy the rope with a pat on the back. Colt Cutler never smiles, but he always lends a helping hand.

When I saunter up to him, he slaps my shoulder. "You ready for the draw? I hear Diablo's a tough one, so watch out if you get him. That bull's got a wicked spin and a mean snarl, so put all that two-stepping to good use. Stay loose and—"

"Flow like good tequila. Smooth and steady," I finish, strapping on my chaps. "I know, Pops."

He squeezes my shoulders hard, like he's trying to transfer all his love, concern, and unspoken worries into me. My dad isn't physically affectionate with many people, but he is with me, and I'm the same way.

I'll never hug a stranger—not after Boone called me an awkward hugger because I let go too soon. The only two people I like to hug are my dad and Wyatt, and Vienna too, so I guess that's three people now.

My dad gives me pointers for the next fifteen minutes while I stretch and then plants a scruffy kiss on my cheek. "I love you, darlin'. More than life itself."

"Love you more, Pops."

He taps the brim of my hat, his brown eyes crinkling in my favorite way, but in their depths, I can see all that worry he tries so hard to hide. Our incessant *I love yous* might seem like a lot, but it's a tradition I'll never break. If something ever happened to me, I want my last words to be *I love you* to my dad.

Navigating the dusty corridors of the animal stalls, I weave through the bristling horses and head toward the bull riders' section for the draw.

That familiar spark of excitement flashes in my chest and quickly grows into a flame of adrenaline as I imagine all those people watching me ride, and that feeling is why I keep doing this. When things go right, and you stay on for all eight seconds, there's no better high.

It makes all the lows worth the climb.

I find my open seat smack-dab in the row of cowboys. No cowgirls in sight. As the only woman, I catch several curious stares and hushed whispers that ripple through the dry heat, but I let their doubts roll right off me. I'm feeling good today.

Real good.

Keeping my head high, I settle down next to a cowboy with his black hat tipped down, but when he looks up and those familiar ocean eyes meet mine, I nearly fall off my stool.

All that anger comes boiling back.

I remember the shit he said in that interview about how I'd never make it in this career, and it broke me, having the person I thought I loved turn against me.

I remember sobbing on the shower floor that night, questioning everything about whether I had what it takes to do this.

And then, I remember stepping back into the arena, feeling like an imposter while I told myself over and over that I had what it takes.

I picked myself back up.

And I'm damn proud of myself.

"Well, howdy there, stranger," he drawls, chewing on that damn toothpick like always. I used to worry that thing would poke my eye out.

I dig my nails into my palms. "What the hell are you doing here, Boone?"

32

SMILEY

DAKOTA

"*H*appy to see me?" he twangs out in his heavy accent.

Boone Bowman has always been handsome with his midnight hair, square jaw, and ocean eyes. With that all-black getup, he screams WARNING: BAD BOY COWBOY. But all that previous attraction is gone.

Long gone.

I never loved him. It was all lust. We've both got this intense drive to succeed, a grumpy scowl, and a no-bullshit attitude, so our relationship was us constantly trying to one-up each other.

"Why are you here?" I grit out, trying to keep my voice low in front of all the other cowboys in the row. We've got an audience.

He takes that infuriating toothpick out of his mouth. "I'm in town for a few rodeos, so I'll be here the rest of the month. Thought I'd come say hi to my favorite cowgirl."

"It's bull rider to you."

He snorts. "Still got that attitude, I see. How you been? You miss me?"

"Really? You're asking me that in the middle of a draw?" I demand, annoyed, irritated—you name it, I'm feeling it as I look into Boone's fathomless gaze and feel... nothing but resentment, thankfully.

I like to let shit roll downhill, but I'll never forgive Boone Bowman for making me question everything about my skills. He never even apologized, but I don't have time to deal with him in the middle of a draw.

I could yell, scream, rage at him, but that won't get me anything. I'd rather hop on my high horse and ride out of this conversation. I hear the view's great from up there.

All of a sudden, his sneer morphs into a sad grin that could be genuine, but I don't trust him.

"I just want to talk, Kodie," he pleads. "Please?"

He's normally all rough edges, and I've never heard him sound so desperate. It throws me off for a second, but I quickly put on my steely mask. "I've got nothing to say to you. What's done is done. We don't need to rehash anything."

He almost sounds sincere, but I know better than to believe a word out of his lying mouth. Boone's family is on the board of directors for one of the largest ranches in Texas, so like Alanna, he grew up going to galas, charity balls, and banquets.

He can charm the chaps off any cowgirl when he wants.

He shoves his hands in his jeans, rocking back on the stool with the fucking toothpick dangling from his lips. "Please, Kodie? Ten minutes. That's all I need. I swear I just want to talk."

"Ten minutes is more than you'll ever get. I don't even want to give you ten seconds."

"Alright, folks!" the announcer booms from the podium, thankfully saving me from this conversation. "Who's ready for the draw?"

They begin calling out the pairings. It's always the luck of the draw with the animals. Pun intended. Some days you get an easy bull, some days, a tough one. I keep my focus fixed on the list of bulls on the screen, not Boone's scalding stare as the auctioneer rolls off names.

"And next up, we've got Nash Sawyer riding..." Nash leans forward in the line of cowboys to wink playfully at me. "The wicked Diablo! He's a tough one!" he announces. A murmur of anticipation sweeps through the crowd, and Nash shoots me a blasé shrug.

He needs to take this seriously. That naive confidence is going to get him hurt, and I can't let that happen.

I lean over Boone to look him directly in the eye, and the brims of our hats bump. I push him back, focusing on Nash. "I hear he's got a mean spin. Be careful out there, you hear? I don't want you to get hurt. Good luck."

"Thanks, I'll need it." Another goofy grin. "Alright, I'll leave you to it."

That's the last thing he says to me.

I ignore Boone for the rest of the draw and end up getting paired with a bull named Rogue, and we head back to the animal corrals. I wait to use Nash's protective vest, but it turns out I never get to use his because, true to his name, Diablo gives Nash a ride as wild and unforgiving as any I've seen.

From the sidelines, I watch in horror as Nash gets violently jerked around, my knuckles turning white on the rails. Diablo twists and bucks with a ferocity that sends Nash flying into the air.

As he falls, the bull's horn catches his side, ripping through the leather of his jacket. Blood spurts through his chaps, painting the dirt a shocking, vivid crimson. I'm close enough that a few drops splatter on me. It's horrific, but I force myself to watch out of respect.

Blood is *everywhere.*

The bustling crowd goes silent with a stillness that makes me nauseous. The medics rush in, calling for an ambulance as Smiley Nash writhes on the dirt with tears streaming down his face. They scramble to stabilize him before taking off to the hospital.

Boone and I watch from the sidelines with our hands pressed

over our mouths. For a moment, it reminds me what I saw in him —we're one and the same. We understand the brutalities of this crazy sport, and yet, all I can think about is how I want to make it home to Wyatt and Vi. I need them. They're my sunshine.

"Did you see them take him away?" Boone whispers. "He was pale as a ghost. Fuck. I hope he's okay."

The dirt is stained red, and I keep my eyes on the wet patch. "He was going to let me use his protective vest," I mumble, my voice vacant.

Without a word, Boone shrugs out of his jacket and carefully drapes it over my shoulders. "Here. You can wear mine."

He squeezes my shoulders, and I'm too shocked to push him away. It's a thoughtful gesture, but it doesn't make up for anything he's done.

I glance back at the dirt stain, and uncontrollable bile rises in my throat. I lurch away from Boone, and as soon as I get behind the bull chutes, I'm hurling. I puke up my guts for who knows how long, all while Boone rubs my back.

"It's okay, baby," he keeps saying. "I'm right there with you."

I always hated when he called me baby. "Don't call me that."

He doesn't listen. He just continues to call me baby while stroking my back as I hurl, but the entire time, I'm wishing it was Wyatt here with me.

Once my stomach is empty, I wipe the vomit off my mouth, zip up Boone's jacket, and get on the back of my own bull because that's what we do, even when someone almost dies. It's disrespectful as fuck to quit when someone gets hurt, because if they can do it, you sure as hell can.

But my body won't stop shaking.

My hands won't stop sweating.

My heart won't stop pounding for Nash, Smiley Nash.

I fall off after two seconds.

The rodeo—it's ruthless.

It breaks us all at some point, and that time, it broke Nash.

33

TAKE IT ALL

WYATT

*S*he's late, so I'm panicking.

I'm pacing by the barn door, my heartbeat battering in my chest while I glance at the rooster clock every five seconds. I squint at the ticking needle.

Are those hands moving *slower*?

It's almost nine, so Dakota should be home from the rodeo by now. Vi is finally asleep in her crib, but it took forever to get her there. She could probably sense my anxiety, so I read her five bedtime stories—complete with voices for Tommy the Turtle— just to calm her down. Now the silence feels unbearable as I wait, worry gnawing at me.

Moonlight crawls higher and higher on the wood floorboards while crickets chirp through the open window, and it would be peaceful if my ears weren't ringing. It's always like this when I can't watch her.

See her.

When I don't know if she's safe.

Suddenly, gravel crunches on the driveway, and a minute later, the front door swings open, bringing with it a rush of warm night air and a sight that makes my stomach clench.

Dakota stumbles in, supported by her dad, his strong arm around her waist. She's covered in dirt, sweat, and... is that blood? I'm going to lose my shit if that's her blood. Her face is pale, and her brown eyes are glossed over like she's seen a ghost.

I rush to her side, and she doesn't even look at me, just stares blankly at the floorboards. "What's wrong?" I panic. "Did something happen? Is she okay?"

Colt's face is grim, his brow furrowed deeply as he gently, so gently, brushes a strand of Dakota's brown hair off her face. "We had a bit of a scare at the rodeo, and I think she's in shock. Hell, I'm in shock, but one of us had to drive Daisy Blue home."

"What happened?" I ask, scanning her for injuries. "Did she get hurt?"

"No, but one of our boys got speared by a horn, and it wasn't a pretty sight." Colt winces. "He'll live, but he won't be the same."

I rush out a breath of relief that she's okay, but then I feel guilty for not thinking of the guy.

I clasp my hands behind my neck. "Shit, that's brutal."

Dakota pushes Colt off her and heads straight to the liquor cabinet, her movements jerky and unsteady. She yanks out a bottle of tequila and pours herself a hefty shot with trembling hands.

Colt and I exchange worried glances when she downs it in one go. She goes to pour another, but he stops her with a hand on top of the bottle.

"One shot will dull those feelings, darlin', but two? That'll make those emotions a hell of a lot worse. Trust me. It's a slippery slope when it comes to drinkin' away your problems, and it normally just ends with you feeling all those things you tried to dull in the first place."

She blinks at him, blinks again, and then she slowly lowers the tequila bottle. He kisses her forehead, and watching them be so raw with each other, so real, it's exactly the type of relationship I want to grow with my daughter.

"There you go," he rasps. "Go shower off and get a good night's sleep, alright? A good night of sleep can solve almost any problem."

She nods but doesn't say anything. Colt spins in his boots and crooks a finger at me. I strut up to him but keep my focus on Dakota breathing hard in my periphery.

He peers at me, those dark eyes even darker with concern. "You'll take care of my girl?"

I fight the urge to say she's mine too and nod instead. "Always, sir."

He seems to soften at that, and maybe I've cracked his hard exterior. "Good man. I always knew you were a good one."

After stepping back, he murmurs something low and soothing in Dakota's ear and wraps her in a tight hug, his rugged hands gently patting her. She doesn't hug him back, just lets her arms dangle at her sides like a rag doll. After a moment, Colt sighs and heads out the door, the heavy wooden slab creaking shut behind him.

It's just us, the crickets, and the moonlight now.

I take a careful step forward, searching Dakota's face for instructions on how to handle this situation, but I find nothing. She's still panting, breathing hard, and she's a mess.

"Come on, honey," I try to soothe. "Let's get you in the shower."

"Okay," she mumbles, but it's like she doesn't even hear me. Her eyes glaze over, staring right through me as if I'm invisible.

I wrap my arm around her waist, and she clutches me like a lifeline. Pushing open the back door, we stumble into the warm Texas night while I try to hold her up.

The air hums with crickets and rustling leaves as I guide her to the outdoor shower behind the barn. The wooden panels offer the perfect amount of privacy under a blanket of stars, and there's no need for light with the full moon brightening the inky darkness. I've always loved the stars in the Hill Country. You can't see the constellations in the city.

I turn the bronze faucet, and water cascades down.

Dakota jumps, startled by the noise.

"It's just the water," I murmur in my most calming voice, sticking my hand under the stream. "I'm checking to make sure it's warm for you."

She looks down at her hands, caked in a grimy mixture of dirt, sweat, and blood. She stares until her hands start trembling. That tremble ripples through her entire body, and she starts shaking violently, her teeth chattering as if she's freezing to death. I've never been so scared for her.

Suddenly, she clutches her stomach, her breaths coming in rapid, shallow gasps. "So much blood. There's so much blood."

In reality, there are only a few droplets, but she seems trapped in a daze, fixated on the thought. She's not moving into the water, and the shower's still running.

I lift her chin, forcing her to look at me and not the blood droplets on her hands. "Come here, honey. Let's get you out of those clothes."

She remains motionless, lost in some faraway thought. I step closer and gently tug on her jacket zipper. "Do you want me to help?" I whisper softly, hoping to break through her daze.

She gives me an absent nod.

"Are you sure?" I ask again.

She nods a yes, more forcefully this time.

"Okay," I say, kissing her forehead. "I've got you."

I slowly tug down the zipper, the metallic sound slicing through the night. Carefully, I peel off the dirty leather, but it's different. Bigger. I squint down at the fabric. This isn't her jacket.

"What happened to your protective vest?" I murmur. "This doesn't look like yours."

All she does is shake with chattering teeth. It's like I'm

speaking into a void. The jacket doesn't matter, so I slide it off her shoulders, dropping it with a soft thud, which leaves her in nothing but a white tank top.

I swallow, thinking about all the clothing coming off next. "Arms up."

She listens.

She raises her arms, and in one fluid motion, I peel off her sports bra and tank top so she's topless in front of me. She's still shaking, so I grip her hips to steady her. I catalog all the bruises and cuts on her skin before I bend down, kneeling in front of her until my eyes are level with her bare stomach.

"Hold onto my shoulders," I say. "I'm going to get you out of these jeans."

She clutches me in a desperate grip, like how I imagine she holds onto the bull rope. I press a gentle kiss to her abs to let her know I'm still here. I've still got her.

With a soft snap, I undo the button on her jeans and carefully drag them down her legs, coaxing her to step out of her dusty jeans. "Lift your leg for me."

She listens but keeps repeating the phrase, "So much blood." Her voice trembles more with each repetition until she's standing in nothing but her white cotton underwear, the moonlight highlighting her every curve.

I let myself look at her bare chest for one second, and then, squeezing my eyes shut, I gently tug down her panties, not allowing myself to look anymore. Once she steps out of them, I move to the stream of water. I test the temperature of the shower to make sure it's warm enough before turning to head back inside.

"Alright, I'll leave you to it."

At my words, she jerks out a hand, panic flaring in her amber eyes. "No. Don't leave me. That's what he said," she repeats over and over again as she curls in on herself.

I don't know what *he* she's talking about, but I'm back at her side in an instant, crushing her to my chest. "Hey, it's okay, honey. It's okay. I'm not going anywhere."

She seems to go from feeling nothing to feeling everything. Her body starts to tremble, and her face contorts with panic. She clutches her chest, panting like she's drowning in her emotions.

I've never seen her feel so much. She's not like this with anyone else, just me.

"I can't breathe," she gasps, her voice rising in desperation, each word choked out between rapid breaths.

"In and out," I say, my voice steady but filled with urgency.

Her entire body starts shaking as she stares down at the dirt and blood on her hands. "I can't breathe! Get it off!" she screams, voice cracking like a whip. Tears stream down her disheveled face, carving rivers through the dirt.

I wrap her up in my arms, clutching her fiercely to my chest, and do something reckless because I don't know how else to help —I drag us both beneath the stream of warm water.

Her, completely naked.

Me, completely clothed.

"Hey, you're okay. I've got you," I whisper, holding her tight as the warm water cascades over both of us.

She continues to sob against my chest, her shoulders shaking uncontrollably as the water washes away all the dirt, blood, and mess on her skin. I hold her tight, so damn tight, the water soaking my T-shirt and jeans, but I don't care.

She needs me, so I'm here.

We sink to the concrete ground of the shower, her straddling my lap, and all I do is hold her, stroke her hair, rub her back as the water soaks her naked body, and all the while, I murmur *"It's okay, it's okay"* in her ear. We stay like that for so long, my fingertips shrivel into raisins.

But then, with a sudden movement, she kisses me.

It's not so much a kiss as an urgent attack against my lips, and it's wet, making her lips slide over mine. For a second, I'm so caught off guard that I can't help but kiss her back, tugging the strands of her hair. Until I remember that the last thing I want is for her to regret anything that happens between us.

"Dakota, hey, hold on," I say, pulling back slightly to cup her cheeks. Droplets of water cling to her dark lashes.

"Please, Wyatt," she begs in a cracking voice. "*Please.* I just need to feel something good. Just let me feel something good tonight."

She twists her fingers in my soaking shirt, pressing into my chest. She starts biting my neck, sucking, pulling my hair like she needs me, desperately. She's making me ache for her, but this isn't how I imagined this happening.

"Dakota, I can't…" I let out a broken groan. "This isn't how I wanted anything to happen between us. Don't beg for me. It makes me want to give you everything."

"Please," she begs anyway. "It's never… I've never…"

"You've never what?"

She sucks in a shaky breath. "It's never meant something before, but you do. You mean something to me, and I just want you tonight."

She presses little kisses to my stubble, and then she bites my bottom lip. She's destroying my self-control with her pleas.

I feel like an absolute bastard when I get hard.

She notices and reaches down to unbutton my soaked jeans, but my fingers form handcuffs around her wrists. I can't tell her to stop because part of me doesn't want her to stop, even though we should. I've wanted her for so long that my control is in shreds. She seems to sense that I want this just as much as she needs this.

She grinds all over me as the water pours down beneath the blanket of stars. "Please, Wyatt."

"I didn't think it would happen like this," I say through the shower rain.

She sniffs, and fuck, she's killing my resolve. "Just… *please?*"

Her eyes fill with a pain that cuts deep. I can't stand it, her being in pain because of me. She needs this, and I've never been good at denying her, but I don't want to give it all up yet. "I don't have a condom. We can't."

Dumbass. I carried around the same condom for five years when I was a virgin, but of course I forget it with the woman of my dreams.

"I don't care. I'm on birth control, and I've never had sex without one. I trust you more than anyone in the world," she begs, fingers twisting in my wet shirt. "I want you. Only you. Do you…" She hiccups. "Do you not want me?"

That breaks my resolve.

"Dakota," I growl, forcing her to look at me in the shower rain. "You're the only woman I want. Hell, you're the only woman I *see*. I'm desperate for every part of you."

With a heavy groan, I surrender myself to her. I kiss her fiercely and slide two fingers into her, feeling the intense, velvety heat of her pussy, and I nearly come in my jeans at the warmth. I have to sink my teeth into her shoulder so I don't lose control.

She loses all control and starts thrusting against my hand.

This is too much.

It's all too much.

The friction against my cock makes it throb, the pleasure bordering on pain, but I like it almost as much as her nails digging into my back. With my other hand, I clutch her ass, pulling her impossibly close, our bodies melding together under the cascade of water, her wetness coating my fingers.

"Take what you need from me," I groan against her lips. "I'm yours, so take it all."

34

IT'S A PRIVILEGE

DAKOTA

I'm an open wound. Every part of me is raw.

But this, *this* is what I need tonight. To feel something good, something real. After what happened today, I need to feel someone's heart beating against mine.

And not just anyone's—Wyatt's.

I throw my head up to the moon, straddling his hand as I try to drown out my dark thoughts and focus on the man beneath me. His hot tongue tracing up the curve of my neck.

Water droplets cascade down my flushed skin in the heat of the night. The cords of his neck are taut, his jaw clenched in concentration as he rubs my clit with the pad of his thumb.

But I need more.

So much more.

His hand pumps inside me, and I close my eyes, furrowing my brow in concentration. But in the darkness, thoughts of the rodeo, the screaming, the sirens all creep back into my mind.

"Hey." Wyatt grips my chin, forcing our eyes to connect. His gaze darkens to pools of moss, filling with an intensity that makes my breath hitch. "Eyes on me. I don't want you thinking of anything else when you're with me. If you need something to focus on, watch *me*."

The command in his tone sucks the worries right out of my mind. I've always had a hard time focusing during sex, but not now.

Not with him.

His mouth crashes down on mine, hard and fierce, like he's been waiting for this moment forever. He stands from the shower floor, picking me up right along with him, all while keeping his lips locked with mine. It's like he doesn't want to stop kissing me even for a moment. He tries to take off his wet shirt while keeping his lips on me, but when he can't, he groans in frustration. He only pulls back for a second to rip off all his clothing, and then his lips are back on mine.

I barely hear his belt hit the floor.

He steps out of his wet jeans, leaving the rest of his clothing in a puddle on the ground. I don't even get a chance to appreciate all those naked muscles in the moonlight, but his drugging kisses are worth it.

His hand slams against the shower slats like he's trying to hold himself up. That noise, knowing *I'm* the one doing that to him, making it sound like he can't handle any more, turns me on more than anything, but it's not enough.

"Please, Wyatt. I need to feel you inside me."

That seems to make him more feral. We're both standing, so he grips the back of my knees and lifts me off the ground, forcing me to wrap my legs around his strong waist. He cradles my head as he slams me against the shower wall, protecting me. Something about that gesture is so sweet it brings tears to my eyes. Embarrassment simmers in my chest because I never cry during sex, but I'm feeling all kinds of raw, so I kiss him harder.

"Are you sure?" he breathes against my lips.

I tangle my fingers in his wet hair, clenching my legs tighter around his waist. "I've never been more sure of anything in my life."

In one movement, he lines himself up with my center and then slides into me—deep, deeper, deepest. I've never felt so full. When he reaches that farthest point inside me, he groans, biting my shoulder.

"Oh, fuck," we both moan.

Well, he moans it. I scream it.

"Are you okay?" he pants, letting me adjust to him. "Tell me you're good."

He's taking in deep rugged breaths like this is too much for him, but that doesn't matter. It's too much for me too. I cling to his shoulders, clenching him tight. "So good."

I can barely get the words out without whimpering. He begins moving inside me, slowly at first as the water drenches us. We're so damn wet.

He kisses my temple while pumping into me, and it's the perfect balance of sex and romance. He somehow manages to know exactly what I need without me having to tell him.

It's really hard not to explode into ecstasy right then and there. He dives back into a kiss all while thrusting into me, and the entire time, he never once stops kissing me. The base of his cock rubs perfectly against my clit, sending sharp jolts of pleasure through me. My thighs tremble, and *my* moans make *him* moan.

I cry out. So does he.

He thrusts up against me, and then his mouth is on my neck, biting and sucking, leaving marks on my skin. They're a possession, and I wouldn't let anyone other than Wyatt claim me.

His thrusts become more intense with the rhythm of rough sex. Skin slapping together, brutal and hard. We're loud enough to drown out all the worries in my mind. Every water droplet that lands on my skin feels like a caress, and the wetness between us makes our movements slick and raw.

"Fuck, fuck, fuck," he groans, the words all stringing together. His pumps turn faster, harder, driving me wild. "Come on, honey, get there with me. You're gonna make me lose it the way you're bucking against me like that. Tell me you're close."

I raise my voice over our slapping bodies. "So close."

"Where do you want me to come?"

"Inside me."

"*Fuck*," he moans.

My eyes roll back, and he releases a guttural, slightly frustrated groan, and then I feel it, that warmth. His release fills me up and seeing him so unleashed, knowing his control is snapping because of me, it pushes me over my own ledge.

My panting turns to screaming as the intensity of my orgasm crashes through me. It's never been like this, and I don't know whether it's because I've never needed an orgasm so badly or because it's Wyatt.

Probably Wyatt.

"That's it," he murmurs, coaxing wave after wave from my body. "Goddamn, I can feel you clenching around me." My body convulses, and he makes sure to draw out every last bit of ecstasy.

When it's all over, we're a wet, panting mess, and I already feel better. More like myself.

His eyes are on me, glinting with primal satisfaction, but there's also something deeper, something tender, so I stroke his rough cheeks. "I needed that. Needed you."

His arms tighten around me in a desperate hold, but he doesn't say anything as he pulls me impossibly close, his lips find my temple in a wispy kiss.

"Did you…" he trails off, sounding nervous. "Was it good for you? I wanted it to be good for you."

"It was more than good." I kiss him. "It's never been like that for me."

I don't ever want to let him go, and I could kick myself for not doing this with him sooner. I can already feel my craving for him growing, and I know I won't be able to keep my hands off him for the rest of the summer. There's no way I can stay emotionally detached, so this is going to hurt when it's all over.

I can't even think about him leaving, so I won't. Not tonight.

We untangle our bodies, and his hands move with an almost reverent touch as he washes me, rinsing away the evidence of our passion. He lathers shampoo into my hair, massaging my scalp, and I close my eyes, finally letting myself relax.

As he conditions my hair, the rodeo, Nash's smile, it flashes through my mind again because I'm an overthinker who can't shut her brain off at the appropriate times—like post-shower fuck.

That so easily could've been me. My brain speeds off with my worries, spiraling into the abyss. I'm going to end up dead by the age of thirty with a tombstone that reads: *Took the bull by the horns... and lost.*

Life's brutal out there, but then I think about how I can't give up this dream. I can *never* give up because without the rodeo, I have nothing. I've poured too much of my life into this career to give up—missed birthday parties, failed friendships, forgotten Christmas presents, declined wedding invitations.

Boone told me I'm an obsessed workaholic who doesn't care about anyone but herself, and maybe he's right. I've sacrificed too much to quit, and if I give up now, all that hard work will be pointless.

I'm in too deep now.

Wyatt seems to sense my thoughts have veered off because he murmurs softly, "Let's get you to bed. Like your dad said, a good night's sleep can solve most problems."

He wraps me tight in a towel and lifts me effortlessly into his arms. I've never had anyone handle me so gently, and it's something I didn't know I needed in a man. Everyone treats my body like it's indestructible, but Wyatt's holding me like I've got caution tape wrapped around me, not a towel.

I thought I needed a man who could handle me, but maybe what I really needed was a man to hold me.

As he carries me to my room, a tight lump forms in my chest. We both get dressed, but as he's about to lower me onto my bed, I look up at him and whisper, "I don't want to be alone. Can I sleep with you and Vi tonight?"

Softness flickers in his eyes, and without a word, he carries me to his room, holding me a little tighter this time. Luna follows behind us because she can't sleep without me, and I need my little shadow too.

He kicks open the door with his foot, stepping over the sea of toys. His room is a disaster. Piles of laundry are stacked on the floor. So many clothes. The laundry must never end, and I make a mental note to throw some of his stuff in with mine.

Vienna's stuffed animals are everywhere, but she's snoozing in her crib. She hasn't had the chance to love me yet, but I'm falling for the way she squeals Dee-dee when I walk in the door.

My eyes start burning at the thought of Vi. This barn is going to feel so much emptier once they're gone. If something like this happened again, I'd have nothing to come home to but a bottle of tequila. And coming home to Vi's laughter is a trillion times better.

Wyatt gently tucks me into his bed, the cool sheets enveloping me as he slips in beside me. I curl against his warm side with Luna nestled comfortably at our tangled feet.

"How're you feeling?" he whispers, stroking my hair in the moonlight.

I'm feeling all kinds of things I can't sort through, and I'm really wishing I could have another shot of tequila just to dull my thoughts, but my dad's right, that never works. Because it's Wyatt asking, and this is the most peaceful I've felt since the rodeo, all my fears pour from my lips.

"I was so scared," I admit into the darkness. "I'm starting to think it's just better if no one loves me. That way, fewer people get hurt if something happens."

"Don't say that," he demands in a hot voice, tightening his arms around me. "Don't even think that. Loving someone as brave as you could only ever be considered a privilege."

My eyes start to sting again. "There's a reason all those bull riders sleep around. It's just easier not to get attached in case something happens. It's why I've never believed in happy endings."

He wraps me up in his strong arms, holding me close. "Then let me believe in them for you."

And I do the last thing I ever thought I'd do tonight—I fall asleep with a smile.

35

GET THE COFFEE

DAKOTA

*T*he following day, I wake up sandwiched between two stifling bodies. One of those bodies feels like cuddling a statue, and the other is, I think, a giant stuffed animal.

I glance over my shoulder to find Luna-Tuna, the ever-so-devious pup, currently sprawled out, laying (or logging, as I call it) against my back like this is *her* dog bed.

The furry diva.

Goodness, do I love this dog and her attachment issues.

The bedroom feels like a cocoon, the dim morning light puddling on the floor and birds greeting the world with chirps on the windowsill. My body's sore, but I can't remember the last time I woke up so well-rested.

That ends fast when memories of last night hit me.

The shower. Boone. Nash.

Wyatt.

My summer boy.

I can't believe I slept with my oldest friend, and everything about it felt natural.

It was raw.

We were *real.*

I'd been so worried about ruining our friendship, but now I'm wondering if we were meant to be more all along. With the way he's holding me sweetly, delicately, I'm scared to let him go.

He pulled me back from the brink of darkness with one tantalizing kiss, but what am I giving him in return? A life traveling from rodeo to rodeo? I don't want to drag my summer boy down into the pits of my despair, but if there's one thing that will always kill my good notions, it's my selfish tendencies, and I want him badly.

I know a good thing when I see it, and Wyatt Patterson is too good to be true. This will probably end in a disaster, but I don't give a shit. Let us go up in flames.

Before I can let myself spiral into worries over the present, the future, and worries of *us*, I reach down, stroking him.

He's already hard.

This man's the best distraction.

A deep groan escapes his lips, his arms tightening instinctively around me, and those mouthwatering forearm veins pop. I'm not sure when I made the switch to describing his veins as *mouthwatering*, but there's no turning back now.

Especially not after last night.

His sleepy groan sparks a burn in my core, and I work him harder. His greens pop open in surprise, but it quickly melts to heat. And when I start climbing down his body, fully intent on taking him in my mouth, that spark turns into a wildfire. A husky noise scrapes through the back of his throat when he realizes my plans for the morning.

"Fuck," he rasps. "You're so much better than my alarm clock."

His voice is thick with sleep, but that only makes it sound rougher. Why are men's tired morning voices so sexy? It's like silky sandpaper rubbing all over me.

"Dada!" a tiny voice shouts from her crib in the corner.

We both freeze.

"Shit." Wyatt yanks up the covers so fast I almost fall off the bed. He whips his head between us, eyes wide like he's worried Vi will remember this moment when she's older. "Is it bad that I forgot she was in here?"

My hands fly to my mouth. "No, I forgot too, so I guess we're both terrible people for almost ruining her innocence."

We laugh at that, our chuckles syncing, but then Wyatt groans and throws his head back into the pillows. "I love her, but my girl's got the worst timing."

I climb back up his body to gently kiss him. "Hey, she'll understand one day."

He grimaces. "Great, and now the moment's ruined. Thanks for that."

This man. He's such a *daddy*. I brush the loose strands from his forehead, smiling. "You're gonna have to let her grow up, you know."

"I know, but she's not growing up today."

He grins at his daughter clutching at the railing, and we both watch her for a moment. After last night, and how awful that was, just looking at her trying to pull herself up in the crib warms me back up, melts all the bad. There's so much goodness in my life now that Wyatt and Vi are back. They're my bright spots.

He rubs his calloused fingertips up my ribcage. "Are you okay after last night?"

"Yeah, I'll be fine. I just have to get back out in the gym. The Tejas rodeo is coming up and there will be a scout there to watch me compete, so I need to practice."

"So, Tejas is a big deal?"

"A huge deal."

"You'll be amazing." He kisses me again slowly before pulling back with a glint in his eye. "And what about everything that happened after?"

"Which part?"

He swallows. "The part where we had sex and basically ruined our friendship, 'cause there's no way I can go back to being your fucking friend after that."

He rumbles the words, so I brush the loose strands of hair from his forehead to soothe his worries. "I'm starting to think we were never meant to be just friends."

He kisses the inside of my palm, and I feel him smile against my skin. "Good. It's about damn time you realized that."

* * *

THE FOLLOWING week whirls into a tornado of training, riding, and weight lifting as I prepare for the Tejas rodeo. Nash spent the last few days in the hospital, so I can get my ass to the gym.

Tejas is a big one because there will be a few PBR scouts there watching, and I desperately need it to go well. If it doesn't, I might not get another chance to impress the PBR scout, and that'll set me back. *And* I can't afford to lose any more time when my biological clock is a ticking bomb, *and...* fantastic, now my thoughts are spiraling into an overthinking web.

The pressure builds and builds as the Tejas rodeo approaches, fraying my nerves. I push myself harder than ever before in the gym, practice on every aggressive bull that I can, and all the while, my dad and Wyatt are at my side.

"Slow down, you wild child," my dad drawls in his comforting rumble as I slam my shoulder into the punching bag, my breaths coming in ragged gasps.

Wyatt had to leave earlier to pick up Vi, but the gym is still bustling with rodeo folks immersed in their own routines. All around me, cowboys, riders, and barrel racers are slapping each other on the back, getting ready for the rodeo next Saturday like nothing's changed. The clang of weights and occasional whoop of encouragement only fuel my frustration. We all found out Nash would be okay, so they're excited, but he's still got a hard path to recovery.

Their whoops shouldn't sound so damn happy.

I punch the bag with all my might. Smiley's face flashes in my mind. *Punch.* "I can't slow down, Pops. I have to keep going. I can't stop."

My dad grabs the punching bag, stopping it from swinging. He gives me his Cutler scowl, the lines of his face settling into a mix of concern and sternness beneath the brim of his hat. "You still thinking about Nash? I found out he's gonna be fine, darlin'. Don't you worry. He won't be the same, but he'll live."

"I know that." I grunt, my eyes burning with tears for him.

"Then what is it? Tejas?"

My chest heaves.

"It's everything, Pops," I admit, punching the bag again. "Nash's accident, and I still can't manage to hold on for eight fucking seconds. I'm an embarrassment, so I need to keep practicing. Keep going. I can't stop."

I punch and punch and punch so hard that my knuckles almost crack. This is going to set Nash back at least a year as he recovers, and I feel for him, for that dream of his that was so close, but just out of reach.

"Darlin'," my dad says, gripping my shoulders. His rumbly voice is calmer than the eye of a storm. "You don't need to sprint after your dreams. They'll be there waiting for you. Take a breath. Get some coffee. Breathe."

"I don't want coffee," I cut out, my frustration bubbling over.

I punch the bag again.

"Well, too damn bad," he grunts right back. "'Cause Lana's in that fancy car of hers, and she's been waiting on you for over thirty minutes. You're being rude to her, so you're gonna take a break, grab some coffee, and bring me back one of those blueberry scones I know Gerald's lady friend makes fresh every morning. Your dreams will always be here waiting for you, but the people? They might not be around forever."

I glance toward the gym entrance, guilt pricking beneath my skin.

I can just make out the silhouette of Lana's waiting figure, hunched against her Porsche.

I've turned down so many coffee dates with her all because I needed to practice, but she never stops asking me to come out. I don't want to be the woman who is constantly saying no. The girl who's so wrapped up in her goals that she forgets to be there for the people who matter. I've spent so much of my life sprinting after this dream that I forgot I have a life outside this sport left to live.

Sighing, I lower my fists.

"Fine," I mutter, slinging my towel over my shoulder. "I'll get the coffee."

He presses a scratchy kiss on my cheek. "Smart girl."

* * *

"I'm so glad you actually decided to get coffee because, holy shit, this is too good. I'm calling it. Boone wants you back," Lana blurts, slamming down her oat-milk cappuccino with extra foam and a shot of pumpkin spice. She drinks pumpkin spice well into the summer.

Lana leans back in her velvet wingback chair. I don't think Gerald, the owner, has updated the furniture in this old house-turned-coffee shop since the forties. He still has the same pink floral wallpaper.

"I don't care what he wants. He doesn't matter anymore," I say, though I'm glad we're talking about Boone and not Nash. I need a light distraction from all that heaviness, and Boone doesn't dredge up feelings.

Not anymore.

She slaps the counter. "Oh, but you matter to him, babe."

Gerald shuts off the espresso machine and points a wrinkled

finger at Lana, effectively saying, *tone it down, young lady* with just his eyes. "I can still hear you, Alanna."

"Sorry, Gerald!" she sing-songs.

Gerald opened Granite Falls Coffee twenty years ago, and he can sum up his entire life in one breath, so by the time you finish ordering coffee, you know he's got twenty-three grandchildren, a wife who died of old age, and a new "lady friend" who makes the best blueberry scones but won't share her secret recipe.

We love the Geralds of the world.

"Anyway," she says. "What're you gonna do about Boone?"

I sip my murky coffee. "Nothing. I don't care if Boone wants me back because I don't want him back. Honestly, I don't know what I ever saw in him."

Lana nods. "Good, because if you chose him over Wyatt, I'd actually disown you as a friend."

"There's not even a choice," I say fervently.

Lana leans back, scrutinizing me with an impressed smile. "Look at you defending the blond men of the world. Since when did you turn over that leaf? I didn't realize you had a thing for golden boys."

"I don't. I just have a thing for Wyatt."

I think the reason I always went for the broody assholes is because I never loved myself enough to fall for someone I deemed worthy. I settled for men who used to treat me like shit because I felt like shit, but maybe all these insecurities were planted in my head by other people, not me. I want to be good enough for a man like Wyatt.

My phone buzzes on the wooden table, and I flip it over to see a text on the screen.

WYATT

I can't stop thinking about you

Butterflies roar to life in my stomach, and I press my lips together to hide my smile. I can't believe this man who I've known for over a decade is giving me toe-curling, feet-kicking *butterflies* like some high school crush.

Another buzz.

Another under-the-table feet kick.

Or last night... on the kitchen counter (;

I'm tempted to snuggle into myself.

Lana slaps a manicured hand to the table, grinning smugly. "Oh, babe. Look at that smile! You totally knocked boots, didn't you? How was it? I need details."

Heat climbs up the back of my neck. I used to give her all the details about the guys I slept with, but Wyatt's different. "It was great," I mumble into my black coffee.

She groans. "No. I need more than this. Pick a different adjective."

"Fine," I say, keeping my voice low. "It was really great, but I don't want to talk about it because it's personal."

"Okay, fine. I get it." Her red lips spread into a smile. "I'm happy for you, babe, and not jealous at all that you're having amazing sex."

I let out an amused snort.

She nibbles her bottom lip, mulling something over as she looks at the old historic marker plaque hanging on the wallpaper. She's always had a thing for historic landmarks and pulls us over anytime she sees one on the highway.

This sign says the rustic coffee shop was the filming spot for some seventies horror chainsaw movie. I'm not sure that's the vibe people want while sipping their morning coffee, but to each their own.

"How's Wyatt feel about Boone being back?" she finally asks.

I shrug, the motion causing his Guardians sweatshirt to slide down my shoulder. He gave it to me this morning, and it smells like his cologne, so I can't stop sniffing the fabric. "I don't think it'll be a big deal. Boone and I are done. He might as well be an invisible part of my past."

"You really think he'll be okay with it?" she prods.

"Yeah, Wyatt's not the jealous type anyway, and I don't want Boone. I want Wyatt and Vi. They're my people now."

It's the first time I've spoken the truth, and it feels so right. There's still that gut-wrenching dread that something's going to go wrong, but I'm trying to be more like him and not let those worries get to me.

"I bet he's gonna hate it when he finds out Boone's back," she says.

I wave a hand, ignoring the stone of unease that just dropped in my stomach. "He'll be fine. They're both gentlemen, so I'm sure they'll be civil to each other."

"Sure," she agrees warily. "As civil as cavemen."

DRUNK TODDLER

WYATT

J can't keep my hands off Dakota for the next week as she prepares for the rodeo. We have sex *everywhere*.

My bed. Her bed. The kitchen counter. We almost get caught by the cops when we fool around in my truck like two high schoolers drunk in love.

We can't get enough of each other.

But on Wednesday, I wake up to an empty bed and step out into the kitchen to find Vienna fed, changed, and playing in her playpen while Dakota flips banana pancakes and the laundry machine whirs.

She's not the domestic type, but I'm not surprised either. When she feels like her life is spiraling out of control, she tries to control the things within her power.

I can't decide what I like more—her in my arms or her with my daughter. She's dressed in her workout gear, biker shorts and a black bra, ready for our daily gym session because she's the most determined woman I've met.

I wrap my arms around her from behind. "Morning. Why's the TV off? You normally like having the background noise."

She shrugs. "Stella told me you were pretty strict about screen time with Vi, so I've been trying to keep it off."

That makes me hold her tighter, and I genuinely wonder how I'm ever going to let her go. I'm beginning to think I need to put in for a transfer to Austin, but I'm worried about telling Cruz.

I brush off a tiny curl on her forehead, still worried about how she's been doing since Nash's fall. "How're you feeling? Are you ready for the rodeo this weekend? I got a babysitter, so my parents and I can come watch you. We'll all be there."

She stirs the pancake batter harder, faster. "I'm ready. I just have to pick myself up and keep going, like always. I can't let the highs go to my head just like I can't let the lows bring me down."

And that's exactly what she does.

Every day leading up to Tejas, we're in the gym, squatting, lunging, lifting. She won't stop, because if there's one thing about Dakota, she will always, *always* pick herself back up no matter how far she falls. She acknowledges her fear, but it's never a roadblock. It's the kind of woman I want my daughter to be one day.

She's so focused during our daily workout sessions, and meanwhile, I can't keep my hands, eyes, or lips off her. Especially now that I know what it feels like to be inside her. It's better than I even imagined, and I imagined it a hell of a lot.

There is nothing, and I mean *nothing*, I would rather do than kiss her all day, but I'm trying to rein in the urge so I don't play my entire hand before she shows her cards.

At the gym, I pretend like my throat isn't parched, watching her squat in the tiniest shorts that should really only be considered scraps of fabric. I can barely get a word out. When I tell her to *add more weight* it comes out sounding like *take your clothes off.*

And now, as I FaceTime Cruz, I'm getting half hard looking at her discarded pink panties on the bathroom tile, so it's a good thing he can only see me from the chest up.

"I slept with her, Cruz."

"Hell yeah!" he erupts on the phone screen, startling me enough that I nearly drop my razor in the bathroom sink. "I knew she couldn't resist a shirtless Patty Daddy."

He wiggles his dark brows, and his brown eyes brighten.

"Yeah, thanks for the top-tier advice." I huff a laugh, the razor gliding precariously close to my skin. "Except now, every time she steps into the arena in those fringe chaps, my dick gets rock-hard, and I can't focus on anything but her."

I almost nick my throat, thinking of those chaps, as I shave my neck beard. Last night, Dakota kept nuzzling up against my scruff. I think she likes it, so I'm leaving the stubble along my jaw and cleaning up the edges.

"So, things have been good with her?" he asks on speaker-phone, his deep voice reverberating against the bathroom tiles.

Good is an understatement. She can't keep her hands off me, and I've never been this happy. Nothing could bring me down right now. "Things have been incredible. Going back to Nashville is gonna be tough, though."

His brown eyes turn down, and I'm tempted to take back my words at the sad look on his face. "But I'm in Nashville."

My stomach drops, but I need to come out and say it. Cruz is my boy, so he deserves my honesty.

"I'm thinking I might put in for a transfer," I blurt to get it over with. "Austin's getting an NHL team, and it'd be nice to move back home."

I wait, carefully analyzing him. Cruz goes silent for a second and then throws his head back onto the pillow on the screen. "Why the fuck is everyone leaving? Tremblay first and now you? I've barely spoken to him since he moved to Argentina, and I don't want to lose you too."

Guilt slithers beneath my skin. "Aw, come on, Micah. Don't do this to me."

He jams his finger at me on the screen. "No. No first-naming me. I want to know why."

"It feels like home for me," I explain, setting down the razor. "I love it down here, man. I've got family here. The schools are great, and I want to be with Dakota. I can't leave her."

Cruz stares at me through the phone, and then heaves a sigh. "Fine. If you need to transfer, then do it, but don't be surprised when I follow your ass down to Texas."

My brows soar. "You'd follow me here? Really?"

"If you or Tremblay jumped off a bridge, I'd jump," he admits, and that's Micah Cruz, loyal to a fault. "You do know it's hot as shit down there though, right?"

"Only in August and September, and even then, you just find a lake, crack open a beer, and fall asleep on a floatie in the water. I got the world's worst sunburn from doing that one summer. My entire chest was peeling off."

"You're really selling me on the whole Texas thing," he deadpans.

"Wyatt!"

Dakota's wild shriek slices through the quiet of the barn, sending a jolt of panic straight through me.

"I have to go." I drop my phone, our conversation forgotten, and the razor follows close behind.

I rush out from the bathroom with shaving cream still smeared on half my face, my towel hastily wrapped around me, trying not to imagine the worst-case scenario.

I burst into the living room, and my eyes immediately dart to her. "What?" I panic, my heart throbbing in that way it only does around her. "Is Vi okay? Are you okay?"

I scan Dakota's body for injuries, blood, something terrible, but she's standing by the stone fireplace in nothing but a thin white tank (that shows her nipples) and boxers (that look a lot like... mine?). Damn, I like seeing her in my clothes. But then, I notice Tuna wagging her black tail and the look of radiant joy on Dakota's face.

Her grin is so blinding I blink to make sure she's real.

"Wyatt," she yells again, pointing at something in the living room. "Stop staring at me and look at your girl!"

My gaze follows the direction of her outstretched arm, and there, right there, on her ABC mat—holy shit—there's my baby girl, wobbling on her tiny feet like a drunk toddler staggering her way toward me. My heart vaults from my stomach to my throat.

She's walking.

My little girl's finally walking.

"She's walking!" Dakota exclaims again, her voice bubbling over with excitement. "She's actually walking, Wyatt. Look at her go!"

Every other worry dissolves as I drop to my knees, my arms outstretched to my girl's toothy grin. "Come here, baby girl. Come to Daddy," I call out, my voice choked with a lump of emotion.

Vi's baby greens lock onto me, her smile widening, and she stumbles her way into my waiting arms. The impact when she bumps into my chest is the sweetest collision of my life.

"Hi, baby," I whisper, peppering her face with shaving-cream kisses—her cheeks, her lips, her tiny button nose. "You did it, sweetheart. You're a little walker. I'm so proud of you, baby girl," I breathe out, my voice thick.

"Dada!"

The wave of relief and awe that hits me is so potent, it nearly knocks the tears out of my eyes.

Dakota's standing by the leather couch, snapping pictures with her phone, and I wish I didn't have shaving cream smeared on half my face, or that I had on real clothes, or that my eyes weren't watering because there's a stench in my baby girl's diaper that's stronger than nuclear waste, but that's parenting for you— never quite camera ready.

Still, I wouldn't trade a photo of me with my little girl for the world, even if I'm a mess in it.

Dakota sets her phone down on the granite counter, studying

us with a half-smile that's full of emotion. "I like this version of you. A lot."

I pick up my daughter, balancing her on my hip. Now that she's mobile, things are going to get a lot crazier. "What version?"

She gestures to my bare chest, nibbling her lip. "The dad version, and basically any version."

I walk toward her with my girl on my hip, dropping my voice to a teasing lilt. "Oh yeah?" I say, tickling Vi's stomach until she squeals. "You think walking around with a baby girl that *definitely* needs her diaper changed is hot?"

Vienna giggles at that, so she thinks my joke is funny, but Dakota doesn't laugh. She looks at me with this warm smile that's half joy, half... not sadness, but something nearby. Yearning? Nostalgia? I can't tell.

"You mean," she starts. "Do I think being a reliable, trust-worthy man who knows how to care for another person is attractive? Yeah, I do. I know what a good father looks like, and you, Wyatt Patterson, are one of the best."

Her words strike me deep.

A lot of the time, I question whether I'm getting this whole dad thing right. I try to shake off the worry that I might be messing up with Vienna, taking it one day at a time, but it gets to me—not having a partner to share these moments with.

I want someone by my side through all the highs and lows of parenthood. I never realized just how much I needed to hear that validation. My throat's too tight to even murmur a thanks.

Vienna makes grabby-hands at Dakota. "Dee-dee!" she squeals, at least, that's what it sounds like to me.

Dakota startles at the noise, like she's surprised my daughter would even remember her, but my girl's got good taste in people.

"Hi, little devil," she says in a choked-up voice, taking her from me to smother her face in kisses. "Or maybe I should call you little walker now. I'm so proud of you. We're gonna have to put a gate on that spiral staircase now so you don't become a little climber."

That one extra thought for my daughter does me in. She's thinking of my girl's safety, and it makes me want to get down on one knee right in this living room, but I need to figure out my future first because I'm not asking her to change her plans for me.

As I watch her set her phone down, her glossy gaze meets mine, and I notice the moisture pooling in her brown eyes.

"Are you crying?" I ask, half joking, but I also need to know because I rarely see her cry.

She swipes at a corner, a small laugh mingling with a sniffle. "Yeah, but I don't know why. I guess I just didn't know little things could feel so big."

She kisses my girl's cheek, and seeing Dakota like this, all vulnerable and open, hits me hard. She's usually so guarded, and I pull her in, giving her a solid hug. "You don't need to give me a reason. I know. I'm glad this moment happened with you, too."

"You know something, summer boy?" she says, keeping her damp eyes on my daughter.

I kiss the top of her hair. "Yeah, honey?"

She breathes in deep and kisses Vi's nose. "I think I'm falling for your little summer girl."

I hold her close at that, my daughter sandwiched comfortably between our bodies. "Fall as hard as you want; we'll be here to catch you."

KEEP THOSE BOOTS ON

DAKOTA

*W*yatt's late.

That man's always ten minutes early. He's more reliable than my Flo app, so something must be wrong. But in a petty twist of fate, Boone's competing, so unfortunately, he's by my side while I pace the Tejas rodeo grounds, waiting for them.

"Have you seen Wyatt?" I grunt at Boone, my eyes darting across the crowded stands, searching for any sign of my family here at the rodeo. "Or my Dad? Or Lana? They should be here by now."

"No, I haven't," he replies, tugging me to a stop by the sheep pens.

I've been trying to avoid him, still vacillating over whether I actually want to hear him out, but our paths keep crossing in this dusty rodeo maze of corrals and trailers. His navy eyes, shadowed by the brim of his straw Stetson, search my face as if trying to read my thoughts.

"Can we talk now?" he murmurs over the jingle of spurs. "I still need to get my jacket back from you. I had to borrow someone else's."

"No," I hiss, yanking my arm out of his grasp. "We're not talking right now, or ever. I have to concentrate."

He holds up his hands. "Okay, I get it. How about we do dinner? I've missed you. Next week or—"

My phone vibrates, cutting him off mid-sentence, and I'm grateful for the interruption. I quickly dig into my pocket, pulling it out to see Wyatt's name flashing on the screen, and lift it to my cheek. "Hey, where are you? I was—"

"Our tire blew out," he shouts, and I jerk, startled by the panic in those few words.

I've never heard Wyatt sound so stressed. It takes a lot to get him riled up, and by *a lot*, I mean a category-five hurricane striking during a nuclear explosion.

"Okay, back up. What happened?" I hammer out, stomping away from Boone to find a private hay barrel by the goats. "Are you okay? Is Vi okay?"

My little devil better be okay.

"No, I'm not." He pants, sounding out of breath like he's pacing. "The truck got a flat, so we're all stranded on some back-country road, waiting for a tow to come pick us up since we don't have a spare, and now the babysitter just called me freaking the fuck out because she invited her lame fucking boyfriend over to 'watch a movie,' and like a fuckwit, he invited his even lamer friends, and now the babysitter's panicking because our barn's turning into a fucking rager, and she can't get them to leave. I'm worried as fuck about Vi, but I can't go get her because I'm fucking stuck, and I should've vetted the babysitter more. Fuck! This is all my fault."

I don't think I've ever heard him say *fuck* so many times in one paragraph, so I try to keep my voice soothing.

"Wyatt, it's not your fault. You did vet the babysitter. Your mom got a recommendation from someone in town," I reassure him, even though I'm feeling just as worried over Vienna, but one of us has to stay calm.

"And I can go check on her," I offer.

He pauses. "No, you can't. You've got the rodeo."

Wyatt has been doing so much for me this summer, helping me train, that I want to be there for him. Not to mention the thought of something bad happening to Vi is actually making me a little murderous.

I'll get another chance to impress the scout.

Wyatt and Vi are more important.

"Let me do this for you," I say. "You do so much for everyone else that I want to help."

"Are you sure?" he says, and the relief in his tone is palpable. I can practically hear his shoulders falling.

"Yeah, I'm sure. I think I'd do anything for you and Vi at this point," I admit honestly, heading to the parking lot. "I'm already getting in Daisy Blue. Want me to pick you up?"

He pauses again, longer this time, like he's thinking. "No, we took the backroads here, so we're out of the way. You're closer. I'll feel better knowing you're at home with her. Thank you, Dakota," he breathes, his voice finally easing for the first time since he picked up the call.

"Of course, I'll be back at the barn in thirty minutes."

"You have no idea how much this means to me," he murmurs again before hanging up.

"Anything for you, summer boy," I whisper into the sunset air, not that he can hear.

As I head to my truck, the bustling sounds of the rodeo fade behind me, and the engine roars to life. One the way home, I break a few traffic violations because my mind races with thoughts of what I'll find when I get to the barn. All I can think about is Vi, picturing her scared, crying all alone.

My grip tightens on the steering wheel. It makes me absolutely furious.

When I was in high school, I gave my dad a stress-induced stomach ulcer with a few house parties, so I know they can get out of control.

The ball of orange sun dips low in the sky as I speed down the sprawling two-lane highway. Finally, the barndominium comes into view, and I pull up to the chaotic scene—teenagers spill out onto the patio, and laughter echoes in the evening air.

I. Am. Fuming.

If something bad happened to my girl, someone's going to prison.

After parking, I slam the truck door, storming toward the barn. The sight that greets me is lighter fluid for my rage. The place is a disaster, littered with trash and empty beer cans, the obnoxious thump of country music blaring from the speakers—really shitty country music, none of the nineties classics.

The moment I step inside, the smell of spilled beer hits me. I scan the living room, searching for Vienna and Luna, but I can't find them in the crowd of solo cups.

The babysitter comes rushing up to me, tears streaming down her face, so she clearly feels bad. "I'm so glad you're here! I'm so sorry. Please don't tell my mom. I didn't think this would happen, and all these people just showed up, and now I can't get them to leave, and I'm sorry."

She wipes the snot from her nose, but I ignore her tears, only focused on my little devil. "Where's Vi?"

She sniffs. "I put her down in her room. I've been watching her I swear."

I'm still in my rodeo gear, so I get a few looks and whistles as I shove my way through the crowd, but they must be afraid of me because the further I walk, the more the crowd seems to part, and the less I have to barrel through them.

Ignoring the stares, I head straight to Wyatt's bedroom. The door is closed, and I fling it open to find Vienna crying in her crib, her face tear-streaked, and Luna curled up in a ball at the foot like she's keeping watch.

When I walk inside, she perks her fluffy head up.

The relief that hits me almost makes my knees buckle, but the rage comes a second later. Who the hell is this babysitter's asshole boyfriend?

Luna's black tail starts thumping when she sees me, and I murmur, "Hey, Tuna Roll," and pat her head as I walk by to snuggle Vienna.

"Hey, little devil," I soothe, scooping her up into my arms. She instantly calms down, her sobs quieting to soft whimpers. That gets me every time. Being the one who calms her down. "I'd be pissed too if I were you; I get it. This music's loud. Come here, sweetie. You want to look at the ceiling fan?"

"Mah," she murmurs into my chest, and that's a new word. I'm not sure if it means she wants more snuggles, but either way I give her what she wants.

She stares up at me with those big, green, tear-streaked eyes, her little face crumpled. I lift her pink T-shirt and wipe the snot on her nose.

"I've got you, girl. I'm here. I'm here," I murmur.

She burrows into my chest, her tiny hands clutching at my leather riding jacket, and I think this toddler melting into me might be the best feeling in the world. I've always wanted to be a mom, and maybe that's why it's been so easy for me to fall for her. But I also think it's because she's Wyatt's.

That one little nuzzle ignites a flare of protectiveness. I might not be her mom, but I'll be damned if I let anyone hurt her. She's mine now. Vienna clings to me, her small body trembling slightly, but I hold her close.

Swaying her.

Calming her in the night with the chirping crickets keeping us company.

I've never been the person someone can depend on because I've been relentlessly going after what I want, but what's that going to get me at the end of my life? I've never felt *needed* like this before, and I think this might be addicting. For so long, I've only had to worry about myself, never anyone else, but her tiny little fists clinging onto me makes my life feel like it's worth something more.

Life is made up of memories you leave with other people, so the more people you love, the more memories you make, and the more you'll be remembered. I want to be remembered by the people I love.

With Vienna on my hip, I storm into the living room like a mama grizzly. I've dealt with enough rowdy cowboys that I can handle some rowdy teenagers.

My eyes zero in on the iPhone hooked up to the speaker. Without a second thought, I march over and yank it out, the abrupt silence hits like a record screech.

"What the hell?" some little asshole shouts. "Who turned off the music?"

I chuck the phone against the wall, hard enough to crack the screen, and the room falls silent as everyone turns to stare at me.

My breath comes in ragged gasps.

"On the count of three," I yell, holding up a finger. "Everyone better get the fuck out of my house, or I'm calling the cops! One…"

They scatter like cockroaches, scrambling for the door.

"Two…." Another finger. More scrambles.

"Three!"

In seconds, the house is empty, the only sounds remaining are the distant hum of cars racing off on gravel and the soft sniffles from Vienna. I take a deep breath, the adrenaline still pumping through my veins, but it's fine—everything's fine.

"It's okay, little devil," I whisper, brushing a curl of gold from her forehead. Soothing her is actually soothing me. "I'm here. I've got you."

With the house finally quiet, I rock her gently, humming "Banana Pancakes" by Jack Johnson until her breathing steadies and her tiny hands relax their grip on my jacket.

I don't know how long we stay like that, but I'll hold her all night if that's what she needs. She falls asleep in my arms, and I tuck her back into her crib, set up the monitor, and start cleaning up the absolute mess those little shits made, picking up empty beer cans and discarded vape pens.

I text Wyatt to let him know everything is fine. He replies a second later.

WYATT

Tow still isn't here, so I don't know when I'll be back. Don't wait up

WYATT

You have no idea how grateful I am. I don't even have words. I think you might be the only person I know who could clear out a house of teenagers on her own

ME

I'll always be the bad cop to your good cop <3

There are dots, then nothing, dots again, nothing, until his message pops onto my screen.

WYATT

Oh yeah?

How bad are you?

ME

You might need some handcuffs (;

WYATT

Already have them (;

ME

Look at you, still surprising me after all these years

WYATT

Just you wait, honey

With the biggest, giddiest grin on my face from those texts, I shut off my phone and get to work cleaning, which quickly has my lips turning down.

As I pick up red solo cups, Luna shadows me around, and I think about how much worse this could have been. It surprises me just how furious I am on Wyatt's behalf, and by the time I finish cleaning over an hour later, the house is spotless.

I take a quick shower and put on my cowboy boots and an old, massive rodeo T-shirt because I need to repark Daisy Blue since all those cars were in the way. But then exhaustion hits.

I plop down on my floral bedspread with the baby monitor against my chest, and before I know it, my eyes are drifting closed, my boots still on my feet.

"Dakota."

A soft whisper into the night, so quiet I can't be sure it's real.

The next thing I feel is something warm pressing against my bare legs, climbing higher and higher, and... my eyes fly open. Wyatt's nestled between my thighs, dropping kisses up my skin as he tugs up my shirt. I glance around my moonlit bedroom, still half-dazed.

"You're home," I murmur, my voice thick with sleep. "Where's Vi?"

"She's safe and sound, asleep in her crib. I've spent the past thirty minutes rocking with her, calming us both down, but then I came in here because..." He kisses my hip crease, and *his* breath hitches. "I figured I owe you a thank you. A big thank you, for taking care of everything. You just..."

He drops his head between my legs, shuddering fiercely. "You have no idea how much this meant to me. I owe you everything for what you did tonight. I completely forgot that the PBR scout was going to be there at the rodeo, or I never would've let you come, and the whole drive home I felt so fucking shitty when I remembered."

I tangle my fingers in his golden strands, pulling him closer, desperate to comfort him. "Don't worry. I've still got the qualifiers at the end of the summer, so this wasn't a make-or-break-it thing. You don't owe me anything."

He jerks his head up, and there, I find a wildness in his glassy eyes I've never seen before. Something loose and free, and it makes me a little feral, too.

His grip tightens around the backs of my knees. "I owe you everything, and I think I know exactly how to thank you."

In an instant, he yanks off my T-shirt so I'm left in nothing but my white cowgirl boots. He stares at my naked body with so much lust in his eyes that I get swept up in the moment. I reach down to take my boots off, but his hand flies up to stop me.

"No," he commands, his grip tightening around my wrists, eyes flaring with desire. "Keep those boots on, honey."

MY FAVORITE TEMPERATURE

WYATT

$\mathcal{I}$ hook my hands behind the backs of Dakota's knees, gazing down at her bare, wet pussy in the moonlight. I never thought I'd be waxing poetic about moonlit pussies, but I'll wax poetry all night if it means keeping her like this.

Naked.

Looking dazed and needy in those sexy white cowgirl boots.

There's some leather riding jacket at the foot of the bed that's not mine, and it doesn't look like hers either, but I'm too focused on her to care, so I shove it off to the side.

Her tousled hair frames her face, casting shadows against the soft glow. This is how I always want her. "Turn that pretty ass around and ride my face. I bet those cowgirl boots will look even better wrapped around my head."

Her honey eyes pop in shock, and I love that, surprising her with my demands. She makes me feel like a man in the best way.

"What?" she breathes out.

I'm not in the mood to explain myself. All I want is to lose myself in her. "Don't make me repeat myself," I say in a low voice, kissing the crease of her hip. "You heard me the first time. Ride. My. Face."

My command seems to wake her up. Her eyes widen at my tone, but then a sly smile curls her lips. I hook my hands on the backs of her knees as I slide down her body, bringing her pussy closer to my mouth. Her thighs are getting big from all our workouts, and she's never looked sexier. And that ass of hers?

I want to bite it.

"Okay, then," she purrs, her voice dripping with need. She lifts her hips up on the bed to grind against my jaw, teasingly torturous, like she knows exactly how to push me to the edge of insanity.

"No," I demand, flicking my tongue against her clit. She tastes... Christ, she tastes so fucking good. I don't think I'll ever get tired of going down on her, and I haven't even started. "Tell me this is what you want. I need to hear you say it."

"Yes," she moans, tugging my hair to drag me closer to her center. "It's what I want."

I lightly scrape my teeth against her clit, earning a sharp gasp from her. "Yes, *what?*"

"Oh, god," she groans, her body trembling. "You're really gonna make me say it?"

"Yes, ma'am. If I can use my manners, so can you."

"Fine," she grits out. "Yes... *sir.*"

I press a kiss to her center. "There you go. Who knew you could be so polite?"

Her eyes flash with a challenge, but I knew she wouldn't like being called polite when she's as rowdy as they come. A second later, she kicks my chest back with her boot, hops off the bed, and pushes me down on the mattress so I'm the one on bottom.

But I don't mind letting her take control.

I grip the backs of her thighs, forcing her to straddle my cock. She unbuckles my jeans and rips off my shirt. This woman is undressing me at lightning speed, and it's making me so hard for her. Once I'm naked, she flips around, straddles my face with her boots, and takes my cock deep into her mouth.

So.

Fucking.

Deep.

We just soared right into sixty-nine territory, and I couldn't be happier about it. I fucking love this position.

It's intimate.

It's hot.

And you can really only do it with people you feel comfortable in bed with, which is saying a lot about how she feels.

It's like she's determined to prove just how impolite she can be as she suffocates me with her pussy. The feeling of her warm, wet mouth sucking me off is almost too much.

I moan into her warmth, digging my fingers into her ass so I don't lose control in less than two seconds. She swirls her tongue around my tip, and goddamn that's sensitive.

I'm drowning in the intoxicating scent of her. I can't help but think this would be the best way for a man to go. Her mouth works my cock, each stroke and suck driving me closer to the edge. She's going to have me coming in five seconds if she keeps up that suction.

I can't help but smack her ass, the sound echoing in her moonlit bedroom. "Slow down, honey. I want to take my time with you."

To make my point, I grip her thighs firmly and shove my tongue deep inside her, leaving her clit untouched on purpose. I know it's driving her wild, being a hairpin short of ecstasy. She continues to suck me off, her moans vibrating around my cock while she rides my face, soaking my scruff. The sensation is almost too much, but I want this to last.

Her scent, her taste, the way she grinds against me—it's everything. I was worried about jumping into the physical part of our relationship and thought it might take her a while to get there, but everything between us is so natural.

I knew it would be because I was made for this woman, and

she was crafted for me. No one else could've barreled through the house and taken control of that situation. Hell, I don't even know if *I* could've handled it the way she did.

I keep playing with her, licking, sucking, listening to her moans grow louder and more desperate right alongside mine. The harder I suck, the more she sucks. Heat races up my spine, my balls tightening as I edge closer to release. When I know I've reached the point of no return, I lean forward, sucking her whole clit into my mouth with just the right amount of suction to get her there.

I know what sets her off because I know my girl.

It doesn't take long for either of us to come.

She bucks against my face as she cries out around my cock. The vibrations and the fact that she's still in those sexy-as-shit boots send me over the edge, and I explode in her mouth, groaning, panting, legs twitching. We ride out the waves together as she trembles around me, her legs shaking with the force of her orgasm.

She comes all over my face.

I lap up every drop, savoring the taste of her. By the end, we're both loose and relaxed, and I, for one, feel a hell of a lot better.

It strikes me that we both tend to come to each other during the difficult parts of life. She needed me after her traumatic experience, and I need her now. I'm not sure if that's a good or a bad thing, but I think it's a *real* thing—needing someone during the hardest parts of life. We're not perfect, we're messy, and that's okay.

I wrap her in my arms and pull her close as we come down from the high. I fucking love cuddling. I kiss her hard, wanting to taste myself on her lips. She looks so satisfied, and it feels damn good to know I'm the man who put that dazed and satiated look on her face.

"Do you feel thoroughly thanked?" I murmur against her temple.

"Oh, definitely. You sure know how to express your gratitude." She toys with my chest, drawing little circles that send pleasant shivers through me. "You seemed like you *really* liked that position."

"It's one of my favorites." I smirk. "Why do you think I keep the AC set to sixty-nine?"

39

DADDIES

WYATT

I'm never going to sit down again.

Now that Vi's walking, she walks everywhere.

She doesn't want me picking her up because she wants to *"wah!"*—which sometimes means walk and sometimes means water—so I'm constantly juggling water bottles while holding her tiny hands to help her balance. I miss the days when she was a crawler, but Dakota's been helping me keep an eye on her.

On Saturday, I pry myself from Dakota's arms because I promised to help my parents with some flower deliveries around town. She's got her skills session with Colt anyway, and it gives Vi the chance to stretch her tiny legs (and hopefully tire her out) as we go from shop to shop in our old red pickup truck. The truck is thick with the scent of flowers from our deliveries, a mix of zinnias, lavender, and eucalyptus.

That's a trendy plant now.

Mama adjusts her straw sunhat from the passenger side, fixing her blonde hair in a braid. "I can't believe she's finally walking! You're gonna miss those crawling days, sweetie."

"I already do," I grumble, leaning back against the ripped

leather headrest. "That girl won't sit down unless she's sleeping. I'm never going to have a quiet morning again."

She leans over the console to kiss my cheek. "You'll get your quiet mornings back, but then you'll end up missing the hectic ones, so just enjoy what you have now."

"You're probably right, but the days seem so long."

It's our routine delivery day, bringing fresh bouquets to all the small shops around town, but each delivery is taking triple the time because everyone wants to *ooh* and *ahh* over my girl.

I can't blame them.

She's looking especially cute today in her mini cowgirl hat and matching pink booties that Dakota bought for her, and I love seeing her fawn over my baby girl. I'm so damn happy all the time. I don't think there's anything that could bring me down.

My mom shouts something outside the Granite Falls Bakery, so I crank down the hand-rolled window. "You ready to go?"

"In a minute!" she says, propping Vi up on her hip, who's trying to rip Mom's navy Guardians cap off her head. "Ms. Thompson here is gonna give us her apple pie recipe. You need to use Granny Smith apples because the Honeycrisp makes it too sweet!"

I didn't ask, but that's small towns for you—go to deliver flowers and come out with a homemade apple pie recipe from the local baker. The sweet aroma of cinnamon and apples drifts to the truck as we chat for the next fifteen minutes.

The sound of the car door creaking open interrupts our conversation, and I turn to see my mom cradling Vi. "Okay, we're ready to go. She's getting a little fussy."

She gently places my squirming girl in the car seat. Long drives normally calm her down, so I start heading home as we talk about the upcoming hockey season.

"I hear the new goalie's pretty good," Mom says, popping her head up from the backseat. She likes talking stats and players. "But he's no Tremblay."

"There will never be another goalie like Rhode Tremblay," I say, thinking of our retired veteran player.

I always thought Tremblay had been crazy, giving up his dream to move to Argentina for his girl, but maybe he had it right. As I stare out at the rolling hills stretching beneath the wide blue sky, I'm hit with how much I don't want to leave Texas.

"I'm thinking I might put in for a transfer," I blurt as we drive. "Austin's getting an NHL team, and it'd be nice to move back home."

"Oh my goodness!" Mama shouts, clapping her hands. She tends to respond to everything with an excited squeal. Vi starts clapping her hands in her car seat, trying to mimic her, and I smile at her in the rearview.

"We'd love that," Mama continues. "Wouldn't we love that, Jessie? I've always wanted to come back home. We could offer tours of the farm!"

My mom, being the serious planner, presses her lips together as she scrutinizes me. "How do you feel about that? Is that really what you want?"

She's always getting me to dig deeper into my thoughts. I hated it in high school because she loves playing the devil's advocate, and that made writing my philosophy papers hell, but I know she does it to try and help.

"It feels like home for me," I say, glancing at her brown eyes in the rearview mirror. "I love it down here."

"And there's a girl you love too," Mama adds with a knowing grin.

I smile. "That too."

The memories flood in—the nights we spent under the stars, the feel of Dakota's hand in mine. I think back to all our almosts —almost kisses, almost admissions, almost touches. Our past is too full of tangled what-ifs and could-have-beens, and I need to make it permanent.

Mom scans my face from the backseat, and whatever she finds in my expression has her sighing. "Then I guess we're moving back to Texas."

My heart jerks.

"You'd follow me here?" I squeeze the steering wheel, hopeful. They've helped me out so much that I don't know what I'd do without them. "Come back home? Really?"

"Sweetie." My mama rolls her eyes. "If you think for one damn second I'm going to live more than five minutes away from my grandbaby, you're sorely mistaken."

Mom leans over from the back to kiss her cheek, and then she kisses mine. "There's nothing you can do to keep us away. You're stuck with us forever."

My throat goes tight, thinking of all those summer memories —Mom teaching me how to fish, Mama taking me to Sweet Berry Farm to pick strawberries. And now, I'm doing all that with my little girl, and they're still by my side.

"I love y'all," I say. "You know that, right? I don't know what I'd do without you."

Both their eyes go glassy.

"You're our home, sweetie," Mama says.

"That's right," Mom adds. "Where you go, we go."

* * *

"Here's that bouquet of roses and bronze leaf wax begonias, Willie," I say, setting the giant arrangement of pink sherbet flowers on the bar counter.

His Caribbean eyes narrow on the flowers, and he stares at the bouquet like it's about to explode into pink confetti. "I didn't order these."

"Hey, don't look at me. Alanna said the bar could use some 'prettyin' up.' Her words. Not mine, and I think there's something else in there for you too."

He digs around the white box I used to stabilize the bouquet and pulls out the embroidered apron. "What the hell is this?"

I hold up my hands. "She's the one who told me to put it in there."

He pulls out the pink floral apron with an image of a cartoon man with oven mitts on his hand that reads, *Always Use Protection.*

It must be some inside joke because I don't get it.

He stares at it, but I can't read his expression under all that dark hair. After a few seconds, he scrunches up the apron, throws it behind the counter, and mutters something under his breath that sounds like *Fuckin' Barbie.*

The door suddenly bursts open with a bang.

Colter Cutler strides inside the bar, clad in Wrangler jeans and a plaid button-down. He scans the crowded bar beneath his cowboy hat, and when his eyes land on me, he cuts through the smoky haze. A few patrons give him a nod of hello.

This man turns more heads than his daughter.

Once he reaches the counter, he scrapes out a seat, turns it backwards, and straddles the wood. "Mind if I join you?"

Colt has finally started to ease up on the scowls directed at me, so I slap his shoulder. "I've actually got to finish some flower deliveries, so I was just heading out, but I'm glad I caught you. I wanted to talk to you about the Granite Falls rodeo in a few weeks."

"What about it?" he asks, nodding to Willie who hands him a long-necked beer.

"I know Dakota lost her shot with the scout because of me, and I want to get her another chance. Think you could get me a meeting with him so I can convince him to come watch her at Granite Falls in a couple of weeks?"

He takes a slow sip of his beer before answering. "I'll try. He's a hard-ass, though. Fair warning. I already tried talking to the man, and he gave me nothin'. You might have to beg."

"I'll beg for her."

He appraises me, piercing me in the way he always does, like he's staring at my soul, not my face. "You'll do whatever it takes for my little girl, won't you?"

I dip my hat. "Yes, sir, but she's not so little anymore."

"Some part of them will always stay little. You'll see," he says, creaking back in the stool. His eyes seem to fill with memories. "You'll always be her daddy, no matter how old she gets, but instead of asking you to tuck her into bed, she'll ask you if she can stay on the family phone plan because *it's a better rate.*"

I groan a chuckle. "I can't even imagine Vi having a cell phone right now."

"You best believe it. They grow up too damn fast." He tosses back the beer. "One minute, you're holding them, trying to keep them from falling off the petting zoo pony. And the next, they're giving you a heart attack on the back of a bull, and you're feeling all kinds of proud. But you also know she's gonna put you in the ground early from all the worryin' you have to hide from her 'cause, at the end of the day, her dreams are more important than yours."

A wave of chills rattles my body, and my eyes burn.

"Well, fuck," I sniff like a man. "Thanks for that. I'm gonna cry now."

Willie clears his throat. "Me too, and I don't even like kids."

Colt salutes us with his empty bottle, the corners of his eyes crinkling. "Welcome to fatherhood, gents. It's the worst best thing that'll ever happen to you. The only person who can make me cry on this Earth is my little girl."

Love isn't a big enough word to encompass what I feel for my daughter, and I don't want her to grow up too fast. Every day, she seems to change, learning new words, discovering new things, falling, standing, getting back up.

I want her to always need me, but I guess one day, she won't. Even then, I hope she always knows she can come to me for anything, because she might not always need me, but I'll *always* need my little girl.

I swallow. "So, the worrying never goes away?"

"Never. You just learn to deal with it, and then eventually you get to share that worry with the person she chooses to spend her life with." His brown eyes spear me, and he waits, holding onto whatever words he's going to say next just long enough to get my heart racing. "That gonna be you, Wyatt?"

He doesn't bullshit me, so I don't hesitate. "Yes, sir. I've always been hers."

He gives me a long appraising look and seems to come to some internal decision before giving me a hard nod. "Good man. Now enough with the 'sir.'"

"No can do. My mama would kill me." I wink at him on my way out. "Once a gentleman, always a gentleman, sir."

40

"NAMA"

DAKOTA

One lazy Sunday morning, a tiny squeal stirs me awake.

I roll over to face Wyatt, who's snoring peacefully in my ear with his heavy arm draped around my chest. He doesn't stir, so he must be exhausted after the four rounds of sex last night.

This man can go all night.

All I want to do is have sex with him in every position imaginable. I've never had a hard time having an orgasm, but normally if I don't have one, it's because I'm too lazy to tell the guy what I want in bed since I'm not into whatever's happening.

One of the best things about sleeping with a man I've known for years is I don't have to pretend with him. If something isn't working, we talk it out, which means every time keeps getting better and better.

My phone buzzes on my nightstand, and irritation flares in my chest when I see the message on the screen.

BOONE

I still need my jacket. I'm going to have to show up at your place if you don't text me back (;

ME

Don't even think about it. I'll give it to you at the
Granite Falls rodeo.

BOONE

Okay... I miss you Kodie

I grind my teeth together, clicking off my phone. Everything
about that text is pissing me off, but Boone would never have the
audacity to show up here, and I don't want to deal with him. It's
not that I avoid confrontation, it's just that I only choose battles
worth fighting, and Boone's not worth my energy.

"Ma! Fah!" Vi says.

Fah means fan. There's another giggle-squeal, and I turn to
see Vi slapping the bars on her crib, staring at the bedroom
ceiling fan and pointing. She loves her ceiling fans.

I carefully shift out of Wyatt's sleeping grasp and tiptoe to her
crib, still feeling a little shaken after everything that happened
with the babysitter.

I'm surprised by how long this rage is lasting, but every time I
think about the party and how it could've been so much worse, I
get furious all over again. Sure, I'm angry that I missed my
opportunity with the scout, really pissed, but it's nothing
compared to the potent, gut-wrenching worry I felt when I
stormed into that party.

This little girl is worth missing my shot.

I scoop her up, and she clings to me like a little koala instead
of a little devil. I nuzzle my head right back into her, giving her
some extra snuggles this morning.

"We match, rodeo girl," I say, looking at her clothes.

Wyatt put her in her *Rodeo Girl* shirt with the little lassos, and
I've got on my *Rodeo Queen* shirt that I bought to match, so we
look darn cute together. "You hungry, little devil?"

"No!"

I've learned *no* is her word for *yes*. Actually, it's her word for everything. I kiss her cheek. "That's a yes. Let's get you some food. How does oatmeal sound this morning?"

She claps her baby hands. "Mo, Mah!"

She burrows into me as I head to the kitchen, and I love having her here, tucked against my chest. Luna lifts her head from Wyatt's feet, ears perking up. She stumbles off the bed, her tail wagging, and trots after me into the kitchen.

I heat some wet dog food in the microwave for her because my fur baby deserves a gourmet breakfast just like my real baby. Then, I place Vi in her highchair, and pull out some of the cinnamon overnight oats I made for everyone.

I set a bowl on her highchair and plop spoonfuls between her tiny pink lips, wiping up the dribbles with a napkin. "Here you go. You'll like this. I put some peanut butter in too, now that you're all done with your allergy tests. I know it's your favorite, so it's extra yummy. Open up."

Her tiny lips pop open, and I scoop some oatmeal into her mouth. She gets the most surprised happy grin on her little face as she chews. When she swallows, she screams, "Mo!"

I chuckle at her, scooping up another bite. "Yeah, I'm glad you like my oatmeal because it's one of the few things I know how to cook."

"Ma, mo. Wah," she demands, flailing her cute baby fists.

As I feed her spoonfuls, I try really hard not to think about how much I'm going to miss my little devil when she goes back to Tennessee. Wyatt and I are used to doing long-distance, and I can talk to him on the phone, but it won't be the same without Vienna. The barn's going to feel so much emptier without all her toys I keep stepping on. Without her little laugh-squeal. Without those baby snuggles.

I never knew one tiny human could take up so much space in my heart.

I blow out a breath to combat the burning in my eyes. "I'm a little sad you're leaving, girl," I admit, kissing her head while she chomps on her oatmeal, making an absolute mess. "I'm gonna miss you and your daddy too, but we'll be okay, won't we? You won't forget me? And you'll be back next summer, right?"

"Ma." She jerks her little head up and stares right into my eyes. "Nama."

I freeze, my breath catching in my throat. It sounds like she's combining the words Nanna and Mama. That one word drowns out all the other sounds in the world. "What did you just say?"

"Nama," she repeats, all proud of herself as she slaps her highchair.

"No, I'm Dee-dee," I correct gently, my heart pounding. "Can you say Dee-dee? Dee-dee. And that's Luna, but we like to call her Tuna. Can you say Tuna?"

"Mama," she shrieks happily. "Mo!"

She said it. She said Mama this time.

It feels like I'm being bucked off a bull and dipped into a Texas sunset all at once, but I try to stay calm. With a trembling hand, I scoop another spoonful of oatmeal into her mouth. She chews happily, completely oblivious to the avalanche of emotions she just unleashed on me.

I'm melting—completely melting. The world seems to slow down, as if it wants me to remember this moment. Here's this adorable, chubby, smiling little girl calling me Mama, or Nama, whatever, and... Tears blur my vision.

I've been chasing this PBR dream for so long that I forgot what it felt like to have someone rely on me. To feel needed. There's no better feeling than being needed by the people you can't live without.

A door creaks.

"Hey, look at that. We're all matching," Wyatt says, rubbing the sleep from his eyes. He steps into the living room in his *Rodeo Daddy* shirt and boxers, with his dirty blond hair sleep-mussed around his shoulders. "How're my girls doing this morning? All three of them," he adds, scratching Luna-Tuna's ear.

A smile starts to form, but it pops when he sees my face. "What's wrong?"

I sniffle, unable to find the words for a moment. "She, uh, she just called me, um, Mama, or Nama. I'm not sure, but she probably didn't mean it. We don't have to make a big deal about it."

"What? Really? She said that?" His eyes widen in disbelief, swinging between me and her, and then he gets this nostalgic, knowing grin on his face, as if he can feel the emotions pounding through me.

"Yeah," I confirm in a trembling voice, swiping a corner of my eye.

I don't cry in front of many people, but Wyatt's one of the few. He crosses the room in four quick strides and wraps me up in his solid arms. "Are you okay? How do you feel?"

I clutch him fiercely. I thought I'd feel scared, nervous, worried about her calling me that, but the only thing I feel is this gut-wrenching ache when I think of them leaving, and now my throat's tightening for an entirely different reason. "I'm feeling like I don't want you to go, and I want you and Vi to stay right here with me."

He searches my face, and so very slowly, the biggest smile I've ever seen starts to spread across his mouth. "What if I came back? Transferred to Austin? They're getting a new NHL team, and I want to be close to you too."

There's that *dipped in a Texas sunset* feeling again. "You'd do that for me?"

He kisses the tip of my nose. "Honey, you should know by now that I'd do anything for you."

I smile into the morning light, and looking at him and Vienna, I think I'd do anything for them too. His dry gaze bounces between my damp one, and he adds, "I love seeing you like this."

The way he says the word *love* has those butterflies flying.

"Like what?"

"Soft for the people who matter." He squeezes me. "You might be this badass bull rider, Dakota Cutler, but I know you ordered that Rodeo Queen T-shirt online because you wanted to match us."

"Yeah, I did." I bite my bottom lip to trap my smile and shift my focus to Vienna, who's now using her hands for spoons to eat the oatmeal.

"Do you... Do you think she meant it?" I whisper. "Calling me Mama?"

I hope she meant it.

He kisses my temple. "Would it make you feel better if I told you she calls my parents Mama too?"

I choke out a laugh. "No, actually, it wouldn't. I wanted to be someone special to her."

"Good. Because she doesn't." He lifts my chin with one finger and looks at me with such adoration that I can't help but grin back at him. He dips his thumb into my cheek. "There are those dimples. You should flash those around more often, *Mama*."

I giggle, actually giggle, the sound bright and airy.

His eyes bounce between mine, seeing something, before he kisses the tip of my nose. "Careful with that look, honey."

I tangle my fingers through his loose hair. "What look?"

"That look in your eyes."

"How am I looking at you?" I ask.

He flashes me a casual smirk. "You look like you might be fallin' for me, and it's giving me all kinds of hope."

His positivity is contagious, so I press a gentle kiss to his lips.

"I think you might be right," I say.

There's a difference between falling for a stranger and falling for someone you've known forever. When you fall for your best friend, you're falling for their secrets, their backstory, and every skeleton in their closet. It's a heavier kind of love, but it's the kind forevers are made of.

He gets serious as he strokes a hand down my waist, resting

his forehead against mine. "Do you want to know why I named her Vienna?"

I tilt my head. "Why?"

He walks over to the vintage record player we bought at an estate sale and digs through the records. He finds the one he's looking for and places it on the spinning wheel. "Vienna" by Billy Joel fills the living room.

"That's my favorite song," I murmur, my heart glimmering.

He winks at me. "I know it is."

He starts dancing with me then, leading me around the kitchen in a slow two-step. "You love this song, and it always makes me think of you. Always rushing ahead, never taking the time to slow down, and I always knew that I could be so good for you, if you'd just let me be that man, because..." He dips me low, brushing his nose against my neck. "I slow you down."

Suddenly, he picks me up by my waist and spins me around, the kitchen blurring. I can feel his breath warm against my ear as he leans in, whispering softly as he sets me back on the floor. "This song always reminds me of you, and I wanted my little girl to have a piece of the strongest woman I know. Dakota and Vienna. Two people that have my heart."

41

BAD BOY COWBOY

WYATT

"Well, would you look at that? Pocket kings." Dakota fans her cards on the outdoor patio table that Colt Cutler himself carved out of an old oak tree. "Unless any of you fools have pocket aces, these bad boys are gonna take the winnings."

"The Gambler" by Kenny Rogers plays over the sunset hum of the cicadas as we sit around the Cutler's wraparound porch. It's a balmy Saturday night, so we're all playing poker like old times, our laughter mingling with the soft clink of chips.

She's bouncing Vi on her knee, ripping plastic chips out of my girl's hands as she tries to stick them in her mouth so she doesn't choke. My girl only wants to be with her now, which isn't all that surprising. They're attached at the hip.

Alanna tosses out her cards with a huff and takes a hefty swig of her ranch water because she went on a ten-minute rant about how she can't do the sugar in a margarita. "Eight-two off-suit."

"Brutal." Dakota whistles, patting Alanna's shoulder in a solid effort gesture. "That's one of the worst hands you can get."

Alanna shoots her a glare. "Thanks for the commentary, babe."

Dakota smiles.

Vi laughs in her arms.

It's perfect.

"Ace-high," Mr. Cutler says, chewing on the tip of his unlit cigar.

Willie tosses his cards on the table with a gruff grumble. "Seven-two off-suit."

"Hah!" Alanna shouts. "At least I beat Sasquatch."

He sips his whiskey neat. "Don't get used to it, Barbie."

My mom begrudgingly lifts her navy Guardians cap, revealing the short gray strands that she brushes out of her face. "Damn it all. Three of a kind."

Mama flicks her blonde braid over one shoulder and downs the last of her margarita, the glass catching the sunlight as she finishes her drink. "I've only got a two pair."

Dakota swings her beautiful brown eyes to me, propping up a brow while popping a kiss on Vienna's cheek. "Well, Patty Daddy? Let's hear it, 'cause unless you're hiding pocket aces, there's no chance in hell you're beating me."

Fuck.

Hearing her call me *Daddy* makes me want to drag her to the nearest bedroom. One wink from this woman is enough to get me half-hard.

It's ridiculous.

She stares at me with a challenge set in her smile, but what she doesn't know is I've never minded losing if she's the one doing the winning.

I flip over my pocket aces with a grin. "Three-eight off-suit."

Those dimples pop, and I'll lose to her every time if it means seeing that grin.

"Look at that," Dakota drawls, scooping up her chips. "Guess I win that round. Again. Who wants another margarita? I spent over an hour picking those prickly pears out in the fields for the homemade syrup, and the tiny thorns got all up in my gloves, so please tell me y'all want more."

Everyone at the table slumps up a sad, defeated hand because we're all losing. This is the fifth round she's won, or at least she thinks.

"Dammit, Colt," my mom playfully chastises. "Did you have to teach your daughter *every* trick in the book? You raised a poker prodigy."

Colt smiles proudly at his daughter, as he should. She's won almost every round besides this one. "Course I did. She's my girl, and my girl's got to know how to beat 'em all. Oh, and would you make my margarita a ranch water, darlin'?" he grunts, the cigar wobbling from his lips. He pats his flat, muscular stomach. "Gotta watch my weight to keep up with you."

"Pops. Stop it," she sighs, dropping Vi into my mama's waiting arms. "You're more fit than a Clydesdale horse."

"Can you make mine a ranch water, too, babe?" Alanna asks. "I'm also trying to watch my weight, so I don't need the sugar."

"Why the fuck would you do that?" Willie grunts, pulling down his bandana on his forehead. "I don't want to watch your weight go anywhere."

Alanna tosses her hair to the side. "I didn't ask for your commentary on my body."

"Here, I'll help you with the margaritas," I say, pushing back from the porch table as they continue bickering.

Dakota makes the world's best margaritas (her secret is pickled jalapeño slices), but I'll take any excuse to be alone so I can get my hands on her.

Mr. Cutler lets out a gruff harrumph, cutting me a glare. "I didn't realize slicing limes was a two-person job."

He's playing the grumpy dad, but he can't fool me. He's starting to like me again.

Dakota flicks an airy hand. "Stop it, Pops. We'll be right back."

Looping her fingers through mine, she guides me from the

wraparound porch into the vintage kitchen with a giant wooden island. As she washes the cutting knife at the sink, she gazes out over the sprawling fields highlighted in sunset shades of pink while I gaze at her.

Standing behind her, I brush my scruffy cheek against hers. "You know what I'm thinking about?" I whisper, the warmth of my breath dancing along her ear.

She nestles into me, resting her head against my shoulder. "What're you thinking about?"

I sway, rocking us in a quiet rhythm. "I'm thinking about getting you home, to bed."

She tilts her head back, letting the cutting knife clatter to the sink. "Oh? And what would we do at home?"

Smiling into her warm skin, I slide my fingers just under the edge of her jeans, teasing the delicate lace of her panties. "Well, for starters…" I murmur, my voice a husky whisper, "I'd slip you out of these Wranglers."

"Oh?"

The word is nothing more than a quick gasp, like she can't spare any more oxygen for a longer sentence.

"Yeah, and then I'd watch those jeans fall to the floor." I lick up her neck, gently grazing her earlobe with my teeth, and she lets out a sexy little moan that has heat rushing down my body.

I drop my voice to a hopefully seductive hum, singing in her ear. She laughs, loud and addicting. "Are you serenading me, Wyatt Patterson?"

With a swift move, I spin her around to face me, her back against the kitchen counter, and capture her mouth in a slow, leisurely kiss.

Her lips meet mine eagerly, and she tugs on my hair, but I try to slow her down, tease her with my tongue. She's gunning ahead while I'm always trying to leave her wanting more of me, more of *us*.

She tastes like the tang of margarita salt and lime juice, and it's difficult not to drag her back to a bedroom, but I remind myself there are people on the front porch—namely, her perpetually grunting father.

A throat clear slices through the kitchen, breaking us apart.

I pry my lips from her to see Mr. Cutler leaning against the kitchen doorframe with his scowl looking more intimidating than usual, flicking his pocketknife. "So, this is what was taking so long, huh? And here I thought you were just putting a little extra love into my ranch water."

Dakota rolls her eyes. "Me kissing Wyatt has nothing to do with the love I put into your ranch water, Pops. I'll always put *all* the love into yours."

Mr. Cutler flicks his knife with a sharp snap, eyeing me like we're fixing to go head-to-head in a face-off, but I'm starting to realize that's how he looks at most people. It's not personal. He's like Dakota. His grumpiness gets mistaken for callousness.

I nudge Dakota in front of me—not just to shield the obvious bulge straining my jeans, but also because I can't let Mr. Cutler think I'll let his daughter slip away now that I've got her.

He might be intimidating, but being afraid of a woman's father? That's the sign of an insecure man who doesn't know how to treat a woman. I've got nothing to fear from Mr. Cutler because I'll do right by his daughter. I'll treat her like a queen, so no small blade or scowl is going to rattle me.

The doorbell rings, cutting through the tension with a cheerful jingle. I let go of Dakota. "I'll get that."

Mr. Cutler tips his hat at her. "Why don't you get that, darlin'? I think this man and I need to have a little chat."

"Okay, but y'all play nice, Pops," she says, pecking me on the jaw before floating over to do the same to her father's cheek. She saunters down the hallway, and I can't help but watch her hips sway in those tight jeans as she goes.

"You better be looking at my daughter's face, boy," Mr. Cutler grunts.

I snap my eyes up to his narrowed gaze. I'm not about to tell him I was staring at his daughter's perfect ass, but I can't lie to him either. "Actually, sir. I was admiring her legs. She's been working hard this summer. All those workout sessions are paying off."

Mr. Cutler snorts like I'm bluffing.

I'm not. Her legs look damn good in those jeans.

He stalks toward me, the old floorboards creaking under his heavy boots. "Look here, I'm not one to beat around the bush, so lay it on me straight. What's going on between you and my daughter?"

I've always held a deep respect for Colt Cutler. He's protective without being overbearing. Kind without being a pushover. Commanding without being *demanding.* He's exactly the kind of father I want to be to Vienna—but I'll add in a few more smiles.

My moms gave me everything I needed, and they're some of the best parents, but Mr. Cutler was always a role model, and he deserves my honesty.

I check the hallway. Dakota must be occupied with whoever is at the door because I hear low voices, and it sounds like... a man? I turn back to her father, ignoring the voices. "Sir, I'm completely in love with your daughter, and I have been since the day she pulled me out of that creek."

He chews on his lip, and I wait, and wait, and wait some more. By the time he steps forward, I'm sweating, but he claps a hand on my back. "Well, it's about damn time you admitted that, son."

Son.

That takes me by surprise. "You're not going to give me a hard time for dating your girl, sir? I wouldn't blame you. I'm a father too."

"Now, why would I get mad at a good man for loving my daughter? Any man who looks at her the way you do is fine by me, but I wanted to make sure you were all in," he rasps, the sound filled with more emotion than I expected. "You've got my blessin', son. I couldn't think of a better man for her. I always had a feeling it'd be you with how you followed her around every summer."

I swallow hard at the thought that this man, who loves Dakota just as fiercely as I do, sees me as being worthy of her.

"Thank you," I scrape out the words. "That means more to me than you know."

Colt's brown eyes melt to chocolate pools. "Just promise me you'll love her with everything you've got. She deserves nothing less."

Dakota might have rough edges, but when she cares, she cares deeply for her people. She's bold, caring, driven, all the qualities I want my little girl to grow into, and if it weren't for her, I wouldn't have gone after my own dreams.

She sharpens me, but I soften her, and she deserves a man who's going to support her goals. I'm not saying life will be as breezy as a flower farm, but I'll never try to squash her dreams.

"I promise," I say, and I know that'll be the easiest promise I ever keep. "I don't know any other way to love her, sir."

He pours us each an amber shot of tequila. "And I think it's about time you started calling me Colt. Enough with the 'sir.'"

We clink our shot glasses, the tequila burning down my throat, and seal our agreement with a firm handshake. I'm feeling good, really good, about where things are headed.

There's even a bounce in my step as I walk to the front door, but when I see who's waiting in the hall, all that positivity dries up. The ominous black cowboy hat casts a shadow on his face, but I'd recognize that annoying drawl anywhere.

I freeze in my tracks.

"Get the hell out," Dakota's voice rings, clear and sharp. "I told you to leave, Boone."

42

FIVE TIMES THE MAN

DAKOTA

"*R*eally, Boone? You're just showing up unannounced? We're busy," I cross my arms, pissed off that he has the audacity to strut up to my dad's front porch.

He takes that damn toothpick out of his mouth. "I need my jacket for a rodeo this weekend, so I thought I'd stop by. I warned you."

"Well, I don't have it with me, so go on, now."

He rocks back in his boots, frowning a little like that comment hurts him, and I have no clue why he looks like that. I don't trust that look. "I just want to talk, Kodie."

"The last thing I want to do is talk to you," I cut out. "We're done."

The unmistakable heavy thud of footsteps thumps behind me, and instinctively, I know it's Wyatt. I've memorized the sound of his reassuring cadence over the years.

The heat from his body meets mine, and he places a steady hand on my lower back. I'm not sure if it's meant to be possessive or reassuring, but either way, his silent support is comforting.

"When a woman tells you to leave, you leave," Wyatt rumbles

in his *dad voice*. That's what I call it when his drawl takes on that deadly calm tone.

It's my favorite voice of his.

And the sexiest.

"Patterson," he scoffs. Boone's eyes flick between Wyatt and me, his jaw tightening. "Of course you'd be here. Figures you'd finally move in on her. You never could stay away from her every summer."

There's a pause.

"What can I say?" Wyatt rasps, confidence rolling off him in waves as he pulls me closer. "I've been obsessed with this one for a while now."

I just about rip his jeans right off. I don't know why him claiming me in front of my ex is the hottest thing that's ever happened to me, but it is, and I'm relishing in this moment.

Boone scoffs. "That much was obvious, man."

Wyatt's body tenses behind me, a ripple of protectiveness radiating through him. Then, he wraps his arms around my shoulders, his chest to my back, drawing me against his muscular frame.

I feel his breath tickle my skin before he presses a gentle kiss to my neck, and I lean in. Partially to seek more of his warmth and partially to drive the point that we're together home.

"You want him to go, honey?" he replies nonchalantly, looking down at me with tender eyes, but his jaw is tight.

"Yes," I say, not even having to think about my answer. "You best be going home. We've got to get back to our poker game."

Boone's expression hardens, and he opens his mouth, but before any words can escape, Wyatt's voice cuts through the air, silencing him mid-breath. "You heard her. Go on, now."

"Well, I'll be damned." Boone smirks, annoyingly calm as his eyes linger on the way we're wrapped around each other. "Didn't know you had it in you, Patterson."

He narrows his eyes in my periphery. "Didn't know I had what in me?"

Boone ambles closer until he's right in Wyatt's face like he's about to deliver the blow of all blows. I never realized how much taller Wyatt was until this very moment.

"Oh, nothin' really," he sneers. "It's just that I never pegged you for a guy who'd steal another man's girl. Looks like you've actually got a backbone after all."

We both rush forward, but I'm smaller and quicker, so I move faster. I pull myself out of Wyatt's grasp, getting all up in Boone's face. I might let shit roll downhill when it comes to me, but disrespect the people in my life?

Yeah, I get angry all right.

"Leave, Boone," I spit out, pointing to his truck. "You've got no business being here. Wyatt's five times the man you'll ever be."

That wasn't the fanciest declaration, but I'm sure I'll come up with a beautiful romantic speech three days from now when I'm washing my hair.

My chest heaves, and then slowly, so slowly, Wyatt's hands form a possessive cage around my waist, and I feel his thumbs brushing *everywhere* on my body.

Wyatt drawls with an arrogance I rarely hear from him, "You heard her, Bowman. Five times the man. You better hope she's not talking about size."

I sputter a laugh, wishing I had his comebacks.

Luna hobbles from the hallway and growls a low rumble. She never much liked Boone, but he wasn't a dog person like Wyatt.

I scratch the spot behind her ear with a proud grin. "Good girl."

Boone looks between us with narrowed eyes and exhales a heavy sigh. His shoulders slump in defeat as he trudges back to his pickup truck, kicking up dust in his wake.

"Oh, and Bowman," Wyatt calls out over my shoulder, tucking

me against his hard chest. "You can't lose something that never belonged to you in the first place."

All Boone does is shove that toothpick back in his mouth. The setting sun casts long shadows across the rugged fields, painting an orange glow that highlights Boone's lonesome figure. He slams the door, but he doesn't start the truck. He stays right there in the gravel driveway, watching us.

No one's ever stood up for me like that, had my back. I lean up to give Wyatt a thank you kiss, but he only smiles against my lips, slow, tantalizing.

"So, five times the man, huh?" he teases. "It kind of sounds like you've got a little crush on me, honey. When did *that* happen?"

There's a note beneath his playful voice that I think he's trying to hide, or maybe downplay, and I can't tell if it's pride or something else, but it sounds like angels blowing trumpets.

I circle my fingers through his belt loops, using the leverage to bring him closer, playing along. "I think it started when you took your shirt off."

"And here I thought it was 'cause of my ass dimples."

"Those too."

He chuckles, but then nods to where Boone's still sitting in his truck. "What'd he want?"

"Do we really have to talk about him?" I groan, looping my arms around his neck. "I don't want to waste any breath on him, and things are long over between us."

"Mm-hm. Maybe for you, but he's still out there in his truck, so I don't think they're over for him." He skims his hands up my waist, driving me absolutely wild. "Talk to me. I want to know what's going on in that head of yours, then maybe you'll get the kiss you so desperately want."

He playfully nips my bottom lip.

I try to pull him closer for more, but all he does is smile against my mouth, keeping me wanting, yearning.

"Fine," I grumble. "He needs his protective vest back for some rodeo. That's all. Now, can I have that kiss I so desperately want?"

He smiles, though it doesn't quite reach his eyes, and it's almost a little too quick. A flash of a grin. "Then you better make sure you bring it, but..." He trails off, eyes falling to my lips, staying, sticking.

"But what?"

He looks back at where Boone is still waiting in his truck, cocks his head, curls his lip, and then jerks me forward by my hips. I crash into his hard body.

My lips part in shock when Wyatt goes in for a demanding, feral kiss. His hand cradles the back of my head, pulling me in deeper, closer, fusing our bodies together. His tongue invades my mouth with a wild urgency, exploring fervently, and it's everything I never thought to want in a kiss.

God, he's the best kisser.

A rough, needy groan breaks free from him, sending shivers rippling over me, and this kiss isn't just intense—it's untamed, voracious, wild.

If a kiss were a middle finger, it'd be this one.

His hands find the backs of my knees, lifting me effortlessly until I'm sitting on the front porch railing. Coming closer, instinctively, I wrap my legs around his waist as I anchor myself to him, using my fingers to latch onto his hair. I tug on the strands, desperate, and I can feel him hardening against me, right over my center.

I try to move, just needing friction to ease this building ache. My nipples stiffen to peaks, and I can feel this clawing heat sinking lower and lower, pooling between my thighs, and then, all of a sudden, he drops me back down on the porch.

"But the next time you meet up with him," he growls, his breath almost as heavy as mine. "I hope you're still thinking about that kiss."

THE SCOUT

WYATT

I'm jealous as hell—there, I admit the damn thing.

I'm trying not to show it because I don't want Vienna growing up thinking that's the sign of a healthy relationship, but it turns out that I'm jealous about *everything* when it comes to Dakota. More than anything, it's annoying, so I'm doing my best to ignore the feeling.

The next day, I head straight to the rodeo grounds to hunt down the scout, with every intent of doing whatever it takes to get him to come back next weekend to watch Dakota compete at the Granite Falls rodeo.

I draw the line at sexual favors because the only person I'm getting on my knees for is her, but I'm willing to do pretty much anything other than that.

After three hours of back-and-forth negotiation, a *lot* of schmoozing (mostly about his llama farm), and a fair amount of begging, I finally convince him to come to the Granite Falls rodeo next weekend to watch Dakota compete.

"Thank you, sir," I say, shaking his calloused hand. "You won't regret watching her. She's a sight to behold."

His gray mustache twitches with a grunt. "I better not."

"You won't."

Pride swells in my chest as I strut back to my truck with the birds chirping, the sun shining, until I run smack into Boone Bowman's black cowboy hat in the middle of the rodeo's parking lot. That damn toothpick nearly pokes my eye out.

His eyes narrow under the shade of his hat. "Patterson."

"Bowman."

We stare each other down, neither of us willing to break first.

I never much liked the guy.

He has an ego bigger than Texas and thinks he's hot shit because he never misses a shot to flaunt that his dad is on the board of directors at Regal Ranch, as if that makes him some kind of cowboy royalty. I never understood what Dakota saw in him. She doesn't care much about money, so maybe he's got something decent hiding beneath his all-black getup—not that I care to find out.

I start to head to my truck, but his bitter voice stops me in my tracks. "You know she's just gonna leave you, too, right? That woman can't be tamed. She'll leave your heart broken like she left mine."

If he means to set me off, it won't work. I turn around as slow as possible, letting my eyes travel over him from hat to boots. "See, that's the difference between you and me, Bowman. I'd never try to tame her. The only thing you can do is hold on tight to women like her."

With that, I head to my truck, but not before Boone calls out behind me. "I'm gettin' her back, Patterson! I fucked up, but I'm gonna make it right."

My fists clench. "Like hell you are. I'm better for her than you ever were."

I slam the door with more force than usual. The engine roars to life, and I take the backroads home because I need to cool down after that.

As I drive down the winding Texas roads, I can already feel

myself relaxing. The sunset paints the sky with flames. The vast expanse of open land stretches out, dotted with grazing cattle. I drive ten under the speed limit, soaking up the beauty as the warm breeze blows through the open windows of my truck, carrying the scent of wildflowers.

I can't wait to come back.

Texas has always been more than a home. It's my favorite escape. The pace is slower. The people smile more. It's a place to come back to when the daily grind of training, workouts, and stress gets to be too much.

By the time I pull up to the barn, I'm already feeling more levelheaded.

I spot Dakota watering the pot of mint leaves on the front porch, dressed in nothing but her sports bra and shorts. The late afternoon sun bathes her in gold, making the sweat on her skin shine. She's sipping her carbonated water, and she's clearly just finished a workout.

I park my truck and walk up to her, needing to feel the warm reassurance of her body in my arms.

"Guess what?" I whisper into her ear.

She leans back into me, her body fitting perfectly against mine. "You had a quarter-life crisis and bought a boat."

I laugh into her ear, tugging her closer. "Try again."

"You... won the lottery on a scratch-off?"

"That'd be nice, but no."

"Okay, what?" she asks, curious. "Tell me."

I kiss her very bare, very sweaty shoulder. "You better dust off those chaps because you're gonna have a PBR scout watching you compete in the Granite Falls rodeo this weekend. Buckle up."

She drops the watering can to the ground with a dull thud, jerking around to face me. "What?"

I lift a shoulder. "You heard me. You're riding. I talked to the scout for you, and he agreed."

She spins around fully, and the most beautiful smile breaks

across her face. Dimples and all. She flings herself at me, wrapping her legs around my waist as she climbs onto my chest and squeezes me hard.

"Thank you, Wyatt," she says, showering kisses all over my face. "Thank you, thank you, thank you! Holy shit. How'd you make that happen?"

I hold her tight. "It just took a little convincing, wasn't too bad. Let's just say I complimented the hell out of all the llamas on his farm. I never knew I could talk for hours about how those all-natural, organic mineral feed supplements make their coats shine."

She laughs at that. "We need to take Vi to the llama farm. I think she'd love the llamas."

This woman. She's always thinking about my baby girl.

She pulls back to cradle my cheeks, searching my face for something I hope she finds. "You have no idea how much this means to me. Sometimes, I wonder what I did *right* to get saddled with a man like you."

She starts kissing me with hungry lips, and I kiss her back, just as eager. That one sentence eases all my worries about Boone. She moans into my mouth, and I'm hard for her in an instant. My tongue slips between her lips, exploring, teasing, swiping the roof of her mouth, and her happiness quickly turns to need. She tastes like salt and sweat, and the tang of her workout is all over her skin.

I start walking us to the outdoor shower, her legs still wrapped around my waist, every inch of her body pressed against mine. She grinds against me like she needs me to give her some relief, and I will.

"Where are we going?" she whimpers against my lips.

I kiss her sweaty skin. "*You* need a shower."

44

SHHH...

DAKOTA

*W*yatt drags me beneath the stream of running water, kissing me while he cups the back of my head. I *love* the dichotomy of Wyatt Patterson. He's hard, but soft. Rough, but gentle. Dominant, but caring.

Our teeth clink.

Something falls to the ground. A bucket, maybe? Or my self-control.

"I figured we could shower together," he says, stripping off my bra. "Get nice and clean."

"I thought you liked me dirty?"

Another teeth knock.

Another smile.

"I like you any way. Really, this is just an excuse to get you naked." He deepens the kiss, reaching behind me to turn up the heat knob.

"Okay, but you better get the job done fast, cowboy," I murmur into his lips. "Lana's picking me up for dinner in ten minutes, and I promised her I'd go. I'm not canceling on her again."

288

He yanks down my workout shorts. "Fast and furious, got it."

"You did *not* just compare sex with me to a movie."

"Fine. Quick and dirty, then. Turn around, put your hands on the wall, and spread those pretty legs for me. I want to see all of you."

Bossy Wyatt might be my favorite Wyatt.

Heat blazes through me. He gets me naked and rips off his own clothes in record time, all the while watching me with a ravenous gaze, eyes bright with anticipation. That hungry look always winds me up, makes my body taut with a need only he can release.

Wyatt has sex like every time is the last time—intense, vigorous, insatiable. Like he might never do this again. He doesn't just make me feel good, he makes me feel precious.

Once he's naked, hard, and ready for me, he spins me around and pushes me into the wooden shower slats before sliding into me. There's a height difference, so he has to bend his legs, but he makes it work. I moan into the sunset sky when he reaches a spot deep inside. "Oh my fuck. Why does it feel better every time?"

He bites my shoulder, rolling his hips against my ass. "I don't know, honey, but I can't stop. Christ, you feel so fucking good."

For a few seconds, we're slow, tender, but the needy ache eventually sweeps us both away until Wyatt's pumping into me so hard the wooden slats are shaking. I'm crying out, my entire body burning in the cool water.

He reaches around to pinch my nipple, and all that does is make my clit ache for his fingers, but he doesn't touch me there, not yet.

"Put your leg on that wooden stool for me," he commands. "I want to go deeper."

With one foot on the shower floor and the other hitched on the wooden stool, Wyatt's able to push so deep inside me that my eyes roll back a little. He's ruined me, which suits me just fine since there's no one else I want. When he reaches around and starts circling my clit while rubbing my nipple, I nearly come apart right then.

"Not yet," he commands, pinching my center a little too hard to stop me from shattering. "Wait for me. I want to come with you."

"I can't," I whimper.

"You can." He smiles wickedly into my neck, rolling his hips tantalizingly slow. "If I can wait ten years to have you like this, you can wait ten seconds to come on my cock."

He kisses me then from behind, holding me tight like he's worried I'll fall to the ground if he lets me go. I just might. The feeling of him throbbing inside me, the way we're connected, the way he's biting my shoulder to control himself while I'm screaming into the sky, there's no turning back from this.

Our bodies, our hearts, they're puzzle pieces.

I can't believe I got this lucky, to have a man my family loves, who makes me laugh, who supports my dreams, and goes down on me every chance he gets. People would be jealous as hell if they ever knew how amazing he was, but he's mine.

All mine.

The water cascades over us, mixing with the sweat and heat of our bodies, drenching us both. It makes his fingers glide effortlessly as he circles my clit, and when he moves deeper inside me, he hits that furthest, most sensitive part.

I almost break. "Oh fuck, I'm close."

"I know. I can feel you," he grunts, picking up his pace. "Me too. You make me so damn *needy*."

His hips slam into me, driving deep with each thrust, and I lift my head, gazing at the sunset through the mist of the shower. Wyatt's movements match the rhythm of my heartbeat until his circles on my center become harder, faster, and my moans turn to cries of ecstasy.

"Yes, Wyatt. Don't stop. Please."

He bites my neck. "I love it when you moan my name. Scream it again for me."

I do.

And again, and again, and again.

Until I hear footsteps crunch on the grass.

"Babe!" Lana shouts. "Where are you? You're late! Are you seriously just now showering?"

Wyatt stiffens, but he doesn't stop pumping into me, almost like he can't. I'm right on the verge of a life-changing orgasm, so I can't stop the breathy sound that slips out of my mouth.

"Dakota Rae Cutler!" Lana's voice suddenly rings out. "Are you fucking your cowboy in an outdoor shower when you *promised* you'd be ready for dinner by now?"

Wyatt's hand flies up to my mouth, trapping in my moans. "Shhh," he whispers, his breath hot against my neck. "Normally, I like you loud, but she's going to steal you away if she thinks you're in here, and I need you to come for me. Can you do that and be quiet?"

I nod against his hand.

He smiles into my neck. "That's my girl."

He continues pumping into me from behind, clasping his hand over my lips, sucking, licking. His thrusts become more deliberate, one hand circling my clit while the other keeps my moans trapped against my lips. The dual sensations drive me wild, and I start trembling against him.

"That's it, honey," he moans quietly. "You're being so good. Just like that. Come for me."

Wyatt's relentless rhythm pushes me closer to the edge, and despite his muffling hand, my moans spill out in gasps, and despite him telling me to be quiet, he can't stifle his groans. I feel him spill himself into me, his release sending me over the edge as I scream into his hand.

"I can still hear you!" Lana says, sounding amused. "Damn, people would pay good money to hear those moans."

"Don't get any ideas," Wyatt growls into my ear, his dick twitching inside me as he rides out his release. "I want you all to myself."

LET'S RODEO

WYATT

"She's gonna have to ride 'em hard."

My eyes slide to the two guys next to me. They blend into the crowd of cowboys with their Wranglers, boots, and cowboy hats.

At least they're straw this time.

"She will," I interject, resting my elbows on the metal fence of the arena. "She always does."

The Granite Falls rodeo is packed to the brim tonight, the air overflowing with the smell of dust, sweat, and manure, and the scout is right in front, waiting for Dakota to ride. Despite the whoops and cheers of the crowd, all I can do is stare at her and Boone, stretching off to the side together.

The sight of her in those fringe chaps and worn boots is making my thoughts veer in a naughty direction, and based on how Boone's broad frame keeps moving toward her, it seems like he's having those same damn thoughts.

He keeps reaching out for her leather-clad shoulder, and each time, she shoves him away, her jaw set in a hard line that matches my own. I clench my beer bottle, trying to tamp down this possessive energy in me.

This is Dakota's big ride, and I'm not going to ruin it with my irrational jealousy. She's all mine—I know it. Still, it doesn't mean I like watching another man go after my girl.

"What's got you scowling like that, son?" Colt grunts, resting his elbows next to mine as people fill the stands. Reaching forward, he steals a sip of my lukewarm beer, wincing. "That's not the good stuff."

"They ran out of the good stuff," I explain.

"Figures." He sips it again. "Did I tell ya she got matched with Diablo in the draw? It's that bull that hurt the poor boy, and I'm worried sick about her."

My stomach drops, and a rush of worry surges through me, but I have to believe with every fiber of my being that she'll be okay. I tighten my grip on his shoulder. "She'll be fine, Colt. You raised a tough as nails woman. She's got everything it takes, and then some."

The worry is still there, but there's nothing I can do. She's riding that bull whether I like it or not.

"Yeah," he agrees, nodding like he's trying to convince himself. "Yeah, you're right. She'll be fine. Let's talk about somethin' else. I don't want to dwell on the negative."

"Same here."

Colt scans the rodeo crowd beneath his cowboy hat, earning a few nods of respect from onlookers nearby, but when he spots Boone, his face plummets into a glower that matches mine.

"You scowlin' 'cause my little girl's still talking to that prick out there in the arena?" he asks, gesturing to where Boone and Dakota are standing too close for my liking.

I take a long swig of my beer. "You don't like him either?"

"Never have. Never will," he grunts, gripping the metal railing. "I had to keep my mouth shut when she wanted to marry him 'cause she had to make her own mistakes to learn. There are some men that'll be boys until they're eighty. Boone's one of 'em. You aren't. You've always been more man than boy."

I straighten under his compliment. "Thank you, sir. That means a hell of a lot coming from you."

"Just tellin' the truth, son." He pats my shoulder. "That boy was always a pit-stop, and she knows it. You're her destination. It just took her a little longer since she took the backroads to get to you."

I laugh a little. "She should've taken the highway."

"Yeah, but the scenic route always makes for a better story," he says with a grin, his swagger carrying him away.

I turn to find my family in the bustling crowd. The stands are alive with energy, everyone buzzing with anticipation for the bull riding to start. My chest throbs with pain as Dakota prepares to climb onto the back of a raging bull, strapping on her chaps, dusting off her boots.

The black bull thrashes in the chute, and I hold my breath as I watch her strut up to the metal corral. It never gets easier watching her face off against a bull, and as much as it scares the hell out of me, I can never look away.

Because I've always been hers, and this time, she's mine.

"Get ready," some guy drawls next to me, nudging his friend. "This one's gonna be a wild ride."

"Yeah, all two seconds," some other asshole says.

"Eight seconds," I state, ignoring them, even though my heart is thrashing around in my chest like the damn bull. "She's got this. I know it."

I repeat the phrase like a prayer, lifting that mood ring to my lips like I do before every ride. I kiss the metal, thinking about the day I got down on one knee and asked her to marry me. She said no, but I promised to keep the ring, and keep it I did.

And once I move back to Texas, I plan to get down on one knee and give it back to Dakota.

"Wyatt! Over here!"

I spot Alanna with my mom, who's gently pushing Vi in her stroller. I make my way to them and scoop my daughter into my arms. Her tiny hands clutch the stuffed longhorn Dakota gave her weeks ago.

She never lets go of that thing.

We all take our seats on the bleachers of the crowded rodeo stands. Alanna's sitting beside me, her eyes glued to the arena, and my parents are squeezing each other's hands, eagerly waiting. We're all keeping our fingers crossed that she stays on for those eight seconds as we wait for her to ride.

The mustached cowboy next to me leans over to his friend, scoffing, "Twenty says she falls off in the first five seconds."

Look at that, another asshole.

"Thirty says she only stays on for three," the other chimes in.

Make that two assholes.

I lean over to them, pulling out the crisp bill I got from the ATM earlier. I hadn't been to an ATM in over a decade, but I went just for today so I wouldn't have a repeat of last time. "One hundred says she stays on all eight seconds and then some."

Lana digs through her Prada purse—which I only know because she made sure to tell me—and pulls out two crisp hundreds. "Make that three hundred on our girl."

My mom digs into her jeans and adds a twenty. Mama adds her own five-dollar bill, and I'm shocked we're all carrying cash. But then again, we *are* a family of poker players. "Make that three-twenty-five."

I take all the bills and shove them in the cowboy's shocked face. "Guess we're going all in."

Our entire group has matching smug-as-hell smirks as we glare down the mustached cowboy.

He frowns. "You're willing to go all in on a bet for Kodie Cutler?"

"I'll always bet on her," I add, leaning down to kiss Vienna's cheek. "Isn't that right, baby?"

She squeals, playing with her fluffy longhorn. I pull Vi to my chest and point out to Dakota, who's stretching off to the side of the dusty arena with the cowboys.

"You see her, baby?" I whisper into her ear. "That's the kind of woman I want you to be one day. Strong. Fearless. Soft. Kind. I don't care what you want to do with your life as long as you go after it with everything you've got. Take life by the horns, baby girl. Just like her."

I plant kisses all over her flushed cheeks and she giggles in my arms. "Dada! Ma!"

Oh, do I love my little girl.

When I first held Vi, I was overwhelmed with the responsibility of being two role models rolled into one—a mom *and* a dad. I wanted to be everything she needed, but I think Dakota's right. Just being there when she needs me is enough. I tried so hard to be everything for her that I ended up giving too much of myself away. Now, being back here, I feel like I've finally found a part of myself again.

"I told you to give me some space, Boone!" Dakota's shout pierces the air from the distant arena. My eyes snap to them, catching Boone and Dakota locked in a heated argument, faces inches apart. He grabs her arm roughly, way too rough, dragging her toward the animal trailers and out of sight.

Oh, fuck no.

I jump up from the stands.

"Can you watch Vi for a minute?" I hammer out to my mom, heart pounding. "I need to go check on Dakota."

"Of course, sweetie."

I'm on my feet a second later, heading straight for her.

HELL NO

DAKOTA

"*I* told you I don't want to talk, Boone," I shout, my voice echoing off the metal grates of the animal stalls at the rodeo.

Ever since I found out I'd be riding Diablo, I've been a nervous wreck. It's making me more jittery than normal, and I need to settle down. My cuticles are bleeding I've been picking at them so much, and I just need my summer boy.

"All I'm asking for is dinner. I just want to explain." Boone's voice is pleading, but I can see the stubborn set of his jaw.

"I wouldn't even go through a drive-thru with you," I snap back, folding my arms across my leather vest. The words come out sharp and satisfying.

Hell yeah. That was a decent comeback.

His ocean eyes narrow, a rogue black curl tumbling across his forehead. He doesn't brush it out of the way, almost like he knows it makes him look a tad dangerous. "Can we please just talk?"

There's a desperate edge to his voice that has me curiously nibbling my bottom lip, debating. Arguing is only going to draw this out longer, and I need to prepare for my ride, so with a huff,

I lean against a hay bale. "Fine. Whatever you want to say, just say it."

Boone's eyes flash with something like regret. "Damn," he mutters, that muscle twitching in his cheek again. "You sure know how to kick a man when he's down, Cowboy Killer."

Irritation burns in my cheeks, and my fuse snaps. Boone and I used to argue all the time, and it seems like we're falling right back into that old habit. He made me question *everything* about myself, and now he has the audacity to put this back on me?

"Did those words actually come out of your mouth?" I demand. "*You're* the one who kicked me when I was down when you said I couldn't do this. *You're* the one who made me question everything about myself. I've spent the better part of this whole year trying to pick myself back up, and it wasn't until Wyatt came back that I started believing in myself again."

I expect him to bite back like always, but instead, he looks down at his boots, avoiding my gaze. He seems a little guilty for once, and that has my shoulders slumping, regret prickling.

He pulls out a toothpick from his jean pocket and sticks it between his lips before sucking in a deep breath. "I know. I never should've said what I said in the interview or treated you that way. It kills me, and I'm so damn sorry. And I miss you. Miss us. That's all I wanted to say."

I rear back in absolute shock.

He did it. He actually apologized, but I'm not letting him off the hook just yet. "Then why did you do it?"

Boone scrapes a hand through his black hair, a gesture I've seen a thousand times and don't want to see again. "I was in love with you, and you broke my heart, Kodie. I was so angry after that. I wanted to hurt you as much as you hurt me, so I said something that I knew would hit you hard, but it was a mistake. You've got everything it takes to make it, and all I wanted to say was that I'm sorry."

"That's not a good reason," I say. "You don't just spew bullshit about people 'cause you're angry. You come to me, and we talk it out."

He seems to sink in on himself. "I know, and I'm sorry. I really am. I think you can do anything you set your mind to, Kodie. You've got this."

His nice words do nothing for me, even though they're kind. For so long, I placed my self-worth on the validation of other people, like Boone. We were one in the same, and I wanted to impress him, but now I know that if I try to please everyone, I'll never be good enough for anyone.

I blow out a heavy sigh, wanting to put all of this behind me. "I didn't mean to hurt you. It's just that we never would've worked. You asked me to give up my entire dream for you. To pick up my life and move to Vegas. What'd you expect?"

"I guess…" His throat bobs, and he stares at the animal trailers in the distance. "I guess I thought you loved me more than you loved bull riding. I thought you'd pick me."

"If you really loved me, you wouldn't have asked me to choose," I say, softening my words. "You would've supported my dreams no matter what. Like Wyatt."

Wyatt could come up with a million reasons for us not to be together, but instead, he's looking at the one reason he wants to make this work.

Boone gives me a sad look, his eyes searching mine. "So, it's him, then?"

I might be standing here with Boone, but my mind is back with Wyatt and Vi, snuggled on our leather couch with Luna-Tuna at my feet. With Wyatt, I can have everything: my dream, a family. Sure, there are things standing in our way, but I want to be the type of person who believes in the goodness of the world, just like him.

I always thought love meant finding someone who makes you stronger, but for me, I think love is finding someone who makes me softer, and that's Wyatt. It took me too long to see it because no one gets that lucky. No one meets the love of their life at ten years old, but I did.

I met the love of my life so young that I didn't realize he'd be the love of my life.

I nod, a smile cracking across my face like a sunrise. "Yeah, it is. He's so good for me. Too good, really, but that's how I know he's the one."

Life dealt me a royal flush with Wyatt Patterson. He's soft where I'm hard. Calm where I'm intense. Caring where I'm focused. He was crafted so perfectly for me, slid so effortlessly into my life, that I never realized he was meant to be there all along.

"I think it's always been him," I murmur to cushion the blow. "I just didn't see it before, but I do now."

His fists ball up at his sides, and I can't tell if he's angry, hurt, determined, or all of the above.

"You know he's going back to Nashville, and what about his kid?" Boone's question is laced with concern, whether it's fake or not, I can't tell, and I don't care—it doesn't shake my resolve.

"We'll figure it out. I'm not worried, and I love that little girl," I reply, surprising myself with the ferocity in my tone.

I'm normally the overthinker, but all I feel right now is this resolute certainty, so maybe Wyatt's chronic positivity is rubbing off on me.

"You?" He arches a brow, his expression settling into disbelief. "Not worried? That's shocking."

I lift a casual shoulder. "What can I say? He brings out the best in me."

Boone meets my gaze, and then gives me this sad little smile that reminds me we did have some good things, but we didn't have enough of them to last.

"You know," he eventually says, his eyes locking onto mine before dropping to my lips. "I think you'll always be the one who got away from me, Kodie Cutler."

He'll eventually realize we were all wrong for each other, so I shrug. "You'll find someone else. You're a looker, Bowman. I'm not worried." And then, because I want to put this behind me once and for all, I add, "You're not a bad man, Boone. You're just not the man for me."

That seems to ignite something within him, and his eyes spark with intensity.

I start to pull away, but in an instant, his hands meet my waist. He pulls me into his chest and goes in for a kiss like he's landing a plane on my face. Shock surges through me, and without thinking, I lift my hand to slap his cheek.

He stumbles back.

"What the hell?" I say, wiping my mouth off with the back of my hand, even though he didn't even kiss me. I don't want any of his breath particles on my lips. "Why would you even kiss me? That's disrespectful as hell, and I told you we're done. It's always going to be Wyatt for me."

"I'm sorry, sorry," he mumbles, rubbing his cheek. "Shit. I just thought I could change your mind and remind you what we had."

Slow, heavy footsteps thump behind me.

"You should listen to her, Bowman," a familiar voice grits out, and I feel the heat of his body at my back. "Every gentleman knows you *never* disrespect a lady unless she's begging for it in the bedroom."

INDECENTLY PUBLIC

WYATT

*H*e tried to kiss *my* lady.

Rage boils inside me, a white-hot jealousy that threatens to consume every shred of my self-control. I do my best to casually saunter forward, stuffing my hands deep in my pockets to keep my composure.

Boone's eyes bulge when he sees me towering over him, but his confusion quickly turns to irritation. "What're you doing here in the back pens, Patterson? You always seem to show up at the wrong times."

"Or the right ones," Dakota interjects from behind me.

That settles some of the boiling irritation in my chest, but I still grip his shoulder hard enough that Boone winces.

"I think you and I need to have a little talk," I drawl, the veins in my arms bulging with the force of my clenched fist.

I'm pissed that he tried to kiss Dakota, but I'm also angry because I'd never want someone treating my daughter that way, and I feel like it's my duty to set this guy straight once and for all.

All he does is chew on that goddamn toothpick.

I pluck the wooden toothpick from Boone's lips and throw it into the hay bale. "Listen up, Bowman."

"What the hell, man?" Boone tries to rip himself out of my grasp, but he can't. He might be a bull rider, but I've got a decade of hockey under my belt.

I lower my voice, getting so close to his face that my nose bumps his. "Where's your dictionary?"

He cocks his head like Luna when she hears a high-pitched noise. "What the hell are you talking about?"

"Your dictionary. Where is it?" I punctuate each word with a sharp snap.

"Do I look like the kind of guy who owns a fucking dictionary?" Boone frowns, trying to break out of my grasp, but I hold him tighter.

I glance at Boone's black button-down, the fabric pulled tight, too tight, over his broad chest. "No, you don't," I admit. "I'll make this easy then."

I pull out my phone from my jeans and start typing. Now that I'm a dad, there's this strange urge to educate the assholes of the world. Dakota peers over my shoulder at the screen. When I finish typing, I shove my phone in Boone's face.

"Read this," I command.

Boone grumbles something under his breath, but he reads the screen with pinched brows. "No, meaning no. Not any. There is no excuse. Used to give a negative response..." He looks up, more irritated than confused now. "What the hell am I reading?"

"Watch that tone." I shove my phone back into my pocket. "You're reading the definition of the word 'no,' because apparently, you need to learn the meaning of it. So let me educate you, when a woman says no, she means hell no. You got that, or do you need to read that definition again?"

"God*damn*," Dakota mumbles, fanning herself in my periphery. She sounds a little breathless, a little impressed.

It makes me a little hard.

Boone gulps, darting his eyes to her. "Yeah, I got it. You don't need to shove your phone in my face; I get it. I'm sorry."

We stare at each other for a few tense seconds. Images of him trying to kiss her flash through my mind, fueling my irritation. But I can be the bigger man.

Boone might've made some mistakes, but people deserve second chances. I know if I stay, I'm going to do something I regret, so with one last squeeze of his shoulders, I say, "She's right. You're not a bad man, Bowman, so act like a good one."

I release him, striding away to a more secluded area outside the animal corrals. I need some breathing room to cool off. I hear Dakota's footsteps behind me, soft but persistent, and soon it's just us among the hay bales and horses, the familiar scents of straw and leather cocooning us.

I lean against a hay bale and pinch the bridge of my nose. Deep breaths. In and out.

"You're mad," she blurts the obvious, sounding worried as she grips my forearm. "Nothing happened between us. I swear, Wyatt. I would never do something like that to you. I pushed him away."

"I know you did. I saw. I'm not mad," I lie because this isn't her problem. I'm the one who needs to calm the hell down. This is her big day, and I don't want to ruin anything. She has to ride in less than an hour.

She loops her arms around my waist, burying her head against my chest. "You seem really mad."

The smell hits me.

Sandalwood cologne. *His* smell—on her.

The muscles in my back tense. I don't want her smelling like him, which I know is ridiculous, but I'm not feeling all too level-headed right now.

I catch her wrist and tug her deeper into the shadows behind the hay bales, away from prying eyes. Grabbing her hips, I lift her up on top of a hay bale, earning me a surprised intake of air from her. Every heavy breath brings our chests closer together.

"Fine. You're right. I'm mad," I say, pinning her against the hay with my hips. "I'm *mad* because you smell like him. I'm *mad* because he still wants you. But most of all, I'm *mad* because I've been in love with you since the day you saved my life, and I want everyone in this whole damn world to know it."

I don't give her a chance to respond. I kiss her hard—just to make sure she gets the whole goddamn point.

My lips crash onto hers, rolling and rolling, our breaths mingling. She twists her fingers in my hair, and the sensation sends electric sparks down my spine. She meets my kiss and raises me one better, sucking my tongue into her mouth.

The feel of her in my arms, it's everything and somehow not enough. I reach down and grip the back of her hips, my fingers digging into her soft flesh. I push her down onto the hay behind her, the rough straw poking at my jeans. All I'm thinking about is how I need her, right here, right now, but I can't.

Maybe I can.

No, I can't fuck her on a hay barrel in the middle of the rodeo grounds.

She moans into my mouth, and that sound vibrates through my entire body. "I want you, Wyatt. Please. Now. There's only you."

I groan into her neck, nipping at her shoulder with pent-up frustration. It's the only thing I needed to hear from her.

"We can't," I whisper, my breath hot against her skin. "There are people around, and these chaps of yours are gonna be hell to get off."

"I don't care about anyone else," she breathes against my lips. "And I think you can handle taking off my pants just fine."

My breathing is ragged, and this idea of hers is starting to sound brilliant. "You want me to fuck you right here on this hay bale?"

Her hands are already at my belt, and her fingers slip as she tries to undo the buckle. "Yes, right here. There aren't that many people around, and if someone randomly walks by, well..." Her lips curl into a wicked grin.

Her movements are frantic, and her desperation, that need I feel in her touch, it's all the convincing I need. She pulls out my cock, and for a second, I think about how if one of those security guards sees this, I could go to jail for public indecency, but then she swipes her finger around the tip, and I think Dakota Cutler is worth jail time.

My mind is a haze of desire, consumed by how much I want her. Her fingers tease my dick, sending jolts of pleasure through me. It sets me loose, and I undo her belt buckle and then the zipper, but these jeans are impossible to get off with the chaps. There's no leverage for her to wrap her legs around my waist, but she's had these jeans for years, so the fabric is pretty worn.

Bet I could rip them.

I struggle, fumbling with the zipper. The damn thing won't budge. "You know what? Fuck this. I'll buy you some new pants." I grunt, ripping the fabric of her jeans right down the middle inseam, giving her a satisfied smirk. "Much better."

Her mouth falls. "Did you just *rip* my jeans right down the middle? How's that even possible?"

I roll my eyes at the surprise in her tone. "You've had these for years, honey. The fabric is so worn, it's like paper. I think it's time for a new pair."

I barely shove her panties aside before I pick her up by the backs of her knees and press her ass into the hay bale. She guides me in, and I slip into her wet warmth, deeper, always so deep. I bite her neck to muffle my groan.

The feeling of her is too much.

Once I'm fully inside her, I still, letting her adjust to me. I always need this to be good for her. She throws her head up to the orange sky, moaning. "Oh god, I mean Wyatt. Holy shit. Don't ever take your cock out of me. You stay right here forever."

I chuckle against her, and that vibration makes me all too

aware of being inside her, so it quickly escalates into another breathy groan. I hiss in a breath, the sensation almost too much to bear. "You're so fucking tight, honey."

And then we really start moving.

Her warmth wraps around me, and this right here, there's no better feeling in the world. She clings to my back as I roll my hips, sinking deeper into her. She clutches her legs around me, scraping up my back with the blunt tips of her nails. The sound of our slapping skin echoes through the rodeo grounds, louder than the crowd's cheers.

It's wild and fast, and I wish I had the self-control to savor this moment, but I can't. All I can think about is the way she's biting my neck and how she's screaming even louder than I am, and how she won't stop looking into my eyes, and I can't stop staring at her because I want to see exactly how I make her feel.

I need to watch her shatter around me.

Each thrust drives us closer to the edge, and I can feel my control slipping. The way she clutches at me, her nails digging into my shoulders, her pussy gripping me, tells me she's just as close.

I thrust deeper, my hips snapping forward as I pull her down onto me at the same time. Her legs start to tremble around my waist, and a searing heat races up my spine, electrifying every nerve.

We're both shaking, teetering, burning, and then we plunge over the edge together. Her moans mix with mine, raw and loud, and the sight of a few people glancing our way only makes me come harder.

God bless hay bales and their perfect height.

She clenches around me, her body pulsing in time with mine, and I pour myself into her. We scream our moans into the sunset, our voices melding with the sounds of the rodeo, until there's nothing left but our ragged breathing.

"Look at you," I say, stroking her cheek as I soften inside her. She's flushed, her skin glowing with satisfaction.

"I think some people are." She smiles against my lips, her breath still coming in soft pants. "Wyatt Patterson, who knew you were so dirty, fucking me in public like that?"

I kiss her, slow and tender this time. "What can I say? I wanted this whole rodeo to hear you screaming my name so they know you're mine."

"Oh, summer boy," she drawls, resting her forehead against me. "I think the entire *world* knows I'm yours now."

48

DIABLO

DAKOTA

"**G**ive it up for Kodie Cutler, the Cowboy Killer! Let's see if she can stay on the wild and wicked Diablo!" the announcer's voice slashes through the arena's applause.

The crowd erupts while my stomach swarms with nerves. I'm glad I packed an extra pair of jeans in my bag after that little romp in the hay bale with my summer boy. I was feeling good after that—calm, settled, ready—but now all those worries come rushing back.

But I can do this.

I've got this.

Even if I am riding Diablo. The bull who almost broke Nash Sawyer.

I don't even want to think about that day because it was the last time I ever saw his goofy grin. He came back from the hospital, sweating, pale as a sheet, with his smile petrified into a grimace, but at least he survived. Only from then on, we didn't call him Smiley…

We called him The Ghost.

That made him grin a bit when he got his new nickname. It's

actually an honor in the bull riding community to earn one based on the hellish ride you survived. Only the toughest riders get a badass nickname.

Cheers fill the late-summer air, but I tune them out. Same as always. I can't afford to be thinking about Diablo just like I can't afford to be thinking of the crowd's applause. I need to ride out my emotions in that middle lane, not too fast, not too slow.

My dad strides up to me through the relentless heat with that same grumpy scowl under the brim of his hat. Leaves might be changing everywhere else, but September is still brutally hot in Texas.

"You ready to ride Diablo?" he grunts, but I see the worry there in his eyes.

"I'm ready to hurl behind the chutes." All bulls can be mean, but that Bramer's especially tough.

It's got me all twisted up, but it also means if I do well, my score will be even higher. He's the most aggressive bull out there, so if I can just stay on, I've got a good shot of impressing the scout today.

My dad doesn't crack a laugh at my joke. He takes me in his arms, gripping me fiercely. "Remember, you stay loose and—"

"Flow like good tequila. Smooth and steady," I finish for him, our well-rehearsed mantra washing a familiar wave of calm over me.

"Right you are." He taps the brim of my hat with a trembling finger. "If you stay on this round, that'll be one hell of a score. You'll have a shot at making the Austin Rattlers one day, you hear?"

I straighten at the thought, imagining sitting in the draft and them calling out my name. It's everything I've wanted, but now the thought of saying goodbye to Wyatt and Vienna taints the dream a little. I need to figure out how to make them part of my world. This dream won't mean anything if I can't have them by my side.

My dad eyes the snarling bull in the chutes. "Diablo's got a wicked spin though."

"I know."

"And an even more wicked kick."

"I know, Pops. I'll be fine."

He nods, but his eyes keep darting to the thrashing black bull in the chute. One of the flank men shouts, "Woo doggy, that kick almost got ya, boy! Back off now, back off. Give 'em some space! Goddamn, Cowboy Killer, this one's gonna get ya!"

They all chortle obnoxiously.

I might piss myself.

My heart jumps into my throat, and it feels like all the blood drains from my face. My dad shoots them a murderous glare before he tightens his grip around my shoulders.

"Hey," he commands. "Don't listen to them. You listen to me now. You've been practicing every day this summer. You've got everything it takes. Just remember those lessons."

Suddenly, he tugs me close into his leather jacket, leading me in a quick two-step, and then spins me around right there in front of the chutes.

"Pops!" I shout as he twirls me, stumbling into his solid chest. "What are you doing?"

He continues leading me in a confident two-step, and I forgot how good of a dancer my dad is. "Just making sure you're nice and loose. You might be dancing with that boy now, but don't forget who taught you how. I love you always, darlin'."

I gaze up into his shimmering brown eyes. "I'll never forget who taught me how to dance."

He kisses my cheek, his whiskers tickling my skin, and quickly walks away, almost like he can't bear a longer goodbye. As his figure fades down the animal corrals, a tightness grips my throat.

My mom might never miss a Sunday night phone call, but my dad never missed a bedtime story, never forgot to pack my lunch, never missed the matching prom pictures, and never missed a rodeo. He cheered me on through every high and caught me at every low. If it weren't for him, I don't know where I'd be.

"Hey, Pops?" I call out, just as he's about to round the corner by the horses.

He looks over his shoulder, the setting sun casting an orange halo around his hat. "Yeah, darlin'?"

I try to keep my voice steady. "I'm the luckiest girl in the world, getting you as a dad. You know that, right? You're my reason for riding."

He swallows hard and looks down at his boots. He pulls out a handkerchief from his jean pocket to wipe his eyes.

"You're my reason for everything, darlin'. I still remember when you were just a girl, and anytime we'd have people over, you'd ask them to buck you around on their backs, piggy-back style. People always thought you were a little wild, but you've always been my crazy child. Now, stop making me cry like a fool and go kick ass in that arena."

We don't have time for long-winded goodbyes, so I salute him, swiping away the tears. I put my best smirk in place, confidence with a dash of fake arrogance. "Always, Pops. I'm your girl. What else do you think I'd do?"

"That you are. Raise hell, darlin'." With a final nod, he strides away.

I'm my daddy's girl through and through, which means I can handle Diablo. I *will*. This time is different. Now, I have people who need me to stay on. People I'm riding for. Specifically, two very important people.

Steeling my shoulders, I head to the chutes and turn to face off with the beast. The massive black bull snorts and smashes his hooves at the dirt, muscles rippling under his dark hide. The rodeo arena buzzes with the cheers from the crowd, the distant calls of cowboys, and the snarling bull.

"You sure you got this one, Cowboy Killer?" the flank man asks.

I bend down to get eye-level and glare right into Diablo's fathomless black eyes. Doubt will get you killed in this sport, so I growl right in his huffing face, "Yeah, I got this one."

After securing my helmet, I climb up onto the metal chutes, gripping the cool steel beneath my hands. I swing a leg over the rail and settle onto Diablo's broad back, feeling his muscles tense beneath me.

He instantly tries to buck me off, but I grip the rope, thinking of Vienna, thinking of how desperately I want to stay on for my little girl. For Smiley. Pops. And Wyatt, always for my summer boy.

"Alright, folks!" the announcer shouts. "Give it up for the Cowboy Killer!"

The crowd goes wild, but all I'm thinking about are my people. No one else matters.

"Let's dance, you big ol' brute," I mutter to the snarling bull beneath me. "I'm not letting you take this round, you hear me?"

My ears ring loud enough to drown out the crowd. I use one hand to grip the bull rope, and the other is poised and ready in the air. I take a deep breath, adrenaline pumping through my veins.

The world narrows to just me and Diablo.

The gate man unlatches the metal chute, and I tighten my grip, feeling the rope bite into my palm. "All right," he says. "Three... Two... One!"

The metal gate shoots open, and we're off.

Diablo bucks around like Satan has a tight hold of his balls, and I'm whipped left, then right, then left again. The behemoth is a whirlwind of muscle, snot, and fury. I'm clinging on, every fiber of my being fighting to stay perched atop this raging beast, but I stay centered, loose, and fluid.

It's terrifying.

It's exhilarating.

It's intoxicating.

Diablo kicks me around the arena, and I thought I'd be mentally chanting my dad's tequila phrase or thinking of all those two-step lessons with Wyatt, but the only thing on my mind is my little devil and how I have to stay on for her. I never thought I'd fall in love with someone else's kid, but I love Wyatt, so of course I'd fall hard for his daughter.

The crowd's roar grows louder and louder with each second I hold onto the beast, until finally, the buzzer rings through the arena.

Holy fucking shit.

I did it.

Eight seconds.

I made it all eight seconds—and then some.

A rider comes to help me off Diablo's hide, and I run away in the dirt so the bull doesn't come after me. A grin spreads across my face as I search for Wyatt in the stands. He's the first person I want to see, so I keep scanning until I find him. He's standing alone in front of the rails with his knuckles clenched tight, but he's grinning bright.

I fucking did it, I mouth.

You fucking did it, he says like he knew I would all along.

His smile has me smiling, but it drops when his eyes narrow on something over my shoulder. The air shifts and I feel it, the crowd sucking in a collective gasp.

"Dakota!" he booms out, eyes wide with panic. "Run!"

49

MINE

DAKOTA

I whirl around just in time to see Diablo barreling toward me, a hurricane of snot and rage. The meaner ones always charge. The barrel men are trying to rope the animal, but it's no use; he's a fast one, and he's headed right for me.

There's only one option in times like this—run, and run like hell.

I don't hesitate.

I sprint straight for Wyatt's waiting arms because I know he'll always catch me.

I'm not even thinking about the bull gunning for me. I hear a snarl behind me, but the adrenaline drives me forward, pushing me toward Wyatt.

With a heavy grunt, I heave myself over the metal railing separating the arena from the crowd and tumble into his waiting embrace, pushing him down onto the stands. This happens more often than you'd think at rodeos—having to jump the railing to safety to escape a runaway bull.

I fall into him, and he wraps me up in his arms, breathing just as hard as I am. "You're good. I've got you. Holy shit. Diablo was this close to getting you, but the barrel men roped him just in time. You okay?"

The words rush out of him so fast I barely catch them all. All he does is hold me, but it's the only thing I need right now. To feel him against me.

"I'm okay," I pant. "You're here."

I search the arena to see the barrel men leading a kicking Diablo back into the chutes by the rope and release a heavy breath, but a second later, I scan the scoreboard for my score.

The judges award a score of up to twenty-five points each for the rider's performance, and up to twenty-five points each for the bull's effort for a total score of one hundred, and when I see the 95.25 score next to my name, I scream in excitement.

"You did it!" Wyatt shouts, matching my enthusiasm. "Holy shit, that's one hell of a score. I'm so glad the scout was here to watch you."

The adrenaline, the relief, the pure-fucking-joy, it all barrels into me at once, but it's nothing compared to what I'm feeling for Wyatt. It's crazy to think that I've been chasing success for so long, only to realize it never really mattered without having the right people in my life. I lift my leg, straddling his lap in front of everyone on the bleachers, but still keeping it somewhat tame.

His brows shoot up.

Someone whistles.

"You, Wyatt Patterson, are my absolute favorite person in the world," I say heatedly, cradling his scruffy cheeks. "And Vienna. Her too. You make me feel like I'm breathing, and you make me look at the bright side of things. I'm not great with words, so I'll probably think of an amazing love declaration next week when I'm in the shower, hopefully with you, but I just need you to know that I don't ever want to live in a world without you because I'm so damn in love with you and our little girl."

A look of complete awe lights up his face, but I kiss him, hard and demanding. The cheers of the crowd fade until it's just me and him. The fame, glory, recognition—I'll take a proud kiss from the man I love over their praise any day. My people are more important than any scout, any world championship, or any fleeting moment of glory.

I can feel every eye in the arena on us, which only has me kissing him harder. I want everyone in this little ol' town to know this sweet, kind, loyal, sexy man is *mine*.

And his daughter—she's mine too.

All mine.

Everyone in the crowd starts hooting and hollering. He meets my kiss stroke for stroke, and it's messy and sloppy and so fucking perfect that I never want to stop. Maybe we shouldn't be making out like teenagers in front of everyone, but my man makes me feel young and reckless.

With a raw moan, he pulls back first. "Careful, there. Keep kissing me like that and these jeans aren't gonna fit anymore."

"I can't help that I get carried away with you," I say, our noses bumping. "You're mine, Wyatt Patterson. You and Vi. You're my whole world."

I really did get lucky, stumbling upon the love of my life at such a young age. He's my happy beginning and ending. We might have one of the best love stories of all time, but I think about everyone else falling in love across the world, yearning, hoping, finding their happy ending, and that might be the most beautiful thing—that everyone thinks their own love story is the happiest of all.

He tugs me closer, catching my bottom lip with his teeth. "It's about time you realized that, 'cause honey, I've been yours since the day you pulled me out of that creek."

ONE YEAR LATER

WYATT

I can't stop sweating.

It's been six months since I moved back home to Granite Falls, so this September heat has nothing on my nerves. These damn nerves that won't go away because I'm proposing to the woman of my dreams tonight.

The General is bursting with people, beers in hand, laughing, nodding their heads to the twang of country music, and as I look through the haze, happiness slams into me. I can't believe I managed to make my way back down south.

I didn't expect my heart to heal this much coming back home, but I hoped, and I've never been more grateful for being a glass-half-full man.

This heart of mine is no longer black and blue, it's as healthy as they come.

But Dakota and I have had to work hard for that. This past year hasn't been easy for us. It's been a whirlwind of plane rides, late-night FaceTime calls, and figuring out how to navigate our long-distance lives. But we made it work because when something's worth it, I'll always make it work.

I glance at Dakota, getting tugged and hugged by everyone in this town, shouting *Congrats!* and *You did it!* in her face. The Granite Falls baker even made her a peach-crisp with *PBR Bound* spelled out in Fredericksburg peach slices.

She deserves all their praise for making the Austin Rattlers team—and then some.

"You did it! I always knew you would!" Alanna shouts, wrapping Dakota up into such a tight hug, I'm worried she'll crack her ribs. "I knew you could do it, babe, but watching you ride is intense. I don't know how I'm gonna watch you compete in the PBR every day. I'll have to borrow grungy Willie's bandana to shield my eyes."

She yells *grungy Willie* loud enough for the man in question to give her the finger while jerking a cocktail shaker. Willie is working triple-time making cocktails since it seems like the entire town squeezed into The General to celebrate Dakota getting drafted into the PBR. Even Boone came. He's sulking in a corner, but he's not a threat to me now that I've got the girl.

The same girl I've barely spoken one word to tonight because my throat is so dry from the thought of getting down on one knee. I keep fiddling with the mood ring, making sure it's still chained around my neck.

"No, Vi!" Dakota shouts, and I jerk my head on reflex to find her chasing after our stomping little girl. She picks up her squirming body, yanks a plastic cake knife out of her hands, and looks at her with warning eyes. "I told you not to touch that. What did we talk about?"

Damn.

I don't think there's anything hotter than the *stern mom* version of Dakota. Her voice takes on this raspy quality, and I can't help but think this woman's just what I need in a co-parent. I can already see Vi growing into a teenager and me wanting to give her everything, but Dakota will be a good balance for me.

She's the no to my yes. The spice to my sweet.

She kisses Vi's cheek and struts over to our group by the bar counter.

"What the hell is in this martini?" Alanna says with a glare at Willie. "I asked for *black* blue-cheese-stuffed olives. These are green olives sans blue cheese. Aren't all bartenders supposed to know how to make martinis? Isn't that like, a prerequisite?"

She holds up the martini glass in Willie's face.

He glowers at her, and then yanks a bottle of Jägermeister off the counter. He dumps a shot into her martini, turning the whole drink black.

"There," he shoots back, sliding it across the sticky counter. "Now they're black olives. Have at it, Barbie."

Alanna gapes at her drink. "Did you seriously just dump *Jägermeister* in my martini?"

"You bet your ass implants I did."

"I do not have *ass implants*," she grits out. "Only my tits are faux. My ass is au-natural and the result of a lot of pilates."

Willie blatantly checks out her ass, pursing his lips. "I don't know about that. Looks too good to be real. I'd say jury's still out on the implants."

Her face turns a violent shade of red. She glances at the drink, then at Willie, and back at the drink. Dakota snatches it from her grasp just as she's about to hurl the entire drink at his face. "Stop that. You be nice. That's Wyatt's cousin, and he's my man now, so you better get used to hanging around his people."

That'll never get old—her calling me her man.

She shoots a stern warning at Willie, but all he does is shrug. Alanna cuts him a glare. "I'd have a better shot getting along with a rattlesnake than I would this grizzly man. Seriously, when was the last time you got a haircut?"

Willie snaps his teeth at her in an audible click. "Careful there, Barbie. I like to *bite.*"

"I'd probably get rabies from your bite, Face Beard." Alanna tosses her red hair over her shoulder, and without a word, struts away.

Willie doesn't take his eyes off her as he watches her go. It's only when some cowboy puts an arm around Alanna that he goes back to making drinks.

My mama walks by, trying to take Vienna, but she makes grabby hands toward Dakota, clearly wanting her. That was another reason the long-distance was hell. Vi cried every single time she had to say goodnight to Dakota, and then Dakota teared up, and it was a whole ordeal.

"I've got you, little devil," Dakota says, hitching her up like a natural. "You're not going anywhere."

"Mama!" she shrieks happily, nuzzling her chest. "Mama, I wan mo!"

We're finally progressing from garbled words to garbled sentences. So much changes in a year. This time last year I was so focused on getting her to walk, and now I'm starting to have real conversations with my little girl. It blows my mind. She's turning into her own person.

"Do you know where her water bottle is?" Dakota asks. "She's thirsty."

"I'll get it," my mama offers, tugging Vi's cowgirl booties.

I thought I'd get used to this, watching Dakota with our little girl, but I never want to take having this woman in my life for granted. I pull them close into my chest, dropping a kiss to both their heads. "I love watching you with Vi. It makes me want to rip those pants off and make another baby with you."

"Wyatt Patterson!" She mock gasps, covering Vienna's tiny ears. "You can't be saying naughty things to me like that in front of our daughter."

Our daughter.

It gets me every time.

"Why not? I want Vi to know what a healthy relationship looks like, and no man should ever stop flirting with his girl, no

322

matter how long they've been together." I kiss her again. I can't seem to stop. "I'll always be flirtin' with you, honey. Even when we're eighty years old, and I can't get it up."

Her eyes flick down to my jeans, and heat flares in her gaze. "I don't think you'll ever have a problem with that."

"Good point," I agree with a wink, already shifting to stop the blood rushing to my groin. "My jeans are always a little too tight around you."

She takes a long swig of her margarita, smirking at me over the rim. "How about we go somewhere so you can take off these pants? I'm pretty tired of wearing them."

"Those Wranglers are wearing *you*." I brush my thumb along her bottom lip, swiping off a purple-pink droplet.

Vienna tugs on her dark curls. "Mama! Uh-oh!"

Dakota kisses the tip of her nose, bouncing her in her arms. "Uh-oh is right. Daddy is being very naughty."

She smushes Vi between us and kisses me—thoroughly—tasting of lime and salt. She shudders against me, muffling an *I love you* against my mouth that sounds like she's saying *olive juice,* but I know what she means. I'm just about to lose myself in the kiss when the door suddenly bursts open, hitting the wall with a loud smack.

Everyone in the bar jerks their heads at the noise, and Micah Cruz struts into The General, spreading his arms wide around the room with an even wider smile on his face.

He's exchanged his hockey jersey for a button-down and jeans, so he looks nothing like our black-haired center.

"I finally made it to this small-ass town!" he booms. "So the party can finally start."

Cruz spots me a second later and launches himself across the room—and I mean *launches*. He flies through the crowd and pulls me into a bone-crushing hug. "Patty-Daddy! I missed you, man. Fuck, it feels good to hug you. It's not the same without you on the team. And look at you, little Vi!

Looks like your daddy finally figured out how to braid hair. 'Bout time!"

We had to break out another bottle of Japanese whiskey when I told Cruz I was transferring to Texas, but he understood because he's got one of the biggest hearts of anyone I know.

"Cruz!" I slap his back. "What the hell are you doing here? Damn, it's good to see you. Missed you, brother."

"Figured I'd surprise you since Tremblay's still off in Argentina, and you know..." He pats my shoulder, giving a look to the ring on my neck. "Big day and all."

Dakota's brows come together. "Why's it a big day?"

I send Cruz a glare that I hope he translates as *shut the fuck up*, so he doesn't ruin my mood ring proposal, and tug Dakota into my side. They've met over FaceTime, but never in person, so this is a first.

"Just a big day to celebrate you," I say, changing the subject. "Cruz, this is my Dakota."

I expect her to make some snappy retort about calling her mine, but all she does is hold me tighter and kiss my cheek. Cruz appraises her with his brown eyes, and she appraises him right back. After a moment of silence, they seem to come to some agreement, both deeming the other worthy.

He wraps her up in a bear hug, lifting her off the floor with Vi in her arms. "Oh, I've heard all about you. You put my boy here through hell."

"What can I say?" she teases, still snuggling my squirming little girl. It seems like she doesn't want to let her go, which is doing things to me. "I give as good as I get."

Cruz sets her back down, and she looks up at me with a softness in her eyes that she only reserves for me. "But we found our way to each other eventually, didn't we?"

I kiss her temple. "That we did. You just took the scenic route."

She lifts on her toes to kiss me gently. "I do love taking the backroads. Forces me to slow down."

Colt eventually pulls Dakota away, whispering something that looks like *I'm proud of you* in her ear. She hands off Vi to my mom when the song "My Little Girl" by Tim McGraw comes on the speakers, and Colt Cutler drags his daughter out onto the dance floor, leading her in a slow two-step. Damn, and here I thought I was good.

The man's got moves.

Cruz whistles a breath. "So, you're really doing this, man? Proposing to her?"

I tug the mood ring around my neck. "Yeah, I've been ready since the day I met her, so it's time. Let's hope she says yes."

"She will. She hasn't stopped looking at you all night. It's like you're the only guy in this room. She's obsessed with you."

Just then, I meet her gaze across the bar to find her already smiling at me. She cuts her way through the crowded dance floor to get to me.

When she reaches me, she throws her arms around my neck, flushed from the prickly pear margaritas. "Hi, summer boy."

Obsessed is right. We both are.

I kiss her good, the brims of our hats bumping. "How are you holding up under the spotlight? Am I gonna have to steal you away to get some alone time with you?"

She likes being the center of attention, and I've always been happy in her aura, but I didn't think getting down on one knee in front of all these people would be this nerve-racking.

Her face lights up with the most beautiful smile I've seen. *Dimples.* "Only if you steal me away to an outdoor shower."

This woman. *My* woman.

"Tupelo Honey" by Van Morrison comes on the speakers, and that's my cue. It's time.

"I think I can make that happen." I wrap her up, lifting her off the floor to kiss her. "Dance with me?"

Her lips curl in a half-smile. "My two-step skills aren't as rusty as they once were, you know. I have a really good teacher."

I loop my hand through hers, leading her out onto the dance floor. "Then this time, I can step on *your* toes."

I guide us in a slow two-step, the soft lights casting a warm glow around us. From the corner, Colt Cutler watches with a small grin playing on his lips. She loops her arms around my neck, her eyes shimmering with happiness. As we dance, my nerves get the better of me, and I actually do end up stepping on her toes a few times.

"Well, look who's a little rusty now?" she teases, but I don't say anything because my heart's pounding in my ears.

Do it, Patterson. Do it now.

I pull back, take a deep breath, and slowly sink down to one knee. Her hands fly to her mouth, and everyone in the bar turns to stare. I yank off the mood ring from the chain around my neck and hold it up for her, opening my mouth to say my rehearsed speech that I've been practicing all week.

And then, my mind goes absolutely fucking blank.

Here's something they don't teach you in the school of life—it's unnatural as shit to get down on one knee for a woman, and it's something you don't realize until it's too late, and you're down there on one knee, proposing to the woman of your dreams. I'll stay on both knees for her all night, but one knee? No one warns you how wobbly this feels.

Why is it so hard to keep your balance?

"Wyatt, what're you doing?" she asks, eyes wide with surprise, but she's smiling. That's good.

Buckle up, Patterson, and keep it simple.

Every eye in the room is on us, and I swear if I topple over, she's never going to let me live this down. I take a deep breath, steadying myself.

"Dakota Rae Cutler. I've loved you from the day you saved my life in that creek, and I want to spend the rest of my life loving you." My voice shakes slightly, but I press on. "For me, it'll always be you. Anytime I think of the woman I want my daughter to grow up to be, it's a woman as bold as you. I know you still have that dream of yours to chase, so…" I pull out the mood ring I kept all those years ago. "You don't have to marry me today, but will you marry me someday?"

Her eyes water as she looks down at me and whispers, "You kept the mood ring?"

"Told you I would."

A grin slowly spreads across her face, her eyes glossing over. "You know I'm not good with words, but yes, Wyatt Patterson. I'll marry you someday. Now, get up here and kiss me. Let's give the people what they want just like we did for that fiddle player."

It feels like I'm being bodychecked in the heart when she holds out her left hand. I press my lips to her bare finger. "Can I let you in on a secret?"

"Always," she whispers.

I smirk up at her. "I set that whole thing up with the fiddle player just so I could kiss you."

Her mouth falls, and she laughs, big and happy. "Wyatt! Now I know where Vi gets her devilish tendencies from."

"You needed a little bit of a push," I say with a shrug. "You were taking too long to get there, honey."

I slip the mood ring onto her left index finger, but it won't go past her knuckle. She laughs with tears in her eyes. "I don't think it's gonna fit since you've kept it for so long, so maybe just put it on my pinky 'cause I still want it."

And I do.

I stand and swing her around the bar, kissing her like no one's watching—with a hell of a lot of tongue. Everyone claps and whoops and cheers. Cruz even wolf whistles, so I know it's a good kiss.

"All right, all right, all right," Colt Cutler drawls, but he's grinning that rare smile. "That's enough of that."

"Sorry, sir," I shout over Dakota's head. "I'm never gonna get tired of kissing this one, so you better get used to it."

Vienna runs across the dance floor to us, and I lift her up in my arms. Dakota hugs her tight; the three of us forming our own little home.

"I can't believe you proposed like that," she says, pulling me closer by my belt loops. "Especially in front of all these people. You're gonna have the whole town talking about us until Christmas."

"I figured I had to go big or go home, and since I'm already home…" I trail off so I can kiss her again, keeping my baby girl tucked between us.

She chuckles. "You figured you just *had* to go big?"

"You should know by now, honey…" I flash her a wink. "Everything's bigger in Texas."

COMING SOON

Thanks for reading! If you enjoyed this book, I would appreciate you leaving a review on Amazon, Goodreads, or wherever else! I have so many fun stories planned. For more updates on future couples, sign up for my newsletter at the link in my Instagram page or follow me on social media: @authormeredithtrapp

DAKOTA'S PRICKLY PEAR MARGARITA

Ingredients:

- 1 shot of tequila. I use LALO!
- 1 shot of fresh squeezed orange juice, or if you really want to be on the floor, add one shot of Cointreau (not Triple Sec)
- 1 shot of lime juice (I always do a little more because I like the extra tang)
- 1/2 shot of prickly pear syrup (Making it homemade is a NIGHTMARE! Buy an all-natural organic bottle online. The less preservatives, the better. If you like it sweeter, do a full shot)
- Add in a few slices of Trader Joe's Hot & Sweet Jalapeños
- Tajín seasoning for the rim (I like to sprinkle some into the shaker to give it a little spicy kick)
- Top with Fever Tree light tonic water or club soda for less sweetness

Directions:

Step 1: Pour Tajín onto a small plate. Wet the rim of a margarita glass and dip rim into Tajín.

Step 2: Fill a cocktail shaker with ice; pour tequila, Cointreau, lime juice, jalapeños, and prickly pear syrup over ice. Cover shaker and shake the drink. Strain into the prepared margarita glass and top with tonic water.

Step 3: Find yourself a body of water and scarf that bad boy down!

ACKNOWLEDGMENTS

First off, thank you, dearest reader, for taking a chance on my book! I hope you loved Wyatt and Dakota's story as much as I loved writing them.

If you did, I would be so forever grateful if you left a review on Amazon and Goodreads. Positive reviews work magic for authors!

Writing is a joy, but it's also a lot of hard work. I would've pulled all my hair out if not for the people below.

To my family and friends, thank you for being so understanding when I turned down events to write and holed up for months. This book never would've made it out of my head without your unwavering support.

To my beta readers: Alysha, Morgan, Nicole, Kristen(s), Amanda, and Selene. Thank you for your valuable feedback and honesty. This book is a thousand times better thanks to all of your help.

To the book community, thank you for your positivity, support, and excitement. It kept me going when I wanted to give up!

ABOUT THE AUTHOR

Meredith is a professional daydreamer who writes romance stories full of spice, smooches, and swoons. She lives in Texas with her favorite person and one lazy poodle. When she's not writing, you can usually find her walking beneath the Texas sun or spending time with her family outdoors. To stay up to date on Meredith's upcoming projects, connect with her on social media, @authormeredithtrapp.

Printed in Great Britain
by Amazon

45503033R00199